To Leyton,

Thank you for the support! This one is for a new chapter in our lives!

♡ Megan Payne

THE GOD OF PEACE

Book 2 in the Bearer of Bad News Saga

Paul and Megan Payne

Interior Image Credit: Megan Payne

Exterior Image Credit: Scott Fisher

ISBN: 978-1-71602-987-5 (sc)
ISBN: 978-1-71602-992-9 (hc)
ISBN: 978-1-71613-000-7 (e)

Library of Congress Control Number: 2020905252

Lulu Publishing Services rev. date: 3/17/2020

Contents

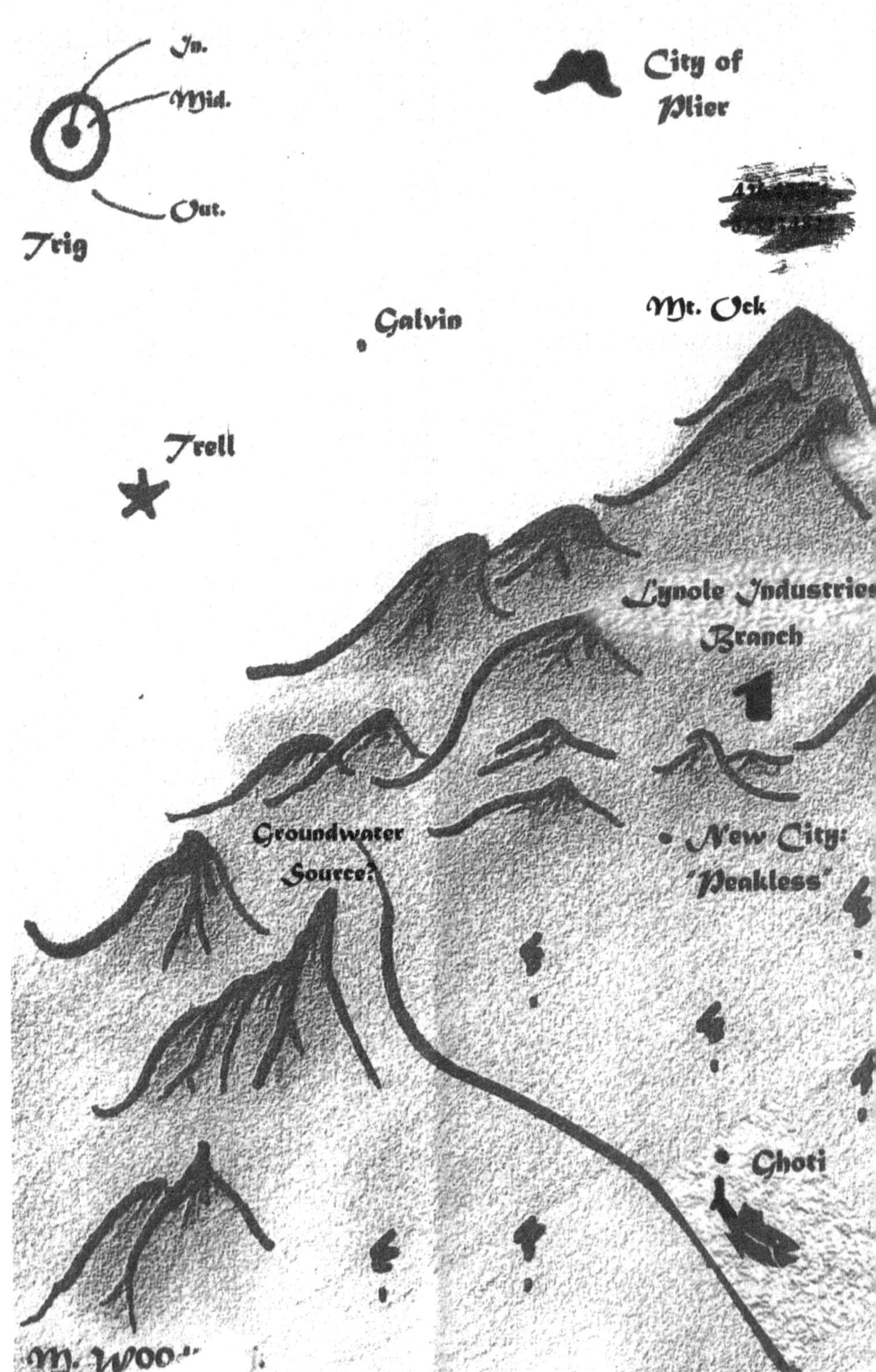
In.
Mid.
Out.
Trig
City of
Plier
Mt. Ock
Galvin
Trell
Lynole Industrie
Branch
Groundwater
Source?
New City:
"Peakless"
Ghoti

Notes:

- Heavy woods at base of mtns.
- Lynole Ind. Mtn. Branch unoccupied
- Possible fracture leads to Underworld
- Still no sign of 'Heaven'

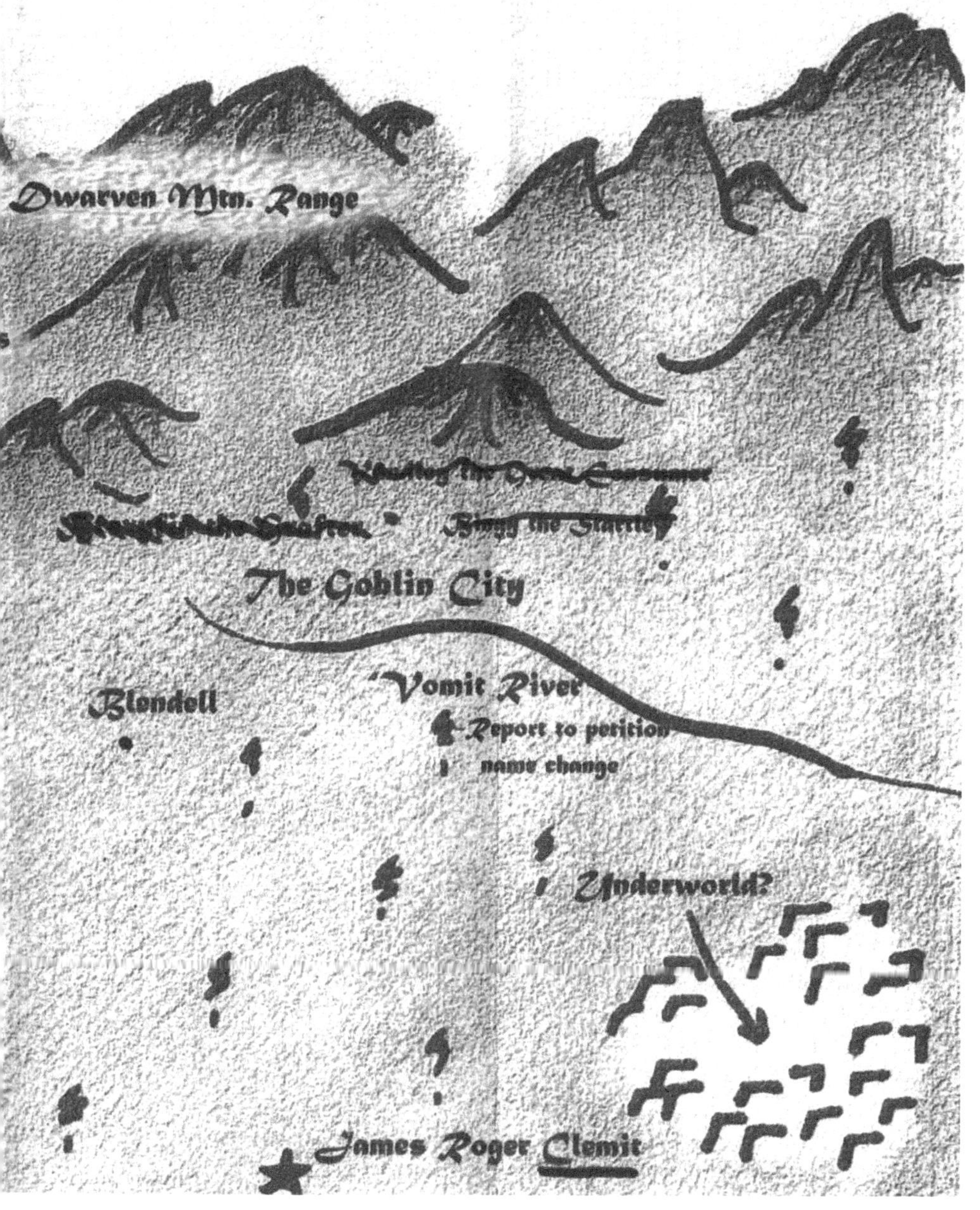

AUTHORS' NOTE

THANK YOU TO EVERYONE WHO has been patiently waiting for the release of this book. Truth be told, writing this has been extremely difficult, even now as we struggle to write these final touches before release. This book has been in production for a few years now, and it was honestly due to some paranoia of wanting to make the perfect sequel and getting through negative criticism. One of us is very good at handling naysayers, while the other isn't. The other struggles with associating any form of criticism with ones they have faced in the past, such as being a terrible student because of a sickness, or being told they will never, ever have a career in music despite the efforts being put into it. It was why the book was written in the first place, because it was the one thing that made everything okay, and having the opportunity to expand it beyond a simple self-publishing tool and into a small business has been the most amazing experience.

But we learned something important out of this, and that was learning how to achieve confidence when it runs empty. Admittedly, there were many nights when writing turned into tears, when blueprinting turned into deep discussions of whether or not this is something we want to do, pockets full of cash became full of lint, or those missing earbuds we'd been searching for, and faith turned into doubt. It wasn't until we finally laid out our final draft to ready it for production that we realized it was all worth it, and until we saw the people we look up to also waiver in their confidence. The truth is you have evidence all around you that proves how amazing you are as a person. For us, it's an app that shows us our published works and works waiting to be published, but for you, it could be that degree on the wall, that work of art you put hours into, that instrument waiting to be practiced, that open video game tab with a list of your achievements, that sports trophy, or even that math test you studied for. It doesn't matter how little achievements you have, how low that grade is, or even the place on that trophy. The point is *you* achieved it, and you can achieve it again, or you can achieve something better because *you are capable.*

That being said, we came across a lot of amazing people in this endeavor, but also some immensely poor ones that lead to some intense self-doubt and discouragement. It has definitely been a new experience. This note was meant to be something of an apology and an explanation for forcing those that have been so good to us to wait, but the reality is we don't really need to explain ourselves. We could say we had some challenges and leave it at that. We don't even need to go into the details of how mental illness has severely changed our lives because we are our own people with our own business, but that isn't what we are about. The family, friends, and fans that all told us to keep moving forward have told us to ignore those negative comments, but it's been such a challenge to do so because we care about what other people have to say. We want to hear what we can improve on, what you want to see in future books, what you liked, and what you didn't like because you each have voices that deserve to be heard. The problem is that some of this ideology conflicts with the authors' roots to the story, because if we cave and give you what you want, the ending and story is expected, and we lose our passion because the story is no longer.

We can't write the perfect book series, mostly because it doesn't exist, but damn it, we want to try and give you something that accurately depicts real problems, something that will make you laugh and cry, and something that you will remember every single day because each of these book characters are based upon your individual emotions and unique challenges. We want them to be heroes to you the same way each and every reader has been a hero to us.

If we can encourage you to do anything, we encourage you to stay true to yourself, and there are many ways to do so:

1. Listen to the naysayers, because they have a voice just like you do.
2. Allowing negativity into your life isn't going to define your future. What defines your future is holding onto your passions and personality with all your might, because you don't have to give it away.
3. Hold the positive experiences over the negative ones. The individual that read your entire book in one day and came back to rave about it will leave a bigger impression than your first negative review on Good Reads.
4. Be educated. It doesn't matter if that education is a Bachelor's degree hanging on your wall, or the five web tabs open on the internet. Learn about the world, yourself, and others. That is the best way to achieve survival.
5. Laugh even when it feels impossible. Perhaps you place being serious over being silly, and that's okay. We just solely believe that your most memorable moments in life are going to be the ones where you are smiling, and the ones you will recall the easiest. Those moments ease the bad days when it feels like they won't get any better.
6. You don't need to justify why you lack in certain areas. You just need to try. The people who don't need justifications

are the ones who matter. Your friends just care that you are happy.

One last thing before we present this long-awaited book to you: Thank you.

Thank you for your support. Thank you for being yourself. Thank you for giving us the opportunity to share this story with you. Thank you for walking this road with us. There are far too many people to dedicate this book to, since our parents have been helping us get on our feet, our fans have inspired us to reach new levels, our friends have organized days to help us be successful, and the best boy didn't make it to the publication. So, if anything, this book is to all of you.

Payneful Reads proudly presents: *The Bearer of Bad News: The God of Peace*

Chapter One

Fool Me Once

"EVERYTHING I JUST RECITED TO you a moment ago are the rights that the dead have; however, you are not dead, and therefore, have no rights. Upon that information, I suppose I just wasted my breath for nothing… I hope that you know that you are infringing on *several* legalities just by existing."

Ignoring the speaker before him, James gazed at his surroundings in awe, and not necessarily sure how he had gotten into his current predicament. He appeared to be riding in some sort of stagecoach with a white, leather interior.

Didn't I... die? he thought to himself.

"… Are you listening?"

James turned his attention to his well-dressed companion in the stagecoach with him. The man was clearly irritated with James' lack of response as he clung to a sleek, black briefcase until his knuckles turned white.

James shook his head. "I'm sorry… where am I?"

The man sighed loudly. "This again. I don't know why I'm reiterating this explanation to you, since your ears obviously don't work." He leaned forward. "Read my lips: you are about to appear on trial and I, Jeremy Huxley, have the 'delightful' opportunity to accompany you."

"What?" James exclaimed as he stood from his seat in astonishment, but immediately fell back down after hitting his head on the roof of the stagecoach.

"Gods, I hate it here," Jeremy muttered.

"Why am I going on trial?" James continued as he rubbed the top of his head.

"It's illegal to be alive in the Underworld."

"The... The Underworld? I'm alive, and I'm in *the Underworld?"*

"Yes! Good Gloric, we've discussed this *dozens* of times already!" Jeremy placed his hand on his forehead and muttered while his thumb and middle finger massaged his temples. "Like talking to a broken record."

Horribly confused, James saw the Sword of Lord Krag sheathed and resting across his lap. "What's going on?"

I don't know, Lord Krag replied.

"You seriously need me to repeat this again?" Jeremy demanded.

James looked up at him and gave him a dirty look. "No, I wasn't talking to you."

"Well, whom else would you be talking to? I'm the only one on this stagecoach with you."

"I was talking to Lord Krag."

Jeremy slowly blinked. "Excuse me?"

"Lord Krag. He's in the sword."

Jeremy scoffed. "Great, I'm trapped in here with a crazy person. It's everything I've ever wanted."

Bewildered by the man's terrible attitude, James sat up a bit straighter. "For your information, this sword is enchanted, and I can communicate with the man infused to it freely through my thoughts. In fact, this isn't just any blade. This is the Sword of Lord Krag."

"Yeah, I figured that out after you called the sword 'Lord Krag,' stupid."

"Well, if you're so smart, then you should understand that *I* am it's chosen wielder, and maybe you should think twice before you decide to open your rude, loud mouth."

"Being entitled to magical, talking swords means nothing here. Now, if you happened to be a king or a friendly CEO of a friendly company, you might be able to land yourself a house with a *whole* broom closet; however, by the looks of you, I'd say you are just short of being the embodiment of insignificance itself, and you're not even dead."

James blinked for a second as Jeremy's words stung him a bit. Then again, "stung" wasn't really the right word to describe how the offense felt, but James grew rather irate, and his stomach churned like he had just eaten something far too salty.

"Who is this fetching guy?" James whispered to his sword.

I don't know... a fetch, like you said?

"I am a lawyer."

Close enough.

"I have a lawyer?" James looked up at Jeremy once more. "You're my lawyer?"

"I'm *a* lawyer provided for you since you didn't provide your own. Now, will you at least try to be competent for five minutes?"

"Good lord, who decided that you should be allowed to work with people? Then again, who decided that a sack of crap[1] can be paid to hold someone's life in their hands?"

---

[1] Little does James know that crap can get many people out of a lot of bad situations. James is already a sack of crap himself and tends to "BS" his way out of certain situations. Hell, if "BS" was a commodity, James would find himself quite wealthy for once.

"Yeah, yeah, go ahead and fill my ears with senseless complaining. It's nothing I haven't heard before. I'm pretty sure my clients all have their own club where they fill out poor survey cards and hand out t-shirts describing their so-called 'woe.' You should go join it, you know, assuming you make it out of this trial dead."

James let out a frustrated shout. "Look, I'm not trying to be difficult. I have no idea where I am or what I am doing, and to make matters worse, I'm stuck on a stagecoach with a guy that's done more insulting than explaining!"

"I've explained your situation to you several times already."

"Well, buddy, you're about to do it again."

Jeremy let out long sigh. "Fine… I'll explain it all again."

"Thank you."

He cleared his throat. "When you died in the Ugly Horse Bar, you weren't allowed to take your body with you, hence the rules of the Underworld. Now, since you obviously still have your body, the Council of Thirteen will decide what to do with you."

"You mean my trial?"

"Correct."

"… How do you *know* I still have my body with me?"

"You mean other than the horrible body odor?"

James groaned. "Never mind. So, what is the Council of Thirteen?"

Just a bunch of old codgers! Lord Krag exclaimed.

"You know them?" James directed towards his lap.

Jeremy stared at James blankly. "Are you stupid? Of course, I know them!"

"I wasn't talking to you," James retorted

"Oh, right, 'the sword can talk.' My apologies, I should've asked if it had an opinion on the matter, since it seems to be more important than the reality happening in front of you."

James rolled his eyes and allowed them to stare out the window of the stagecoach. He marveled at the pitch-black sky above him. It was empty, devoid of any stars, clouds, or signs of anything more, but was decorated with a large, slightly yellowed moon that glistened above this world of the dead and illuminated the way forward for the aimless, nomadic souls.

"Tch. You're a lost cause anyway." Jeremy said as the doors on the side of the stagecoach opened abruptly. "You get out first."

Reluctantly, James stepped out of the stagecoach, gripping the sheath of his sword. As he placed the sheath across his back, he felt his stomach drop as he glanced upward at a large, monolithic building. A cold sweat formed on the back of his neck as this obsidian tower mocked him and the so-called "rights" he didn't have as a being of warm flesh and blood. The grandeur and size of this building reminded James of somebody, but he couldn't quite put his finger on it…

Muttering complaints and not-so-subtle insults towards James, the lawyer walked ahead while clutching the handle of his briefcase tightly. James followed behind as they entered the tenacious building. The hallway before them emanated a golden hue, adding to the lavishness of the place. Feeling intimidated by everything around him, James managed to match his pace with Jeremy's in hopes that he might find a bit of consolation to his insecurity. After what seemed to be about ten minutes, James sheepishly spoke up. "This hallway is really long."

"And?"

"It's just taking forever to get to the Council."

"Well, as cute as your exaggeration is, there isn't a concept of time here."

"Seriously?"

"Think about it, what is time to the dead?"

"So… you have no perception of time?"

"It's not like we need it. We're all dead. There is, however, someone trying to bring time back here, but it's completely impossible. Plus, I highly doubt it will become a trend down here."

"Who is it?"

"Don't know, don't care."

For another space of time that didn't particularly matter, the hollowness of the hallway was filled with the hypnotic footsteps of both James and Jeremy.

"... When do you know when it's time for lunch?" James suddenly asked.

Jeremy gave him a dirty look. "We don't eat here. We're dead."

James furrowed his brow and covered his forehead with his hand. "Does that mean you don't go to the bathroom here, either?"

"Yes."

"Then what the hell am *I* supposed to do?"

"Die?"

James huffed.

"For goodness' sakes, you have to be the most ignorant person I've ever encountered."

James hung his head slightly and pouted as they continued walking. After another non-existent eternity, James kept his head down and developed a strong appreciation for the textile design of the ground until the two men finally arrived at a court room. James nervously clenched his fists as he walked into the oval-shaped auditorium, and he was at center stage. Rows of seats circled this vast place and were raised at least five feet off of the ground, in addition to balconies that extended towards the ceiling like they had no end. Seats were speckled with different lives that once were, each of them eager for the fate of the living one, or as far as they knew, the troubled, dead one. At the far end of the room, raised even higher off of the ground were thirteen gold seats, filled with thirteen old men.

They stared him down condescendingly, as if they had better things to do in their dead states than to deal with this unwarranted interruption. Each of them wore pure, black suits, and were encased in a pale, sunken skin that emphasized nearly every bone and crevice of their skeletons. Some of them were bald, while others still had a little bit of hair, which looked as thin as particles of dust that glimmered with silvers and whites in the light above. Their frailty almost convinced James that they had taken their decomposing corpses with them to this terrible place, and they still continued to rot away in fragile egos and inconveniencies.

James gulped as he approached the center of the room, feeling the weight of everyone's eyes upon him. The centermost man leaned forward, looking James square in the eyes. James assumed he must be the leader and was genuinely surprised that the man could see him at all with that bulbous nose on his face.

"What sins has this convicted one committed in the presence of the Council of Thirteen?" the man spoke, with a harsh, scratchy voice.

"This man is alive," Jeremy monotonously and carelessly said as he approached James' side.

The eyes of the Council members widened as the audience surrounding them erupted with gasps and whispers of shock. The man in the middle, or "Big Nose" as James has decided, simply closed his eyes and let out a frustrated sigh. "Plea your defense before us."

"We don't have one."

James shot the lawyer a nasty, slightly astonished look. "The fetch? You're *my lawyer!* You're supposed to be defending me!"

Jeremy raised an eyebrow and glanced at James. "No, I'm *a lawyer,* and, surprise, your crime is being alive. How am I supposed to come up with a defense for someone that doesn't have any rights here?"

"Well... you're the worst lawyer ever, then!"

"You're the worst case ever. You should've just died like the rest of us."

"I'm beginning to understand why you have a fan club—"

"Silence!" Big Nose shouted, bellowing throughout the room unaesthetically as he slowly stood from his seat. "You stand before the mighty Council of Thirteen, boy! The overarching judicial system of the Underworld! Humble yourself before your elders!"

"… What?" James asked as he finally broke his attention away from the lawyer.

Big Nose's eye twitched as he found himself perplexed at the idea of having to repeat himself, especially to someone of the living persuasion.

"… Uh" —James cleared his throat— "sorry. Despite what this 'lawyer' said, I *do* happen to have a defense. May I present it?"

Big Nose upheld his angry look.

"… Please?"

He looked to his left and to his right, with his fellow Councilmen murmuring to one another and to himself. His gaze returned to James. "Permission granted," he replied as he slowly sat back down.

James took a deep breath. "Look, I don't know why I am here, or how I got here, but unfortunately, here I am, alive and well. So, would it be a bit far-fetched to let me return to where I came from? It will be as if this encounter of ours never happened."

Big Nose arched a brow, as if waiting for James to continue.

James narrowed his eyes and coughed uncomfortably. "That's all I got…"

With a sigh, Big Nose batted a dismissive hand at James while turning to the other Councilmen. More murmurs and whispers were conceived among them. James held his breath as they conversed, his mind occupied by the thoughts of another.

You really couldn't come up with a defense better than that one? Krag said.

"Well," James said quietly while glancing around to see if anyone were listening, "you could've suggested something better?"

I'm an old man trapped in a sword with a pack of one-hundred wolves and you want me to come up with something believable?

James smirked. "Are you doubting your own lore?"

Oh, not at all. I'm just saying that coming up with a defense that you got from your "talking sword" may not get you taken seriously. It's more of a concern for you than for me.

"… I wouldn't have said that *you* came up with the defense for me."

But yet, here you are, asking for this old heap of metal for help. Plus, you are a terrible liar. You'd slip one way or another to these people.

"No, I wouldn't!"

Really? Look up.

James did as Krag said and noticed the Council of Thirteen giving him confused looks.

... *Fetch,* James thought as he gave the Council an innocent smile.

"… Do you have something further to say?" Big Nose asked.

James shook his head. "No. Forgive me for… interrupting."

The man to the right of Big Nose, as James lovingly named "Buck Teeth," whispered a few words to Big Nose. After Buck Teeth finished what he had said, the two looked into James' eyes once again, sending waves of ice down his spine.

"Either way, the Council has come to a conclusion."

James wiped his sweaty palm on his sleeve.

"Since your only defense is that you don't know why or how you have arrived here to this realm of the dead, we shall be more merciful in your punishment."

James sighed with relief. "Thank you!"

"That being said, we shall release you of your physical form."

His face immediately fell. "… Excuse me?"

"In the history of the Underworld, a mortal man has never visited us before. What better way to welcome him than with a public execution? All in favor?"

As the thirteen men raised their hands, James' anger festered inside until he had finally snapped. "Are you serious? That's so unfair! I have no control as to whether or not I'm alive, but here I am, in the flesh! I have a chance to continue living my life and you're going to kill me?"

Do you even have a life to return to? Krag asked.

Whose side are you on? James thought in return.

Geez, sorry I said anything.

"You're not a Council member," a man on the far left said, whom James named "Wide Eyes," for his freakishly wide eye gap. "Your opinion does not count."

"Then, how do I become one? Is there an election or something?"

"… Well, no—"

"Then how did *you* become one?"

Exasperated, Wide Eyes stumbled over his words. "It doesn't matter how I got here!"

"I'd accuse you of bringing your body here, too, since I can smell your rottenness from over here—!"

"That's enough!" Big Nose bellowed. "Court is dismiss—"

"Now wait just a minute, you old bags of gas! This whole bit is garbage and I'm not going to take it!"

Several of the Councilmen gripped their chests and exchanged horrified glances as the profane insults grazed across their ears.

"Riddle me this," James continued, "if the last thing this 'mortal man' remembers is being *murdered*, then what could it possibly be that kept his heart beating?"

More gasps and whispers could be heard among the audience.

Big Nose looked at his comrades, back at James, and then sighed. "There appears to be a divine bid being gambled here," he said calmly.

"Sir," a man directly to the left of Big Nose said, who James decided to call "Crumpy Face," for his crumpy face.

You're stupid.

Don't you judge me!

"Could this be the work of Gloric?"

James rolled his eyes and stuck out his tongue.

"Why does it matter if it's Gloric?" Wide Eyes shouted. "This... mortal" —he gestured towards James as if he were a heaping pile of fetchwork— "has violated our laws by entering the Underworld as a living being! He must be punished for his crimes!"

"'Why does it matter if it's Gloric?'" James piped up. "Well, if there's some damn, cosmic reason why I've been spared by 'the gods,' then surely you must abide to that!"

"We don't have to do anything!" Buck Teeth retorted.

"So, what happens to you then? What if 'Gloric' did spare me for some convoluted reason? Do you think you're just going to get away with executing me? You're going to disobey a god just because you're jealous that I'm alive and you're not? Fine, pursue your cruelty and prejudice! Just consider what a couple of dead, aged men are to a deity."

The Council as they gritted their teeth and tapped their fingers on their seats, knowing that any argument they could compose would be invalid.

"Fine, I propose an alternative to your punishment." Big Nose pointed a wrinkled, bony finger at James. "When you are summoned, you will face the executioner, not as prey, but as a competitor. Should you prevail over him in a duel, we will grant you your freedom, and you shall continue to live your life as you have been."

The rest of the Council erupted in disagreement.

"Do you wish to face the wrath of the Holy One?"

With his words, the Council fell silent.

"However, should you fail," he continued, "you will be among us in this land of the dead, as you should be."

James nodded sheepishly and sighed. "That's fair."

"Of course, it is! Court adjourned!"

Members of the audience and the Council filed out of the courtroom. Jeremy Huxley stretched his arms above his head and yawned. "Well, I'm going home now."

"You have a home?" James asked.

"Of course, I do, idiot. I live here."

"Well, where am *I* supposed to go? Is there a bar or something I can go to?"

"A bar?"

"Or… something?"

Jeremy stared at James, convinced he was a new species of stupid. "Do you think this place is some sort of hick-joint 'or something?'"

James looked at the grandiose surrounding him. "Not even slightly."

"There aren't any bars in the Underworld."

James blinked and shook his head. "What fresh hell is this place?"

"Hell is a different realm from the Underworld—"

"Just go home, Mister 'Technical Tilly!'"

Jeremy sighed. "Well, wherever you end up, the guards will find you and bring you back here."

"How will they find me? After all, this seems like a pretty big place."

"Well, you're the only one that's alive, so…"

"Good grief, I never knew being alive would be such a pain in the butt."

"It probably wouldn't be so bad if, you know, you weren't breaking the law."

Why is this guy still here? James thought.

To James' surprise, there was no reply.

... Krag?

... Oh, sorry. I forgot that you can't see me shrug or whatever. Geez.

"But, I digress, it's been a tedious trial and I'm tired of dealing with… this." Jeremy gestured his hand at James. "and, I really need a nap, so" —he spun on his heels, began walking away, and raised his hand slightly— "good luck."

"You take naps, but you don't eat food?"

"Goodbye."

James pouted, folded his arms, and found himself alone with only a few other people left in the room. "What do I do, Krag?"

Sorry, bud. I really don't know how to get you out of this one.

James sighed and hung his head.

... Those people have been staring at you for a while now, though.

"What people?"

James glanced around and noticed a couple standing at their seats, almost waiting for James to have a free moment. The woman waved at him, tears seemingly forming in her eyes.

A smile spread across James' face as he felt a warmth in his heart. "Mom?"

Chapter Two

A Hypothetical Day at the Clemit's

HOUSES ARE KNOWN TO BE lovely human dwellings with several purposeful rooms and quaint decorations that have their own style to reflect the culture of the family living there. The Underworld houses are very similar, except there are no families "living" in those units, since everyone in the Underworld is dead.

It is also certain (and obvious) that these poor, unfortunate souls have been horribly screwed over. The Underworld houses are approximately as large as a size seven shoe, in children's, consisting of a sitting room and about one to two bedrooms. The Clemit's residence, unlike most Underworld houses, had a broom closet, which is a bit pointless since the dead have no chores.

The broom closet was a courtesy to James Lynn Clemit, one of the founders of the Bureau of Bad News and initial sole owner. He had taken residence with his son's family, since he was a bit of an outcast, so their home was upgraded to one with a broom closet, considering he was a "friendly" CEO of a "friendly" company that changed the world.

In this humble abode, the infamous instigator was sitting at a desk in his room, tinkering with a dysfunctional clock, desperate for some sort of way to tell time again. As he was trying to fit the gears of the clock together, the cramming of parts into a small space caused springs and gears to scatter across his desk and onto the floor.

"Fresh furnace of hell," he muttered as he reached down to collect the gears. He heard his family return as he continued cursing under his breath.

"Dad!" his son called. "Dad come out here! You'll never believe who we found!"

James Lynn Clemit let out a heavy sigh, gathering the remnants of the broken timepiece as he reluctantly left his room.

Mr. Clemit, the father of James Roger Clemit, stood merrily in the doorway as he allowed his wife and son to enter the home first. "We found our son, Dad! It's James!"

".... Okay?" James Lynn Clemit replied unenthusiastically. "Am I supposed to be surprised that there is, yet again, another dead Clemit?"

"No, Dad, he's still alive!"

"So, I *don't* have to share my room?"

"Um, no—?"

"Super…"

"Why don't the two of you get to know each other?" Mrs. Clemit, mother of James Roger Clemit, said to try and break the awkwardness abiding in the atmosphere. "Besides, young James here wanted to ask you some questions."

James Lynn Clemit let out a disgusted groan as he took a seat in a plush armchair.

Feeling rather nervous, James Roger Clemit hesitantly took a seat in the armchair next to his grandfather as his parents seated themselves in a couch across from them.

"So, you're James Lynn Clemit?" James Roger Clemit asked.

"Call me Jim."

"… Not grandpa?" James said with a slight laugh.

"My name is Jim," he replied, more sternly.

"O-Oh. My apologies."

Jim didn't respond. Instead, he set the clock onto his lap and began fiddling with it again.

James tilted his head. "Is that a clock?"

"No, but it will be when I'm done with it."

"I thought the dead have no concept of time."

"They will, when I'm done with this damn clock!"

"It's a loss cause, Dad," Mr. Clemit piped up.

"I will not be dictated by this ignorant patriarchy! We will have time, again!" Jim exclaimed, waving a screwdriver at his son as he did so.

"And what will that accomplish?"

Jim gritted his teeth as held on tighter to his screwdriver. "I don't have to explain myself to you. You're a simple-minded peon!"

Mr. Clemit rolled his eyes. "Fine, I'll just go into the kitchen and grab a snack."

"We don't have the need of food! Nor do we have a kitchen!"

"Then, we don't need a clock." Mr. Clemit smirked.

Jim muttered something under his breath, seemingly defeated.

Dumbstruck, James fumbled to get back to the matter at hand. "Anyway, I… I heard you're one of the founders of the Bureau of Bad News."

Jim scoffed. "Never thought I'd hear the name of that damn place ever again."

"Right… well, you hypothetically you were the only one that *truly* owned it, right?"

"Does it matter?"

James bit his lip. "Well… there may have been a quarrel about who technically 'owns' the Bureau, and if it was you, wouldn't the current owner technically be me?"

Jim looked up from the clock. "And how would you come to such a… seemingly rational and logical conclusion?"

"I… may have worked there for a little bit," James nervously replied.

Jim scoffed and returned to his work. "Typical Clemit, stooping to a new low every generation."

James winced. "Well, on the way here, Mom and Dad said you were living with them, so I just thought I'd get a sure answer—"

"Listen" —Jim looked up at him again— "I'm sure you're a nice kid, but I'm not particularly interested in developing a nice, family relationship with *you.*"

James raised his eyebrow and blinked. "Excuse me?"

"Quite literally, if you weren't a stupid little kid, my son wouldn't be here in the Underworld with bitter, old me. But like I said, we stoop to a new low every generation."

"Jim." Mrs. Clemit scowled.

"What? If we're all here asking questions and getting to know each other, then you should know that I'm quite disappointed that my son risked his entire family just for a boy who didn't have what it took to live a normal life. Imaginary friends, shadow monsters" —Jim scoffed— "a load of bull crap. Before I knew it, your parents were here, without you. The bastard child lived—"

"Hey!" James intervened. "That's enough! So, what if I was a troubled child? I wasn't the cause of my parents' deaths! It was that company you so 'lovingly' founded! You ruined lives, and *I'm* the bastard here?"

Jim chuckled. "You have a point. Perhaps I was being a bit unfair, but isn't that what'd you'd expect of a man that 'owns' the Bureau? Unfair? Cruel and heartless? I sent the entire world to Hell, James." He stood, cradling the clock in his arms. "Like I said,

I'm sure you're a nice kid, but I stand by my beliefs that my children are here because of you. Perhaps another time I'll humor you, answering whatever questions you want… over your dead body." With that, Jim stood and returned to his bedroom, closing the door and himself off from the rest of the world around him.

James sat back in his seat, not believing what he had just heard,

Even if it was true.

Your grandfather is a fetch.

Thanks, Krag… I appreciate your input there.

"Don't take anything that man says personally, son," Mr. Clemit said. "He's like that to everybody. He just called me a 'simple-minded peon.'"

"I doubt it," James replied. "That was some pretty deep hatred."

"Well, I strongly believe that the hatred isn't towards you, but himself."

James huffed and shook his head. "I guess, but still, that was a blow below the belt. So far, my time here has been nothing but that… or rather my *experience,* because of that weird time thing."

"Well… we're still proud of you, James! You've always been such a good boy," Mrs. Clemit said as she smiled sweetly.

James gave his mother a wry smile, observing his parents more closely. He noticed that they haven't changed a bit since he last saw them, as if their bodies had been frozen in time. He was relieved when he beheld no blood stains, bullet wounds, or snake bites on their clothes and throats, but just barely noticed that his own suit was shredded from the fight with Mr. Finch, and had several crimson holes from being shot by Henry Chase.

While James didn't have all the answers, he was just glad that could remember his parents like they were trapped in a photograph. Smiling and happy, with nothing seemingly wrong with life.

Then again, nothing can be wrong if there isn't a life to live.

“I… really miss you,” James said.

“We miss you, too,” Mrs. Clemit said while reaching her hand out.

James reached back and was surprised that his hand faded right through hers, as if he were a ghost.

“Oh dear, I already forgot about that,” she said, observing James’ confusion. “The living cannot interact with the dead, but at least we can speak to one another!”

James felt cold inside. His mood took a turn for the better when he saw his parents again, but it changed direction at the sudden realization that the last time he ever truly held his mother’s hand would always be the last time.

Before he could manifest tears, James turned to his father in an attempt to change the subject. “That reminds me. I’m supposedly sentenced to ‘execution’ just by being here, do you have any idea what might be executing me?”

“Well” —Mr. Clemit bit his lip— “the last time anything similar to this situation ever happened was when this… monster-looking thing showed up here.”

“A… monster?”

“Yes. It had its own disgusting aura about it, so the Council decided to deal with it by trapping it and locking it away, saying it would ‘probably’ leave some day… or die.”

“How did they trap it?”

“Cardboard box and a string.”

James stared at his father.

“Yeah… The sad part is that it worked.”

“That’s another thing. If, supposedly, the living cannot interact with the dead” —he slapped his hands on the armrests of the chair— “how is this happening?”

“Perhaps… furniture is the temporal realm between the living and the dead…” Mr. Clemit looked down at the sofa. “The fibers between the upholstery must be the thing that holds these worlds together, millions of anchors spanned throughout all of existence…"

Mr. Clemit stared out into space as Mrs. Clemit stared at him blankly. "Seriously, dear?"

"Oh, right!" Mr. Clemit snapped back into reality. "Uh… The Underworld is a mysterious place."

James chuckled. "'A mysterious place,' if anything, this place is more… fan-fetching-tastic!"

"Language, dear," Mrs. Clemit said with a stern tone.

"No, I'm being serious. This place and everyone here is just… awesome."

Mr. Clemit folded his arms. "I understand that you're upset, son, but please try to calm down and drop the sarcasm."

"It's impossible, dear, since he probably got his attitude from you," Mrs. Clemit off-handedly said.

Dumbfounded, Mr. Clemit turned towards his wife. "Excuse me? Why in the world do you think he got it from *me?*"

"You're always sarcastic with me!"

"Name one instance I was sarcastic with you."

"Just the other day, when I asked what time it was, you responded with 'half past time doesn't matter.'"

Mr. Clemit tossed his hands up. "Time doesn't matter! I still don't understand why you asked me that!"

"Well, *sweetheart*," she began, "you've dismissed the fact that I've been alive much longer than I've been dead, I think, and if I've learned anything, people have shorter lifespans than old habits. You didn't have to be so snide."

"Fine, dear. You caught me. Our son got his wonderful attitude from me. Sure nailed that one on the head."

Mrs. Clemit gestured towards him with her hand. "Perfect example, right here!"

James began laughing, and his parents looked at him oddly.

"I'm sorry. This just brings me back to how things used to be. Dad would make a snide comment, Mom would get upset, and eventually, bickering turned into sweet nothings." He almost teared up again. "Damn… this place is nothing but a constant, nostalgic heartbreak."

"… That may be," Mrs. Clemit said after a moment, "but, most people don't have the privilege of closure, and to see their beloved ones once more before life resumes. This is a good thing, James. At least, we think it is."

The words of his mother melted James' heart, and the family exchanged adored looks. James' smile quickly faded as he remembered his current predicament. "Seriously though, what do I do? I mean, it isn't like I don't miss you or anything, but I don't want to die!"

"I think you're overreacting," Mr. Clemit replied.

James scoffed. "I'm sorry, I'm 'overreacting?' This is serious, and you think I'm overreacting?"

His father chuckled and shook his head. "No."

James huffed and leaned back in his seat. "Unbelievable."

"You were raised in this world as a Clemit," his father continued, "and a Clemit you shall be for the rest of your life. We have a strong lineage of determined leaders, intellectuals, and brave warriors. I have no doubt in my mind that you can continue that legacy, and whatever happens tomorrow doesn't matter, because you will be victorious."

James gave him a skeptibrow.[2]

"Your father is right, James," Mrs. Clemit began. "Whatever you will be facing tomorrow, you will have the advantage. The strength in your blood will sustain you. If you can face whatever is executing you tomorrow, and win, then nobody else here will be

[2] For those of you who are either uneducated or uncultured, a "skeptibrow" means arching an eyebrow skeptically. The word itself is a portmanteau.

able to kill you. They will have no choice but to give you your freedom. You can be my brave, young man, right?"

James sighed with dismay. "You've always said that... especially when the things I feared *weren't there.* Any hope that I could be even slightly successful is ridiculous."

"James—"

"No, Mom, 'Jim' is right. I'm flattered that you think I could carry on this Clemit legacy, but I'm probably the greatest failure among us. And all of this, like every fetching other thing, is probably a dream."

"Sweetheart..." Mrs. Clemit's voice strained with pangs of sadness.

"Forgive me, but, I just..." He stood from his seat and headed towards the door. "I'm going for a walk. I'll be back in a little bit."

And with that, James entered further into the abyss which was the Underworld. Perhaps he'd get a reassurance that all of this nonsense was real.

At least, he hoped that someday he'd know for sure.

~

Mr. and Mrs. Clemit looked at one another, and simultaneously let out a sigh. Mr. Clemit chuckled. "Still a difficult one, I see."

Mrs. Clemit slowly nodded as she stared at the carpet. "This... is all my fault."

"How in Gloric's name is any of this your fault?" Mr. Clemit scoffed.

"W-Well, I'm his mother! I shouldn't have left him, *a child*, alone to fend for himself!"

"You just saw him, he's a healthy, grown man!"

"That doesn't make a difference!"

As she wiped away tears, her husband's temper subsided, and he wrapped his arms around her. "James is a grown man."

"You've already said that, dear."

"And, it is very obvious that he has held onto your every word as he has made his way through the world. Tch. Your fault. Perhaps to some degree, you are right. It's your fault that he turned out to be so fine, brave, and everything we could ever hope for him to become."

With wet and shimmery eyes, Mrs. Clemit hopefully gazed at her husband. "Do you… really believe that?"

"I really do."

She rested her head on his shoulder as he held her tighter. "We have had such a simple death for… Gloric knows how long. Then, a little bit of life comes along and makes it all the more exciting."

He nodded. "Interesting how that can happen…"

CHAPTER THREE

WHAT A "WONDERFUL" WORLD

WHAT A STRANGE PLACE, JAMES thought to himself as he continued down the road. The streets, instead of asphalt, were made of black bricks, and gas lamps towered over the sidewalks, with benches carved in a lovely fashion out of dark wood parked beneath them. There were pallets of beautiful, richly colored flowers set daintily between the benches, along with stray dogs happily running and greeting people while cats walked atop fences. Horse drawn carriages also made their way through the streets, dropping off the recently deceased into their new settlements. The rest of the dead visited their neighbors and lost relatives upon a near infinite block.

Bewildered by this scene, James continued pacing through this town, or Underworld, with passing anxieties nipping at his mind. He shook his head and decided to take a seat on a bench. A nearby cat hopped up next to him and tried to crawl into his lap but was astonished when it just phased through him. It meowed as it clawed at him, seemingly flabbergasted at these odd physics while James merely chuckled.

My wolves don't like cats, Krag said.

James shrugged. "What are they going to do? They're in a sword."

Just trying to make conversation... you fetch.

James sighed, sat back, crossed one leg over the other, and stared up at the moon.

"Excuse me?"

James looked up to his left and found a red-haired, slightly bulky, middle-aged man standing next to him.

"May I sit here?" The man pointed to the other side of the bench.

"Oh, go ahead," James said, not with much care.

The man awkwardly sat next to him. The cat nervously walked over to this new character and crawled into his lap. The man stroked the cat's back, happily looking at his surroundings. "How did you die?" the man asked.

James chuckled. "I was bit by a snake, then shot several times."

"Oh my. What a terrible way to go."

"Yeah, except I lived."

The man gave James a horribly confused look.

"I'm not dead."

The man's eyes narrowed for a moment, and then lit up. "Oh, so *you're* the living that showed up here!"

"That would be me."

"Wow! How interesting! Especially since you've been so brutally attacked!"

James shrugged, not really wanting to make conversation with this guy. He seemed a bit odd. Although well-dressed in button up-shirt and vest, he was very disheveled. A few buttons on his shirt were undone, his tie was loose, and words were written on the inside of his cuffs with pencil. His shoes were untied, and one of his pockets was turned inside out.

"I remember when I died. Unfortunately, I was murdered." He grabbed a dirty handkerchief out of the unturned pocket and wiped a smudge off of his glasses.

"That is unfortunate."

"Oh well, a thing of the past. No need to worry about that. After all, I'm here in this lovely place, aren't I?" The man chuckled.

James gave him a quick smile of acknowledgement and then looked away.

The man pulled out a notebook and began jotting down a few thoughts. "Forgive me if I made you uncomfortable, I thought a fellow like yourself wouldn't mind my presence," the man commented.

James arched an eyebrow and looked back at the man. "What do you mean by that?"

"Well, any man who talks to himself is surely mad."

James' cheeks turned pink and he looked away, embarrassed.

"But, that's okay. Some of the smartest people have a bit of madness about them. For example, I talk to myself sometimes, too, and I'm a scholar."

James scoffed. "Yeah, but that's different"

"How so?"

"It's just..." He paused, unsure if he should disclose something so personal to a stranger.

"Just...?"

Then again, the stranger might not have been real.

James let out a defeated sigh. "I dunno. This all seems impossible. I don't know if this is real or not. This could all just be a figment of my imagination."

"Trust me, my boy. The Underworld is a very, very real place."

James shook his head. "How am I supposed to know that you're real, too? You could just be some manifestation of my mind trying to convince me otherwise. For all I know, I could be sitting in a padded room with a straight-jacket mumbling this entire conversation."

The man seemed taken back by that one. He looked out into space for a moment, as if reflecting if he truly were a figment of another man's imagination.

James sighed, placed both feet on the ground, leaned forward, and put his heads in his hands. "That's my biggest fear, you know? One day, I'll snap out of this and wake up somewhere completely different, and that everything I've become so attached to never even happened."

"That's okay."

James lifted his head, giving the man a dirty look. "'That's okay?' With all due respect, sir, but why the fetch would you say that? What if everything you've seen up to this point ended up being a lie?"

"Then, it ended up being a lie."

James huffed with perplexity, not believing the audacity of this crazy guy.

"What's your name, boy?"

"… James."

"Well, I have a similar fear, James."

James sat up and his mood calmed as he grew intrigued by that statement.

The man smiled. "Not a lot of people believed me, either. Granted, it was along the lines of personal belief, but my colleagues still viewed me as a socially impaired madman, and that my findings were merely conspiracies. I couldn't afford being viewed as incapable or unfit, after all, I had a little girl to take care of. As you can see, that worked out fine."

James felt a pang in his chest as he said that.

"I could tell you anything that you want to hear, James. I could say that all of this isn't a part of your imagination, and that I'm just as real as the skin on your bones, but what good does that do if it doesn't ease your anxieties?"

James didn't reply.

"If I were in your shoes, I say just to live. Even if all of this is unreal, what an interesting reality we live in! Just look at this place!"

James scanned the streets once more, recalling the feeling of awe he had before sitting down on the bench. The man had a point. The vastness of the Underworld seemed to continue indefinitely in all directions and with unique intricacy as it housed dead cultures, extinct species, and people of all personalities, the good and the bad. It should have reached over-capacitation millennia ago, but it has room for everyone, and everything, as if it were some entity of mercy that allows even the smallest particle to find rest in some way, shape, or form. The sky was dark, but the world, itself, had some sort of light about it, an aura of peace and reverence.

"Even if you woke up in a padded room, or returned to the world above, how many people could say that they've seen this? This may or may not be reality, but you can at least admit that it isn't a bad one to live in?"

James smiled. "I guess it isn't so bad."

"There you go!" The man placed his notebook into his pocket, picked up the cat, and stood from his seat. He held up the cat in front of him and shrugged. "I guess this is my cat now," he said. "If you'll excuse me, I have some things to attend to."

"Forgive me for asking, but what things do the dead have to 'attend to?'"

"My research never ends, James." He allowed a hand to give him a short wave. "I'll be attending the public execution, so I wish you the best of luck."

James scoffed. "Thanks."

As the man began to walk away, James spoke out once more. "Sir! You never told me your name!"

The man turned and smiled. "My name is Kyle."

"Well, it was nice to meet you."

"It was nice to meet you too."

When the man took his leave again, James sighed and took a deep breath. "Well, that was… interesting."

He wasn't that bad, after all, that was some rich advice, Lord Krag said.

Thinking back to what his mother said just before he left, James began feeling guilty. Never for a moment did James doubt what his mother told him. The counsel she gave him was always the one thing to help him surpass the impossible as he lived his life paranoid and haunted by his psychosis.

In all honesty, James, don't worry about a thing, Lord Krag said. *After all, you should be able to trust in an ancient, sentient blade.*

James nodded. "Yeah, but it has a little bit of rust around the edges."

Shut up, boy!

James laughed to himself as some people walking by gave him odd glances. Feeling in high spirits, he clasped his hands together. "You're right, and Mom was right. As long as we defeat whatever it is we are facing, we're home free. As long as we focus, I think we can do this."

Not to be the bearer of bad news here,[3] *but you should go back to your family now, especially since they could send for you at any "moment." It's like your mother said earlier, not everyone has the opportunity to see their dead loved ones.*

James nodded, stood up, and headed back to the Clemit residence. "Oh wait" —James stopped in his place— "do you have any loved ones?"

James… I literally killed tens of thousands of people with this sword… and I also have a mom.

---

[3] Roll credits.

"Do you… want to go see her?"

There's a reason why I'm messed up in the head... and let's just say… I may or may not have cooled this sword in her blood.

James held onto strained breath.

Don't worry, I cleaned up my act.

"… Okay."

CHAPTER FOUR

MORTAL FOLLY

LIKE MOST TIMES WHEN JAMES was determined, the feeling was immediately diminished by another run of bad luck, assuming you believe in luck. The instance James returned to the Clemit residence also happened to be the instance when six of the Underworld guards came to take him to his execution.

The guards were all dressed in different uniforms, but were too primitive for James to identify. As they surrounded him and led him back to the courthouse, James kept his head back and moaned. "Fetch my life… Fetch my life!" he shouted a few times over and over.

"Okay, can you stop saying that?" the guard behind him piped up. He was dressed in a black and gold uniform with a lion crest over his heart. "It's kind of offensive."

"What's the matter, can't handle the word 'fetch?'"

"I don't care about that, you just keep saying, 'Fetch my life,' when none of us here have lives. It's a bit insensitive."

Perplexed, James peered over his shoulder and gave the guard a dirty look. "I'm sorry, you ripped me out of my dead parents' house before I even got a chance to say goodbye to them, along with threatening to do them harm if I didn't comply, and decided to *walk* me to the courthouse because, and I quote, 'the horses need rest,' and you're calling *me* insensitive?"

The guard's face twitched as he tried to come up with a response. "W-Well… it wouldn't be so bad if you didn't word it that way—"

"I just stated what happened."

The guard stuttered and averted eye contact. "J-Just keep up the pace, criminal!"

"Forgive me, I forgot that involuntary vital signs were forbidden." James smirked before eyeing all of the guards. "You know what *really* should be forbidden, gentleman?"

The guards ignored him and continued to move at a rhythmic pace.

"Holding the living here against their will."

"You are in violation of the law for trespassing in a realm that is not your own," the guard walking in front of him said in a deep, gruff voice. He wore black garbs and a silver mask. The mask had somewhat of a distraught expression, with a weird emblem engraved in it. James assumed it was some sort of bird claw. "Should you have stayed where you belonged, there would be no trouble. You have made your bed, now you must lie in it."

The four guards walking beside James all nodded in compliance.

"Does everybody here seriously think I pulled some heist to get into this place? First of all, this place is horrible, and I don't know why anyone would *want* to come here at all! Second, I was fetching shot! And it's because of your stupid Council, and not providing a valid defense for somebody who manifested here against their will, that the so-called 'living' must lie in beds that weren't even theirs to begin with! It's unfair!"

The four guards all glanced at one another, shrugged, and nodded in agreeance with James.

The guard in front of James chuckled. "Well, unfortunately, that's just the way the things are here. Tell you what, kid, if you manage to fight your way through your little dilemma, you won't have to lie in a strange bed anymore."

After he said those words, James and all the guards arrived at the courthouse. James made his way through the long corridor once more. As he took in the grandeur, he snapped his fingers. "Frank!"

"What?" a guard to the right asked.

"That's who I was thinking of earlier! Frank!"

The guards all exchanged confused glances.

"You know, the war general for the Bureau of Bad News?"

"… The what?"

"Never mind," James muttered, a bit disappointed that nobody could relate to him.

When they arrived at the courtroom, James observed that it had transformed into some sort of gravel pit, or rather, arena. The guards stood in the hallway as James entered this coliseum, with large, obsidian gates rising from the ground behind him, preventing any form of escape. The black sand and rocks shifted underneath James' feet as he felt the stares of the audience and Council members, leering at him from above.

Big Nose leaned forward. "Young mortal, are you ready to face that which you've inflicted upon yourself?"

James held up a finger. "I just have… one question."

Unamused, Big Nose simply raised an eyebrow and stared back at him blankly.

"How come everyone else has nice, fixed clothes while my clothes are still torn up and stuff?"

Big Nose blinked. "It would be a waste to answer such a simple, irrelevant question."

“A waste of what, time? First of all, time doesn’t exist here. And second, you literally dumped a bunch of rocks and dirt into the courtroom just so you could watch me die… again… ish.”

Baffled at this sarcastic imbecile’s response, Big Nose’s face turned red. “Enough! Your stalling is of no use, for as you have recalled, time does not exist here. Your maker patiently and inevitably waits.” The old man cackled, almost manically. “We’ll see how clever you are when you submit to defeat.”

James felt a pit in his stomach when a pair of doors manifested in the wall under the Council, and slowly and tediously opened. With his heart rapidly beating from the suspense, James quickly drew his sword and held it out in front of him. To his dismay, it wasn’t some demonic monster or six-armed executioner that entered the arena, but found himself furrowing his brows when some punk kid walked through the doors.

“… Are you kidding me?” James said with a scoff. “*This* is supposed to be my ultimate demise?”

Before James could continue his, he felt his sword rapidly fluctuating in weight. He shifted his attention to it and could feel the wolves’ fur standing on end, snapping their jaws at the sight of the boy.

“What in the world?”

Something’s wrong, Lord Krag said.

“How could something be wrong? He’s just a child!”

No, James, this *is no child.*

Feeling almost as uneasy as the wolves, James glanced back at the boy. He seemed to be flesh and blood, just like James; however, he also seemed to be rotting away, as if he were a living corpse with veins of ice and maggots. Then, James thought back to the conversation with his father, how there was only one other living person that has been here before,

But they weren’t exactly human.

Just as James had put two and two together, the boy across arched his back and a snarl began to formulate in the back of his throat. Silent hissing transformed into a deep, loud growl, and the boy's eyes traveled up and down James' body, just like a lion hungering for its next meal. Within seconds, the flesh had torn off of the boy's body, and a black badger the size of a lion emerged.

James shook his head and pointed at the creature with his sword, and shouted, "WHAT IN GLORIC'S NAME IS THAT THING?"

Realizing he had drawn far too much attention to himself, he saw the creature barreling towards him. Before he could even move out of the way, the creature had tackled him into the wall, and imprinted an indentation of James' body into it. As the wind was knocked out of him and he fell to his knees, James groggily but swiftly raised his sword. The creature batted it out of the way and eagerly tried to make contact with its teeth to James' sweet, tender man meat.[4]

Quickly, James fell to the ground, the creature's head plummeting into the wall. James was able to scurry away and put some distance between him and the creature. It pulled its head away from the wall, as in it moved its head and took the wall with it, then turned to give James a horrifying glare, seemingly unfazed by the blow,

And the wall acting as a necklace.

James held out his sword again as the creature slowly approached and bore its rotting fangs. Getting a better look, James observed that this badger-like thing was rather sickly, with patches of fur missing and limbs revealing muscle tissue and bone. He grew nauseous as he closely observed its unhinged lower jaw, but despite its decayed appearance, he couldn't deny the creature's impeccable strength.

---

[4] A.K.A. his face.

The creature lunged for another attack. James tried to block its claws with his sword as he fell flat on his back. He pushed his legs against its chest, preventing its head from closing in on him; however, James was not spared entirely by the claws. They swiped at the sword as James continued to desperately block the blows. It was almost like a game of tug-of-war.

A very convoluted game of tug-of-war.

The creature let out a roar while looking at James intensely. "*The smell of living flesh and blood is one I have grown to miss,*" the creature said.

"I-It can talk?" James exclaimed

"*You bear the face of the one we hate, and for that, I will devour you for the glory of our god.*"

"I don't understand."

"FOR THE GLORY OF OUR GOD!"

In one swift motion, the creature bit James' coat sleeve and threw him up in the air. As the sleeve was ripped away, James continued to soar into the air, and he flailed from the unexpected maneuver. Before he hit the ground, the creature head butted James into the wall again, and his head smacked against the granite, resonating with the sound of a loud "crack!"

James groaned as he stood up from the ground, feeling like his shoulder was dislocated.

Actually, that was an understatement.

James groaned as he stood up from the ground, feeling as if his whole body was dislocated, but mostly his shoulder. He angrily looked up at the creature, his head pounding as a hint of blood trickled down his forehead. The creature attacked again. James quickly snapped his shoulder back into place, in an unflinching matter, even though he was internally screaming like a rabbit during the Thin Man Crusade of Trell.[5]

As he stood on his feet, he felt a bit more agile and he was able to dodge, but he kept losing his footing due to the instability of the ground beneath his feet.

"Why the hell would you put gravel into an arena?" James shouted towards the Council of Thirteen.

"It was my idea," Crumpy Face said. "I think it looks quite pretty from this angle."

"Pretty?"

"It also puts odds in our favor," Big Nose said. "If I were you, I'd do something before you lose your mortality, and yourself."

James huffed and went in for an attack, but as soon as he swung the sword, the creature brutally swiped its paw again, chucking the sword across the arena. James quickly rolled out of the way as the creature bore its fangs towards his face once more. He was able to put a bit of distance between himself and the creature, but it still stood between him and the Sword of Lord Krag.

Fetch, what do I do? James thought. *My sword is all the way over there while this hairless wonder has me nearly cornered.*

Silence.

Great, I'm talking to myself and expecting a response from a dog man trapped in a sword! I'm crazy!

He dodged another attack. The creature swung a paw towards James face, and he quickly ducked and hopped to the side.

Okay, it seems to be using its claws to get around. Maybe if I had claws? Or, something...

He once again dodged another swing, using his weight to slide across the gravel.

---

[5] A religious official during the Third Eon had given his followers the impression that a rabbit was an unholy creature that would lead the nation into a famine. In turn, the Crusaders of Trell had destroyed every rabbit within a fifty mile radius.

Hmm... the ice archers taught me that an arrow moving at full speed will never stop soaring if it weren't for the target. If I can get this thing moving at full speed, something has to stop it eventually... Good Gloric, I hope this works.

"Hey, you!" James shouted at the creature. "Fetch you!"

While James hoped to spark an angry reaction from the creature, he didn't expect what he got instead. The creature gasped loudly and offensively as its eyes glared into James', as if searching for a soul to burn with its stare on its own.

"*How* dare *you?*" The creature demanded in an airy voice, as if reflecting its own light-headedness and the Council's.

"What are you going to do about it?" James challenged.

The creature broke into a full sprint, muttering over and over, "*For the glory of our god!*" James, in turn, barreled towards the creature with a bit of a war cry. As the creature launched into the air at him, James dove into the gravel and slid towards the sword on his belly like a penguin.

In awe at the boldness of this man, the creature lost its footing upon landing and plummeted into the wall, the stone slab around its neck crumbling in the process.

"Stop ruining the pretty walls!" Crumpy Face shouted.

James grabbed the sword and stabbed it into the ground, stopping his momentum. He looked up at Crumpy Face. "Fetch you, too!"

Furious, the creature quickly stood up and burst into another sprint. At the last moment, James held out the sword in front of him. The creature dug its claws into the ground at the realization of what was about to happen but realized too late as its heart met the blade. With a crippling cry, the creature fell onto James, impaled and motionless.

Well, that was dumb. I didn't do a damn thing! Lord Krag commented.

James pushed the dead creature off of him, rolled onto his knees and stood. The courtroom was completely silent, as everyone stared at James, dumbfounded at what just happened. Then, clapping from a single person could be heard.

"Yay, James!" Mrs. Clemit cheered.

"That's my boy!" Mr. Clemit followed.

The two exchanged a glance and noticed that they were the only ones in the courtroom applauding. Mrs. Clemit's clapping slowed as the two awkwardly sat back down into their seats.

James let out a giggle and looked up at the Council of Thirteen. He smirked as every member reflected complete and utter shock.

He thought that they might die again!

As the arena reverted back to its lustrous, heinous, court-like state, with a golden pew rising in front of him, James sheathed his sword, and with a charismatic voice, said, "And that's why you don't let a mortal do battle in an Underworld folly."

"Boo!" someone in the audience shouted. "Bad pun!"

James pointed his sword at the source of the voice. "Fetch you, citizen!"

"You smell like one!"

"Who the hell even are you?"

"Better than you!"

"That's not an answer to the question!"

"Excuse us!" Big Nose hollered.

"Sure, you're excused," James said with light wave.

"You're a stupid mouth breather!" the heckler shouted.

"Why don't you come down here and say that to my face!"

"For the love of Gloric, just shut up!" Big Nose's voice bellowed.

James jumped at the sudden, oddly informal shout. "… Sorry." Big Nose sat back in his seat, and the Council fell silent for what seemed like several minutes.

"… Are you not going to say anything?" James asked.

They stayed quiet, appearing rather confused, and frustrated.

James let out a sigh. "I'm just going to start breaking things until you let me go."

"You can't break anything!" a Councilman on the far right said.

"No?" James drew his sword, and in one quick motion, slashed the golden pew in half.

The Council grew even more appalled as James continued slashing at the golden pew until it was nearly obliterated. James almost broke into a dance as he skipped towards the newly refurbished granite walls. He walked along the walls for a few feet, stopped to etch the words "James waz here" in a large, neat cursive, and finished the sentence with a little heart.

"ENOUGH!"

James smirked as he glanced back at the Council. Big Nose had turned several shades of red and shook with anger.

"So, are you going to let me go?" James asked.

"Absolutely not! You have just violated—"

James chucked the sword towards the Councilman. He immediately choked on his words and was overcome with fear as the sword landed on the wall below, missing him by inches. James, calmly, approached the Council and climbed up to their level.

"Lct mc rcphrasc that," hc said as hc pullcd thc sword out of the wall. "I want three things."

Big Nose narrowed his eyes and let out a huff of air. "What do you desire?"

"First of all, I want my parents to have a better house. The one they're in right now sucks."

"… And the second thing?"

"The living can visit the dead, and it won't be against the law."

"That is preposterous!"

"Is that so?" James rested his sword on his shoulder. "It seems like a pretty reasonable request to me."

"There are laws that we need to follow, and the living being able to freely visit the dead isn't one of them."

James shrugged. "Seems to me like we've violated many laws since my visit here. What's one more?"

Big Nose sighed. "The third?"

"Where is the fetching exit? I'm tired and I want to go back home, well, homeless…"

"… It's the moon."

James skeptically raised his eyebrows. "The moon?"

"… I-It takes a certain process—"

"Well, guess what you're doing today, friend?" James said as his hand phased in and out of the man's shoulder as a sad attempt of a pat on the back. "Let's all go on a nice field trip to the moon!"

~

You do realize "was" isn't spelled with a "z," right?

Of course, I do, Krag. It's slang and used in a joking context. I'm not stupid.

You're not that *stupid.*

Whatever.

The Council of Thirteen led James out of the courtroom (being held by sword point) and into the bustling Underworld, with the entire audience following behind. He playfully swung the sword around, with the Council before him tense and nervous.

"W-Will you stop swinging that damn thing?" one of the Councilmen shouted.

"Are you serious?" James asked. "I'm alive and you're dead, how could *this* do any harm to you?"

He playfully poked at the man's shoulder. The man cried out in pain, gripping his hand around his shoulder as a bit of blood began to stain the fabric.

James felt his face drain and his stomach drop. "Wh-What? How—?"

Well, James, I am a spirit in an enchanted sword. You can't bring them harm, but I can.

You seriously could've hurt them this entire time?

"Could've," yes, "would've," probably.

Then why didn't you?

It's so much more fun to watch an innocent man be tormented than to kill people.

... I hate you.

"I-I am so sorry! I had no idea—"

The man spun around furiously. "Will you just get the fetch out of our Underworld?"

"Y-Yes sir..."

Well, would you look at that! They hate you so much they won't press charges for your attempted assassination! You're a lucky man, James.

Shut up!

With a huff and a puff, Big Nose raised his arm, implying for everyone to stop in their tracks. He stepped to the side, gesturing for James to go in front of him. "We are here."

Before James was a clearing set perfectly underneath the glowing, yellow moon. The beams illuminated the entire area, but one beam acted as a spotlight, dead center of the clearing. James slowly approached that center beam, looking back at the Council as soon as he reached it.

"So... what am I supposed to do?" James asked

"Grab it!" Buck Teeth shouted.

Confused, James reached out towards the beam of light, surprised when his hand brushed against golden silk. "Ohhh..." He pulled his hand away and looked back at the Council. "Before I go, can I say goodbye first?"

"GET OUT OF HERE, BOY!" the injured Councilman yelled.

James tilted his head and held up his sword. "Are you sure you should be denying me?"

The Councilman gritted his teeth and glared at James. "… Fine. Say goodbye." He walked to the side and began muttering to himself. "It's almost like dealing with Gloric all over again…"

James sheathed his sword and glanced about the group of people. Mr. and Mrs. Clemit fought through the crowd to come forward. James ran over to them as Mrs. Clemit looked up and smiled. He tried to reach out to hug her, but the physics of this place seemed to slip his mind once more. Slightly dismayed that he couldn't touch his mother's silhouette, she simply smiled, letting her hand hover against his cheek. "We knew you could do it," she said.

Trying to fight back tears, James nodded. "I… don't know if I should leave."

"What do you mean, son?" Mr. Clemit asked.

"I have nobody up there waiting for me, and I'm not really the best kind of person…"

"To us, you are," Mrs. Clemit replied.

James sighed. "I mean, at least down here I have my family."

"If you can't live for yourself, then live for us," Mr. Clemit began. "You're lucky to be alive, son, and I know every one of us here are a bit envious of that."

James glanced past Mr. Clemit's shoulder at the rest of the audience, even locking eyes with Kyle, who smiled and gave him a nod.

"Hey."

James looked back at his father.

"You don't quite understand the capacity you hold for talent and intellect, son. Go out and find it."

"For us?" Mrs. Clemit asked.

James smiled and nodded. "I will. I love you guys."

"We love you, too," his parents replied in unison.

Giving one more wave, James turned back towards the silk beam and approached it. He grabbed on tightly and began to climb. *Hey, Krag, that old guy compared me to a god for a second!*

Gloric could be a fetch sometimes, whereas you are a fetch all the time.

James furrowed his brows as he reached upward and continued to climb. *Why do you have to be a jerk?*

How do you think an ancient warlord would reply to that question, James?

Touché...

~

After what seemed to be miles (and probably were miles) James, with shaking arms that could give way any minute, finally reached the moon. The moon, to James' surprise, ended up being just a hole to the Surface. With a wholehearted struggle and a slight leap of faith, James immersed into the world of the living. He crawled weakly and buried into a whitish gray sediment. His face was red, and his panting was rhythmic to the throbbing that occurred in his arms.

Holy... fetch, he thought to himself.

You know, I thought you wouldn't make that last stretch, Krag said.

Wait a minute, couldn't you have leant me strength?

What do you mean?

You know, like when I ran all the way back from Trig in a matter of hours instead of days. Couldn't you have helped me climb up here without getting tired?

Yes.

Then why didn't you?

I wanted to see what would happen.

... I hate you.

Yet, you still need me.

James rolled his eyes, then rolled over onto his back and coughed before raising his arm to shield his eyes from the sun. *Hah... the sun... almost forgot what it looked like,* he thought, before falling asleep for a few hours,

Because, news flash, time is a thing now.

That's pretty cool.

CHAPTER FIVE

KIDS THESE DAYS

JAMES AWOKE TO A JABBING sensation in his side.

What the heck, he thought to himself as he groaned and slowly opened his eyes.

An old man, with a twinkle in his eye and a pleasant smile on his face was standing above him. "Hello," he merrily spoke.

James let out a startled shout, sat up, and crawled a few inches away.

"I didn't mean to frighten you there, fella," the man continued with a chuckle. "You were rather motionless, so I was checking to see if you were alive."

The man gently poked James in the chest with a wooden cane.

"Uh… thanks… I guess." James took a deep breath as an attempt to calm his rapid heartbeat. He rubbed his eyes and glanced at his surroundings, observing a white rock quarry before him. "Where am I?"

"Not sure. I just happened to stumble across this place. I was quite surprised to see another person, though. This area seems rather vacant."

"Oh…" James replied, still trying to gather his bearings.

"I am quite curious about this large hole. Do you think it must be some bottomless pit?"

James glanced to his side and noticed the hole as well. The fogginess began to diminish as the recent events returned to his mind. "… The Underworld."

"What was that, young man?"

"Uh... I said I'm not sure either."

"Oh, that's unfortunate." He scowled. "I was hoping you might know a thing or two about the area."

"… May I ask why?"

"Well, I consider myself a bit of an explorer. This plane of existence is constantly evolving, as well as the people that live on it. If I happen to come across somebody who seems just as lost as I am, then we may as well work together to find out where we are and what has changed."

James furrowed his brow and mashed his lips together as he examined the man more intently. His white hair was far too maintained for someone that spent their time wandering the wilderness, not to mention that his white dress shirt and beige slacks didn't have a single hint of dirt on them. His heavy backpack and hiking boots made him look legitimate, in addition to the honest sparkle of good will in his metallic blue eyes, but James didn't understand what the benefits of being overdressed out in nature would be,

And that made him nervous.

"… That doesn't make any sense," James carelessly whispered as his mind raced with questions and concerns.

"… Oh, I get it," the old man indignantly replied. "You think I'm senile and that my judgment is off. Well, I've been around here a lot longer than you've been, sonny, and I think I know a thing or two about how this world works!"

"I-I didn't mean to offend you! I just thought—"

"Just thought you could pull a fast one on me? Let me tell you, boy, it's one thing to find a traveler in this region, but it's another thing to come across an unmaintained clod with no supplies, tattered clothing, and passed out at the edge of a mysterious fracture in the ground!"

James winced, knowing that the man had every right to be just as wary,

Perhaps more.

"Well?"

"Um…" James averted his gaze. "You're right."

"Of course, I'm right! Here I am, being nice, and you're just being uncivil!" The man groaned as he got down on his knees and plopped down onto the ground next to James. A bit winded, he pulled out a sandwich bag from one of his many pockets. "Trail mix?"

"… Excuse me?"

"Do you want some trail mix?"

"… What do you mean 'trail mix?'"

"It's an assortment of nuts and raisins, with little bits of candy. I bought it from Blendell." He shook the bag. "Trail mix?"

It could be poisoned.

James, it's just trail mix. Stop being so paranoid.

But—

No.

I—

Stop. It's trail mix. It's fine.

"Um… okay?" James hesitantly reached into the bag and pulled out a peanut. "Thank you."

"No, *thank* you."

"… Why are you offering me food? I was just really rude to you. I thought you'd be mad."

"When you get to my age, you come to find out that people use most of their time to assume rather than to acquaint themselves with others. Since I look old and grumpy, I often get deemed as unfriendly and angry. But I promise you that I do my best to be a good-hearted fellow! Why do you think I haven't left you for dead? What kind of responsible citizen would I be if I didn't assist someone in their time of need, especially a man with nothing but the clothes on his back? He must be beside himself with depression, and not just the one in the ground."

James snickered at the man's pun. "Well, thank you for going out of your way to help me."

"Well, the circumstance of your satisfaction pleases me!"

"… What?"

"It's my pleasure."

"Oh," James looked back at the hole, "okay, then…"

The man tilted his head. "Now… to find out what this hole is."

"… The Underworld," James spoke up.

"What?" the man exclaimed. "The Underworld you say?"

"Yeah, that's the hole that leads to the Underworld…"

"Fascinating! Absolutely fascinating!" The man shoved the trail mix in James' hands and unfolded a piece of parchment paper from another pocket. He pressed a button on the handle of his cane, causing a pen to emerge from it. "And you just… woke up here next to it?"

"No, I actually climbed out of there."

"How did you manage to do that?"

"A silk trail attached to the hole."

"Exhilarating!" The man wrote down James' words. "On silk you say? I wonder why silk of all things…"

"… It looked like the moon from down there. Maybe it's" —James scoffed— "'moon silk,' or something like that."

"Interesting, moon silk, how in the world did they get moon silk?"

"N-No, sir, that was more of a joke than anything. I wasn't trying to give you the wrong idea—"

"Oh, but my dear boy, moon silk is a material that actually exists.

James raised his eyebrows, feeling rather impressed with himself. "Really?"

"Yes. There existed a species of spiders that were able to capture the beams of the moon in silk strands. In fact, the silk, itself, could seemingly imitate those moon beams, and bring light to all of those who came across such an exceptional treasure."

James' eyes lit up. "That sounds really cool."

"I'm quite surprised, though. The spiders went extinct thousands of years ago, and you say that there was enough moon silk to climb out of that hole? Peculiar, I say! Absolutely peculiar!"

James shrugged. "Actually, it wouldn't be so farfetched."

"No?"

"There were animal and plant species down there that I didn't recognize, so it isn't unbelievable that there would be moon silk spiders down there."

The man nodded and wrote down more notes.

"So… yeah" James awkwardly placed the peanut in his mouth then reached into the bag for a raisin.

"What were you even doing down there anyway?" the man asked, his face suddenly closer to James.

James let out another startled shout and some of the trail mix flew out of the bag when he jumped.

"Sorry, sorry. I can barely contain my excitement when I discover something new."

"I-It's fine," James said while tightly clutching the bag.

"You know what, young man, I like you!"

"… What?"

"There isn't a lot of youth out there that would take a moment to have a chat with an old man about the world. I appreciate your time."

"Wow, um, thank you," James said. He felt happy that someone, other than his parents, thought he was slightly decent.

"What's your name?"

"It's James, sir. James Roger Clemit."

"James Roger Clemit," the man marveled. "I've known a few Clemits in my lifetime. Such a strong name."

James smiled. "What's your name?"

"My name is Mr. Woodstock."

"Mr. Woodstock? That's a nice name, too."

"Thank you, Mr. Clemit."

Mr. Woodstock slowly got up on his feet, then extended a hand towards James. Assuming it was merely a handshake, James firmly grasped his hand, and was surprised when the old man effortlessly pulled him to his feet.

"Now then," Mr. Woodstock began, "where are you traveling to?"

"Uh… I'm not too sure. It's kind of a long story as to why, but so far I don't have any set destination."

"Well, do you mind traveling with an elderly man for a short while?"

"I don't know," James nervously replied. "You just met me, and I'm spouting a bunch of mumbo jumbo about visiting the Underworld. For all you know I could be crazy."

"Would a crazy person admit to insanity?"

James bit his lip. Mr. Woodstock was right, but James didn't have the heart nor the guts to say that he wasn't too fond of strangers, not anymore anyway.

"I completely understand if you are uncomfortable, I just thought I'd offer since you have nowhere else to go."

"U-Um, I guess I could travel with you for a little bit—"

"Perfect!" Mr. Woodstock took the large backpack off of his shoulders and handed it to James. "You can carry this for me."

"… Of course."

"Now, we must hurry along, now. I promised I'd be done with this map by the first of Glorin and it's already the third of Mittelan."

"… Third of… Mittelan?"

"Yes."

"What's that?"

Mr. Woodstock stared intently at James. "You're not pulling my leg, are you?"

"N-Not at all!"

"You honestly don't know what Mittelan is?"

James hung his head in embarrassment. "No."

"My goodness boy," Mr. Woodstock walked closer, "did you hit your head or something?"

"Not that I recall."

"Then, how do you not know what Mittelan is?"

"Uh…" James narrowed his eyes. "Why don't you explain to me what it is… then I'll tell you why."

"Mittelan is the fifth month of the year."

"What's a month?"

Mr. Woodstock stared blankly.

You cannot be this stupid, Krag said.

Shush, I'm trying to look sane to an old man.

You're doing an awful job.

You're an awful job!

The fetch?

"I-I mean… I, uh… I never really paid attention to months. My… adopted father, for lack of better words, would always respond with 'today' when I asked what day it was."

Mr. Woodstock laughed. "Oh, that is an unfortunate predicament. You don't know about months, but you know about years?"

James shrugged. "I tend to focus on other things.[6]"

"I suppose that's a valid response. I would love to hear more about you James, since that is quite an interesting trait. I haven't met anyone quite like you, not in a while anyway," Mr. Woodstock said as he started towards one direction, gripping firmly onto his parchment. "Now, then, how did you end up all the way down there?"

James looped his arms through the straps of the backpack.

"Ugh, where do I even begin?"

"Well, at the beginning, Mr. Clemit. It's silly to start a story halfway through it. Too many loose ends! What are they doing? Who's Carl? I don't know!"

"Wait, Carl?"

"My point exactly! Nobody knows who Carl is!"

"O-Okay."

"Always start at the beginning, Mr. Clemit. *Always*."

"Right…"

~

"So," Mr. Woodstock began, "you got into a quarrel with a man at a bar, he shot you several times, but somehow you managed to arrive at the Underworld and still be alive?"

"That's what happened," James said, feeling a bit guilty that he purposely left out what his previous employment was, and that the quarrel was with Chancellor Henry Chase.

"What a curious, curious predicament you found yourself in! Did you meet the Council of Thirteen?"

James scoffed. "Unfortunately."

---

[6] There are ten months in an entire year on Tor, each consisting of thirty days. The order of the months are First Dawn, Lyndnol, Maw, Vrenic, Mittelan, Glorin, Falter, Trimble, Slivic, and Nox.

"Ah," Mr. Woodstock nodded and sighed. "I'm not much of a worshipper, nor a follower for that matter, but I will admit that Gloric did the world a service when dealing with them."

"What is the legend regarding them anyway? Nobody ever really told me."

Mr. Woodstock cleared his throat. "Well, many, many, *many* years ago, there lived a judge with the most gruesome, condescending demeanor, with his personal jury from hell."

James raised his eyebrows, intrigued.

"The judge was cruel and unfair in his punishment. Nobody was innocent until proven guilty, and no defense came to anyone's aid. He was quick to point his crooked finger and didn't see anybody beyond his nose."

Literally, James thought to himself.

"He handed out as many death sentences as the amount of filn he kept in his robes of gold. It was the goal of the judge and the jury to rid the world of simple commoners, and that they only deserved the same amount of mercy as an unwanted fly on the wall.

"When word of this jury reached the ears of the God of Peace, he disguised himself as a common man, or rather an orange farmer, and entered the forsaken city they reigned over. Quickly, he was called out, saying his oranges were overpriced, and sentenced to death over false crimes."

"How much were the oranges?"

"They were free."

James rolled his eyes and shook his head. "Bastards."

Mr. Woodstock nodded in agreeance. "The instant the gavel gave verdict, Gloric revealed himself to the people of the court. Since they seemed to be such lovers of death, the punishment inflicted upon them was to pass judgment in a world where death is no longer an option. The jury and the judge became known as the Council of Thirteen, where they now obey the laws of a god."

"Whoa…"

"Like I said before, I am not an advocate of Gloric, but he does have a unique way of punishing people." Mr. Woodstock stared out into the distance instead of at the parchment for the first time since the two began their journey together. "He strips people of their power, allowing them to live out the rest of their eternal lives in complete humiliation while he continues to reign supreme. I'd admire the god if he weren't so pompous."

"… Mr. Woodstock, have you met Gloric?"

Mr. Woodstock shuddered. "Ugh, to my dismay! Not my cup of tea, that one!"

"Wait, you've met him?" James exclaimed.

"You just asked that question."

James blinked. "Sorry, I wasn't expecting you to say 'yes.'"

"And I wasn't expecting to be traveling with a dead man, but here we are, traveling together, and exchanging stories as if we were old buddies."

James gave a light laugh. "You've got me there."

"Anyway, like I said. He's not my favorite person."

"Yeah, he seems to be a bit of a fetch."

Mr. Woodstock cringed at the word as it passed James' lips.

"Oh, um, sorry. I sort of use that word a bit too much. I forget that it's a swearword sometimes."

Mr. Woodstock simply nodded and looked back at the paper. "I understand. It's a word that tends to be… overused. May I politely request that you refrain from using it around me?"

"I'll… I'll do my best."

"Please do."

Feeling a bit embarrassed, James decided to change the subject.

"So… you're making a map of Tor?"

"Yes. I am in need of an update of what this wretched place looks like," Mr. Woodstock replied.

"'Wretched place?'"

"Yes. This entire planet is nauseating, but home is home I suppose."

"Right..."

"Nobody here has any respect anymore." Mr. Woodstock turned around to face James. "That's what I like about you, young man. It's quite rare to find a chap like you eager to help out his elders."

"Well, I'm always happy to help out others," James boasted with a slight smile on his face.

Mr. Woodstock muttered to himself, pointing at different trees with his pen and cane in one hand, and then would pause to make notes in the map. He then took a glance at the sun, and then looked down at his sundial.

... Sundial?

"Mother of Gloric! Is that the time?"

"Oh right, time," James said, reminding himself that he's out of the Underworld. "What *is* the time, Mr. Woodstock?"

"Horribly *late!* We must set up camp!"

It's literally seven-thirty... Krag said.

How do you know?

I can see the sundial, James. I'm a sword, not blind.

You can read sundials?

How old am I, James?

Touché... but where are your eyes?

Everywhere, James. I have a hundred sets.

James shuddered. "Do you want to set up camp here, then?"

"We're going to have to," Mr. Woodstock begrudgingly replied.

James removed the backpack and gently set it on the ground. Mr. Woodstock folded up his map, returned it to his pocket, put away his pen, and then tossed the cane to the side. He approached the backpack, unzipped the largest pocket, and pulled out a small tarp and a few stakes. Then, he glanced up at James, almost as if he had forgotten about his existence. "Oh, would you go look for firewood?"

"I don't mind helping set up camp first. That way the time to set up is halved and you can just relax while I get firewood."

Mr. Woodstock sighed. "You have such poise, James. Your parents raised you well."

"... Actually, my parents didn't raise me. I was raised by a chieftain."

"Then, what a fine chieftain he was!"

Not really, James thought.

"But, I insist, I can set up here, you can just go get the wood." Mr. Woodstock flicked his hand towards James dismissively.

"O-Okay." James reluctantly submitted.

James ventured out into the surrounding forest. The sun hadn't completely set yet, and he felt warm in his tattered, dress shirt. As he rolled up his sleeves, he noticed that the bullet holes in the shirt were quite prominent. He sighed, still confused as to how the whole ordeal even happened. Then again, he was technically alive, or rather he was never dead, so, he should go ahead and drop the issue, right? After all, it's just another weird event to add to his mental book of remembrance.

James shook his head and began gathering sticks and dry plant material. The forest was rather pretty as it echoed with the eloquent sounds of quivering trees and life chittering at every nook and cranny. James smiled widely at a squirrel and a hummingbird chirping loudly at each other in a nearby tree.

They're like a married couple, he thought to himself.

He closed his eyes to listen to the subtle growls of a body of water nearby, and the crisp, delicious air broke through the heat of the evening, sweet against his tongue. The scuffing of his boots against the dirt rang harmoniously with the sounds of the forest, and he felt full at the thought of no longer being subject to the desolate world existing underneath him.

After about ten minutes, he returned to the camp to see Mr. Woodstock sitting on the ground next to a pitched tent, rummaging through his backpack.

"I got the firewood," James declared.

"Good, good." Mr. Woodstock didn't look up from his bag. "Go ahead and start a fire while I see if I can find any food."

"… Do you not have any food?" James asked as he began arranging branches on the ground.

"Of course, I do! I just… may or may not have enough for the two of us… and the size of this bag doesn't help my search one bit!"

Doesn't he know how to organize? James thought

Cut him some slack, he's elderly.

You raise a valid point. After all, he's not as senile as you are.

What did you say, boy?

You heard me.

"I'm pretty sure I heard some water running when I was looking for wood. Maybe I could fish for us?"

Mr. Woodstock grumbled something and then sighed. "Fine. That seems to be the better option. Thanks, lad."

James diverted from starting the fire to venturing into the forest once more. He listened for the sound of running water again and hoped that it was a bit larger than just a small brook. To his delight, he came across a river, and excitedly eyed some fish swimming in the crystal, clear water.

You seriously thought this could've been a brook? Rivers are loud. *Do your ears not work?*

"Shut up. Look, if we work together, I think we could muster up a couple of fish."

Lord Krag grew silent.

As James unsheathed the sword, it suddenly grew heavy and caused him to fall backwards on his rear.

"What the fetch?" James shouted

Oh, sorry, did I do that?

"Yes! What the hell are you doing?"

I just can't seem to think straight.

"Well, just lighten up!"

Okay.

James stood and was able to easily pick up the sword. "Okay, I'm going to count to three, and we're going to jab that fish right there. One—"

The sword grew heavy again and James fell forward into the river, scaring away the fish.

"Krag!" James shouted as waded towards the shore, completely drenched.

Oh, sorry, I thought you said on "one"

"What has gotten into you?"

Don't know. Perhaps I've just grown too senile…

"… I hate you so much right now," James stood on his feet

While James couldn't see Lord Krag, he could tell that he was enjoying himself far too much and was probably smiling at James' inevitable karma.

"Humor me this one time?"

Mm… no.

James huffed.

However, I suppose I've had my fun, for now. As you were, stupid youngster.

"Thanks, old man…"

~

"My goodness, what happened to you?" Mr. Woodstock asked as he was sitting on the ground next to a blazing fire.

James, holding tightly onto his fish-skewered sword, simply smiled. "I fell," he said with water still trickling down from the tips of his hair.

“You fell?”

“Yep. I fell.”

“I’m sorry… at least you managed to grab—” Mr. Woodstock’s face fell at the sight of James’ sword. “Is that dinner?”

“… Yes?

“Mother of Gloric.” Mr. Woodstock huffed as he began going through his backpack.

“Is everything okay?”

“Ah-hah!” Mr. Woodstock pulled out a small tackle box. “You’re lucky I happened to have lures on me.” He handed the box to James. “Go back and try again.”

“What?” James exclaimed. “What’s wrong with the fish I brought?”

“There is a process, young man, an intricate process that effects the entire outcome, taste, and nutrients you receive from the fish. What you are doing now is absurd! Not only did you fail to gut the fish, but you stabbed straight through them, rupturing their organs in the process. The fish is ruined due to your recklessness!”

James felt himself sinking with embarrassment. He had been so used to living off of scraps most of his life that he didn’t even know there were processes to certain things. How was he supposed to know, anyway?

“Go back and get more!”

James groaned as Krag’s laughter echoed in his head, and he returned to the river. He managed to fashion a makeshift fishing pole by attaching a lure to a string and trying it around a stick

“This is going to be impossible,” James said to himself. “The string is just going to be whisked away with the river, assuming I even find bait. How am I going to attract fish like this?”

Go find some insects, Krag said.

“Insects?”

Just look through the ground and find a handful of insects.

"And I just keep them in my hand this entire time?" James exclaimed.

Yes.

James huffed, but he didn't argue. He dug through the ground and found worms, maggots, and other variety of bugs. He tried to keep himself from gagging or flinching at their slimy writhing in his hands. "Now what?"

Throw them into the river.

James did as Krag said. After a few seconds, he noticed that some fish swarmed from upstream just to get some of the bugs.

Now, put the lure in the water.

James hesitantly lowered the lure into the river, and before he knew it, a fish had already snagged onto the hook. Quickly, he yanked it out of the water and watched it flail at the end of the hook.

Congratulations, you now know how to fish with limited resources.

James marveled for a second at Krag. "How did you know how to do that?"

Some of us actually took the time to learn how to survive in the wilderness.

James rolled his eyes but felt grateful for the advice as he put the fish in the sack. James repeated the process of dangling in the lure and throwing more bugs into the water when the fish finally scattered. Once he had about six fish, he returned to the camp to see Mr. Woodstock sitting by the fire with two knives, a few large leaves, a couple of lumpy, orange fruits, and some herbs.

"Did you get the fish?" Mr. Woodstock asked when James was in sight."

James nodded an held up the sack.

"Did you do it right?"

"I-I believe so," James stammered.

"Good, now come and sit."

James did as he was told, and Mr. Woodstock proceeded to teach James how to prepare the fish for eating. He was in a significantly better mood as he taught James how to properly gut the fish by holding it upside-down, cutting it from the belly to the head, and scraping in a V-shape while cutting out black spots.

As they began to stuff the fish with herbs and the orange fruit, James' question of why the fruit was shaped the way it was triggered a tangent out of Mr. Woodstock.

"Limes, lemons, and oranges are not naturally occurring citrus," he began. "They were adapted genetically by man with these." He held up the fruit. "This is what real citrus is, James. *This* is naturally occurring, which means it's *real.*"

"Real?" James reiterated.

"Yes. Now, wrap your fish in the leaves. The greener the leaves are, the better it is for cooking because it distributes the heat better."

James nodded and did as he was told.

"Now, place it on the rocks."

"How long does it cook for?" James asked as he did as he was told.

"Ten minutes for every inch."

James nodded. "Got it.[7]"

Mr. Woodstock sat back. "See how you just learned a new skill? Man has become too dependent on technology to learn all of this information. What if the world was thrown into the dark ages? Mankind wouldn't know what to do in order to survive…"

Mr. Woodstock continued his rant about mankind being too dependent, which transitioned into a tangent about the environment, with a rant about air quality beginning to form in the crevices of the argument.

James found himself quite amused at Mr. Woodstock's small complaints. Being in the Underworld was the first time he had ever

---

[7] Payneful Reads: Teaching readers how to cook fish in the wilderness since 2020.

really met Jim, and he didn't have any other grandparents to entertain him the tales of the golden times before the now. Despite the peace in the air and the last of the sunlight scattering across the ground, James felt himself growing extremely nervous the longer he was with Mr. Woodstock.

When it was time for them to share a meal with one another, James observed that Mr. Woodstock hadn't eaten a single bite. He wanted to believe the reason for that was simply distraction of these thoroughly contemplated grievances, but he found his mind wandering back to when Mr. Woodstock didn't have any food in his backpack, or the fact that there was an old man wandering the woods by himself with no trace of weariness. James found his appetite wavering as his thoughts raced faster. He started jumping to outrageous conclusions, such as Mr. Woodstock being some sort of monster that only transforms at night, and he wanted to go to bed early so he could murder James when he least expected.

What if he wasn't a monster, though? What if he was in cahoots with the Tri-bore and the Bureau with an agenda to betray him at the last minute and turn him over to the government? What if he was some sort of thief and wanted to rob James of his belongings in the night. Granted, James didn't have much on him, but he did have the Sword of Lord Krag, and perhaps Mr. Woodstock found value in the blade without even knowing its history.

The conclusions James came to made his shoulders feel like rocks with overwhelming feelings of stress and panic beginning to form in his stress knots. He was crazy to wander into the wilderness with some man he didn't even know. James knew his mind was beginning to take things too far, so he took a deep breath to try and repress the thoughts, to try and repress the sense of reality. After all, the last time he assumed the worst about a person, he nearly murdered an innocent man.

"Young man?"

James' attention snapped back to Mr. Woodstock, who was staring with genuine concern.

"Are you alright?"

James nodded. "Yes, sorry. It's just been… a very long time since I got a good night's rest."

"I see. Fortunately for you, the night has fallen upon us. We will begin our journey again in the morning."

James nodded again and felt himself choking with unease.

Mr. Woodstock was kind enough to offer the tent to James, but he declined and claimed that he preferred to sleep under the stars anyway. While Mr. Woodstock was asleep, James rested on the ground and stared at the stars. He found himself counting them to keep himself distracted, but he felt like the number of stars in the sky began to match the number of concerns growing in his head.

Would you just calm down? You're making the dogs all antsy, Krag complained.

James sighed. *I know, but the last time I carelessly agreed to do something, it ended up being the near-death of me. He seems okay, but it was stupid of me to just agree to travel with someone I barely know.*

... I'm sorry... isn't that literally what you did with that one kid?

Reggy was a minor. I felt irresponsible just letting him roam the wilderness like that.

That also justifies abandoning him?

James winced.

Make a decision, kid. Are you going to be cautious, or are you going to calm the fetch down and realize that not everyone is out to get you.

... Calm the fetch down.

Are you sure?

He pouted slightly. *You're not just saying that so you can torment me?*

Okay, yes, I'm a recovering serial killer, but no, I'm not saying things to torment you. I promise I won't put you in danger. I learned my lesson.

James pursed his lips and started to feel a bit more reassured, but not entirely.

Sleep well, you stupid youngster.

Goodnight old man.

Chapter Six

Ghoti-y Ordeals

THE TOWN OF GHOTI WAS absolutely beautiful.

It was one of the first settlements apart of the Kingdom of Plier that eventually grew independent. The pink-haired citizens were speckled among different walks of life that all congregated to trade their invaluable goods. The river running through it flourished with various species of fish. Thick oak trees surrounded this serene location in addition to cherry blossoms popcorning into bloom, and the green of the atmosphere blended with the logged buildings.

It was stunning.

But the smell was nearly intolerable.

This so-called "merchant hub," as Mr. Woodstock described, used fish as a primary resource. It was obvious that people traded rare and expensive things for the delicacies being sold at every corner of the town, but the stink was terrible. James felt himself gagging with every breath he took and debated between vomiting for eternity or to just stop breathing. He tried for the second option, but he couldn't seem to hold his breath long enough.

"Well, I believe this is where we part ways," Mr. Woodstock said.

James turned to the old man, astonished. "You mean, I'm not going to continue traveling with you?"

"You are an ambitious, young man, James. I can see a lot of potential with you. It was a nice three days, but you don't need to be wasting time doting over someone like myself."

"Yeah, but…" James scratched his head. "I don't really have anywhere else to go."

"Here"—Mr. Woodstock handed James a pouch full of silver filn— "buy yourself a couple of fish and get to know the people around here. Someone might have a bit more to offer than myself."

"I-I can't accept this," James replied.

"Do you have money of your own?"

James reached into his pockets and frowned, embarrassed at their emptiness.

"Consider it a payment, for your assistance."

James averted his gaze. "Th-Thank you."

"Oh, and it probably wouldn't hurt to buy yourself a change of clothes first." Mr. Woodstock pointed his cane towards the bullet holes in James' suit. "Someone might think you looted this suit off a dead body."

James smirked. "I mean, it did go with me to the Underworld."

"That may be, but you don't have to go advertising it. Despite the greatness of the tale, you don't want the wrong ears to come across such news. That would be *quite* detrimental."

James nodded, trying to maintain his smile while hiding his anxiety.

"Good luck, Mr. Clemit. May your journeys treat you well." He gave James a pat on the shoulder.

"I hope the same for you." James returned the gesture.

With a wave, the old man turned around and walked away, the large backpack shifting with every step he took. James, unsure of what to do, looked around the town. He had no idea what kind of fish he could buy, or even should buy, but figured he should try and find some work first.

Then again, Mr. Woodstock was right about his appearance. James didn't know if anyone here sold clothing, or if the clothing they provided was made from the scales of fish. The thought of fish-scaled clothing reminded him that maybe finding work in this particular town wouldn't be the best, since he would rather die than breathe in the rancid air all day,

And that was saying a lot.

James had no other option except his last resort. He looked to his right and called out towards a random man gutting fish. "Excuse me?"

The man halted his work. "May I help you?"

"Is there a bar here?"

~

"Is this your first time to Ghoti?" the bartender asked as he wiped the counter down.

"Um" —James pointed his thumb at the exit— "the sign outside of your town says 'Gho-ti.'"

The bartender narrowed his eyes. "Yes… and it's pronounced Ghoti."

James opened his mouth to argue but stammered over his confusion on the pronunciation of this town's name. Nevertheless, he shook his head. He was never one for linguistics anyway.

"So, I take it this *is* your first time here."

Defeated, James nodded. "Yes, it is."

"Ah, well let me tell you, this place is heaven on Tor! Better than the realm of Heaven, itself, if I may say so!"

"I agree that this place is beautiful, but how do you tolerate the smell?"

"What smell?"

"… Never mind. Heaven on Tor?"

"Oh, yes. You'll never find a paradise quite like this one!"

James nodded, agreeing that there definitely wasn't a place quite like this one.

"Do you plan on staying long?"

"I'm not sure. I thought maybe by coming here I would be able to find some work or at least something to do."

"Dressed like that?"

"Justifies me needing a job, doesn't it?"

"I suppose you're right." The bartender put the rag away. "What are we drinking today?"

"Um…" James examined the shelves behind the bar tender. "… I'll just have water."

The bartender raised his eyebrow. "Really? You're going to drink water in a bar?"

"I stopped drinking recently. Besides, I'm mostly here for direction, not scotch. I'm sure your liquor is great, though."

"You're damn right. At least let me get you a soda? I have all sorts of flavors you can add to it. You can make it your own! You can even have our trade-marked fish flavored soda!"

James laughed nervously. "Yeah… about that…"

"Quitting soda, too? What are you, some health nut?"

"Hell, no. Gloric have mercy, I may be a fetch but not to that extent. I'll be frank, you'd rather deal with an aggressive drunk than me on caffeine. I literally bounce off of the walls."

The bartender chuckled. "Fair enough. Tell you what, how about a sparkling water with a lemon? Unless you have something against lemons or bubbles?"

James smiled. "No issues there."

The bartender pulled out a glass. "I hope you don't mind me asking, but did you get into a street fight with fifty cats or something?"

James looked down at his clothes and then back up at the bartender. “Yes… Yes, I did.”

“And how did that happen?”

“… When you get into a car accident with a truck transporting catnip?” James anxiously said, hoping the bartender believed him.

“That’s quite the story.”

“Indeed, it is.”

“Guess I’ll have to be warier around transport trucks should I ever own a car. This region is outside of the Bureau’s jurisdiction, so we haven’t the resources to build roads or fuel cars just yet.”

James sighed, relieved that the bartender seemed to believe him, and that there wouldn’t be any Red Knights to whisk him away to an electric chair.

“By the way” —the bartender began pouring the sparkling water into the glass— “if you decide to leave town, you need to meet our mayor before you go.”

“What’s so great about him?”

The bartender’s head shot up with an offended look spread across his face.

“S-Sorry! I didn’t mean it like that! Sometimes I just sort of blurt out words without thinking about how I may come off to other people.”

“Well… I’ll cut you some slack because you’re new, but other people here might not be so easy on you.”

“You must really admire your mayor.”

“Oh, he is a *novelty!* Our feelings for him are greater than just admiration!” The bartender put the lemon wedge on the edge of the glass, set down a napkin, and placed the drink in front of James. “It’s because of him that we have such a successful economy.”

“Really?” James picked up the lemon wedge and squeezed the juice into the water.

"Yes, our humble, vibrant town was once a makeshift dump. We came to him, unsure of what to do, and he simply replied with a joke: 'Where do fish keep their money? In a riverbank!'"

James, a bit thrown off at where the direction of the story was going, snickered at the terrible joke.

"So, we got the idea to make our main output fish. We quickly escaped poverty, awarding him with the title of 'Mayor of Ghoti.'"

"That's… an interesting story. Very inspiring," James commented as he began to nibble on what was left of the lemon.

"Isn't it?" The bartender smiled. "Anyway, I need to tend to my other guests, but I'll let you know if I hear of anybody in need of a worker."

"Thank you."

The bartender traveled down to the other end of the bar, leaving James with his beverage. He took a sip of the sparkling water. It was weird sitting at a bar with no subtle buzz, and by buzz, he literally meant ringing in his head.

The last time James had a sip of alcohol was before he delivered his last message. He could return to that life, using hopeless, insensitive fibs as a way out.

... So why do I still have this lemon water? he thought

Perhaps, deep down, James succumbed to the idea that he didn't have to be a bum. He could be a free, hard worker for someone like Mr. Woodstock. Then again, it would be easier to play on the ignorance of others, including himself. It was his ultimate fail safe, but that would render everything that happened to him worthless. He went from being a sewer rat to an aristocrat, so it wasn't impossible to be whatever he wanted.

But what if he began seeing things again? What if he was seeing things in this moment? What if the journey he's holding a standard to didn't even happen? He knew for a fact he wasn't in Trig anymore, so perhaps he made up everything on a walk here, but was Trig even a place to begin with? Ghoti doesn't seem to be real so why would Trig be real? Was the lemon water real?

James tried to push the thoughts out of his head and was reminded of his experience with Kyle in the Underworld. Even if all of this was fake, he could still enjoy it; however, what if "Kyle" just told him that so he wouldn't leave this perpetual state of dissociation? What if his mind didn't *want to* wake up?

James trembled as he brought his hands to his ears. The fog in his mind turned his head into a cloud as his vision grew blurry and his tongue developed fuzz. There it was, that familiar buzzing and the sensation of his stomach practicing its square knots, but not from a toxic drink, it never was. James grew sick from a much more horrifying poison: a mind toxic with racing thoughts of uncertainty.

"Hey, James."

"Not now, Reggy."

The two sat up straighter. James let his hands down and slowly looked to his right to see an unwashed boy with a gaping jaw and twinkling eyes.

"Hey! James!"

Reggy threw his arms around James and nearly knocked the two out of their seats at the bar. James awkwardly returned the hug by patting his back lightly.

Reggy let go. "What are you doing here, man? You're supposed to be dead! I should know, I saw your pool of blood!" he exclaimed, maintaining his enthusiasm.

"… You saw my pool of blood?"

"Yeah!"

James blinked. Reggy saw his pool of blood so, that meant it *did* happen.

But… was Reggy real?

"You okay buddy? You're looking pale. Are you having one of your little 'is it real' gambits?"

"… The last time I saw you we were *days* away from Trig," James challenged.

"Yeah…" Reggy scratched his head. "I was actually looking for you. I felt bad really bad about what I said to you during that fight and wanted to apologize."

"Oh," James said quietly, not sure exactly how to feel.

"It turned out that you were right about that Trellish guy. He *was* a member of the Tri-bore."

"H-He was?"

"Yeah. When I came back from gathering the water, he was talking to some other guy. He was *super* pissed at the Trellish guy for compromising the Tri-bore's position. So, the new guy killed him, and I went looking for you before they could find you."

I told *you!* Krag piped up.

You didn't tell me anything! James retorted.

Oh? Didn't I specifically say that the sword will not harm innocent blood?

James' thoughts grew silent.

That's what I thought.

"I felt awful about the way I treated you," Reggy continued. "You had just let me into your twisted, screwed up brain the night before and the next day I outright betray you? That wasn't very cool of me, and I'm sorry."

James didn't reply. Instead, he stared deeply into his water cup, trying to comprehend everything that just happened.

"So…" Reggy placed his hands on the bar and began drumming. "That's all I got, man."

You really are pathetic, Krag said.

James maintained his silence.

I thought you were going to calm the fetch down.

James took a deep breath and turned to Reggy. As he opened his mouth to speak, the bartender suddenly made his way to the two.

"Hey!" he shouted. "I told you that you aren't allowed back here anymore?"

"What did you do now, Reggy?" James irately asked.

"You know this guy?"

"Yeah" —James looked over at Reggy and smiled— "we're good friends."

Reggy smiled back with the reflection of relief shining in his eyes.

"This kid is a fetch," the bartender continued. "He comes here on a near daily basis asking for gasoline!"

"Reggy, gasoline isn't for drinking! We've been over this!"

"Gentlemen, gentlemen, please." Reggy held up his hands with a smirk on his face. "For the record, I am not here for a round of gasoline. I have a shopping list."

The bartender sighed. "For her again?"

"Yup!" Reggy handed the bartender a small piece of paper.

The bartender rolled his eyes, then walked behind the counter and rummaged around for whisky and rubbing alcohol. "You do realize that I'm not a grocer, right, kid?"

"So… I can't get everything on the list from you?" Reggy whined.

"No, I can only give you the alcohol, not the rest of the supplies. We've been over this, kid!"

Reggy shuffled awkwardly in his seat. "Well… I figured if I asked enough times, you'd start stocking the things that I need."

"Unbelievable," the bartender muttered. "Sorry, kid, but business doesn't work that way. Quit asking me for things I don't provide."

"Moose poots! Can you at least tell me what you *can't* give me? I haven't mastered my reading yet."

"I can read it for you, Reggy," James piped up.

Reggy gasped. "Aw, sick! Thanks, man!"

The bartender pulled out a cardboard box and walked to the back of the bar towards his inventory.

Reggy swiveled in his seat towards James. "So, what have you been doing for three months, you know, besides pretending to be dead?"

"I wasn't pretending, I—wait—*three months?*"

"Yeah… it's been about three months since I've last seen you."

"Mother of Gloric…" James rubbed his temples as he felt the impact of having his mind blown. "… I can't believe I've been in the Underworld for three months."

"Wait, you were in the Underworld? That's so cool! How'd you escape? Did you see my people?"

"W-Well, when I got there, I was apparently still alive, so I was put on trial to find out if I could leave or cease from existence."

"Oh." Reggy's grin left, and he gave James a disappointed look.

"… I did, however, have to fight a ruthless monster to earn my freedom."

"WHOA!" Reggy exclaimed. "So cool! Did you win?"

"… Yes."

"Aw, that's so sick!"

The bartender returned with the box stocked with various bottles of alcohol. "Well, here you go. That will be three silver."

While humming, Reggy reached for one of the several pouches wrapped around his waist and pulled out the necessary filn. "Thank you, sir!"

The bartender grunted.

"Welp, good to see you, James!" Reggy hopped off the stool, grabbed the box, and headed for the exit.

"Reggy," James said sternly.

Reggy stopped in his tracks.

"… Aren't you forgetting something?"

Reggy stared off into space for a second and then gasped. “Oh yeah! You need to help me with the shopping!”

James chuckled then looked back at the bartender. “How much?”

The bartender waved his hand. “On the house for newcomers.”

“Thanks, man.” James reached out and shook the bartender’s hand.

“Good luck, and welcome to Ghoti!”

~

“Let’s see here…” James carefully read over the list. Whoever wrote it had really pretty handwriting, and the bartender took the courtesy to cross off the items he provided. “So, it looks like all you need is some rope, scrap metal, and one ration of trout, salmon, and bass each.”

“Oh, well, that doesn’t seem too hard.”

“I just got here today, so you’ll have to lead the way.”

Reggy nodded. “As long as you carry the box.”

“That’s fair.” James reached for the box. “So, who are you running errands for?”

“Oh, I got a job!”

“Really? What kind of job?”

“Well, I mostly travel with this lady. I help her out by digging up stuff and running errands for her.”

The duo approached a station selling strictly bass. James did his best to hide his destroyed shirt with the box, but it couldn’t stop people from staring and whispering. At least Reggy didn’t seem to mind, or even notice.

“One ration, please!” Reggy asked the man working the station.

“That will be fifty silver.”

Reggy handed him one of the small pouches around his waist and the man gathered some fish, gutted them, and wrapped them in some butcher paper.

"Geez, that's really expensive for fish," James commented.

"It's really good fish," Reggy replied.

"You must be making pretty good money if your boss can afford this stuff."

"Oh, I don't make any money."

James furrowed his brow. "So, you have a job, but you aren't making any money?"

"That's right!"

"Isn't that just volunteering?"

"Here you go." The man handed Reggy a package of fish.

"Well, not really." Reggy set the package in the box. "I mean, she feeds me and lets me have a place to live. Oh! And she is also teaching me how to read!"

"To be honest I didn't know you couldn't read until today."

"Yep! I'm completely illiterate!"

James couldn't help but chuckle at how proudly Reggy declared that.

"I learned what that word meant yesterday!"

"Good job."

"Thank you!"

They moved over to the next station, which was selling salmon.

"Seventy silver," the merchant there replied.

Again, Reggy handed them one of the pouches and they proceeded in the same manner as the first.

"So, this lady," James began, "is she hiring?"

"Well... she's not much of a people person. She only hangs out with me because I'm a Hunter, and apparently 'somebody has to document their history,'" he said with a tad of sarcasm.

"Oh," James replied with a bit of dismay. "I was kind of hoping I could find some work around here. It would've been nice to work with somebody I already knew instead of a strange—"

"You mean you want to be travel buddies again?" Reggy exclaimed.

"Well… I guess. Yeah, I want to be travel buddies again!" James said with a nod.

"Awesome!" Reggy grabbed the package from the seller and placed it in the box with the other. "I'm sure she wouldn't mind too much since you're my friend. Ah man, this is so great! I'll have to admit, when I met you, I honestly thought that something really cool would happen if I hung out with you and was really disappointed when you died in such a lame way."

"Hey," James commented, slightly offended.

"But, now you're back! So, that means something cool might still happen, right?"

James shrugged. "I suppose so… but it might be best not to mention that I used to be a Messenger to your boss."

"You want to lie?"

"Not necessarily *lie,* I just want to start anew. Besides, how will I be able to work anywhere with that kind of burden tarnishing my name?"

"Well, *you* were the one that volunteered, James."

"Could you just do me this one solid and keep it a secret, please?"

Reggy huffed. "Fine, I guess so."

"Thanks, Reggy."

"Just don't get all upset when you get your butt kicked for lying."

James scoffed. "Sure."

They traveled to the final station, payed another ridiculous amount of silver for some trout, and received another package.

“Okay, so, that’s all the fish. We just need rope and scrap metal, right?” Reggy asked.

“Yeah, just that,” James confirmed.

“Sweet! The place to get that stuff is near where the mayor is.”

“Oh, that reminds me, the bartender told me I need to meet him before I leave town.”

“Ah man, that guy is a riot!”

“Really?”

“Yeah! Here, I’ll take it from here. You go talk to him. Just go straight, and I’ll meet you there afterwards!”

“O-Okay!”

Reggy grabbed the box and frolicked away towards his next item of business. James had to admit that he was a bit excited. He had heard so much about this mayor of “Ghoti” that he had to be great. James went straight for a few minutes, and to his surprise, found himself in a line. “Excuse me, what is this line for?” James asked a couple in front of him.

“This is the line to see the mayor,” the woman responded.

“Oh, wow. He’s a pretty busy guy.”

“Of course, he is. People always ask him for wisdom. There’s always some sort of conflict going on, and he is so good at handling these situations.”

“That’s amazing.”

After about five minutes, James found himself almost to the front of the line. He was quite surprised at how fast it moved.

“Water, waiter! What’s wrong with this fish? Long time, no *sea*! Bah ha, ha, ha, ha!”

What the hell? James thought to himself as he heard a man with an old Trigan accent crack a really terrible joke. He glanced around the couple as two men walked up a few stairs to an oak wall. Hanging on the wall was a fish mount. The fish was wearing a floral, button up shirt and a black top hat taped to its head. Right underneath the mount was a plaque reading, "Mayor McBassypants."

"Sir," one of the two gentlemen directed towards the fish mount, "me and my competitor here both want the same station. The station is located near the market entrance, and many people in the past have tended to gravitate towards it. I feel like I deserve it because if I don't meet my quota, I cannot afford a bigger house for my growing family."

"*However,*" the second gentleman piped up, "I feel like *I* deserve it because if I don't meet *my* quota, I can't afford to buy new furniture to replace the tattered ones we currently use for beds."

"What wisdom to you have to offer us?" The first gentleman pushed a red button underneath the fish.

The fish head on the mount turned towards the two men. "Did you hear about the fight at the seafood restaurant? Two fish got *battered*! Bah ha, ha, ha, ha!"

The first gentleman turned towards the second. "I finally understand now. We've been at each other's throats for years, one always rising above the other. In order for both of us to reach success, we need to become business partners."

"We will be more successful than we ever could be on our own."

"Thank you, Mayor McBassypants!"

"… What?" James exclaimed, feeling thoroughly confused.

"Next!" A gentleman dressed up in a black suit and sunglasses standing next to the fish gestured towards the couple in front of James.

"Mayor McBassypants," the man began, "Rose and I have been dating for quite some time now, but both of us feel conflicted and confused. What is the next step we should take in our relationship?" the man stepped forward and pushed the red button.

"What does every fisherman want? A *gill*-friend! Bah ha, ha, ha, ha!"

"I see now! No longer do I have any doubts or concerns. Rose, I love you more than anything in the world! Will you please be by my side forever, as my wife?"

"Oh, Joel!" The woman threw her arms around the man. "Yes! Yes, I will! I love you!"

The two embraced one another before skipping off together.

"Next!"

James' mouth gaped as he watched the couple skip away.

"Next!"

James turned towards the man in the suit. "Are you kidding me?"

"You're wasting time, young man."

"The mayor of your town is a talking fish toy named 'Mayor McBassypants?' He's not even wearing pants!"

"Listen, bub, if you're going to criticize our mayor, then you best be leaving."

"No, I'm just… thoroughly confused! You based your entire economy around a joke a toy made? Not just an economy, but your lives?"

"What's your point?"

"You guys are crazy if you're worshipping a talking fish mount!"

"For your information, young man," a woman with an "I'd like to speak to a manager" haircut piped up behind him, "we don't 'worship' him! We just happen to respect our mayor and the advice he provides us! So, if you're going to be rude and stand around ridiculing us, then get out of our town!"

The line behind the woman erupted with shouts of agreement.

"Fine, fine!"

James approached the fish. *I can't believe I'm doing this,* he thought.

"Um… Mayor McBassypants." James cringed. "Am… I as crazy as I think I am?"

Reluctantly, he pushed the button. The fish head turned towards him. "Nobody is more suf-*fish*-ent than me!" After cracking that pun, random music started up. Cheers of excitement roared behind James.

"What the fetch?" James shouted.

"He sings every ten thousand jokes," the man in the suit said. "Whenever he does, we throw a big festival. Since he started singing after *you* pushed the button, you have to attend as the Guest of Honor."

Lord Krag burst into laughter

"No! I don't want to be the guest of honor for anything!"

"Everyone bands together to give you supplies, and five rations of every fish."

Feeling embarrassed and defeated, James let out a sigh. "Fine."

CHAPTER SEVEN

HER SUBTLE GLOW

NEVER HAS JAMES EVER PRAYED to Gloric,

But in this moment, he was beyond desperation.

Reggy, come on, where are you? he thought to himself. *Gloric, if you're real, let Reggy some find me and free me from this living HELL!*

For the past three hours, James had been sitting on a throne with Mayor McBassypants mounted above him singing the same song on loop. Apparently, he only stops singing when somebody presses the red button again.[8] The only person who gets to press that button is the Guest of Honor, and they cannot press the button until the festival is over.

Feeling as if this was what being driven to insanity felt like, James was forced to try various fried foods, puddings, and other pastries while wearing a silly party hat. The food wasn't too bad, or rather, wouldn't have been too bad if half of them weren't based off of fish,

---

[8] In reality, this is a terrible mechanism. Should something ever be given the ability to sing, make sure that it stops after one song. This can be applied to most pop artists; however, they *do* make a great amount of money more than we do…

Including the pastries.

Nevertheless, James sat for three hours, praying that either Gloric send Reggy, or send James back to the Underworld.

Unfortunately, the Underworld was not expecting anymore live visitors anytime soon.

"Next!"

When yet another person came to pay their respects to James, he felt a glimmer of hope as relief delicately rested upon his shoulders. "Reggy! Where the fetch have you been?"

"Oh! James! I had no idea you were the guest of honor." Reggy had at least twelve skewers of meat kabobs in his hand. He stuck an entire one into his mouth and pulled all the meat off of it. "Want one?" he mumbled through a mouthful of food.

"No! I want you to get me the hell out of here!"

"Well, I'm sorry, James. I was waiting for you back at the trout station, but you never showed up."

"You were supposed to meet me *here,* you dumb fetch!"

"Oh." Reggy shrugged. "Well, my boss was waiting for me, so I had to get back. Fortunately, she said I could go back and enjoy the festival, so, here I am!" Reggy mumbled while he chewed and smacked on the food.

"I don't care! Do something!"

"Well" —he swallowed— "I could tell everyone here that you were a Messen—"

"No, no!" James interrupted. "Not that, I could get killed, and lose all of my gifts…"

"Okay, I have another idea."

"Do it! I don't care what it is, just do it!

Reggy dramatically fell to the ground.

"R-Reggy?"

"Oh, Guest of Honor" —Reggy reached for James— "I think I'm going to die, unless you come back with me to my camp and help me finish eating all of these meat skewers!"

"You imbecile!" James angrily whispered. "There's no way that's going to—"

"And, I'm dead." Reggy closed his eyes and stuck out his tongue.

As soon as that happened, Mayor McBassypants' singing suddenly slowed down, the music dropping one octave at a time, until it stopped completely. The crowd behind him began crying in agony.

"No, our beloved mayor is dead!"

"The death of that young boy must have been too rough on him!"

"What do we do?"

"Calm down, everyone!" James shouted. "Reggy's fine, and your mayor is fine! He just ran out of batteries!"

There was a silence, and then a huge sigh of relief from everybody. The man in the suit removed Mayor McBassypants from the wall and replaced the batteries. "Guest of Honor?" He gestured towards the fish mount.

James let out a sigh, stood up, and pressed the red button. The fish head turned towards James, eerily faster. "What do you call a fish that performs operations? A *sturgeon*! Bah ha, ha, ha, ha!

"He saved our mayor!" the crowd cheered.

James groaned and observed everyone dispersing from the line.

"Well, that was fun," the gentleman in the suit said. "Our mayor stopped singing, so, you're free to go."

"Oh, thank the gods!" James shouted towards the sky.

"We have a cart full of rations and other gifts for you."

"Thanks."

"Anyway, you need to leave." He took the party hat off of James. "I need to get the stage ready for our mayor to hand out advice again."

James helped Reggy up off of the ground. "Come on, Reggy, let's go before another song starts playing."

"We hope you enjoy your stay in the town of Ghoti!"

So, are you a believer of Gloric now that he answered your prayers?

Shut up, Krag.

Can't shut up if I have no vocal cords to silence.

... You're the worst.

Hence, why I chose you.

~

The gifts in the cart were tied down with a tarp, and despite the courtesy the town displayed, the cart was excruciatingly heavy. James grabbed tightly onto the pulling bar while Reggy pushed on one of the wheels. They moved slowly, and tediously, but somehow managed to get back to Reggy's camp before dark.

"Well, here we are," Reggy panted as he let go of the wheel.

It was a nice, quaint camp as far as James could see. There weren't any tents set up, but somebody had built a fire pit and set up some logs to sit around it. There was a mobile home off to the side but didn't have a vehicle attached to it.

"Wow," James muttered. "You… really came prepared."

"Yeah, she did!" Reggy exclaimed.

"I'm curious as to how you got this mobile home here with no car."

"She'll want to explain that one."

"Where is your boss anyway?"

"Well—"

As Reggy began speaking, a young woman with bright, red hair and two sheathed swords at her side exited the mobile home.

"There you are, Reggy. It's getting late, I was—" She paused mid-sentence as her eyes widened and lit up.

Not in a good way, though.

Not at all.

"… Who is this?" she asked in a passive aggressive manner.

Oh my gosh, James thought to himself, *it's the woman that bought me a drink before I delivered my last message…*

"This is James," Reggy replied. "Say 'hi,' James."

"H-Hello—" James nervously began but was quickly interrupted.

"Reggy, I told you not to bring back strange animals to the camp," she said.

James gave her a few perplexed blinks.

"He's not an animal, though! He's my friend!" Reggy defended.

"People you immediately meet aren't friends. Friendship takes time to grow."

"But I *have* known him for a long time!"

"More than three hours?"

"Like, a few months!"

The woman let out a long, disdainful sigh. "I guess that qualifies as a friendship. So, stranger, I take it you won't just be joining us for dinner?"

She doesn't recognize me, James thought with relief. *This is my chance to start over.*

He let out a light laugh. "No, unfortunately. Reggy was telling me a lot about you, and I have hit a bit of a rut, so I was hoping that you would be willing to at least consider my employment."

She folded her arms. "Employment, huh? I guess that's better than being some moocher."

"Oh, I'm not a moocher," James replied. "In fact, I brought my own supplies." He gestured towards the cart.

The woman approached the cart and lifted the tarp. "That's beneficial," she began, "but not enough. What makes you qualified to be here?"

"What qualifies me?"

“Well, other than being physically able to lift, dig, and trek for several miles at a time, you need some experience with Mythical Theorem.”

James arched his eyebrow. “Why is that?”

“I’m a Theoremist, and I like to keep company that has an understanding for the occupation. It provides more of a drive to work. That being said, what’s your experience with Theorem?”

James smirked. “Well, I *do* happen to have this.” He unsheathed his sword.

Her eyes lit up brighter, except in a significantly better way. “That’s the Sword of Lord Krag!” she exclaimed. “You’re the worthy one that gets to wield it?”

“Yes.”

“My gods!” She pulled out a small journal from her pocket and a pencil from behind her ear. “I made the journey for that sword months ago, but I got sidetracked for a job in Trig. To think I nearly wasted my time, but now I get to speak to the champion that wields it, himself!”

When are you going to tell her you were a Messenger?

Shh!

Please, shush the guy no one else can hear.

If no one can hear you, then don’t talk.

You don’t have to be a fetch.

“What happened? How did you do it?”

“That’s actually some confidential information that I would love to tell you, for the small price of employment, that is.”

She stopped writing and looked up to give him an icy scold. “Will you at least let me look at it?”

“All part of the package deal.”

“… Fine.”

The woman put her notebook away and drew the two swords from her back. As a flash of red and white neared his neck, James frantically faltered backwards and withdrew his own sword barely in time to protect himself. As he held his block against the woman, the two locked eyes. She challenged him with a hungry fire that ignited the brown in her eyes, and gave him a daring smile as she harshly slashed her swords at him again with enough power to break his block. James frantically tried to recover, but the woman fought swiftly and ferociously as she struck the two swords at him like lightning. He faltered and blocked and blocked again in an attempt to put more distance between himself and her, but found himself beginning to fail.

"Are you sure that's the Sword of Lord Krag? I would've never imagined the sword would choose a wielder that's such a wimpy fighter like yourself!" she eased

Hah!

You do realize she's insulting you by saying you picked a crappy wielder!

I did.

Before James could think of a response, the sword's weight began fluctuating and quickly deflecting every hit made by the woman.

The woman hopped back a bit and smirked. "That's more like it! Let's up the ante just a bit more."

She flicked her red sword towards James, and the composition of it seemingly changed as the sword grew in length towards him. As James squinted his eyes, he noticed that the sword no longer had a point, but the head of a python headed directly towards his face.

"Whoa!" he shouted as he swung the sword upward. The snake's head redacted as the two blades made contact. James made eye contact with the woman and felt a pit in his stomach as she smiled psychotically at him.

"... Oh, no," he muttered to himself as the woman began wildly swinging her swords at him again, with two snake heads biting at him instead of one. The Sword of Lord Krag fought back furiously, but the swords would transform faster than the blades could make contact, making it impossible to chop of the heads.

James could hear Lord Krag scoffing at him, and he felt a bit ticked off by that. “You know what? No! *This* is how you wield a sword, Krag!”

He quickly reigned control over the sword and began countering the blows quicker than before. He moved his head out of the way as the white blade tried to make contact and he quickly swiped at it. While the snake’s head retracted, it was enough force to knock the blade out of the woman’s hand and send it flying across the clearing. Without acting distracted, the woman swung her red sword at James, yet despite her quick recovery, James parried the sword, and also sent it across the clearing.

The woman gave a shocked glance but smiled and panted excitedly. “Excellent.”

James smiled and panted as well, feeling overconfident at his one move that ended the fight.

“Fine, you can stay with us,” the woman submitted.

“I’m glad you can finally see reason.”

“So, can I borrow your sword?”

“I’d be more than happy to let you *look* at it—”

James looked down and realized that the sword had already left his hands. “What the— hey!” James called as she went after her.

“Rule number one, rookie, never assume you’ve won a battle until your opponent is dead.”

He huffed as he finally caught up with her. When they approached the side of her mobile home, a table suddenly swung out from its side.

“Oh.” James paused in his tracks. “Is that automatic?”

“Something like that.”

“I didn’t think that sort of technology existed outside of Trig.”

“It doesn’t.”

James furrowed his brow. "Then *how* did the table swing out like that?"

"It knew I wanted to examine your sword."

"It… knew?"

"Yeah. It's smart."

James tilted his head and observed the table with a baffled expression. The mobile home suddenly shook and let out a deep, trumpeting sound. James shouted and quickly took a few steps back.

The woman laughed at his reaction and rubbed the side of the home. "Do you need to sit down for a minute?"

A couch adorned with intricate fabric and plush pillows suddenly emerged next to the entrance of the mobile home.

James looked at it in horror. "No, that thing looks dangerous!"

"I promise you it's completely safe."

James nervously took a seat as the woman instructed, but didn't feel any safer in the least.

"So… you're saying that the mobile home is… sentient?" James continued.

"The mobile home has nothing to do with all of the mind-blowing things occurring here."

James head grew light with confusion and he rested it on an armrest that suddenly emerged without his knowledge. "The mobile home *is* smart, or *isn't* smart?"

"The mobile home isn't smart; *the Cougar* is smart."

The mobile home purred deeply.

James sat up and looked at it in awe. "This thing is... a cougar?"

"No, it's a mammoth."

Another trumpeting sound echoed through the air.

"Then why is it called 'the Cougar?'"

"That's what the label on the side of it says."

James stood up and backed away from the mobile home, realizing that "Cougar" was definitely written in the side of it, but was old and faded.

"… Need a hint, buddy?" Reggy suddenly appeared at James' side.

James jumped and looked between him and the woman. "C-Can someone just explain what's going on?"

Reggy and the woman laughed. "This is the Cougar, my greatest Mythical Theorem yet," the woman said.

"The Cougar… is *Theorem*?"

"Yes."

James placed his hand on the side of the Cougar, and it whirred to life once more.

"She likes you," Reggy said.

"S-She does?"

"Totally."

The two disregarded James' shock and resumed their current tasks, with Reggy rummaging through the handcart, and the woman examining the Sword of Lord Krag. She gently set the sword on the table and put on some work gloves. James noticed that the table had been concealing tools mounted against the home and a sealed shelf full of various powders and chemicals. The woman opened the shelf and removed a white powder of curious substance, then applied it to the sword with a brush.

"J-Just be careful with that."

"I received a PhD in the Mythical Arts when I was twelve years old. I know what I'm doing."

James' jaw dropped in awe. "Twelve years old?" he exclaimed.

"My father was a professor at the university in Galvin. Needless to say, I was a bit ahead of my class."

James chuckled lightly before reverently staring at her face. He took in all of her features, from her freckles, the smudge of dirt on her nose, and her intense brown eyes covered by red lashes. Her red hair radiated in the last bits of sunlight and she was seemingly prettier compared to the first time that he saw her.

"It's rude to stare, you know," she said.

"S-Sorry," James replied. "I was just thinking about how I don't know your name."

"That's a secret."

"It's Alexis!" Reggy shouted from the hand cart.

"… Thanks, Reggy," the woman shouted back, with an expression of regret and guilt on her face, for she had forgotten about Reggy's existence for a hot minute.

"You're welcome!"

"That's a nice name," James said.

"Thanks. Should I ask Reggy for your name?"

"It's James."

She looked up at him. "Is that it?"

"… Should there be more?"

Alexis shrugged. "I guess not."

"… Okay."

Alexis resumed covering the sword in powder, and seemingly began to disregard James' presence altogether. Feeling a bit awkward, James decided to join Reggy at the handcart, with the thought of the fire in her brown eyes kindling like a candle. He also thought about the glow that radiated from her presence, it was just too subtle to notice.

CHAPTER EIGHT

MELODIES OF THE STARS

"CHECK THIS OUT!" JAMES EXCLAIMED as he pulled out a toy cork gun. "I thought they stopped making toys like this after the War Bane."

"They did," Reggy replied. "They're super rare to come by. This is way cool!"

"I used to have one as a kid, back in the Far North anyway. The man that raised me was a High Priest of some sort, so he had a ton of old trinkets, like this one, that he let me have. I didn't really have any friends growing up, so, I didn't have to worry about any of the other kids stealing it. It's a shame though, I wonder what happened to it."

"At least you got another one."

"Yeah, but sheesh! These people really must think highly of this so-called 'Guest of Honor' if they're willing to get rid of something like this."

"Speaking of guns, whatever happened to that one you were holding onto?"

"… I don't know. I kept my clothes and my sword in the Underworld, but I think I dropped the gun in the bar—"

James suddenly paid closer attention to his pockets. "… No way." He pulled out the antique handgun. "It followed me down there! And back up here!"

"Sweet!" Reggy leaned in closer.

"… Ugh," James groaned.

"What's wrong? You still managed to hold onto that thing after all this time and you're disappointed?"

James shrugged. "I mean, I only held onto it to seek revenge on Mr. Finch, who in the end was nothing more than a man. There's really no value to it anymore, especially because I used the last bullet."

"Oh," Reggy said, sounding a bit bummed.

"… Do you want it?"

He furrowed his brow. "Really?"

"Yeah. Hold onto it for me. Consider it a gift from one best friend to another."

Reggy scoffed and laughed a little bit.

"Why does everyone keep laughing at me today?"

"Dude, just because I'm your *only* friend doesn't mean I'm your *best* friend. Besides, if you do the math, we've only really known each other for how long, a week? Less? That isn't really enough time to determine if someone is a best friend."

James couldn't believe his ears, especially after the argument Reggy made towards Alexis regarding "friendship," but instead of arguing, he shrugged his shoulders. "Okay."

"… What?"

"We're not best friends then."

"… But what's time except, you know, a unit of measurement and relativity?"

"Okay, you can't read, but you know what 'measurement' and 'relativity' mean?"

"You hang out with Alexis for three months and not have a change in vocabulary!"

“Touché.” James reached into the cart for a violet wad of yarn. He stared at it for a moment and then stuffed it into his pocket. Reggy laughed nervously as James continued looking through the handcart.

“This is nice.” James held up a brown leather jacket.

“Hey, did you know that the guy currently holding a sweater is my best bud?”

“Well, then, thank Gloric that I’m the guy holding a *jacket*.”

“Jackets and sweaters are basically the same thing.”

“No, they aren’t—”

“Okay, fine! Stop begging, James! I’ll be your best friend if it means that much to you!”

James laughed to himself. “You’re the embodiment of mercy.”

“So… that gun you’re holding…”

James rolled his eyes and lightly held the gun up. “Here.”

“Yay!” Reggy swiftly took the gun and turned it over in his hands. “So cool!”

James smiled, but felt a chill go down his spine. He shook his head and blinked a few times.

“You okay, buddy?”

“Yeah, just got a weird chill there.”

“Then put on that raincoat!”

James scoffed, but wasn’t going to argue. He tried on the jacket, and to his surprise, it fit perfectly. The sleeves were lined with straps and had two big pockets on each side, in addition to two more on each of his breasts. “Huh… not bad.”

“You’re a bit of a sap, you know that, right?”

“I’m not a ‘sap!’”

“Yeah, you are! From one best friend to another, let this be symbolic of forever being honest with each other.”

“Well, then, I’m honestly telling you that you’re a bit of a jerk.”

“And I accept that.”

James chuckled, but for some reason, he believed every word Reggy was telling him. He didn't think he was a sap, but he felt like what Reggy told him was, for lack of better words, real. He watched Reggy fumble with some other antique toys and could say that he knew for a fact that it was happening. James had no idea what the fresh fetch was going on, but he felt relieved, and for once, didn't care.

Among other fun things, James came across a bottle of rubbing alcohol and a liter bottle of decaffeinated soda, with a note saying, "Enjoy, random guy that's a health nut but not really." He chuckled, set the soda to the side, and continued to rummage through the cart. Just as James reached for a button-up shirt and denim jeans, he flinched as something bright caught his eye. He looked to his right to see the red katana still impaled into the ground.

Oh yeah, he thought to himself. *She was so excited about my sword that she left hers...*

Knowing how valuable the swords must be to her, James approached the red katana and pulled it out of the ground. He held it up to the light and admired the scales. He felt a bit warm and content, almost as if he were full.

Interesting.

He turned around, looking for the white one, which was only about ten feet away. He approached and pulled it out of the ground. The swords were nearly identical, but he felt a bit more dismal with this one as he held it up to the light like he did with the other and observed the similar glistening scales...

And red hilt...

And an unpleasant memory of a previous encounter with this same sword about three months ago.

"Fresh furnace of hell!" James shouted as he threw the sword back towards the ground.

Alexis laughed from her workstation. "What are you? An old man?"

"Do you know what the fetch this thing is?"

Letting out a sigh, Alexis calmly set down the Sword of Lord Krag and looked back at James. "Yes, that's my katana."

"No, it's not! This is the katana of Mr. Finch, the evilest man in the world!"

"I know, and now it's mine."

James scoffed. "This is just great! This blade almost killed me! No, it did! That's why I shattered it!"

Alexis ripped her goggles off of her head, folded her arms, and gave James a glare hefty with anger. "Oh, so *you* were the one that destroyed this beautiful blade, not to mention killing Mr. Finch, who just so happened to be the man I was hunting. I swore I'd seek vengeance on whomever killed him before me."

"Why?"

"*Why?* First of all, you destroyed the sword! Second of all… I don't like the guy. *I* wanted to be the first to kill him!"

"… In my defense, my sword sort of became more sentient than it already is, and Mr. Finch died from the teeth of one-hundred wolves. Something about it being 'not my judgement.'"

She huffed. "I guess I can't argue with that, but it still took me three weeks after repairing that sword to coax the python out! The poor thing was traumatized from being so brutally destroyed like that!"

James threw up a baffled gaze. "I still don't understand why you wield that thing! It's *evil!*"

"No, it isn't." She left her station, gently picked up the white katana, and ripped the red one from James' hand. "This blade right here" —she held up the red katana— "is called the Hope. It can only be wielded by those with good intentions in this world. No evil is worthy to wield it. This one here" —she held up the white one— "is called the Terror. It can only be wielded by those who are corrupt and susceptible to evil. No good is worthy to wield it. However, when you put them together…" She brought her two hands together and allowed the swords to touch side by side.

A beautiful steel clang rang through the air. James was astonished as the expectation of hissing snakes was shattered as something almost as sweet as a nightingale resonated instead. In fact, it may be even sweeter than that. For a moment, there were no vile, slithering beasts, but two glistening entities singing in perfect harmony. He could no longer behold any sign of separation, but one wholesome being spiraled in crimson and ivory ties.

"The original owner of these swords inserted his goodness and his evil into these blades, so that when he wielded them, he would be a balanced warrior," Alexis continued. "Should they be separated, they will turn on anyone who tries to wield them without a similar alignment. I've spent years tracking the Terror, and I was absolutely mortified when I found it in pieces. You really are a despicable one, you know that, right?"

"Look," James strained as he got on his feet, "it was an accident, and I'm really sorry for that. I won't be destroying anymore magical weapons, okay?"

"These aren't just 'magical weapons,' James! These are Mythical Theorem!"

"What's the difference?"

He flinched as Alexis held her swords at his throat. "You ignoramus punk! These weapons are alive, and they are beautiful! Each one has something unique about it, which is why I'm so surprised that you, not only wield one, but wield something far more powerful than any piece of Theorem! That sword of yours is the very first piece of Mythical Theorem! *The very first one!* It's almost shameful to think that of all people, it's wielded by somebody that calls Mythical Theorem 'magical weapons!'"

Overwhelmed with embarrassment, James decided to change the subject. "How did *you* manage to pick up the sword in the first place? It destroys anybody that isn't its chosen wielder."

"Just because I'm *holding it* doesn't mean I'm attempting to *wield it,* James! Sweet Cirlock, dude! The gods gave you a noggin for a reason, just use it!"

James groaned. He obviously wasn't going to win against this one.

"Whoa! Check this out!" Reggy shouted from the hand cart.

Alexis and James both looked over at him. In Reggy's hand, proudly raised towards the sky, was a recorder.

"… Reggy, put the flute down," James warily said.

"Why?" Reggy whined.

"Because we're not keeping it! Put it back!"

"I don't see why he can't have it," Alexis intervened.

"Yeah, *you* would say that! You won't be the one that has to listen to him play it all day!"

"Exactly." She smirked. "You can keep it, sweetie. You might get good at it if you practice enough."

"Yes!" Reggy immediately stuck the recorder in his mouth and blew as hard as he could.

James threw his hands over his ears, concerned that they might actually be bleeding.

"Aw man! I'm a natural at this! I'm going to be an expert in no time!"

~

James wandered into the forest to change into the clothes he had found, then took the liberty to start a fire in the fire pit despite the pounding migraine induced from explosive levels of high-pitched resonation that hadn't stopped since Reggy's discovery of the recorder.

This has to be the worst day of my life, he thought to himself.

He sat against a log near the fire pit, covering his ears and closing his eyes with the hood of his jacket poorly muffling out any additional noise. He couldn't believe Alexis. She was just whittling away at his sword, as if this terrible, ear-screeching music was nothing more than something playing in the background on a radio. James shook his head, getting sick to his stomach.

Why me?

"Reggy!" Alexis shouted over the playing as she set the Sword of Lord Krag gently next to James.

Reggy, leaning against a log on the opposite side of James, stopped playing his recorder and looked up at her. James uncovered his ears and opened his eyes.

Sweet silence.

"Are you okay?" she asked, seemingly concerned.

Reggy shrugged. "Yeah… why?"

"You seem… different."

"Different how?"

She undid her main braid, allowing her hair and her smaller braid to loosely flow. "I don't know, you seem… bigger, I guess? I mean, your arms aren't as thin as they used to be, you seem taller, and you look like you've gained ten pounds out of the blue."

James tilted his head to observe Reggy. Alexis wasn't wrong. He was the same, scrawny kid he met at the base of a Thingy's carcass when they reunited, but he seemingly transfigured into a beefier… Reggy.

"Yeah," James agreed, "she has a point, Reggy."

"W-Well…" He sunk down. "I sort of… ate all of our food," he said quickly then shut his eyes tightly.

"What?" Alexis exclaimed.

"I'm sorry! I was sooo hungry!" He almost started crying. "I couldn't resist! Once I started, I couldn't stop!"

Alexis kicked the log Reggy was leaning against, then huffed. "Well, there you go, great sword wielder. One more thing you get praised for. Congratulations, you saved us from a food shortage."

James smirked. "You're welcome—"

"Shut up!" Alexis inhaled deeply, took a seat by Reggy, then placed a hand on his shoulder. "It's okay, sweetie, accidents happen."

James threw his hands up in the air.

"D-Do you forgive me, then?"

"Of course, I do! Are you ready for our session?" she asked while pulling out her journal.

"Yes! The best part of the day!"

"You're seriously going to let him off that easy?" James asked as he sheathed his sword.

"Yes," Alexis said snidely. "He's only a kid. You can't be too hard on him."

"No, he's not! Look at him! He easily knows what he's doing!"

"He is a part of a lost culture, James. And since he has maintained youth since the loss of said culture, he obviously hasn't reached a sure sense of maturity."

"Unbelievable," James scoffed.

"Anyway" —Alexis dismissed James— "is there a chance we could talk about the stars tonight?"

"I don't know…" Reggy hesitantly said.

"What's so great about the stars?" James asked.

Alexis shot him a dirty look, and James already found himself getting used to the taste of the foot in his mouth.

"'What's so great about the stars?'" Alexis repeated.

"It's okay, Alexis," Reggy intervened. "Remember when I said that my people could read auras, James?"

"Yeah."

“Well, Hunters have the ability, much like the Bureau of Bad News, to determine the fates of others. We utilize those auras people give off and are able to match them to the Map of Fates.”

“… The Map of Fates?”

“… Do you not know what that is?”

James blushed. “No.”

“When Tor was first created, the sky was pitch black,” Alexis began. “The first humans were very frightened when night came upon them because there was only darkness. Gloric, Cirlock, and Vrec implored that the Elements give them the Map of Fates, which determined the future of everyone on Tor. They strung it into the heavens, so that way humanity would know there would still be a tomorrow.”

“Oh.” James glanced up at the sky. “I always thought stars were just… distant suns in a faraway place.”

“That’s stupid,” Alexis replied. “The stars are representations of individuals on Tor. Everyone knows that, except for you, apparently.”

James rolled his eyes. “Anyway, your people can read stars?”

“Yes, and, unfortunately our process of doing so is a trade secret, so…” Reggy blew some raspberries,

To break the awkward silence, of course.

Alexis moaned. “Okay, but I’m going to find out how you do it eventually!”

Reggy let out a half-hearted laugh. “Trust me, you don’t want to know how to read the stars.”

“Why wouldn’t I want to read the stars?” Alexis exclaimed. “The capacity to interpret the Map of Fates is impeccable, and your entire culture is based around it!”

“Do you really want to know when you’re going to die?” Reggy solemnly asked.

Alexis paused, her excitement diminishing with her sinking heart.

"Why do you think there is no history of my culture? It's a burden to know what's going to happen to your friends and family. We tried to make the best of it, though. Every time one of our own was approaching their death, we'd all go out and celebrate with a hunt, hence being called the Hunters. It always ended with someone not coming back, but we did our best to make sure that they pass on with honor."

Alexis jotted down Reggy's words in her notebook.

"Then, those Thingies obliterated my village. My home, and everything I didn't know I loved was gone. So, here I am, the last of my kind, waiting for my own impending death."

A silence hung heavily over the atmosphere.

"Reggy… you didn't tell me that it was Thingies that wiped out your village," James said.

"Meh." Reggy shrugged.

"Don't give me that! Is that why you hunt them, then? For vengeance?"

"I used to, until I hunted them to extinction."

"You hunted them to extinction?"

"Yeah." Reggy carelessly waved his hand. "I was afraid I'd be super bored when I killed the last one, but then I met you, and then I met Alexis! Now I can be there whenever cool stuff happens!"

"How *do* you know Reggy, James?" Alexis asked.

"We… encountered one another on miscellaneous journeys," James reluctantly said.

Reggy rolled his eyes.

"Okay, well, how did you find out his village was destroyed?"

"Well, one night at camp, we—"

"Wait, did he tell you these stories near a campfire?" Alexis asked with an astonished tone.

"Yeah?"

"… Did you eat a Pegamoose egg?"

James gave her a skeptibrow. "… Yes?"

Alexis took a deep breath. "Okay, um, that's… really amazing."

"Exchanging stories near a campfire?"

"Hunters only do that with people they most trust."

James felt a pit in his stomach. "They do?"

"Yup!" Reggy said while fiddling with his recorder.

"… What does the Pegamoose egg have to do with it?"

"It's a sign of friendship."

"Wow… um… I'm flattered."

"We were traveling buddies, I *had* to do that with you. Plus, I had to find out your deepest, darkest secrets somehow."

James rolled his eyes.

"Did he tell you how he died?" Alexis asked.

"Nah!" Reggy answered. "It wasn't cool enough to share. I was hoping I'd maybe ride on a bear through a forest and I'm on fire and the bear's on fire and everything else is on fire, but that's not going to happen."

"… What is going to happen?"

"Oh, man! Did I ever tell you guys how my friends and I egged a guy's house?"

Alexis sighed. "No, you didn't, but I'm up for a story."

"Well, let me tell you. Since Hunters know exactly when and where they are going to die, we don't mind being a bit reckless from time to time—"

"You have friends besides us?" James interrupted.

Alexis shot him a dirty look.

"Well, I did thousands of years ago," Reggy replied.

"… What?"

"*Anyway,* the guy we egged is, like, *super* scary! So, it was a bit of an adrenaline rush at the time—"

"Wait a minute."

Reggy rolled his eyes, and then gave James a fake smile. "What is it now, bud?"

“Was your village the only Hunter population on Tor?” James asked and his tone began to rise with astonishment.

“Well, yeah, obviously. Races don’t tend to ‘stray away’ from one specific destination on Tor, James. It isn’t unnatural.”

“So, you egged a scary man’s house?” Alexis spoke up.

“Yes, yes, I did, and this is what happened…”

Alexis wrote down Reggy’s tales in her journal, starting with his personal burden of knowing the fates of everybody around him, and how the biggest complaint of the “scary man” was that he didn’t use cage-free eggs to vandalize his house.

James could understand Reggy’s point of not wanting everyone else to know the same sadness, but also felt that keeping secrets was a bit selfish. After all, wouldn’t it be better to know when and where you’re going to die instead of being paranoid every day about it?

Then again, isn’t that how the Bureau started out?

Isn’t that what he was doing in this moment?

James sighed, closed his eyes, leaned his head back against the log and fell asleep to a story about Reggy’s third Thingy encounter, with the full understanding that knowing the news isn’t as hard as bearing it.

Chapter Nine

Peaked Interest

"... BLEGH!" THE LIZARD BRUSHED HIS tongue against his eyeball.

"... That's disgusting," the seagull said with a voice as calm as a brook, but as unpleasant as a black cloud.

The lizard's tongue retracted. "What? It feels good! You try it!" he exclaimed with a voice as excited as a fire popping with embers.

"I think I'll pass."

The lizard continued to lick its eye as it gazed at the Goblin City below. "I like this place!"

"Of course, you do."

"What's that supposed to mean?"

"This place is disgusting, and you like disgusting things."

"This place isn't 'disgusting!'"

"There is a literal river of puke over there."

"It's efficient! It keeps the place clean by getting rid of all the... excess stuff!"

"Do you even hear yourself?"

The lizard paused, then frantically placed its little hands on its head. "Oh no! I don't have ears!"

The lizard began hyperventilating, then the squirrel slapped it across the face with its paws. "Get ahold of yourself!"

"I hate you," the seagull said, rather blankly.

"No, you don't!" the lizard declared. "You love me!"

"We are literally Fire and Water."

"Gloric said that opposites attract!"

"Attract what? People who deserve so much more in life to idiots?"

"Guys!" The squirrel snapped his fingers. "We need to stay focused on the task at hand!"

"Which is what? Watching them? In case Gloric hasn't noticed, they are armed adults. They're fine," the seagull replied.

The squirrel gave the bird a dirty look. "You *know* they can't defend themselves against him."

"And he probably doesn't give the slightest care in the world about them. For all he knows, they're barely blips on his radar."

"I thought Moo-Moo wanted to meet us here!" the lizard interjected.

"Yes," the squirrel tiredly said. "Moo-Moo *did* want us to meet here, but we've also never been told to stop watching them, and we won't be able to accomplish either one of them if you two keep on with your bickering—"

"SQUIRREL!"

A large, white sheep dog suddenly emerged from the woods behind the three animals and gently picked up the squirrel with its teeth.

"No! Moo-Moo! Put me down! Bad dog! BAD!" the squirrel frantically pleaded as the dog shook him like a toy.

"Hello, Moo-Moo," the seagull said.

The sheep dog stopped shaking the squirrel and looked at the seagull, maintaining its gentle grip on the critter. "Hello, Water." It stared at the seagull endearingly with its big, brown eyes.

"… Can you put down Earth so we can get down to business?"

"Oh" —Moo-Moo spat out the squirrel— "sorry, I thought you a squirrel."

"A squirrel is my animal form," the squirrel replied while dripping with drool.

"SQUIRREL!"

"Stop it, Moo-Moo!"

"Oh yeah. I already forgotted."

The squirrel grumbled to itself as it tried to wipe off the thick saliva. The lizard continued to lick its eyeball while the seagull merely stared at Moo-Moo.

Moo-Moo sat down and looked at the three animals. "Hey guys," he began, and then continued to pant for about fifteen seconds before stopping to speak again. "What doing?"

"… You called us here, Moo-Moo," the seagull asserted.

Moo-Moo paused. "Oh, yeah."

"Is something wrong?" the squirrel asked.

"My master and very best friend want me to meet with you guys!"

"… Why?"

Moo-Moo sneezed, getting a few boogers on the squirrel. "He just want to check on you guys. Hi, guys! I check. Bye." Moo-Moo turned around and began walking away.

"Moo-Moo." The squirrel scowled.

The dog stopped. "What?"

"Come back."

"Okay!" Moo-Moo frolicked back to the animals and sat down. "Hi, guys!" He began panting again.

The squirrel's eye twitched. "Was that really all this meeting was for?"

Moo-Moo smacked his lips and licked his nose. “Oh, I also forgotted! Master is very busy, and I lonely! I want to play!”

“We don’t have time to play,” the seagull replied.

“Why not?” the lizard exclaimed.

“Fire, we have a job to do.” The seagull gave the lizard a crippling glare. “Moo-Moo, I’m sorry, but play time will have to wait,” it said a bit more gently.

“Oh…” Moo-Moo quietly whined.

“Yeah, it really is a shame,” the squirrel muttered as it picked the boogers off of its fur.

“Wait,” the seagull spoke up, “why is your master busy?”

Moo-Moo said nothing.

“… Moo-Moo?”

“SQUIRREL!”

“MOTHER OF GLORIC, DOG! THAT’S EARTH, NOT A SQUIRREL!” the seagull squawked with the ferocity of a raging ocean.

“That’s not a very nice thing to say, Water!” the lizard shouted.

“Don’t tell me what to do, Fire!”

“… I not good boy anymore?” Moo-Moo asked the seagull with sad, droopy eyes.

The seagull felt a pang of guilt in its chest. “Well… if you stay focused and tell us why Gloric is busy, then you’ll be the best boy in the whole world.”

Moo-Moo stood up and wagged his tail. “Really?”

“Yes, now, what’s going on?”

“The shiny god is a bad boy. I a good boy, but he a bad boy.”

The three animals stiffened, even the lizard’s demeanor changed. “What has he done?” the lizard demanded, his tone serious, but calm.

“Big brother want to leave, but he needs his favorite toy. He go get it for him.”

The squirrel sighed and placed its paw against its forehead. "I knew we should have intervened."

"No, Gloric said to have faith, and he's clearly taking care of it," the seagull said.

"What if *we* were the ones he assigned to do it, though?" the lizard inquired.

"My master said that he believes in hoomans to take good care of the toy!" Moo-Moo said.

"So, what are we supposed to do then?" the seagull asked.

"He said to me, 'Now, Moo-Moo, tell our friends that they need to guide them to their next stop.' I tell you. I good boy."

"… Already?" the squirrel asked.

Moo-Moo scratched his ear. "Yes! My master tell me everything! Did you know my master is my very best friend?"

The squirrel sighed. "I guess we need to tell this to Wind and Metal."

"Who will keep an eye on them in the meantime?" the seagull asked.

"What was that about them being 'blips on the radar,' Water?" the squirrel snidely replied.

"Don't you dare—"

"I'll do it!" the lizard valiantly declared.

"No."

"Why not?"

"Because you screw up everything."

"I do not!"

"I a good boy?" Moo-Moo intervened.

"Sure," the seagull said dismissively. "Look, here's what we'll do—"

"I best boy?" Moo-Moo interrupted once more.

"Yeah, you're best boy."

"Yay! I help! I best boy!"

"You can't tell him that," the squirrel said.

"Why not?"

"Because he'll—"

"I best boy!" Moo-Moo exclaimed

"... Never let it go."

"Best boy. Best boy. Best boy."

"... Will he really never stop?" the seagull regrettably asked.

"Never," the squirrel solemnly confirmed

Moo-Moo continued to mutter "best boy" while the seagull shook its head, deciding to get back on track. "Fire, you and Earth can go tell the others, and I'll stay here and watch."

"Master want all you to go," Moo-Moo said.

"That makes no sense!" the squirrel shouted. "Who will watch them, then?"

"Look, I hate to be that person, but maybe we should disregard that last order," the seagull suggested.

"Guys," the lizard began.

"Not now! You and Fire go take care of it, does that sound like a good plan, Earth?"

"Guys..."

"Shh! Yes, that sounds fine—" the squirrel began.

"GUYS!"

"WHAT?" the seagull and the squirrel simultaneously demanded.

"Moo-Moo's gone..."

~

James had a very long day.

The morning began with loading the plethora of supplies he had received from Ghoti onto the Cougar and spent the rest of the day stopping every few hours to dig a ton of holes. Granted, those holes were normally filled with "artifacts," as Alexis called them, and were found along "historic" sites and added to her collection of treasures. He wasn't even quite sure what Alexis meant by "artifacts," but with what he has observed with Alexis so far, she's either expecting a rare but haunted jewel from the Second Eon, or an outdated brand of shoes.

"This is where Sir Sorob experienced his first military blunder," she would say, and then add something along the lines of him starting the Waddlesworth family tree, but was written out of their genealogical history due to the shame he had brought upon his name. Before James knew it, he would be whisked away again by the crazy-sword lady to begin digging holes in another site, where "catnip used to be the crop staple," or "was a breeding ground for an extinct species of beast."

His handcart, empty in the morning, was full of a variety of old weapons, fossilized beasts and plants, and random things, such as watches or fraying strands of discontinued yarn. The last of the daylight barely peaked over the mountains surrounding them, and James swore that frost was already beginning to coat the displaced strands of grass.

"… It's cold," James muttered as he held his shovel tightly.

"Didn't you say something about being from the Far North on the way over here?" Alexis asked as she jotted down some notes into her journal.

"Yes, but that doesn't change the fact that I hate the cold."

"Well, the Dwarven Mountains don't care about your sensitivities, James."

James huffed as Reggy shrugged in agreeance.

"Where are we even at this time?" James continued.

"The settlement of a famous dispute known as the Argument of Peaks."

"'Argument of Peaks?'"

Alexis sighed, and closed her journal loudly. "The argument happened in the First Eon. It involved Vrec and Cirlock, Gloric's two brothers. The Gods of Destruction and Commerce. You've heard of them, Vrec and Cirlock, Gloric's two brothers, right, James? Vrec and Cirlock *do* sound familiar?"

"Yes," James replied, irately.

"Even imbeciles know who they are, so if you don't—"

"I know who they are!"

Alexis snickered. "In the early days of their time on Tor, Vrec and Cirlock had a disagreement regarding how high the peak of the mountain should be."

James looked around at the mountains in the Dwarven range, each of the peaks different heights. "So, which mountain was it?"

"This one."

James scoffed. "We aren't on a mountain."

"*Exactly*, James. Since the argument was over the height of the peak, Gloric decided that there shouldn't be a peak at all."

"But if we are digging for artifacts, why did we come here?"

"*Because,* if you would let me finish, local tribes didn't want to damage their homes and civilians, so they decided to duke it out here. This region of land contains centuries of battles fought between multiple cultures; can you imagine the kinds of things we can find here?"

"Well, if it's so obvious that battles were fought here, don't you think someone already came here and took everything?"

Alexis stared in silence at James for a minute before finally saying, in a frighteningly quiet voice, "What part of 'centuries' do you not understand, James?"

"I'm just saying—"

"A ten-year battle occurred here, James! Do you know how long that is?"

"… Ten years?"

"Yeah, *ten years.* Can you imagine how many other ten-year battles occurred here as well?"

"… A lot?"

"I guess that can be concluded, can't it? Now that we are on the same page—[9]"

"But—"

"What?" she snapped in a threatening tone.

James let out a discouraged sigh. "Never mind."

"Good."

Alexis immediately shrugged off the disagreement, stood tall, and looked around the grounds, which were tinted red from the sunset. "They're thinking of building a city here. 'The City of Peakless.' I'm sure we can accumulate some goodies before they begin construction."

She uses larger words because she's better than you, Krag said.

Shut. Up.

"Who's even thinking about building cities?" Reggy commented. "Didn't people stop building cities after the Thanati-whatever?"

"The what?" James inquired.

"The *Thanatichor?*" Alexis corrected. "Yes, sweetheart, but human progression must go on."

"What's the 'Thanatichor?'"

Alexis took a deep, agitated breath. "Do you even live on this planet, man? How have you been here so long and not heard a single one of these stories? It's like you're opening a book for the first time asking 'what?' every five minutes! You know how you solve the problem, James? You read the damn book!"

James averted his gaze, feeling himself sinking into the earth from sheer embarrassment.

"Come on, Alexis," Reggy began, "cut him some slack. There are a ton of people that don't know what 'Thanatichor' is. I couldn't even get the name right."

---

[9] And so are you!

"Well… I suppose you have a point, Reggy. A bit of a convenient transition into a background story, but whatever. James, you know about the War of Brothers, right?"

"Yes."

"Perfect, then you should know that there were two of them, one where Gloric locked away Vrec, and the other where Cirlock was dealt with. You remember who those people are, right?"

"Please don't go there again."

Alexis chuckled. "That's good. You're learning."

James groaned in frustration.

"The second War of Brothers is often referred to as the Thanatichor, meaning 'death of godly blood,' since it was the literal moment where Gloric, Vrec, and Cirlock were no longer kin, but enemies, forever."

"Oh." James grew nauseated. "I didn't realize that… the second war had that title."

"The second War of Brothers has always been called the Thanatichor among scholars. I'm not sure if the rest of Tor stopped using the term because of it being outdated, or out of laziness, since 'War of Brothers 2' is a bit more self-explanatory."

"Well, I'm not sure. I wouldn't want to refer to something as 'the death of blood' either. It's haunting."

"All war is, James."

James' gaze fell down to ground, the weeds and bits of grass taunting him in his remorse.

She gets it.

"As I was saying," Reggy loudly spoke, trying to break the tension in the atmosphere, "who *wants* to build a city here?"

"… Mercenaries?" James suggested.

"Theoremists," Alexis confirmed. "Theoremists are irritated with the Bureau's apathy and interference with their work, so they seek refuge here."

"But… *why?*" Reggy continued.

“Because people can do what they want.”

“Not really, we don’t live in a free world—”

“You know what?” Alexis promptly interrupted. “We’re burning daylight. Time to get to work.”

“It’s six in the evening,” James grumbled.

“And you have just a little over two hours to impress me.”

“… What’s ‘apathy?’”

“The last question you’ll ever ask if you don’t shut up and do your job.”

James let out one last huff before roughly digging along the site. He figured, this being a war ground, that he should be on the lookout for weapons and Theorem, but finding something like a hair tie, a doll, or something foreign to the battlegrounds would definitely be impressive.

For the next few hours, Reggy and James dug for weapons while Alexis took notes on the surroundings and observed the findings of her two “employees.” The musings of nature, orchestrated by rustling leaves and chirping critters, were accompanied by Alexis muttering “garbage,” “worthless,” “trash,” “that’s not bad,” and “ooh… nope, still garbage.” Occasionally, James and Reggy would come across some odd artifacts, like a lone sneaker or a watch, but still resulted in “garbage,” “that’s not bad,” or “garbage… you, James, not the watch. The watch is okay.”

Tired, grumpy, a bit hangry, and sad that watches and shoes weren’t as impressive as he’d thought they’d be, James harshly dug his shovel into the soil, and resulted in a loud, metal “pang!” Dropping whatever artifacts Reggy and James found, Alexis quickly moved to James’ location. “That sounds promising!”

She bent down and used her hands to dig out the weapon. It had a dragon emblem near the hilt along with a tattered rag. The black and red sword reflected in the sunlight almost as if it were brand new. "Ooh! A general's sword from the Fifth Eon! I might be able to get a few gold pieces out of this one! Nice work, James!" James smiled, feeling a bit too confident.

Then, another metal "pang!" sounded through the air, but with a greater resonance. "Hey, look at this!" Reggy shouted.

Alexis stood up and approached Reggy. She bent down and pulled out a black and gold, jewel encrusted blade. Alexis gasped loudly. "Wow! This is from the *first war*! I think… yes! This is *the* sword wielded by Garmosh, the Undaunted!"

Breaker of Gloric's fifth phalanx.

What?

Shut up and listen, James.

"People will pay in platinum for this baby! You're amazing, Reggy!"

She quickly stood up, gave Reggy a kiss on the cheek, yanked off the skeletal hand still clinking to the hilt and threw it on the ground, and then excitedly carried the two swords to her backpack. As she cleaned the swords, wrapped them in parchment paper, and placed them in the handcart, Reggy smirked at James.

James shook his head and pouted, disappointed that Reggy had the better sword.

"Alright, boys," Alexis began as she brushed off her clothes, "looks like the sun has retired for the day, so we should, too."

"Finally," James sighed under his breath.

"Don't you want to explore that shack before we go?" Reggy loudly said as he pointed towards a random, worn down shack near the exit of the battlegrounds.

James bit his lip and scowled at Reggy.

"Not tonight, we have to wake up early. We only have so much time to gather everything."

"You don't think we will be gathering everything?" James warily asked.

"That's the goal."

James blinked perplexedly. "You know that is literally impossible, right?"

"It's about as possible as you coming up with some snide yet depthless remark to try and win this argument."

"Oh, because you're so smart and you think you know me?"

Alexis tilted her head and smiled. "Just as I predicted."

Realizing he had played right into her plans, James decided to stay quiet for the journey back to the Cougar. Upon arrival, James finally mustered up the courage to speak again. "So, are we just going to stay in this clearing until we gather everything?"

"No, we are going to a small settlement to set up camp. It isn't too far from here."

"Why?"

"I have some friends that I want you to meet."

James decided not to ask any further questions. Alexis was clearly trying to be a bit mysterious, so he completed his work of loading up the weapons and traveling with Alexis to wherever this small settlement was. She wasn't lying when she said that it was only a short distance away, since it approximately took them eight minutes to get there, and was probably a good fifteen minutes walking distance between the clearing and the settlement. This settlement, as James discovered, was nothing other than the foundations for the infamous City of Peakless.

While this settlement was known to be the beginning of Peakless, the Theoremists had unintentionally created a high-functioning shanty town with tents scattering across an open field, in addition to mobile homes and rusty trucks. The citizens of this shantytown watched in shock and awe as a mobile home with no vehicle attachment rolled into an empty spot. When the three exited the mobile home, a dark haired, young man with a rich worker's tan made his way over to introduce himself.

"Hey there, Elijah," Alexis said with a chipper voice.

"Is that really you, Alexis?"

She held her hands out. "In the flesh."

"Wow. You look amazing. When I got your telegram that you were coming by, I was ecstatic!"

James ears perked up.

Alexis laughed. "Thanks. You don't look *that* shabby."

"A lady as always."

"Is there a time when I'm otherwise?"

"Not at all."

The two exchanged a laugh and James stepped forward to butt into the conversation. "Hi, I'm James," he said while extending his hand to Elijah.

"Hello, James." Elijah returned the favor. "What's your relationship with this young lady here?"

"Oh, he's just an employee of mine," Alexis answered. "He and Reggy have been doing a good job finding some artifacts for me."

"Really?" Elijah asked with an impressed tone.

"Absolutely," James replied. "What's *your* relationship with Alexis?"

"Oh, we were friends growing up. Both of our fathers worked together at the University."

"So… you probably have a PhD as well?"

"In Theorem? Yes, but Alexis got there before everyone else, me only being six months later."

"That's still really good, Elijah," Alexis intervened.

"Yeah, but we all can't be you."

"You're embarrassing me!"

"Why are you embarrassed? It's the truth that you're amazing."

Alexis' face turned red as she giggled slightly. James felt an anger beginning to boil from the center of his chest.

"Anyway, did I hear you've been artifact hunting?" Elijah continued.

"You heard right. I really do think that some of the people here would like what I have to offer, too."

"I have no doubt you'll have some buyers. In between my time hand feeding the orphaned Pegamoose calves and uniting the sixteen families of theorem, I'll be sure to spread the word."

James stuck out his tongue when no one was looking.

"You do that?" Alexis asked.

"You can be number seventeen."

"Uh," Alexis began, "I'm flattered, really, but we are only here on a visit."

James took in a deep breath of relief.

"Still a free spirit I see?" Elijah continued.

"It's better than being a goodie-two shoes."

"You're so charming."

"As charming as ever."

"I'll make sure I tell people that you're in town."

"Much appreciated, Elijah."

"That's 'Old Elijah' to you," a passing Theoremist said.

"Or whatever you want, really," Elijah said.

"'Old Elijah?'" James piped up. "How can you be 'Old Elijah?' You're like… twenty."

"Well, I have an old person's name."

"That *still* doesn't make any sense. I'd understand if you were a father and had a son named Elijah, but even then…"

"I don't have any kids. I was named after my dad, though."

"Well, then why don't you call *him* Old Elijah?"

"Because he's dead."

James felt his face flush with embarrassment as Alexis gave him a dirty look.

"I'll just… keep doing my Theoremist things."

"That'd be great, Elijah," Alexis said.

Elijah waved once more and returned to his tent.

The Theoremists in the town lived in either trailers or tents, the more fortunate ones having trucks to haul their things, while others relied on horses or their own two legs. Having a mobile home that hauls itself through the use of Theorem made Alexis a bit of a celebrity among the few settlers, and besides "Old Elijah," James could count at least four more Theoremists that stopped by to talk to her about her work.

There were also others in the camp that weren't as kind as they'd express irritable behavior and disgusted looks as they passed by Alexis, as if she were some sort of cult shaman committing the ultimate taboo by creating Theorem out of common items instead of the family heirloom. James could see where they were coming from, for he had never heard of a Theoremist that enchants mobile homes, but at the same time he was flabbergasted that not everyone could see her talents and innovative mindset. He concluded that he knew very little about the Theoremist culture, and that he was probably better off not trying to understand it, but how Alexis saw herself was more important, and she clearly didn't let anybody dictate her nor how she did her work. Upon that revelation, James did his best alongside Reggy to unload everything promptly, so that way when Alexis was finished talking to this next Theoremist, all she would have to do is relax for the rest of the evening and gawk over her new findings.

You sure are putting a lot of effort towards a girl you just met, and not to mention that she is a bit disdainful towards you, Krag said.

James shrugged. *She isn't that bad. If anything, I'm instigating most of our arguments. I also think she might be a bit shy around other people.*

She doesn't seem so shy right now.

But these are people that share an interest with her. Think about it, Reggy was the one doing all of the errands in Ghoti, and the only reason I'm here is because of you. I'm going with the theory that she's shy.

Whatever you say, associate.

Associate? I'm your boss if anything!

Don't take this personally, or do take it personally, I don't care, but this sword tends to wield you more than you wield it. So, technically, I'm *the boss of* you.

You're awfully mouthy for a guy trapped in a sword being guarded by dogs.

You're awfully mouthy for a guy whose life often relies on a guy trapped in a sword being guarded by dogs.

James stood and furrowed his brows at the insult, even if it was a fact.

"James."

He straightened out his back and his head shot towards Alexis.

"Yes?"

"Hand me that sword you're holding," she replied. "Gunther here wants to buy it."

"Oh, sure," James said as he approached her and gently handed her the sword.

She unwrapped the parchment paper and the man standing across from her, or Gunther as James assumed, smiled from ear to ear.

"You weren't kidding, you really *do* have the sword from Garmosh the Undaunted!" Gunther exclaimed with fascination. "How on Tor did you get it?"

"My employee, Reggy, found it."

James rolled his eyes.

"Well Reggy must've been godsent by Gloric, himself."

James tilted his head. "You believe in Gloric?"

Alexis and Gunther gave James a confused expression.

"Yeah, I'm a very strong believer in Gloric. A lot of us here are," Gunther said.

"I don't mean to sound rude, but I thought Gloricism was a dying religion."

Gunther scoffed. "Yeah, if you're a Trigan or a Trellan. Practically anyone who lives outside the Bureau's jurisdiction is a believer in Gloric."

James shook his head and rubbed his eyes. "Sorry. It's just the Bureau had us all believing that Tor doesn't believe in Gloric anymore."

"Well, that doesn't surprise me. Gloric is their greatest enemy."

"Didn't you tell me yesterday that you were from the Far North?" Alexis spoke up, more confused than skeptical or angry.

"I-I did as a child. I spent most of my teenaged years and adult life in the Outer Ring of Trig," James nervously stuttered.

Alexis frowned. "That must have been really rough."

James sighed heavily. "It kind of was."

Alexis diverted the subject back to the transaction between Gunther and herself. To James' surprise, Gunther actually paid platinum filn for the sword.

"This will be the perfect base for my next project!" Gunther happily clutched the sword.

"What are you going to do?" Alexis asked.

"Now, don't tell anybody this, but I'm going to electrify the blade with electric eels."

"Eels? That's a rare soul to use."

"Exactly, and *I'm* going to be the one to make it work perfectly! Remember, it's a secret!"

"Lips are sealed, Gunther. Lips are sealed."

As Gunther practically skipped away, Alexis excitingly eyed the platinum coin, and even James had to take a better look at it.

"Never see a platinum Filn before?" Alexis asked.

James shook his head. "No, only the rich have platinum."

Alexis scoffed. "Only in Trig. *Here* we hold onto our money and keep it within the economy, so it doesn't fall into the hands of a one-sided government. You can hold onto it and look at it a little longer if you want." She placed the coin in his hand.

James furrowed his brow. "You trust me?"

Alexis shrugged. "I've been misjudging you a bit. Had you opened up about your past a bit more, I might not have been as hard on you. I'll have to admit, it *is* kind of fun to tease you."

"That's not fair!" James argued, but couldn't hide his smile.

"Can't you cut me a little slack? After all, my hobbies are limited because I put my career first!"

The two exchanged a laugh.

"It's nice to be surrounded by people just as repulsed with the Bureau as I am," Alexis said.

James nervously nodded. "I do hate the Bureau."

"Well, it's a good thing you're with us and finally out of the hellhole known as 'Trig.'"

James nodded once more, staying silent.

"I'm going to start a fire. Would you like to grab the fish from my ice box?[10]"

"Sure."

Alexis happily grabbed some lighter fluid, a box of matches, and the excess parchment paper and practically skipped over to one of the many firepits in this small town. James wanted to laugh at her joy, but was unnerved by the fact that she was a bit *too*

---

[10] The ice box was another one of Alexis' revolutionary creations. Using the right sheet metal, furs, and a kangaroo, Alexis managed to create an insulated box. This one in particular works for keeping things cold, seeing as there were packs of ice slid into pouches on the inside. It could also work to keep things heated by removing the ice and letting it air out. After it is at room temperature, you place something heated inside, such as a fire stoker after it has sat in a flame. The ice box will maintain the temperature, and the temperature of the object of use, and can adjust to any environmental situation. It's only called an ice box because Alexis hasn't used it for the other option quite yet.

excited carrying that lighter fluid. He turned the platinum coin over in his hand, feeling guilty about keeping his past from her. Then again, he wasn't *really* lying. He's only keeping certain truths from her that will, in the end, only hurt her.

That's called lying.

Shut up, Krag!

James shrugged off his negative thoughts and entered the Cougar.

The Cougar rumbled softly as James stepped onboard.

"Hello to you too, my lady."

The Cougar rumbled again, and James could hear her trumpet slightly.

"I know. All of these long days are keeping us apart. I'm not a fan."

He heard a low, sad-sounding hum.

"Don't worry. I don't plan on leaving any time soon. We can enjoy the small moments we have together."

The door on the Cougar abruptly closed, hitting James in the rear.

"Hey!"

The Cougar rumbled and trumpeted as if it were laughing.

"You're making me blush!"

The Cougar continued laughing, and James merely shook his head, smiled, and headed towards the ice box.

After retrieving the fish, James prepared them in the same manner as he did with Mr. Woodstock, seeing that he had been actively collecting the necessary ingredients during the treks on the way to various digging sites.

"I'll admit, I've grown accustomed to your cooking," Alexis said as she undid her braid.

"I was worried you guys would accuse me of ruining the fish at first," James replied.

"How else would we prepare the fish."

"Touché." James finished his food, pulled out the purple yarn from his pocket, and began to fidget with it. "I'm beat," he added.

Reggy shrugged. "Meh. I'm good."

James shot Reggy a dirty look, because once again, he is making James look lazy.

"I don't know. It might have to do with you burning off that excess intake," Alexis commented.

Reggy bowed his head in shame. "I really didn't mean to eat all of our food."

"It's fine, really. You practically made up for it by bringing James along."

James smirked as Alexis took the last bites of her fish.

"I think I'm going to go to bed, and get the Cougar settled down for the night. I want to be bright eyed and bushy tailed come tomorrow," Alexis said with a slight yawn.

"Are you actually going to help us dig?" James asked, sounding a bit more sarcastic than he intended.

"Depends on your progress, and whether or not I'm more capable of the easy task of digging holes than you are, James."

Reggy laughed.

James shook his head. "I'll leave the science-y stuff to you."

"That's all I want."

Alexis stood and left without another word. James wasn't quite sure if he was necessarily excited about sleeping outside *again,* since Alexis has a very strict "no boys" policy at night about the Cougar like she was some five-year old guarding a tree house. Then again, they were all adults capable of doing adult things, like chess or filing taxes, so he could see how she might feel intimidated.

As the rest of the shanty town put out their fires and crawled into their makeshift homes, Reggy and James opened up a compartment on the side of the Cougar and pulled out sleeping bags and pillows. Just as James was all settled and barely closed his eyes, he felt a drip of water land on his face. He opened his eyes and looked up towards the dark sky, noticing the lack of stars.

"You've got to be kidding me," he muttered as he crawled out of his sleeping bag.

"It's just a little rain, James," Reggy groggily said.

"Yeah, and if we stay out here all night, we could catch pneumonia."

"Well, where else could we go?"

"Alexis will have to let us in."

"Nah, bro, she won't do that."

"Well, then, let's ask some of the other…"

James' voice trailed off as he noticed the trailers and tents of the Theoremists. All of them were seemingly overcrowded with large families and co-workers that decided to relocate elsewhere. He let out a heavy sigh. "Never mind."

"What about that shack?" Reggy suggested.

"Great idea, Reggy!" James exclaimed.

The two quickly grabbed their sleeping bags, pillows, and Lord Krag, and bolted towards the shack in the settlement for the Argument of Peaks, James' heart relieved that he would be able to sleep in shelter for the first time in days.

Chapter Ten

Whiskey for Breakfast, Nails for Dessert

SLEEPING IN THE SHACK WAS a terrible idea.

James had never slept on a more discomforting surface in his entire life. The ground seemed harder and harder with every toss and turn, and whenever he moved to a different spot, he somehow managed to end up under a leak. Not to mention there was a terrible draft, making it feel colder in the shack than it did outside. With more splinters in his arm than hours of sleep, James groggily awoke to a sunbeam shining directly in his eye. His stirring also woke up Reggy, who seemed to be just as tired as James was.

"I don't think I've ever felt sorrier for anything in my entire life," Reggy muttered.

"If it's any consolation, I don't think either one of us could have predicted how terrible this shack would be."

"Still, I think I would've chosen getting sick had I known how bad of sleep we would get."

"I agree."

The two fell silent as they gathered their pillows and sleeping bags, got on their feet, groaned loudly, and took a moment to pop their backs and crack their necks. James put the sheath of his sword across his back, and the two began to exit the shack.

You're stupid, Lord Krag said.

Good morning to you, too.

When they walked outside, they were surprised to see Alexis already out on the settlement digging for artifacts.

"Hey," James called out.

She looked up. "Oh, you two were *here* the whole time. I thought you both decided to run off with my platinum filn in the dead of the night."

"Oh, sorry!" James exclaimed as he reached into his pocket for the filn.

He flicked it towards her with his thumb and she quickly and reflexively caught it.

"… Nice."

"Because I have great reflexes without the need of a sword?"

James sighed. "Must you always insult me?"

"Thus continues the cycle of life."

He groaned.

"I guess you guys can go back to the Cougar, load up your stuff, and grab a quick bite to eat. I'll keep working over here."

"Maybe you should come with us. We might fall asleep… and never wake back up."

"Did you have that bad of a night?"

"It was a *really* uncomfortable shack," Reggy said as he stretched his arms and frowned.

Alexis sighed. "Sorry. I should've let you both in when the rain started, but I figured you were both resourceful enough to find shelter."

"You weren't wrong, it's just that Reggy has poor judgment," James teased.

"Hey!" Reggy playfully shoved James' shoulder.

"Am I wrong? You have me as a friend."

"I suppose you have a point."

Alexis laughed. "Yeah, James can be a little bastard sometimes."

Reggy smirked. "Oh, honey, you have no idea."

"Anyway," James quickly said in order to try to change the subject, "we should all go back together."

Alexis shrugged. "I suppose I could go for a quick break."

James internally cheered as the three returned to the camp. To his surprise, Alexis didn't lead them to the Cougar, but to a completely different mobile home. It was much larger, but also looked like it hadn't been moved in a long time, as if it were already settled in that spot, and someone decided to move in. When they entered this mobile home, there had been a bar set up on one side of the wall and tables aligned along the other. There was a menu with only a few food items on it, such as eggs with toast, a peanut butter sandwich, and just a bucket of peanuts in general, but it mostly had names of alcoholic beverages that were each labeled as original recipes. It was very clear that people didn't come here for the food, since they all had brought sacked lunches, but it didn't necessarily stop them from attending this social hangout.

"… Why are we here?" James asked as the three took a seat at the bar and glanced at the menu. "There's barely anything to eat here. It's only whiskey!"

"Ever have whiskey for breakfast, before?" Alexis asked.

"No!"

"James" —Reggy smirked— "come on."

James huffed. "Okay, fine. Yes, I've had whiskey for breakfast before, but I kind of swore I'd never do it again!"

"Well, that's just weak." Alexis raised her hand in the air and snapped her fingers. "Yo, Thaddeus! Get over here and give us drinks!"

“It’s not ‘weak,’” James continued to argue. “It’s called taking care of your body!”

“Then get a plate of toast.”

“I just don’t see why we can’t go back to the Cougar—”

“Damn, girl” —a man in his late thirties, who James assumed to be Thaddeus, approached the three from behind the bar— “why do you gotta be so got damn loud?”

“How else are you supposed to get service around here?”

“Maybe you should start by being polite. It isn’t too hard to turn away an O’Leary’s business.”

“Is it just as hard as turning away this?” Alexis waved a gold piece in the air with two fingers.

“Got dammit,” Thaddeus complained. “What you want?”

“Glass of Flendin.”

He gave her a dirty look. “You’re kiddin.’”

“Did I stutter?” Alexis said with a scoff. “Oh, and put it on the rocks.”

“Got dammit, girl! I have an array of original recipes and you’re gonna go for that name-brand crap?”

“Your homebrews are disgusting, Thaddeus!”

“That’s ‘cause you and the whole got damn community won’t give ‘em a chance! Forcin’ me to resort to sellin’ them big ol’ fancy name brands just to make a bit of cash instead of developin’ the acquired taste!”

“They taste like donkey piss, Thaddeus,” a patron a few stools down said. “In fact, I wouldn’t be surprised if it was, considering you own a couple.”

“How do you know what that tastes like?” James piped up.

The patron chuckled. “Order one of his drinks!”

Everyone in the bar laughed out loud while Thaddeus grumbled to himself.

“Can I order now?” Reggy asked.

"Of course, sweetheart," Alexis answered. "Get whatever you want."

Reggy placed his hands on the bar. "I would like a tall glass of gas—"

"No," James harshly intervened.

Reggy huffed. "Fine! I would like to try your donkey piss."

"Look, I'll *prove* it!" Thaddeus began. "I'll *prove* that my drinks are good! I'll get you my signature, on the house!"

"… Okay," Reggy continued. "I'd also like a peanut butter and jelly sandwich."

"Would you like that fried today?"

"… Uh." Reggy narrowed his eyes. "… Sure?"

"And what you want?" Thaddeus directed at James.

"Um…" James looked over the menu. "I guess just two pieces of toast."

"And to drink?"

"Do you have any milk?"

Thaddeus gave another dirty look. "Milk?"

James nodded. "Yeah, milk."

"What are you, an infant?"

"Maybe I just like milk with my breakfast, *Thaddeus.*"

"Don't say my name like it's a cuss word."

"Then just do your job."

Thaddeus scoffed. "Fine. I'll get you your stupid milk. Do you want chocolate in it too, since you are apparently an eight-year-old?"

James smirked. "Hell yeah."

"Got dammit."

Thaddeus huffed and walked away to complete their order. Alexis swiveled on her bar stool to face James. "Why did you quit drinking?" she asked.

"It used to be a bit of a bane for me, so now I don't want to give it that power, nor succumb to a life that did absolutely nothing for me."

"Hmm." Alexis furrowed her brow. "That's an insightful statement, James."

James shrugged. "It's just the truth."

"I would've never taken you for an alcoholic."

"Actually" —James looked over her shoulder at Reggy— "I'm not an alcoholic, but I am addicted to the easy way out."

Reggy made eye contact with him and gave him a scowl.

"… It's something I'm still working through."

Reggy let out a sigh and shrugged, but still made his disappointment clear.

"Well, you only fail if you quit, so just keep trying," Alexis commented.

"I suppose you're right."

Thaddeus returned with the toast, sandwich, and milk and then made the alcoholic drinks in front of them. Reggy took a whiff of the home brew and furrowed his brow, definitely unsure if this was an edible poison.

"Go ahead," Alexis urged. "*Prove* that the drink is awful."

"Got dammit, you shut your mouth and let the boy decide," Thaddeus snapped.

Reggy nervously brought the drink to his lips, and as soon as he took a sip, he spat it back into the glass and began coughing.

"Got dammit!" Thaddeus threw his rag onto the ground.

Alexis and a few other patrons burst into laughter. "There's your proof, Thaddeus!" she teased.

Thaddeus mumbled to himself as he picked up his rag, walked further down the bar, and began wiping it down. James looked to his two companions to begin a new conversation, and tried to ignore the unsanitary action of cleaning a counter with a dirty rag being committed by Thaddeus.

“So, you had a bad night in the shack?” Alexis asked as she stole a piece of James’ toast.

“Hey!” He moved his plate so she couldn’t reach. “You can’t just take other people’s food!”

“I paid for it.” She shrugged and put the piece of toast in her mouth.

James huffed. “Whatever, and yes, we had a bad night in the shack.”

“Was the floor just hard?”

“It wasn’t just hard,” Reggy began, “it would, like, move. Whenever we rolled over or something, the ground would shift.”

“Plus, there were holes in the roof and rain kept leaking on our faces,” James added.

Alexis furrowed her brow. “That is pretty odd. I wonder why the ground is so unstable.”

“Not to mention the draft.”

“The draft?”

“Yeah,” Reggy began, “there was a weird draft and it was super cold! Like, colder than out in the storm!”

Reggy finally took a bite of his fried sandwich. His eyes lit up and he happily moaned before stuffing more sandwich into his mouth. Alexis set her elbow on the bar and rested her head in her hand. She delved deeper into her thoughts as she took a sip of her beverage.

“You mean you don’t know?” Thaddeus returned to the three.

“That shack is haunted!”

Alexis scoffed. “The shack isn’t ‘haunted.’”

“Is too! That’s what the draft is for! It’s the ghosts trying to steal your souls!”

James’ head shot up mid bite of toast. “… Ghosts?” he nervously asked with his mouth full of bread.

Thaddeus nodded. "Yeah. Some people *died* in there. I wouldn't be too surprised either, with all them wars that happened over there. Legend says it was a *murder shack."*

"Stop trying to scare us, Thaddeus. It was probably some sort of medical center for the soldiers."

"I'm just being honest. Not my fault you're in nial."

"'In nial?'"

"You know, in the nial."

"It's 'in denial," you idiot!"

"Quit acting like you're better than us, got dammit!"

"I'm not trying to act like I'm better than you!"

"Really? You waltz over here like you're the got damn leader and that's not acting like you're better than us?"

"It's not that I think I'm better than you, I just know all of you too well! Jeb probably packed carrots and a jar of peanut butter for his breakfast."

A man sitting at a table paused and nervously glanced between Alexis and his sack of food.

"And Arthur is probably picking his nose."

Another man at the bar about to stick his finger in his nose quickly put his hand down and averted Alexis' gaze.

"And you, Thaddeus, you are just a tool, and will always be a tool."

"Don't say I didn't warn you, girl." Thaddeus threw his rag over his shoulder. "Don't blame me when you wake up tomorrow with a haunted wagon."

Thaddeus walked away to check on other patrons while Alexis rolled her eyes. Her annoyed expression relaxed as she once again fell deep into her thoughts.

"… Draft… Shifting floor…" she muttered to herself.

"What are you talking about—?" James began

"Shh!" Alexis covered James' mouth with her hands. "Stop your words. I'm thinking."

James pushed her hand away and decided to finish his breakfast. Just when he and Reggy were just about finished eating, Alexis sat up straighter and let out a gasp.

"Come on!' she shouted before abruptly standing from her chair and bolting out of the bar.

James and Reggy stammered before leaving their food behind and ran after her. She was sprinting across the camp at full speed towards the shack.

"Hey!" James shouted at her. "Slow down!"

"Just go to the shack!" she shouted back.

"Can't you just explain what's going on?"

"That draft isn't just a bunch of ghosts! It's a path to treasure!"

James and Reggy panted heavily as they arrived at the shack. James felt himself grow sick as he observed the shack in better lighting and was more coherent. Blood stains painted the floor and bloody handprints decorated the walls. There were old sheets and bones scattered across the ground, suggesting that Thaddeus' theory of it being a murder shack wasn't too farfetched. Alexis was already inside, seemingly oblivious to the horrific scene, crawling along the walls of the shaft, and feeling the ground.

"What in Gloric's name are you doing?" James asked in a pained voice.

"This isn't a shack," Alexis explained as she picked up James' and Reggy's sleeping bags and threw them outside. "It's an entrance."

"How on Tor can you tell?" James asked.

"Look, there is a space between the floor and the wall. That means something is underneath here!"

"How do you know it isn't just erosion and that the floor can give out any minute?"

Alexis huffed and stood up. “Because the structural integrity was *clearly* built to accommodate something more. Think about it, how deceptive is it to hide a treasure underneath a *shack?* No one would think to look there! If only we knew how to get underneath it…”

“What kind of entrance do you think it is? If the platform is small enough, maybe we can distribute our weight to get it to open,” Reggy suggested.

“That’s a good idea! There are four corners and walls in here to experiment with, so we each should man one. I’ll go get Elijah and see if he wants to help.”

“We don’t need Elijah’s help,” James snapped.

“Uh, we kind of do. We need a fourth person to stand on the final corner.”

“We can figure it out on our own. Besides, what if it’s a discovery of a lifetime? We should keep it between the three of us.”

“Well, James, Theoremists believe that we shouldn’t keep information that can improve each other’s work. Whatever we find down here can heavily influence the work of everyone we’ve met so far!”

“Then why is Elijah so special?”

“I think they see him as a leader in a way—”

“Oh, because his name is ‘Old Elijah’ he is suddenly important?”

Alexis scowled at James, laden with anger.

“I bet if I were called ‘Old Jim’ I’d be treated like an elder as well!”

“You don’t know Elijah like I do, James.”

“Why? Because you’re both Theoremists and all I am is a guy with a sword, or maybe it’s because the two of you got fancy PhDs together and I’m just lucky to be able to read and write? Well, sorry I’m just ‘James’ and not ‘Old Tom,’ ‘Adam,’ or ‘Sam!’”

As soon as the words left his lips, the shack began quaking, and a red light emanated between the floorboards. With a loud rumble and an ear-piercing creak, the floor began descending into the ground slowly, before picking up to a moderate speed. The walls surrounding them were black, and no longer made of wood, and the only light they had was from the floorboards. A loud noise suddenly rang through the air and appeared to be coming from the floor itself. It consisted of static and the screams of the damned as it ominously scraped against the party's ears. Each of them were merely startled by the noise, but grew more and more nervous as the lights in the floor began flickering. This continued for quite some time, to the point where all three of them were clinging onto one another, afraid of whatever they had stumbled into.

The lights grew dimmer as some sort of shadow began spreading across the floor. James looked harder at it, and realized that it was some sort of hand, with long, bony fingers, and had something dripping from it. His two companions came to the same conclusion as they all held each other tighter, clung to their weapons, and backed away from the shadow. The shadow eventually turned into shadows, and deep hissing could be heard among the static. The hissing grew louder, and louder, as if the hands were suddenly aware of the party's location. James felt like his chest was going to explode from the screams that had been building up inside him. His stomach and heart fluttered within his core as the hands grew closer and closer. The three took on a fighting stance, but the elevator came to an abrupt complete stop, in addition to the noise and the lights in the floor, leaving the three with the sounds of liquid being squished from a body, and encased in darkness.

James could feel his beating heart pounding against every part of his body, from his head to his toes. The walls in front of them swung outward, like a set of double doors, only to reveal a long, narrow hallway that was slightly darkened, but not completely black. The party glanced at one another, and Alexis took a deep breath, bravely deciding to face the unknown as she stepped into the hallway, with her two employees following her manner, uncertain of their fates.

As they walked down the hallway, lights flickered on with each step they took, slightly illuminating each step forward. They eventually got to a point where the lights no longer lit up whenever they took a step, but Alexis kept moving forward. When the hum of electricity began to grow quiet, the party came to a complete stop as the lights began flickering off behind them, leaving them in complete darkness once more. The three huddled close together again and clung onto one another when the hum grew in volume, and the lights randomly flicked on and off in strange patterns.

Suddenly, a loud "pop" echoed through the air, and the three didn't hesitate to let out screams. The lights in the hallway all flashed on, in addition to the lights in front of them, revealing a large room and a banner draped across the ceiling, reading "Welcome New Employees!" and confetti raining down upon them. The room, itself, tried to set a welcoming atmosphere, but felt like the beginning of a torture session as a black substance clung to the chairs, parts of the walls, paintings, and a guillotine set in the center of the room. After staring at the sight in confusion, a voice began talking over the intercom.

"Welcome to our semi-quarterly employee orientation! From the bottom of the hearts of our office staff, research and development team, managers, and borderline omniscient CEO, who is me, we are excited that you are not only starting your careers, but starting them here of all places, at Lynole Industries."

"What the fresh hell?" James muttered, only to be immediately shushed by Alexis.

"Our next tour guide, known as our famous 'Handy Dandy,' one of the many robotic entities you will encounter at our place of business, will be with you momentarily. We thank you for your patience and encourage you to introduce yourself to your future co-workers and enjoy a slice of cake."

The guillotine suddenly activated, and its blade fell into the headlock, but not cutting into anything.

"Hah, you gotta love that," the voice over the intercom said. "And may I have the pleasure to welcome you all once again to this establishment. Also, keep in mind that none of you would be here if it weren't for me, Cir—!"

"Uh, sir," a background voice in the intercom said, "that's not the slogan we agreed on—"

"I thought I made the decisions around here."

"We do, and in the board meeting, you decided on something else."

"Sam, is that true? Sam? SAM—"

"What?" A woman shouted in the background.

"Is that the slogan we agreed on?"

"Yes! For the thousandth time, *that* is the slogan we agreed on!"

"It is?"

"Yes!"

"Ugh! Fine! All of this brought to you today extends beyond commerce. Happy now, Ron? You dumb fetch—"

The message over the intercom clicked off, and the group of three was left in the company of a quiet, jazz arrangement to fill the silence.

"… What the hell was all that about?" Alexis asked.

"You mean to tell me that you have no idea what this place is?" James replied.

"Of course, I don't. Why would I?"

"Up until this point you've seemed to know everything about each place we've been to."

"Sorry to disappoint you, but I came here to make a *discovery,* and normally prior knowledge in a discovery isn't necessarily required."

"Okay, then let's think about our context clues. The CEO was the one speaking over the intercom, referred to himself as 'omniscient,' and alluded that his name begins with a 'Cir.' Later, he mentions something about 'commerce.' Maybe we are in the, for lack of better words, we are in the lair of Cirlock."

"That's insane. Besides, before he went crazy, a lot of people were named after Cirlock, so it's probably some ordinary dude."

"Some ordinary dude created an underground facility in the middle of nowhere, only for the entrance to be a shack?"

Alexis' eyes carefully observed everything in the room. "Cirlock wouldn't have some 'business' at the bottom of a mountain, let alone one where a giant argument between his brothers happened that Gloric won."

"Well, what is Cirlock most famous for?"

Alexis scoffed. "Bringing lethal, semi-automatic weapons to the humans of Tor."

"And where did he manufacture all of those weapons?"

Alexis' eyes widened. "My gods… everything we've known about Cirlock has been passed down through legend, but assuming you're right, we could know for ourselves whatever we want about him! Think of all the clues, no, all of the *artifacts* we could find here!"

And there she goes again, James thought.

"I wish I brought a bigger backpack, or rather an extra backpack. Do you really think a 'Handy Dandy' is actually going to be arriving soon? What if we legitimately pursue on a tour of Cirlock's *lair*?"

"That sounds fun, it really does," Reggy spoke up, "but I don't think we should spend a minute longer here because there's a disgusting slab of gunk growing on the walls and the paintings have eyes that are clearly watching us. So—"

Reggy ripped Alexis' backpack from her arms. "Hey—!"

"Let's find a way out of here," Reggy finished as he looped the straps through his arms.

"Reggy," Alexis laughed, "*sweetheart,* do you remember who you're working for?" she said through clenched teeth.

"A level-headed Theoremist that recognizes danger when it's right in front of her."

"Then it's a good thing that I'm all of those things you just said, because right now, I think it's okay to progress through the lair, and should danger arise," Alexis unsheathed her swords, "I'll be ready."

A loud scuttle echoed from the vents above.

"... I wanna go home," James spoke up.

Alexis rolled her eyes at James' hypocrisy. "It's like I said, I'll be ready should danger arise."

As Reggy opened his mouth to respond, a pair of doors just beyond the guillotine swung open. A fully metallic robot on a single wheel entered the room and approached the party. Whomever built it paid close attention to detail, as its slender body clearly had several moving parts to make it move naturally, like a human would. The wheel was a bit obtuse, in addition to the face, which had a smile and wide eyes. It also had some of the black goop oozing from its neck and loose panels in its chest, making it look horrifying in the current setting.

Alexis squealed. "A robot? I've never seen an actual robot before!"

"Welcome, new members of our team," the robot said with a light shining on and off behind it's smile as it spoke. "I am the Handy Dandy, an artificial intelligence designed to give you an in-depth history of Lynole Industries, in addition to answering any questions you may have as we explore the facilities and the exciting path of your new career choices. Let's all get acquainted!" The robot turned towards James. "Introduce yourself, new team member."

"Uh..." James warily stared at the eerie robot before anxiously answering. "My name is James—"

"Fantastic! Now that we all know one another, why don't we let the tour commence?"

James threw his hands up in the air as a wide smile spread across Alexis' face.

"See, Reggy," Alexis began, "everything is fine."

"Before we begin, I must warn you that it is against company policy to have weapons out of their places of holding during the tour. For your safety and the safety of our employees and products, we request that you currently put away all weapons and belongings, for Lynole Industries is not responsible for any injury that should occur on your own ignorance, dismembered body parts, or any items lost on the tour."

Alexis frowned and sheathed her swords. "I suppose that seems fair."

Reggy's eyes narrowed as his faith in the crazy sword lady began to diminish.

"Enough with silly disclaimers," the Handy Dandy said. "Let's begin the first day of the rest of your new and improved lives!" The Handy Dandy turned around and rolled towards the doors it entered through, and James, Alexis, and Reggy followed behind. No one else. Obviously just those three, because they are definitely the only ones in this facility currently, and, therefore, no one else should be on the tour with them,

At all.

The Handy Dandy moved at a slower pace in order for the party to keep up with it. The corridors beyond the double doors were pitch black, and fear of the unknown began to seep into James' and Reggy's mind once more, while Alexis continued to beam with excitement. As the Handy Dandy moved further down the corridor, lights began to flicker on above paintings.

"These paintings represent the achievements of our company in chronological order. This painting to your right represents the origins of Lynole Industries, all beginning with a hostile takeover of the previous company."

James took a closer look at the painting. "It's just a picture of a guy standing on top of a pile of dead penguins raising a sword to the sky."

"Yes, you are very observant. Observational skills are imperative when moving through a company."

"But how does this painting represent a hostile takeover of a company?"

"This picture has deep symbolism and is absolutely hilarious! As you can see, it involves the three brothers conquering the industry from the previous owners."

"Who were the previous owners?"

"The previous owners of this industry were the Waddlesworths."

"Hold on," Alexis intervened. "I thought the Waddlesworths were famous for their military control?"

"What a hilarious imagination you have! Waddlesworths are not physically bred for military combat. They are like Guinea pigs, or penguins, meant experimented on and eaten."

"... Excuse me—?"

"However, they do have innovative minds. A Waddlesworth specializing intact would not be an impossible outcome but would be outrageous nonetheless."

Alexis pulled her journal out of her pocket and furiously began taking down notes.

"What's a Guinea pig?" James asked the Handy Dandy.

"The reason we don't have dinosaurs!"

"What the hell is a" —James huffed— "nevermind."

"If you insist."

James irately turned his attention back to the painting and studied it carefully. He thought his mind was beginning to play tricks on him as he began to see a silhouette of hands and a face in the background. He brought his face closer to the painting, and the silhouette became three-dimensional as whatever was behind the painting pressed its body against the back of the canvas. James let out a horrified scream and fell backwards. "There's something in the painting!" he shouted.

Alexis, Reggy, and the Handy Dandy had already progressed further down the hall. "Yes, there is always something that we can learn from art—"

"No, you stupid robot! There's an actual thing *in* the painting!"

Alexis furrowed her brow and rushed towards the painting. She, too, observed it closely before poking at the canvas.

"Now, now, it is against company policy to touch the art in such a barbaric way," the Handy Dandy said.

"I'm just investigating it for signs of danger," Alexis replied.

"What wild imaginations you new employees have! There is nothing dangerous to encounter on the tour." The Handy Dandy then spoke in a quicker voice as it said, "Lynole Industries is not responsible for any danger you may encounter on the tour."

"I don't see anything, anyway," Alexis said as she took a step back. "Maybe the environment is just getting to you, James. Try to calm down.

James' eyes shifted between her and the painting, his anxiety already beginning to rise. "I'll do my best."

Alexis helped him off of the ground and walked back to Reggy and the Handy Dandy, while James decided to keep his distance.

"This next picture is our CEO's top pick, because it is absolutely hilarious," the Handy Dandy said. "It represents an inside joke passed down from previous…"

The Handy Dandy's voice grew deeper and eventually slowed down, speaking in an indecipherable manner. The party of three stopped in their tracks as they observed it closer. The top half of its body suddenly became limp and bent in ways that are usually not deemed as normal, nor healthy. The three let out startled shouts, and the Handy Dandy's voice fired back up to its regular voice.

"Sorry for the inconvenience. It appears that I am currently encountering a disturbance in my script. Running Troubleshoot. Diagnosing… Diagnosing… Diagnosing…"

The Handy Dandy began to mutter that for some time, and Alexis took the initiative to continue this "tour" and observed the other paintings. Some seemed a bit asinine to James, such as the overly embellished picture of a black flamingo surrounded by Cherubs and ivory clouds. Others were a bit more subtle, such as a simple picture of a dark-haired woman, and another picture of a woman on a twelve foot by twelve-foot canvas, simply eating a donut and hiding her face from the artist with her hand.

As they proceeded forward, the Handy Dandy wheeled behind them, continuing to diagnose any problems it was having. The last picture was hanging on a giant wall at the end of the hallway, and was a giant portrait of a lion in a crown, with a large plaque underneath it reading:

"Lynole Industries:
Where the beggars and the barren become kings."

"That's nice," Alexis said as she looked to the path to her left. "I guess we keep going."

"Or, hear me out, we go down this hallway and end this nonsense," Reggy replied as he gestured towards the path on the right, with a giant green sign, with black goop dripping from it, reading: "Emergency Exit."

Alexis huffed. “I’m not leaving here without further exploration.”

“Why?” Reggy exclaimed. “If you’re worried about bringing treasure back, just take one of these stupid paintings! I’m sure they’re worth *something* after you get all of this black gunk off of them.”

“This was once an entire company, and you want me to settle for *paintings*?” Alexis shouted back.

“It’s better than death!”

“Why are you so unnerved by this place?”

“It’s ran by robots?”

“And?”

“The robopocalypse is real, Alexis! The robots *will* take over one day if we let them!”

“Oh, that is just ridiculous—!”

While Alexis and Reggy argued, James found himself becoming more engrossed with the lion portrait. The proud beast had dwindled into a pitiful louse as it seemingly fed off of the despair lingering in the building, for it was the portrait that suffered the most wear and tear. The king had condescended to a state of misery as the shards of his crown were pasted together with the blood and tears the God of Commerce had shed. The saddest thing about this once mighty predator was the pain that emulated from his eyes as he perpetually displayed failure to measure up to the tattered motto written on the plaque, because not only were the beggars and the barren no longer royalty, but they made up the stepping stones that cheaters and murderers use to climb their way up the ranks.

As James’ focus increased on the painting, he began to hear subtle whispers, and instead of shaking them off as usual, he decided to listen, thinking it was a plead for help from the lion, but, oh, was he wrong.

You’re not alone in here.

James removed the Sword of Lord Krag from off his back and set it on the ground beside him.

Of course, I'm not, James thought back. *I have my friends here.*

Diagnosing… Diagnosing…

They appear to be tiny humans that have found their way into this hole… It'd be a shame if we actually crossed paths.

The exit is on the right.

I won't let you hurt them. James felt anger boiling within him.

We aren't running away.

They are being awfully loud. How unwise. They might attract something worse than me.

We'd technically be sprinting towards life.

Then again… there isn't anything in here worse than me.

Diagnosing…

It's a good thing you're nothing more than thoughts, James replied. *That's all you'll ever be: a voice in my head that* isn't *real.*

You're being ridiculous.

The Threshers remind me of myself.

You're being unrational.

The what? James asked.

It's *irrational,* dummy.

All along the walls… all around us.

James' eyes panned across the walls

Their blackness is everywhere.

Diagnosing…

Slowly…

Shut up.

Infiltrating…

This is all your fault.

… Everything.

James felt the pounding of his heart in his head, except the feeling was more intense than when they first arrived. He eyed his arguing friends and the malfunctioning robot, and everything became muffled by the ringing in his ears.

... Up here, little one.

James' eyes slowly looked up towards the ceiling,

But was interrupted when the robot suddenly snapped back into place.

The party shouted at the suddenly revived Handy Dandy, ceasing their arguing and their overthinking. Panting heavily, James reached down and replaced the sheath of his sword across his back.

Care to tell me why you put me on the dirty ground? Krag asked.

... Later.

Whatever.

"I apologize for the stall in our tour. Even Handy Dandies need rest once in a while. Thank you for your patience, and all of you will be receiving a gold star on your paperwork!" Its voice quickened again. "Lynole Industries is not responsible for any endorphins released from the gold stars nor any addictive behavior that may result from it."

"What?" the three simultaneously muttered.

The Handy Dandy spouted out black goop into the air, and the three winced at the sudden action and shielded themselves.

"Confetti canons are the steppingstones for the future. Everything should be made to make another person's day. Follow me, and we will continue our journey through this exciting building."

Alexis huffed and looked at Reggy. "I guess that decides that," she snidely remarked.

"I'm the bigger person, so I'm going to wish that you didn't get infected by the robot plague because of that stupid 'Handy Dan' thing," Reggy said, gritting his teeth slightly.

"Thank you."

"You're welcome."

The group resumed following the Handy Dandy, with James feeling more unnerved than ever. He swore he could hear various clattering in the vents and in the walls, but he didn't know if his mind was playing tricks on him again, or if Thaddeus was right about this place actually being haunted. They were greeted by a pair of large, metal doors at the end of the hallway.

"This next attraction was voted number one on the tour in the year two-thousand five-hundred seventy-seven. It is my pleasure to introduce you to the main showroom of our prized Research and Development Department."

Alexis let out another excited squeal as James and Reggy exchanged concerned glances.

We're going to die here, James thought.

The Handy Dandy raised his arm, and for the first time in millennia, the lights gradually turned on from the start of the room to the end, illuminating the entirety of it before flickering fiercely, and burning out. The group shielded their eyes as sparks emerged from the bulbs. When the room was completely dark, a single red light on the opposite side of the room began fading on and off.

"Geez," Alexis said as she lowered her hands.

"Yeah, a bit underwhelming if you ask me," James muttered.

Alexis turned to glare at James. "What is that supposed to mean?"

"That if we're gonna die, then it should be cooler than that."

"Aw, James" —Reggy placed his hands over his heart— "you do listen."

"Will you two stop it! We are not going to die!" Alexis took back her bag from Reggy and began rummaging through it. "We are going to have a great time" —she handed a flashlight to James— "make brand new discoveries" —handed a flashlight to Reggy— "and have a ton of fun!" then pulled out a flashlight for herself. “Now, quit worrying about the impossible, and find something cool!”

Alexis broke away from the two as she began shining her flashlight over the various tables in the room. They were lined up next to one another, each with some sort of fold out display demonstrating a new invention, or concept. Some had dioramas of the idea, others had the physical prototypes. There were also various glass tanks containing odd inventions as well, each with some sort of plaque next to it with a description. To James' surprise, he came across things that resembled radios and televisions, but seemed to be earlier versions, and didn't come across a single weapon of mass destruction.

“So, what do you want exactly?” James asked. “Are we looking for guns, or tanks, or…?”

“Anything,” Alexis replied.

James huffed. “Okay. Oh, look, a rubber band ball. That sure seems like a new discovery.”

Alexis quickly approached James' side to find the rubber band ball and gasped loudly. “Good job, James!”

James threw his hands up in the air. “I was being entirely sarcastic!”

“But for all we know, this could be a type of rubber band made from a different material, or from a discontinued brand! This stuff has been down here for Gloric knows how long, so even the average is something extraordinary.”

James sighed. “If you say so.”

The party of three continued to search the room.

“I keep seeing notes about a ‘Master Craftsman,’” Alexis declared.

“I do, too,” James replied as he was looking through a portfolio on a nearby table.

“They apparently tutored everybody here. They were some sort of… philosopher, Theoremist, engineer, architect, and nearly everything else. Apparently, they wanted everyone to get closer to achieving the goal of a 'Grand Project.'"

"What's the 'Grand Project?'"

"No clue. Keep looking."

"What do I do?" Reggy asked.

"Practice your reading," Alexis replied.

Reggy sighed. "Okay…"

They continued searching for more evidence on this Grand Project for a few more minutes, but nobody spoke up on whether or not they found something.

"Ugh, this black stuff is everywhere," Alexis observed. "What even is it?"

"Looks like Thresher blood," Reggy said.

Thresher... James thought. *Just like the voice said...*

"Seriously?" Alexis questioned as she took a closer look at the gunk.

Reggy approached a patch of the gunk and sniffed it. "Yep, definitely Thresher blood."

"That doesn't make any sense. Why would there be Threshers here?"

James smiled awkwardly as he gazed at his two companions. "… What's a Thresher?"

Alexis sighed and placed a hand over her forehead.

"… Sorry."

"No, it's my fault. I should be used to this by now."

James' cheeks turned red with embarrassment.

"Threshers are living corpses. What happens is a certain type of fungus will inhabit dead bodies and reanimate it. Its spores won't kill you, but once it is in your system, it will sit there and wait until you die."

James' let out a breath. "Then it's a damn good thing none of us are dead."

"I'll say. I'm confused, though. We haven't come across any corpses quite yet. Why would there be Threshers here?"

James panned his flashlight across the room once more, until he came across an old Handy Dandy covered in the Thresher blood and twitching in the corner.

"Alexis…"

"Yeah, James?"

James gulped. "Hypothetically speaking, could a Thresher inhabit *any* inanimate object?"

"I don't think so, since they primarily attack organic things. What makes you think that?"

After the words left her lips, several black arms emerged out of the sides of the Handy Dandy and the head split in half, revealing a corpse-like face and rows of sharp, black teeth.

"That's why!" James shouted as he unsheathed his sword.

Alexis swiftly turned towards the Thresher. "What the fresh hell?" she exclaimed as she unsheathed her own swords.

James charged at the Thresher with his sword and managed to cut off a few arms as it tried to shield itself, which only resulted in angering the creature as its limbs began regenerating.

"*IT IS NOT ADVISED TO DRAW WEAPONS ON LYNOLE INDUSTRY PRODUCTS AND EMPLOYEES,*" the Thresher robot said in a deep voice.

Fetch! These things talk, too? James thought to himself. *Do you think we can even defeat them?*

The best I can do is slow them down, but I think it'd be better to run. It's not the only one, Krag said.

James looked around the room and noticed several more old Handy Dandies beginning to twitch and reanimate, along with the walls seemingly moving, Alexis trying to fight off two, and Reggy flipping a few tables to detour others. James shook his head and cursed once more as he sprinted across the room towards the other two Threshers. He swung the sword towards the head of one and the mid-section of the other, and as quickly as he arrived, they already began regenerating.

"Run!" James shouted.

The group didn't hesitate to listen as they sprinted off into one direction, with the Threshers behind them crawling at a quick pace. The group ran in several different directions, trying to throw them off their trail, but they either encountered more, or the creatures were just too fast.

"There!" Alexis pointed towards a room with double doors.

The three ran with all of their might towards the doors, quickly grabbing them as they ran inside and shut them on the Threshers. James and Reggy held onto the door handles tightly as Alexis ripped some rope out of her bag and tied the handles together. The Threshers all banged harshly on the glass, but the doors were seemingly impenetrable despite the metal slamming against it.

James, Alexis, and Reggy all panted, but kept their guard up as they observed the room they were in, searching for more Threshers.

"Do you think it was a good idea to potentially lock ourselves into a room with a bunch of monsters?" Reggy warily asked.

"We'll find another way out if that happens," Alexis said as she gripped her swords tightly.

"There you are!"

The three jumped at the sudden voice and turned to their left to see the Handy Dandy that was acting as their tour guide.

"I was beginning to worry," the Handy Dandy said.

Alexis lowered her swords. "Thank Gloric. I was beginning to think we were goners."

"It is important to stick together in a group, for your safety and the safety of our valuable inventions."

James and Reggy maintained their stance, unwavering from a potential attack from the Handy Dandy.

"Now, I will show you where you will be working. Follow me, please. If you are good, you will be rewarded with some 'happy music.'"

"What are you two doing?" Alexis asked as the Handy Dandy began wheeling away.

"That thing malfunctioned earlier and spat Thresher blood everywhere! It's definitely been infected by those things!" James shouted.

Alexis sighed as she tightly gripped her swords again. "You have a point, but I don't even know how to kill these things. You don't usually see them in these areas."

"Maybe you guys can cut it up before it is truly taken over?" Reggy suggested.

"Nuh-uh. I have a feeling we will trigger an attack if that happens," Alexis pointed out.

"Maybe we can lock it in a closet or something?" James suggested next.

"You're on the right track, but I think it will take more than a closet to detain that thing."

Alexis looked around the room before noticing a plant next to the receptionist desk. "Hey, Handy Dandy," she called out to the robot. "I have a question."

The Handy Dandy stopped and turned to face her. "Of course, how may I assist you?"

"What type of plant is that?" She pointed at the plant with her sword.

"Oh, that is easy. That is a Preying Ficus, part of our security system in Lynole Industries. They remain dormant on the tour and are only active after hours."

"What about if they are provoked?"

"It is not a good idea to provoke the Preying Ficus. Much like poking a bear, you do not want to initiate potential threats."

"Just as I thought."

Alexis whipped one of her swords towards the potted plant and the snake wrapped around its base. She swung the sword towards the Handy Dandy, throwing the Preying Ficus at it. As soon as the plant made contact, its leaves began acting as teeth, and its roots began to entangle the Handy Dandy.

"M-My goodness! What are you doing?" the Handy Dandy cried. "Workers in Lynole Industries are supposed to be the top creators and most upstanding citizens of the world." The Preying Ficus wrapped its roots around its neck. "How could you... be... so... cruel?" the Handy Dandy strained.

The Thresher finally let out a shriek and emerged from the robot as it, in turn, tried to wrap around the Preying Ficus. The group watched for a moment as a stalemate occurred between the two creatures, thus allowing the Thresher to be distracted by the Preying Ficus forever.

"Good freaking riddance!" Reggy said

"Nice thinking," James commented, trying to have the same optimism Reggy had about the robot dying.

"Thanks," Alexis said, seemingly shrugging off any guilt she had and turned her attention towards a cubicle. "Are those green paperclips?"

And just like that, Alexis went from a combatant to a fan girl once more.

"What's so special about green paperclips?" James asked.

"Have you ever seen a green paperclip, James?" Alexis replied.

James thought for a moment. "I actually have not."

"Exactly!" Alexis grabbed a clear container full of green paperclips. "They don't make multi-colored paperclips anymore! And if this person had green, then maybe we can find some that are blue, or white."

"Or brown," Reggy added.

"Or pink," Alexis continued.

"Or red!"

"Yellow!"

"You guys are way too enthusiastic about this," James said as he held up his hands.

"You just can't appreciate these ancient artifacts like we do," Alexis retorted.

Reggy scoffed. "Yeah, I didn't even know what a paperclip was until now."

"I can appreciate ancient artifacts, I just don't see the purpose of colorful paperclips, except for maybe the same reason you'd have a red car instead of a blue car."

"Understanding that people used paperclips with different colors tells us something about the culture. People expressed themselves with color then as we do now with cars, I guess. This proves humanity hasn't changed that much."

"Whatever."

The sound of a clatter rang into the room, causing the three to grow completely silent.

Alexis sighed softly. "Just when I think we are finally being left alone," she whispered.

"Do you think it's another Thresher?" James whispered back.

"I'm not sure. Just slowly pan your flashlights around to find whatever it is."

James and Reggy did as she said. There wasn't a whole lot about this room that was special in James' opinion. There was the receptionist desk, a few cubicles, filing cabinets, and a large statue in the center of the room. Then again, he wasn't looking around to find impressive objects, but perhaps an impressive creature to fight, and be thoroughly impressive to Alexis.

... You're not going to make any comment about my motives?

Krag remained silent.

Krag?

It was nice knowing you,

James paused and his heart began to race. *Excuse me?*

I'd tell you to leave right now and run as far away as you can, but knowing you, you wouldn't, and two, you know...

Krag, stop beating around the bush! Tell me what's going on right now!

Calmly turn around.

James obeyed Krag. *Okay... what am I looking for—?*

He felt his heart drop into his stomach when he observed the large statue in the room was absent.

Don't move.

James did as Krag said, but quickly disobeyed as he heard a loud chattering in his right ear, let out a scream, and turned around.

You're so screwed.

James frantically flashed the light around in search for the statue, but began panicking as it was nowhere to be seen.

"What the hell, James?" Alexis whispered as she approached him

James gulped. "The statue."

"What about it?"

"It's gone."

Alexis shined her light towards where the statue was and swore under her breath. "Well, you can't panic like that, James."

James nodded. "How do you lose something that big?"

"Look, we just need to find it before it finds us, and then leave."

He nodded again, certain that, as Krag said previously, it was no use.

James slowly panned the flashlight across the room again until he reached the filing cabinets, and to his dismay, found it. The statue, or thing, was carefully going through the files, individually padding them with its fingers. Whatever it was, it appeared to be human, but James knew better, since ashen skin, a hairless body, being half-naked with only burlap trousers for clothing, long nails, and being over eight feet tall in height were key indicators for identifying a monster.

"Alexis," James whispered.

She continued to examine the room, as if she didn't hear him.

"Alexis, Reggy," he attempted again.

Neither one of them responded.

"Alexis," he said a bit louder.

"What?" she finally replied.

"I found it."

"What?" she walked closer.

"I said I found it," he harshly said threw gritted teeth.

"I can't hear you James—"

"I said I found it!"

Alexis gaped as she looked between him and where his flashlight was shining. As she and James observed an open filing cabinet, she harshly hit him in the arm with her flashlight.

"You dumb fetch!" she whispered.

James winced and gripped his arm. "I'm sorry!" he whispered back.

"You may as well have damned us all! This is all your fault!"

"It's not my fault that you're basically deaf!"

"The way you handled the situation is completely wrong—"

"Guys," Reggy interrupted, maintaining a similar volume as them.

"Not now! Look, we need to get out of here *now*. Turn off your lights so it can't see us."

"Guys."

"I thought you were ready to face danger!" James snapped.

"Just do as I say!"

"Guys—"

James shushed Reggy. "Lead the way then, Alexis. Since you seem so sure about this situation!"

"Don't shush me James, I'm being serious," Reggy snapped back.

"Hush!" Alexis whispered. "Just stay close and follow me."

"Guys!"

"What?" James and Alexis both exclaimed.

"He already found us. He's been watching you two bicker the entire time," he said at a regular volume.

James and Alexis slowly turned around. James felt his heart stop beating when he made eye contact with the thing. It was perched on top of a desk and slowly tilted its head as it closely observed them, its dark violet eyes glowing ominously in the dark.

"... Don't panic," Alexis softly said. "Maybe he's nice."

It stabbed a giant cleaver about as tall as her into the ground in response to her words. James and Alexis unsheathed their weapons and turned to run away, but the being was already behind them, and stood up on its two legs.

"Don't panic," it seemingly mocked. "I'm not going to hurt you."

It slowly walked towards them as it leered over top of them.

"What have we here?" it said in a surprisingly smooth voice. It was almost pleasant sounding, but James could only feel dread at its speech.

"Three little mice have wandered into the wrong nest?" it said as it took a step forward. "Three little children have lost their way?" Its teeth chattered in anticipation. "Or maybe three, small-minded humans that thought they could prove themselves by coming to this place? You shouldn't go looking for treasure in a ghost story, because you might find something else waiting for you." It tilted its head at them again before letting out a hollow laugh.

"You all look so terrified." It backed them into a wall. "I keep my promises. I said I wouldn't hurt you, and I won't. I'm feeling rather... vivacious today. Your deaths will be so fast you'll barely even feel it."

James shook off the nerves and held up his sword. He knew it was a stupid thing to do, but he didn't want to back down, especially if it meant possibly getting Reggy and Alexis out of danger.

The being's eyes moved towards James and met his. "That's cute," it said. "That truly is just… adorable."

In nearly a blink of an eye, the being had already begun to bring the cleaver down on James. Alexis and Reggy jumped out of the way, but James stood his ground as he blocked the blow. A loud "clang" rang through the air like thunder as the two swords collided. James strained at the pressure being brought down on the sword and placed one of his hands near the tip of the sword to get a better grip on it. The being squinted at James before pressing down harder onto the cleaver. James continued to stand his ground, only to notice it becoming unstable underneath him as the floor around his feet began to crack, and before he knew it, the being began to put its full weight onto the cleaver.

"James, you idiot!" Reggy shouted before barreling into James to move him out of the way.

The cleaver stabbed harshly into the ground at the weight of the being, resonating a noise like a steel girder being cut in half. As it moved its head towards James and Reggy, Alexis whipped both of her swords at it from across the room. It immediately noticed the snakes, and it only took a fraction of a second to react, and react calmly, nonetheless. The being reached out and grabbed the two snakes with one hand. Alexis stood in shock at the being and didn't let go of the blades fast enough as she was hurled into the wall at the flick of its wrist. Once Alexis let go and fell to the ground, the being tightened its grip around the snakes. The snakes let out loud, painful shrieks as cracks formed across their faces like shattered glass.

James let out a growl and stood up to charge at the being. It looked down at him and made eye contact with him again. As James was about to swing his sword, the being let go of the cleaver impaled into the ground, reached out with its other hand, and grabbed his neck. The grip was so hard that James swore it had crushed his windpipe the instance it latched on, and the pain was intense enough to make him drop the sword in the act. With an unwavering gaze, the being clasped his other fist, crushing the snakes and shattering the two swords.

"You fetch!" Alexis screamed from across the room, with hints of a Braizen accent in her voice. "How dare you destroy my work like that? I'll make you pay for what you've done!"

The being chuckled as it watched her argue, as if fascinated at her threats despite her lying on the ground hugging her injured body.

"Are you laughing at me? You're seriously laughing at me? I will *kill* you! You will be sorry you were ever born!"

"Be quiet," the being curtly responded as it held up its hand.

As Alexis opened her mouth to continue her rampage, she paused, and her eyes traveled to the ceiling. Cracks began to form as the being slowly opened its fist.

Anger boiled in James' blood at the audacity of this being and he reached up and gripped the being's fingers, trying to pry himself free. The being scoffed, and before James could even think, he was flying in the air, and felt the impact of crashing into several walls against his back. He tore up the ground when he finally landed and slid across the floor into the guillotine from the beginning of the orientation. He opened his eyes, everything was blurry, and the room felt like it was spinning. He saw a dark blur appear overhead and focused on it. Quickly, he somehow managed to gather the strength and roll out of the way as the being came down onto the guillotine with the cleaver.

The being let out a growl as it ripped the cleaver out of the ground and aggressively stalked towards James. "Who are you?"

James opened his mouth to speak, to give out his full name like the fetch that he was but burst into coughing fits as his broken vocal cords attempted to talk.

“Pity,” it said, then chattered its teeth. “I’m *very* curious as to how you haven’t died yet.”

James suddenly sank down into the ground. He looked down and noticed that his thighs were encased by the floor. He leaned forward so his hands met the ground and tried to push himself out, but it was almost as if he were one with the ground.

With its glowing eyes flaring with anger, the being cracked its neck and held the cleaver up over its head. “I guess I’ll have to cut you open and find out.”

James braced himself as the cleaver, once again, swung down on him, but an alarm suddenly began blaring throughout the facility, distracting the being enough for James to push himself with all of his might out of the ground and roll to the side as the cleaver struck the ground.

“Warning, breach detected,” said a voice over an intercom. “Initiate ‘Silver Protocol.’”

The message repeated itself over and over again. Among the alarm and the voice, the deep bark of a snarling dog added on top of the noise. The being let out a loud sigh, brought the cleaver to its side, and then turned around. James glanced behind the being and saw a huge, white sheepdog barking over and over at the being, with the Sword of Lord Krag in its mouth. James tried to ask what the fresh hell was happening but burst into coughing fits once more.

The being kicked James in response to his coughing, with enough impact to push his body towards the wall across the room. The dog charged towards the being, as if infuriated at it for kicking James, and slashed at its legs. The being didn’t wince but looked annoyed as it glanced down at this newcomer. The being looked as if it were raring to kick the dog out of the way, but instead twitched and chattered its teeth. It was seemingly confused at its own action and decided to swing the cleaver at the dog instead, but as soon as it brought it down, it completely missed the dog and impaled the ground beside it.

The being twitched again and seemingly beamed to the other side of the dog. It crouched down onto all fours, arched its back, and began hissing. The dog confusingly shot its head left and right until it turned around and saw the being. It charged at the being and awkwardly slashed at it with the sword again. The being batted at the blade, hissed, and growled, but it wasn't that it *wouldn't* fight back, but as if it *couldn't.*

The being let out a shout, finally pushed off the dog, and seemingly blinked to the cleaver. It gave one last, angry look at James before it dissipated into the air.

I will *find you again...*

The voice carried on the wind like a whisper, and James shook his head as the sound tickled against his ear. He breathed heavily and found himself nearly breaking into a panic attack, but the dog suddenly appeared in front of his face, dropped the sword down in front of him, and began licking his cheek. It took a second for it to register in James' mind that a dog was giving him kisses, but once it did, he wrapped his arms around the dog and started weeping.

"James!" Reggy called.

James looked up and saw Reggy helping Alexis walk as they stepped into the room through the several walls that James' body penetrated. Reggy set Alexis down gently as he ran to James' side to help him up.

"Are you okay?" Reggy exclaimed.

James nodded, shook his head, and then nodded again. He wasn't sure.

"How the…" Reggy let out a huff of air. "How the *hell* did you survive that?"

James shrugged as Reggy squinted at the imprint of the being's hand on his throat.

"Hot damn," Reggy said out loud. "Anyway, Alexis is in bad shape. We need to get out of here fast. I guess it's a good thing that guy threw you through all of those walls. It made a short cut."

"What a good dog!"

James and Reggy looked up at the sudden voice. Another robot had entered the vicinity but seemed different from the others. It was an android of some kind, with a feminine voice and body resembling a metallic human. It had fibrous silver hairs flowing to her shoulders, except on the right side, in which part of her scalp was missing, exposing some gears. Despite its physical appearance, what set it apart from the Handy Dandies was that it wasn't covered with the Thresher blood. The dog left James' side and ran towards the android.

"Good Cow-Cow," the android said as it crouched down to the dog and lifted her hand up and down off the dog's head. "Pat… pat…"

James and Reggy returned to Alexis to help her stand up. She was a bit dazed, but her eyes widened as she saw the robot. "What is that?" Alexis strained.

"Another fetching robot," Reggy said with a scoff.

The robot stood up, looked up at Alexis, and gently approached. Alexis pushed herself off of Reggy and James to try and get closer to the robot but faltered as pain took over her body. The robot reached out and caught her.

"'We pick up what others put down,' that was the first Lynole Industries motto, and the lifelong advice of grandfather."

"What do you mean?" Alexis asked, thoroughly clouded by fascination.

"The Grandfather Star. Shimmer, shimmer."

"Alexis! Get away from that thing! It could be dangerous!" Reggy yelled.

"Oh, I promise I'm not dangerous. The Silver Man is dangerous. He almost annihilated you!" the robot exclaimed as it looked at James. "I am a friend."

"This is amazing!" Alexis shouted before wincing and reaching for her side.

"Analyzing." The robot set Alexis down and then scanned her body with her eyes. "Analysis complete. You are bleeding internally. Bloody, bloody, mush, mush."

"She's speaking backwards! That's the sign of evil!" Reggy shouted.

"She just said she is a friend," Alexis argued.

"We must get you further medical assistance. Gotta put you back together."

"Yeah, we're trying," Reggy mumbled as he went to help Alexis up again. "Come on, James, let's get out of here."

The robot turned and tilted its head at James. "Your name is James?"

James nodded.

The robot walked towards him and held out its hand. "May I shake your hand?"

James shrugged and reached out towards the robot. When they made contact, the robot stared at James intently before pulling away and looking at its hand.

"The blueprints of the future!" the robot exclaimed before turning and following Reggy.

James stood in confusion as to what had just happened, with the sheepdog panting heavily, standing by his side, looking at him admirably with big, brown eyes, and drooling onto his boot. He bent down to give the dog one last pet before returning the Sword of Lord Krag to its sheath and noticed that the dog had a collar.

Moo-Moo? James thought to himself as he read the name tag. He turned it over to look for an address, but only saw the words, "Oh fetch, I'm lost!"

James furrowed his brow in confusion, shook his head, and placed his sheath across his back. As soon as he did so, the wolves in his head erupted with howling.

What's going on? James thought.

Oh, the dogs are celebrating. You were a fetching goner for a minute there, man.

... You keep saying dogs when you told me wolves.

Wolves, dogs, doesn't matter. As long as I sell the product.

That makes no sense! It was me that needed to be worthy!

Maybe I really wanted to kill you, James. In order to do that, you had to pick up the sword.

James tried to growl but ended up coughing again.

Anyway, congratulations, death only made you stronger and the Underworld has a vendetta to keep you out. Good job!

~

Allen Bentally hadn't been doing anything particularly different in his routine. He did what he did everyday: prepared the messages for the Messengers to deliver, record said messages into the Bureau's database on the computer, and, of course, wallow in self-pity. He had to admit his work was cut out for him, since the sudden increase in revenue due to Henry Chase's death. It truly astounded him how much actually got done without him there, but it wasn't like he was doing anything for the Bureau to begin with. Nevertheless, on this weather-less day, Allen continued with his routine as he would any normal day.

"Mr. Bentally?"

Allen sighed loudly when he heard the voice through his intercom. He pressed the red button and responded. "What?"

"Your presence has been requested in the surveillance room. There's… something you need to see."

"What is it?"

"It's just better if you some see for yourself."

"Can't you just tell me what it is now? I'm very busy."

The voice didn't respond.

"Hello?"

Silence.

Allen sighed even louder as he threw down the day's messages onto his desk and stood up. There were only a few times Allen ever stood up from his desk, and it was to grab the messages, take his lunch break, and go home. Working in a crowded, dark workspace brought limited mobility, so this brand-new whelp that they hired is giving him more than just an inconvenience, and an unrequested break in a routine.

He began his treacherous journey out of the rundown building and into the courtyard. He eyed all of the new employees with disgust, and they, in turn, would pause in their conversations to stare at him fearfully and then move out of his way. Allen didn't mind the extra help, and the fact that the Bureau would *actually* act as a functioning company for the first time in years, but each of them were young enough to be considered interns, and far too expendable for his liking; however, it would be easier to promote them to death should they piss him off.

He passed the Messenger housing, which flooded nostalgia into the back of his mind. He remembered when it was just him, then five, then fifty, then one, so seeing fifteen was a step towards the right direction, a direction he had been longing for a while now. With his heart full of solitude, and a really grumpy expression on his face, Allen arrived at the surveillance department, which was a new section in Henry Chase's old building. His knees popped slightly as he walked up the stairs, reminding him that he was not as young as he used to be, and in the time he has left, this moment was a waste of it. He nudged people out of the way with his facial expression, alone, and formed a bubble around his person through his aura of disdain.

Finally, he arrived at the surveillance room and approached a young man in his mid-twenties, who was fresh out of school.

"Okay," Allen began, "I'm here. What's so fetching important that you had to disrupt my entire day?"

The young man typed something into his computer and pulled up a screen. The screen had a list of various locations, such as Castle Plier, Board Building A, and, of course, Lynole Industries. Each of these locations had a green dot underneath their names, except for Lynole Industries, which was blinking red.

"And?" Allen continued. "What am I looking at?"

"Sir, don't you understand?" the young man replied in a grave tone. "There has been a breach at Lynole Industries."

"Yeah, and we scheduled one for today."

"I am fully aware of that, sir; however, there were indications of two separate breaches today, meaning there is a potential that our scheduled one got interrupted."

Allen blinked. "Let me get this straight. You summoned me in the middle of my job to, not only point out something *very* minute, but to tell me something that took less than a minute to explain? Something that didn't even need visuals, nonetheless?"

The young man gulped. "I can see why you'd be upset, sir—"

"Okay."

"… However, it's important that you see this—"

"Why?" Allen exclaimed. "Explain to me why it was so damn important to drag me here when you could've easily told me this over the intercom, and I could've reacted immediately instead of enduring another ten-minute walk to take care of it?"

"Um…" the young man stammered. "I… don't know?"

Allen smiled. "You know what? Everything is okay."

"I-It is?"

"Absolutely, in fact, because you took so much initiative in your job today instead of, I don't know, using common sense and following orders, you've just received a promotion!"

The color in the young man's face drained. "Oh, please, sir! I am so sorry! Please don't—"

"No, no, this is a celebratory moment" —Allen placed his hand on the young man's shoulder— "Messenger #641."

Chapter Eleven

The Hands of Commerce

"It was the most incredible thing!" Alexis exclaimed to her fellow Theoremists as their medics evaluated her. "I thought Thaddeus was pulling my leg when he was telling us about the shack, but it's an entrance to some sort of corporation that was owned by Cirlock, the God of Commerce! It extends miles into the ground and there are so many different relics, and—"

"So many different threats," Thaddeus interrupted.

Alexis huffed. "They were only threats because three people were fighting them off. Can you imagine what would happen if all of us ventured down there with our weapons?"

"Miss, we need you to hold still," one of the medics commented.

"I'm doing my best," Alexis replied as she adjusted her position. "Anyway, if we all work together, we could wipe out the enemies clean and continue to explore the facility!"

Elijah, who was observing the conversation closely, remained silent and stroked his chin, as if deep in thought.

"You expect every single one of us to take out Threshers and not get infected? The only thing that saved you, girl, was some got damn luck!" Thaddeus retorted.

The Theoremists murmured to each other at the comment.

"I expect us *all* to be smart and capable enough to be able to handle an infestation, because we *are* smart and capable. Really think about it, how many of us are fire wielders? Fire could burn and eradicate them quickly. I know at least half of us have a weapon that deals fire damage, imagine if they taught all of us how to make our own! I have plenty of weapons to use as bases, as well!"

The expressions of the Theoremists shifted as they seemingly warmed up to the idea.

"What about that one guy?" Elijah finally spoke.

"We named him 'the Beast,'" Alexis intervened.

"Okay," Elijah dismissed. "You described him as a one-man army. He broke your swords, what's going to keep him from destroying ours? Besides, look what he did to him."

Everyone's eyes drifted towards James. He smiled awkwardly and gave a slight wave, unaware of exactly how bad the handprint on his neck looked. It was like he was wearing a dark, turtleneck sweater underneath his clothing, except it was just a gigantic bruise.

"James was being stupid," Alexis retorted.

"Hey…" James whispered in his defense.

"It wouldn't have happened if he had just stayed put. Granted, it was a nice gesture, but… my swords were going to be destroyed either way."

James felt a pang in his heart as Alexis' gaze fell to the ground.

"Look, just consider, *consider* how great of an opportunity this is, please."

"No." Thaddeus vigorously shook his head and then turned to the rest of the Theoremists. "You heard her, y'all. I was right about that damn shack and the dangers of it! Are y'all gonna be just as crazy as her and put us all in danger?"

Some of the Theoremists spoke up in agreement.

"Then we should seal the damn place away!"

"Now listen, Thaddeus." A Theoremist stepped forward. "Alexis has only been here for a day and she's brightened up the community significantly with her artifacts. You may not see eye to eye with her because of her family tree, but as a person she is incredible and revolutionary. To pass up any opportunity she brings before us is asinine."

"'Incredible' and 'revolutionary?'" another Theoremist spoke up. "That's what you call her blasphemy? She is basically mocking the souls that trust us by putting them into something basic and insignificant. That wagon of hers is an insult to the grand species that is bound to it. And those two swords weren't even hers, she found them. For all we know, she doesn't want this 'research' for the sake of improving her work, but to copy it and claim it as her own. She's a farce with no talent, which is why she chooses to enchant pencils and bandages instead of using Theorem for it's true intention."

"What?" Alexis exclaimed, and then winced and grabbed her side.

"Miss, please sit still and calm down," the medic sternly pleaded.

"B-But—"

"How could you be so cruel? You know for a fact that the O'Leary line is full of talent!" a different Theoremist defended. "It doesn't matter how they do things, it matters that they can accomplish it, and I for one agree that if I could get even a smidge of advice to be more like them, then I'd take it!"

"You've all forgotten, haven't you?" Thaddeus spoke up again. "You've all forgotten the grief we went through because of her father. It's his fault that the Bureau intervened with our work and destroyed what legacies our families had established. If anything, our progress is hindered because of her. Why let the O'Learys do it again?"

The Theoremists erupted into shouts as they disagreed with one another and spat insults and curses at the O'Leary family tree. Alexis shook her head at everyone but didn't appear to be bothered by what they were saying about her family, and it broke James' heart that she was apparently used to it.

"Hey!" Elijah shouted, silencing the crowd. "This isn't about politics! This is about how we handle a discovery. Can we at least agree on that?"

The crowd grew silent as they submitted.

"Thank you." Elijah took a deep breath. "Alexis, you present a great argument, but I think the cons outweigh the pros, and we should seal the place away."

"Elijah—"

"That place is basically a haven for danger, and we can't risk the safety of this community. We came here to seek refuge, not to be annihilated by Threshers and other monsters."

"But… in retrospect, you could technically form the town in the building. You'd be saving extra supplies to fix it up and to clean it out. It'd be a waste of time and resources to seal it away."

"Who votes that we seal it away?"

About three-quarters of the Theoremists raised their hands, including Thaddeus, who was very adamant about his vote as he raised his hand into the sky.

"The decision is final."

"What happened to you people? All of you used to be excited to take risks in order to extend your research or the abilities of your Theorem! I guarantee that this would be the biggest discovery any of you would ever make again, and the fact that you're passing it up just proves how weak you've all grown!"

“Well, unfortunately you’re not the one in charge around here, Alexis.”

“You don’t have to remind me.” Alexis shoved the medics away and weakly stood up on her feet. “We’ll be leaving in the morning.”

“Don’t be like that,” Elijah said as he approached her to help her walk.

“My decision is final,” she retorted as she pushed him away and slowly walked towards the Cougar.

“But miss, if you’re experiencing internal trauma, we need to treat it right away,” one of the medics called after her.

“I don’t need the help of amateurs.”

James and Reggy exchanged nervous glances as they followed her to the Cougar. Upon arrival, she angrily stalked inside, pet the excited dog they decided to adopt on the head, and began rummaging through a cabinet.

“Internal bleeding, huh?” Alexis muttered as she looked through her supplies.

James and Reggy sheepishly followed her inside, closed the door behind them, and watched as she grabbed a box that once held bandages, and pulled out some sort of patch. She peeled off a piece of paper on the back of it, lifted her shirt, and applied the patch to her side. Alexis grimaced as her side throbbed from the effects of the patch, then quickly shook it off.

“What did you just do?” James strained as Moo-Moo jumped on him, begging for attention.

“These patches are my own invention. I infused planarian, a type of flatworm, into them. In search of a new way of medicine, I looked into regenerative properties of animals one day and came across these. Planarian regenerate completely and perfectly, and these patches will help regenerate whatever it is inside me that’s bleeding. After the healing is complete, I replace the adhesive on the back and store it until I have use of it again.”

"So… you're letting worms swim around in your body?" Reggy asked.

Alexis huffed. "Is that what I said, Reggy?"

"You kind of implied it when you taped a bunch of worms to your belly."

"I didn't imply—" Alexis paused and took a deep breath. "The patch releases stem cells into the body, not worms, allowing them to begin the regeneration process."

"So, twigs?"

"Look" —Alexis plopped down on the cot next to the robot they found and lied down on her back— "it doesn't matter what the patches do. The point is that I did more work in one minute than those medics did in ten"

"That's because they have small brains," the robot said.

"You've got that right," Alexis replied while trying to move her face away from Moo-Moo's slobbery, abnormally long tongue.

"Two smalls make one whole, and you can't function on half."

"Alexis, the robot is talking crazy again!" Reggy whined.

"Word salad is nothing to be afraid of, Reggy," Alexis said with a groan.

"So, she's infected you, too? That's just great."

"Will you shut up? There's no reason to be afraid of the robot! We don't know how long she'd been down there, so some of her circuits may be fried."

"How do we even know it's a girl? I thought robots didn't have genders," James spoke up.

Alexis scowled at James before directing her attention to the robot. "So, robot, are you a boy, girl, or neither?"

"I'm Harper."

"Okay, so, is Harper your name?"

"Names say a lot about people, and Mother said Harper means 'daughter.'"

"There you go, James, it's a girl."

Sure, James mentally replied, not wanting to instigate any further arguments.

"Returning to the concept of regenerative properties, how did you survive back there, James?"

James shrugged. "I've always been durable."

"No, this goes beyond durability. I got severely injured just being slammed into a wall, and you were thrown *through* at least twenty."

James shrugged again. "I literally cannot tell you why that happened."

"Maybe it's because you have a thick skull," Reggy joked.

Alexis laughed, and then tilted her head as she eyed James up and down. "Maybe it's that special sword of yours."

"This?" James pointed at the Sword of Lord Krag sheathed across his back.

"No, the other special sword, idiot."

James' gaze fell to the ground.

"There has to be more to the weapon than just being legendary."

James tossed the thought around in his head. "I mean, it did allow me to run all the way back to Trig in a matter of hours from Furthen Ethen Pas."

"Then, I don't see why it wouldn't make your body stronger. If you are the worthy wielder, then maybe the sword prolongs your life, so you don't die like a little wimp once you go out into battle."

"It's probably also why you survived in the Underworld as well," Reggy piped up.

Is that true? Can you really do that? James thought.

I am a man trapped inside a sword with one-hundred dogs acting as my jailers. My actions cannot affect you physically whatsoever.

James stayed silent.

... As far as what the sword does for you, I have no idea. Stuff and things, I guess?

You're the worst.

Okay, Krag scoffed.

"What about the two of you?" James continued. "The last thing I saw was Alexis about to be crushed by drywall."

"The Beast was about to kill us, but noticed you stirring awake, and immediately turned his attention to you. Reggy barely had enough time to grab me before the ceiling caved in," Alexis answered.

"That's it? That thing literally changed its mind about killing you two because of me?"

"Alphas and Betas get along until one survives being hit by a brick," Harper piped up.

"Exactly."

James and Reggy stared at her in silence.

"What? She makes sense—"

"You can understand what she's saying?" James asked with a hint of shock.

"It's not as complicated as it seems. Just break down the meaning of the words to form a new sentence."

"... What did you discover?"

Alexis huffed. "She said that the Beast was threatened by you."

"Threatened? By me?"

"Clearly this is a creature that relies more on animalistic instinct. If something comes along to challenge its strength, then it will become defensive."

James smirked to himself, feeling a bit too proud that he intimidated something as scary as that thing.

"Anyway, if you're going to leave us to travel on an ego trip, you might as well do it now. I need some peace and quiet in order to let the patch start doing its thing, so you two yahoos go outside and do whatever you want I guess."

James coughed. "But—"

"What more do you want, James?" Alexis snapped.

"… Can I get one of those patches?"

Alexis lazily glanced at him. "You're already starting to look better. Besides, let the sword do its job."

James scowled as he and Reggy left the Cougar and went outside, with Moo-Moo following behind them.

"So, shall we get some drinks?" Reggy asked.

"I know you had whiskey with your breakfast, but are you even old enough to drink?" James replied.

Reggy scoffed. "Do you even pay attention to the things I'm saying half the time?"

"What?" James winced as he foolishly poked at his bruise.

"Never mind. Let's just… get some dinner."

"Sounds good to me."

"Do you want me to ask one of these Theoremists if they have a blender to grind up your food."

James furrowed his brow. "Shut up."

~

Do you ever lie awake at night, stare at your ceiling, and reflect every terrible thing you've ever done? You take all of your prescribed SSRIs to get rid of the lingering anxiety, but sometimes that doesn't stop it, and sometimes you don't have to be on antidepressants to face it. Perhaps you could relate to a different situation, like that one time when you were watching a horror film. You shout at the stupid main characters running in the direction of the monster or killer, and you think for a moment how much smarter you are than them and would handle the situation differently, but then you realize that you do the exact same thing except it's tax season and you're running towards an extravagant purchase when you know damn well that hefty return should go straight into savings, but instead you say, "Fetch it, I deserve it!" and then wonder why your life is in shambles.

These are harsh truths, but they're facts. Although, maybe you don't think about reality or failure so much. Maybe you compare yourself to supernatural situations. Maybe you think about how you would get out of a thriller situation and wonder what kind of psychological disorder you would develop as a result of the trauma you just experienced. You probably wonder if you are even in good enough shape to run away, take a moment to think if you've ever experienced true fear, and if you'd ever witnessed any kind of horror to that degree during the course of your lifetime. Don't worry, you're normal enough to wonder all of these things, and you're not alone. Oddly enough, a group of fictional characters think the same thing,

It just hasn't crossed their mind quite yet.

James' mind drifted as the rocking of his hammock soothed his body, but Moo-Moo's snoring was a bit hard to ignore as the dog slept beneath him. The Theoremists were kind enough to put him and Reggy up for the night, and offered him this hammock to sleep in. Using his jacket as a blanket, he clung his sword tightly as he was about to fall asleep, until he had an unsettling feeling, as if he were being watched.

Quit being paranoid, James thought to himself. *There isn't anything there. Just get some sleep.*

Then, he went against his own word and nervously opened his eyes. He let out a raspy shout and broke into coughing fits as he saw Harper standing over him and staring.

"There you are," Harper said.

"What the fetch are you doing?" James snapped as he panted heavily.

"I need your blueprints, but you looked adorable in your hammock. Like a little, sleepy baby, or a sack of meat."

James huffed. "What do you mean you 'need my blueprints?'"

"Follow me."

The robot began pacing away. James nervously sat up in his hammock, set down his sword, and watched as she left. Eventually, she figured out that he wasn't following behind him, and returned to his side.

"Waste can't make haste if you stay and let your thoughts rot," Harper said.

"Look, I'm not just going to up and leave with you. For all I know you could be working with those Threshers."

"I am a friend" —she gently reached down and took James' hand in hers— "and I want to go on an adventure."

"I'm not—"

James paused as he tried to take his hand back, only to realize that she had locked hers into some sort of clamp and was not letting go any time soon.

"This will be fun!"

Harper took off once more towards the direction of the shack, dragging James with her. Instead of fighting, James huffed and decided to play along, thinking that doing as she says in this current predicament would keep him from further danger. Once they arrived at the shack, Harper stood at the center of the room and took a deep breath.

James narrowed his eyes. "Are you seriously trying to breathe—?"

"Sam!"

The elevator immediately began to whirr up, with the floor glowing that familiar red, making the walls look more ominous in the nighttime. James cringed as the screeching noise fired up. He had forgotten about that part.

"Hmm… that's not right," Harper muttered.

The arm that wasn't clinging to James unfolded, revealed two appendages with picks at the tips of them, and opened up a panel on the floor, revealing a speaker. After rewiring a few things, the screeching immediately stopped and a jolly, musical overtone filled the shaft.

"What the hell?" James said aloud as he stared at the speaker.

"We need to be more prompt."

"What's that supposed to mean?"

Harper closed the panel and revealed another. After crossing wires, the speed of the music increased, in addition to the elevator. James felt screams building up in his chest as he slowly started to lift up off the ground but could only muster panicked huffs of air as he clung to Harper. He closed his eyes tight as wind began to blow against his face and through his hair, and he suddenly felt heavier as the elevator came to a stop, revealing the first entrance at Lynole Industries.

James shakily panted as he let go of Harper and got his footing. "Okay," he began, "what do you need me for?"

"Oh, we aren't quite there yet."

"Excuse me?"

Harper opened a panel on the wall and entered a code into the dial pad. The elevator doors immediately shut, and it began to fall at a fast speed again. It went down, then left, then right, then up, and took a few more twists. James' body floated as the momentum whipped him in different directions. He tried to bring his other hand to Harper's so he could stabilize himself but being thrown around so aggressively in the air didn't help his task one bit. Feeling as if he were going to die just from whiplash alone, the elevator descended with one last final drop, then came to a complete stop.

Gravity caught up with James and his body plummeted to the ground, allowing a loud "thud!" to resonate in the air. The doors opened to reveal a glowing orange light through the area. The vastness of the room was hindered meaningless as several pipes and vents crowded against nearly every wall, in addition to piles of scrap metal everywhere along the ground. Harper let go of James' hand and moved forward into the room.

"This is the Great Forge," she began, "where we piece together every important aspect of the Grand Project."

The creaking of the entire room unnerved James as the ceiling vanished in the darkness. He groaned as he shakily stood up on his feet. "What is this Grand Project we keep hearing about?"

"I actually don't know."

"... What?"

"I just know I need your blueprints, because something important is going to happen."

"You mean to tell me that you brought me all the way here and have no idea why?"

"Yes!"

Harper began to wander the area aimlessly and hummed to herself as she glanced around the place.

"Where is the Thresher blood?" James spoke up.

"They like to sleep where it's cold. It's too hot in here. They'll be incinerated!"

"How would they be incinerated?"

"The Forge can reach excruciatingly high temperatures, much like the halo in the sky. Only I am safe down here because I can withstand temperatures over ten-thousand degrees!"

"Hang on," James quickly approached her, "I can't!"

"What was that?"

"I can't withstand a temperature like that!"

"I can't hear you!" She gestured to a vent next to her head.

James loudly groaned with absolute certainty that he would never see daylight again. Harper began to walk around again, and James followed. He paused in his movement as he felt something get caught in his boot. He had been easily able to get over the scrap metal until now, so he was rather surprised when he came across something that nearly penetrated the bottom of his boot. He lifted his foot to see a tiny gear, about a centimeter in diameter, lodged into his boot. He pulled it out and brought it closer to his face.

"How could something like this feel like a giant metal spike?" James asked himself.

Harper paused at his words and then approached him. "Analyzing," she said as she scanned the gear. "I think this is important."

"How important?"

"Like the air you breathe at night, so you don't die in your sleep."

James squinted at the exposed gears on the side of her head, seeing that a few of them were missing, but one particular slot, almost too small to notice, was exposed between two others of similar sizes. "Is this yours?"

Harper grabbed the gear, turned it over in her fingers, and then placed it into the missing slot. The gears began whirring fiercely until she let out a gasp. "I know what this is!"

"What is it?"

"I remember why we are here!"

Harper grabbed his hand again and practically ran towards one direction.

"Slow down!" James exclaimed, but couldn't be heard over the clanking of the metal.

Harper suddenly stopped and her head made a complete one-hundred eighty-degree turn. "… The Night Man cometh," she said in an ominously deep voice.

"W-What?"

Harper let go of his hand and pointed. The sound of metal being ripped apart tore through the air, interrupting the repetitious whirring and rumbling of the forge. A set of heavy footprints followed as a large, dark shadow emerged from the elevator shaft. Quickly, Harper sprinted to the nearest pipe, tore off the opening, and dove inside. Before James could react, a very familiar hand flung him to the left, slamming him into loose metal. The "Beast" growled lowly as it reached into the vent for Harper, discouraged that she had managed to get away as fast as she did. All hope wasn't lost for it, though, as it flung its cleaver onto its shoulder, allowing it to rest there, and slowly let its gaze travel to James.

"You live?" it asked in a calm tone.

Remember earlier when you were presented with questions that hit home a bit too well, and you probably felt personally targeted? Well, fear not, because those same questions finally began crossing James' mind as he reached for his sword and only grasped air.

You have got to be fetching kidding me, he thought as he pictured his sheathed sword swinging in the hammock without him.

It slowly stalked towards him, standing upright, with Thresher blood dripping from the tip of its weapon.

James stood and began backing away. "Yep, I live," he replied, slightly embarrassed at his raspy voice. He gestured at the cleaver. "I see you've been enjoying the plant life?"

The Beast smirked, as if it enjoyed the joke, and in less than a second, it seemingly blinked to James and threw him into the wall. As the wind was knocked out of him, he saw a shadow manifest over top of him. He let out a gasp and rolled to the left as the Beast slammed the cleaver into the ground where James' head was only moments ago. The sound of metal being cut stung James' ears as the Beast landed next to him.

"I'm curious, boy, if you could answer a few questions for me before I rend you in half?" the Beast asked in smooth and methodical voice.

James mustered what was left of his courage and sanity and stood. The Beast stared back at him intently, unwaveringly.

"I will tell you nothing. You're—"

“What? ‘Going to have to kill me first?’ ‘Not as scary as you think you are?’ Something along those lines to sound brave, right?”

James blinked. “… You don’t have to be such a fetch about it.”

The Beast shook his head. “Those are terrible last words.”

James’ eyes widened and he held up his hands. “Wait—”

He was promptly picked up by the Beast and flung through a large window to the left of the main room. The glass was tempered and thick, but of course, it shattered around James’ entry. He bounced off of the guardrail of a balcony and into the main floor of the room, which was filled with dead computers and cubicles. James groaned as he rolled off of a crushed desk.

“Fetching hate this place,” he muttered. “Why are there so many desks?”

His thoughts were interrupted as the Beast gracefully landed on the guardrail above. It closed its eyes and breathed in deeply. “I smell you, little one.”

James clenched his teeth as he felt the air become trapped in his chest. He slowly and quietly crawled away and hid under another desk.

“If you think that hiding, running, or whatever you’d like to call this sad attempt of survival will help you, you’re mistaken.” The Beast jumped off of the guardrail to the floor below. “Once I find you, I’ll disassemble you and that worthless pile of walking scrap to find out what makes you tick.”

Knowing that the Beast would eventually find him if he stayed put, James crawled under a long table connected to the desk. He jumped slightly and held his breath as a “thunk” was heard overhead. He froze in terror as the sound of long nails scraped across the table and creaking as the Beast moved along it. The tapping and scraping of its nails repetitively grazed against his ears, like a clock interrupting the silence of a dead night.

“I can hear your breathing…”

James covered his mouth and nose to stop himself from hyperventilating at the Beast's comments. His muscles grew stiff and tight at the thought of any movement he made next would be his last. The movement above him stopped as he heard the Beast jump off the table, and he peeked his head out slightly to see where it was. As the Beast sat perched atop a cubicle, James seized the opportunity to crawl to a different table covered in a cloth as it searched the work area intently.

When James made it to the covered table, he put his head in his hands and tried to calm his breathing. The ringing of the ears sang a haunting melody with the Beast's rough movements, and James was unsure of how something could make him feel so scared. He had only ever been scared a few times in his life, the first being when his parents died. Growing up, he had his fair share of bad dreams and night terrors, but that was the first time he ever felt truly afraid and uncertain of what was going to happen to him.

The second time was when he was in the Underworld. The only other mortal there was the Chimera, so, was there any proof that if he had died in the Underworld, he would stay, rather than stop existing? It was one thing to question existence, but another thing to question what will happen to your mind when you don't exist, and the thought of not existing ever again scared James to a degree he hadn't quite felt before, and didn't want to wish that on anyone.

The third time was this moment. James had battled many thugs and encountered strange creatures in his life, but this facility and the demons inside of it were beyond any fabrication his imagination could come up with. The familiar phrase began to pound against his skull: "This isn't real."

This isn't real.

He always questioned reality when he felt like he was in danger, mostly because he didn't know if danger was truly there, or if he just wanted an excuse to wake up from another nightmare. But he never woke up, no matter how hard he tried to snap out of it. In his hardest of hearts, he knew he was inches from death, and didn't want to believe it. He didn't want to go back to the Underworld with those weirdos. He wondered if Alexis would miss him if he's gone, and if anyone would even question where the hell he went.

Amidst the distraction of his racing thoughts, his heart stopped at the sudden realization:

What happened to the tapping?

He snapped back to reality as his mind and eyes fixated on the environment before him, making contact with the glowing eyes of violet fury.

"Found you."

"Fetch!" James reflexively screamed as he scrambled out from underneath the table.

The Beast lifted the table effortlessly and threw it in front of James, blocking his way and trapping him where he was. "I won't lie, I thought this would be harder. One would think a person such as yourself is difficult to reckon with if you're still breathing, right?"

James' head frantically shot in different directions in search of an escape. The tip of the cleaver was placed against his chin and moved his head to face the Beast.

"Look at someone when they're talking to you."

James didn't reply but obeyed.

The Beast's head tilted to one side. "As I was saying, *one would think* a person such as yourself is difficult to reckon with if you're still breathing, yet here you are, helplessly face-to-face with me again, and no mutt here to save you. I can admit when I'm wrong, though it rarely happens, but I guess you're a better fighter than you are a hider if you're so strong."

The Beast stared quietly, as if waiting for a reply.

James' mouth opened, but no words came out for a moment. "I'm… just durable," he finally replied.

"'Durable.' Is that what you're calling it?"

"What would you call it?" James retorted as his eyes wandered again and made contact with a glowing pair of mechanical eyes in the vent.

Harper!

The Beast chuckled. "I'd call it 'interesting,' especially because it arouses *many* suspicions on my behalf." Its teeth chattered as it took a deep breath and crouched down to his level. "So, I'll ask you again to answer my questions—"

He's like an animal, James thought as he noticed some of his own blood on his hand.

"—and I wouldn't hesitate in responding if I were you."

"Well, first of all, you're *not* me," James replied a bit too hastily. "Second, you spend a bit too much time talking. Third, I'm incredibly stupid!"

Thinking quickly, James wiped his blood on the Beast's nose. It snarled and faltered backwards as it clawed at its face.

How's that for a sensory overload? James smugly thought as he shoved himself away from the Beast and started running towards a glowing "Exit" sign.

James hadn't gotten very far before he heard an angry howl and his vision went black. When he came to, he was on his knees, and the Beast was right next to his head, sinking its teeth into his shoulder. He let out a scream, far more panicked than in pain. The Beast clenched down harder and shook his head, tossing James into the hallway where the exit was. James let out a cry as he fought back tears, the stale, dusty air stinging at the bloody wound where the majority of his shoulder should be. His blurred vision began to form shapes and he noticed the vent ahead opening up, and Harper waving at him.

He forcefully pushed himself up and ran towards Harper. The Beast slid into the hallway behind him, still disoriented from the blood. In a desperate attempt at survival, James dove towards the vent and reached out towards Harper's hand, and as he was inches away, he heard a loud "pop" echo through the air, and a feeling of fire ignite in his right leg socket. James tried to scream but could only let out air and whimpers at another terrible wound and glanced behind him to see his ankle kept securely in the Beast's grasp. Before the Beast could drag James away, Harper quickly emerged from the vent and bent her elbow, revealing some sort of nozzle.

A mist crudely spouted out of the nozzle, affecting both the Beast and James. The Beast let go of James, roared loudly as it breathed in the chemical, and began clawing at its face again. James, on the other hand, let out a cry as he felt the overwhelming sensation of both pain and euphoria as the mist stung at his eyes and nostrils. While the Beast was distracted, Harper grabbed tightly onto James' arms and pulled him into the vent with her. James took several deep breaths to try and shake off the sensations the mist left him in addition to the panic as he heard the Beast aggressively attacking the wall, trying to get to the two of them. He didn't know how long the two of them were in the vent, but as he was close to coherency, he felt himself suddenly fall and smack against the ground, ten feet below.

James groaned as he rolled onto his back, his vision blurry as Harper came into view. She stuck a small towel into his mouth and proceeded to pop his leg and knee back into place. James bit down and screamed at her quick procedure, panting heavily as she took the towel back.

"Blue Jays are indigenous to the mountain regions," Harper said.

"... What?" James wearily said.

"Click, clack, snapped you back."

"Oh… thanks."

"Now we get back to work!"

"No!" James quickly shouted. "We have to get out of here! That *thing* has a vendetta against me! I think it wants to eat my soul!"

"Silly James, your soul doesn't mean *that* much to it. It just wants you dead!"

James let out a loud sigh. "Thank you, Harper. You're very motivational."

"I'm not programmed for motivational purposes!" she proudly declared.

"Whatever." James shakily stood up on both his legs. "I'm leaving."

"Please don't leave!"

"Look, I can't help you! If you force me to 'work,' I am going to die! Do you even understand what death is? I'll stop existing, and it will be your fault!"

"… Mother stopped existing," Harper said, with a solemn tone. "It was *his* fault. If you stop existing, it will be his fault, too."

James stayed quiet, still feeling enraged.

"I can't do this without you," Harper continued. "Help me fulfill my directive, and things will keep existing, because as long as he exists, everything else won't."

James let out a sigh. "I'm not going to feel empathy for a robot."

"If you can't help me, help Mother."

"… Fine," he begrudgingly submitted.

James took the opportunity to observe the room he was in, noticing that there was a large panel with several blinking buttons and dials at the front of the room, facing a thick window. Harper approached the panel and pressed some buttons, then a voice fired up on an intercom overhead.

"… Can you hear me?" the voice of a woman said. "If so, then you should know that you have initiated the first steps of the Grand Project. If this is correct, enter the appropriate encryption key."

Harper typed a few letters and numbers on a keyboard.

"Okay, this is really happening. Awesome." The woman paused and took a deep breath. "Harper, by the time you get here, I will be long, long gone. You've done a good job to defend it as long as you have. I know it's been hard, and I'm sorry I made you do this, but we all had to make sacrifices so this can happen. Thank you, and as long as you keep working on this Grand Project, I will always be with you."

As the intercom clicked off, James turned to Harper. "Who was that?"

"Mother."

"That was your mother?"

"Yes."

"Okay… well, I agreed to help, so what do you need me to do?"

"I need you to clean out the vermin," Harper said.

"What do you mean?"

She pointed at the window. James looked out to see the Beast emerging from the large window. After doing so, it stood in the middle of the room. It angrily stared daggers at the two, as if waiting for them to come down for a confrontation rather than coming to them.

"What the hell am I supposed to do about that?"

Harper eyed the panel. "Keep it away and I can burn it up."

"How? He's going to kill me—"

He paused as a deep bark interrupted his sentence. "What the—Moo-Moo?" James exclaimed as he looked down to see the sheep dog not only by his side, but also holding the Sword of Lord Krag. "How… how is everything this convenient?"

"Fictional characters do great work when no one is looking." James didn't respond as he took the sword from Moo-Moo and placed the sheath across his back.

You're an idiot, Krag immediately said.

James huffed as he turned his attention to the Beast and took a deep breath.

"Are you ready?"

He nodded. "Yeah, it's time we settled this."

As he left Harper and Moo-Moo in the room, he heard a voice speak over the intercom.

"Ignite lever 1-8 and wait till the shutters are raised as soon as the temperature reaches 'ten' as we discussed…"

As the voice began to fade, James moved slowly and limped, but bravely approached the Beast. It watched him walk, with red, bloodshot eyes following every step he made. When James was only a few feet away, the Beast finally spoke.

"She got you, too?"

James' attention was suddenly brought to his own eyes, which was still stinging from Harper's mist. "... Yes," he replied.

"Dumb thing."

"Hey," James raised his voice slightly, "don't talk about Harper like that. She kept your fetching self away, didn't she?"

The Beast heavily sighed. "Listen, boy, I've spent far too much time chasing my tail in terms of trying to deal with you. I'm not playing anymore, so shut up and submit, because there's no way in hell that you're going to beat me, nor am I going to give you the time to try."

"Well, if you've spent this much time to try and kill me, you're going to need an army to get rid of me, buddy. I'm not going anywhere."

The Beast laughed to himself. "Mother of Gloric, you're a stupid one."

James let out an angry breath and raised his sword, wincing as he tried to operate his injured shoulder.

"Still trying to play the hero, huh? Well, if you want an army, then your wish is my command."

The Beast raised its hand into the air and snapped its fingers. Shortly after, masses of black began pouring into the room from the vents, shutters, and even crevices James didn't know existed. He felt the color drain from his face as he watched them crawl over each other, moaning and oozing as their metal scraped across the walls, the floors, and their own bodies, flowing into the room like wet cement.

"I thought you didn't like the Threshers. You had blood on your sword!"

"Only from the ones that disobeyed me."

James took a deep breath, trying to keep calm.

"What are you going to do, little one? Are you going to waste your time by fighting me? Are you going to let the Threshers get to your little robot friend? Will you finally submit and let me win?" James stayed quiet but stood his ground.

"No more words to say? That's fine. It's probably best if there wasn't anything more said between us anyway."

With that, the Beast quickly swung the cleaver at him. To its surprise, James countered by bringing up his own blade. He winced at his injury and faltered slightly at the Beast's strength, but for the first time since their encounter, James was able to hold his own.

Everyone is right, I really can't function without you, James thought.

Just follow the guy's advice. He's got a point. Words don't need to be said right now.

The Beast went on the offensive while Krag guided James, helping him counter every blow with a dodge or a slight swing of the sword. The frustration in the Beast's eyes began to fester, and the maneuvering of the weapon began to shift as it used less force but was able to get in quicker blows.

Just like earlier, James thought. *There's that cold calculation.*

James took a chance and tried to get a hit in, and the Beast quickly slid to the side. It stabbed the cleaver into the ground and used to momentum to hurl itself at James, taking the blade with it. Surprised at this sudden change intact, James raised his blade to block, but the Beast only used it as a way to jump over him and try to stab him in the back. The sword fluctuated its weight just in time to force James out of the way as the cleaver missed him by inches. This strange swordsmanship continued as it grew more and more difficult to see with the mass of black covering the lights, and the only illumination came from the dim blinking of the Handy Dandies.

James' ears perked at the sound of the Handy Dandies banging against the glass, and the being took advantage of this slight distraction to kick out his legs. James tried to crawl away, but the being used its knee to pin him, and stabbed a piece of sheet metal through his good shoulder, leaving him tacked to the scrap heap. The being raised its cleaver one last time to finally administer the killing blow but paused as a siren began to ring through the air.

James noticed the shutters beginning to open, and a wave reflecting in the air as heat was emitting from them. At the far end of the room, liquid steel poured from two pipes near the elevator and flowed through crevices etched into the floor. The floor was tilted at an angle, which James didn't notice before, allowing this liquid to flow faster and into a concrete block at the end of the room, which was about ten feet in length and five feet in height. The Beast growled under its breath at this process.

"Looks like you won't win after all," James snidely said. "After all, I knew I wouldn't be going back to the Underworld anytime soon, at least without a fight."

The Beast's eyes quickly shifted to James. It picked him up by the shirt and lifted him into the air, the heap of scrap in his shoulder tearing through him.

Fetch! James thought at the idea of another injury.

Before James could cry out or wince at the pain, the Beast brought him closer to its face.

"*What* did you just say?" it spat at him.

James took in a deep breath. "I get the feeling that you heard me."

"Don't get smart with me," the Beast said while shaking James slightly. "You've been to the Underworld and *came back*?"

"Sure," James nonchalantly said, "but I think you have bigger things to worry about."

The cement block began to glow brighter. The Beast's gaze shifted towards Harper, and it cursed under its breath. The Beast let go of James, and then threw its head back. James watched the Beast falter backwards a few feet, slumped over, and remained motionless.

"What the hell?" James said aloud as he heard a loud explosion. James' ears rang from the explosion in addition to the screaming Threshers. The room suddenly flooded with heat, and everything turned white.

This is it, James thought. *The light at the end of the tunnel.*

After at least fifteen seconds, the heat began to dissipate. Surprised that he once again survived, James sat himself up and saw that the scrap metal, the black masses, the Handy Dandies, and the Beast had been completely obliterated, and the only thing left was the cleaver.

James shakily got on his feet and turned around to see Harper and Moo-Moo leaving the room.

"You did it!" James exclaimed as he ran to Harper and hugged her tightly.

"Title IX! Report violation to HR!" Harper shouted.

"Wh-What are you talking about?" James let go and backed away.

"You shed your layers! Exposure is a crime!"

James looked down and noticed that his clothes had disappeared, and the only thing he really had was the sheath across his back and the sword in his hand. He let out a little shout as he covered himself.

"Wait," he began, "how does this offend you if you're a robot?"

"Policies and procedures! No boys allowed!"

"Okay, okay, I'm sorry!" James' face turned bright red and he could hear Lord Krag's laughter echo in his head.

"If you apologize, I can make you new layers."

"Y-You will?"

"And please with extra pretty."

"Okay, um, I'm sorry, and pretty please make me some new clothes?"

"Sure! You're going to look so cute when I'm done!"

"... What?"

Harper's hands suddenly transformed to a ton of long needles as she held them up in the air. "Hold still."

"AH!"

James winced as he heard the needles rapidly clanking against one another.

"Okay, you can open the slits in your face."

James opened his eyes and saw that Harper had fitted bright pink, silk pajamas to his person. They were light enough that he had barely even noticed, including the slippers that were suddenly on his feet. His face turned bright red with embarrassment.

"Was this really necessary?" he asked.

"One can turn a banjo on if they invest with purpose. Fiddle, fiddle strings, and hair."

"Whatever, just lead the way!"

He followed Harper to the cement block, and from the center, a pedestal emerged.

"It will open for you," Harper began, "it just needs your fingerprints."

"*My* fingerprints?"

Harper nodded.

"What's so important about me? Why do I have to be the one to do this?"

"Just because someone burns down your family tree doesn't mean they destroy its roots."

James let out a sigh as he told himself he'd never understand what this damn robot was saying. Nevertheless, he placed his hand on the pedestal. A beam of light shined across it, and the pedestal opened up, revealing some sort of mold that held a smoldering pair of black and gold gauntlets.

"Gauntlets?"

"No, it's the Grand Project," Harper replied as her chest cavity opened up, which was lined with silk, and two icepick appendages, also wrapped in silk, grabbed the gauntlets, and set them inside. "Done."

"'Done?' What do you mean, 'done?'"

"I need to wait for further instructions."

"So, we literally risked our lives just for you to grab a fancy pair of gloves? Who's going to tell you what to do next?"

"I'll know when I hear the password."

James let out a frustrated shout. "Whatever, can we leave now?"

"Cold nibbles on the lesser rung of precipitation."

"I'll take that as a yes."

Chapter Twelve

Ho-Down at the Show-Down

JAMES QUICKLY AND QUIETLY SPRINTED to the Cougar upon arrival at the camp, certain that he was alone. His pajamas maintained their brightness, despite the mud that had caked on the slippers and the bottom of his pantlegs, and the overcast sky tainted with gray. He gripped the handle tightly and pulled, only to learn that his morning had worsened by encountering a locked door. Ignoring the fact that the door was, indeed, locked, James tugged as hard as he could on the handle repeatedly.

"Come on," he whispered to himself. "Fetch… fetch! Mother fetching—!"

James felt his cheeks heat up, matching the color of his pajamas, as the sound of someone clearing their throat interrupted his swearing. He looked up to see all of the Theoremists, the clouds in the sky, and every animal in existence staring at him.

James stood up straight and laughed nervously as Alexis stomped towards him from the back of the crowd.

"Where the hell have you been?" she softly yet harshly spoke.

"Uh," James stuttered, "I was, uh—"

“Cleaning out the dust mites and rodents!” Harper exclaimed, suddenly at James’ side with Moo-Moo. “At ten thousand degrees…”

Alexis’ eyes widened as Elijah made his way over. “You mean that was you?” he asked.

James held up his hands in surrender. “I didn’t do anything—"

Alexis pointed towards one of the mountain peaks, which was pluming with black smoke. James looked between the mountain and the Theoremists and realized they were packing to evacuate.

“Oh… then, yes, that was me.”

The camp sighed with relief.

“Don’t dismiss this so easily,” Thaddeus suddenly spoke, “after all, if this mechanical demon and discolored ragdoll can manage to shake our foundations, then we won’t just have a problem, we’ll have a threat.”

Gasps and whispers erupted among the camp.

“‘Discolored ragdoll?’” James offensively repeated, and oblivious to the situation at hand.

“Shut up, Thaddeus!” Alexis intervened before turning to James and Harper. “You said something about… dust mites and rodents?”

Harper nodded. “Yes, we cleaned up the mess.”

“The mess?”

“Scrubbed away with brimstone. Wash, wash, wishy-wash.”

Alexis nodded. “Ah, I see” —she turned towards the camp— “so, if anything, these two individuals did all of you a service.”

“What in the Sam hell is that supposed to mean?” Thaddeus retorted.

Harper’s eyes began glowing red and her voice deepened. “You can’t take that name in vain.”

“Harper, you’re not helping your case by doing that,” Alexis said as she put her hand on the robot’s shoulder.

Harper turned back to normal. "My apologies. Everything is fine, fine like salt. No need to season the papercuts. It stings like a bee! I'm afraid of flying."

James slapped his palm against his forehead.

"Anyway" —Alexis turned her attention back to Thaddeus— "what she means is that you all don't have to spend resources building a new town. They clearly did… something to wipe out all of the Threshers. You would all be safe in a structure that has existed for centuries and is still holding itself together after causing an earthquake."

"And," James intervened, "all of the Threshers were in one place, so really only one part of the building was burned, and the historical contents were preserved."

"Even better!" Alexis happily exclaimed. "Everything can be put towards improving the building, carrying out your own intentions, and, hell, looking into the research and development the company already made!"

Elijah held up a finger. "What about 'the Beast?'"

"It obliterated into dust." James smirked, before breaking into a fit of coughing.

"Atomized to the core," Harper continued, "like nothing's hopes and dreams."

Alexis gestured towards the two. "There you have it, and everyone is already packed, so the move will be quick."

"How do we know they ain't lyin'?" Thaddeus piped up.

"Commerce isn't here right now," Harper replied.

Thaddeus furrowed his brow. "What?"

"Ignore her. How about you come over here and I'll prove it to you?" James threatened.

"You shut your mouth, you walking wad of fairy floss!"

James blushed again and felt himself sinking.

"Will you shut up?" Alexis intervened. "I'm sick of your comments!"

"I'm just being practical!"

"You're lucky I don't have my swords, because I'd gut you like a fish for always disrespecting me like that!"

"Oh, that's right!" Harper spoke up, "I solved a puzzle."

Alexis turned towards Harper. "You… what?"

A compartment in Harper's thigh opened up and revealed Alexis' two katanas. They were as good as new, in fact, they were better as they radiated in the sun rise as they never have before.

Alexis' eyes lit up as she reached for the swords, gripped them tightly, and held them close to her body. She looked at Thaddeus. "They're telling the damn truth."

Thaddeus scoffed. "Why, because they managed to 'fix' your swords? Anyone here could've done that. And you know what? You've been talking pretty high and mighty for someone of your persuasion, going off about 'disrespect' and whatnot. There's a reason why you'd never lead us Theoremists, or did you already forget? Never trust the word of an O' Leary."

Alexis calmly sheathed her swords, but her eyes burned with rage. "Say that again, Thaddy," she challenged. "Why don't you see what happens if you do?"

"What are you going to do about anything here? You're just another boot-licker for the Bureau, just like your father before you."

Almost as quickly as a strike of lightning, Alexis butted her head into Thaddeus' face. He faltered backwards and slipped in the mud onto his rear. He quickly reached his hand to his nose as the broken thing profusely bled. Alexis stood over him and began swinging wildly at his face. She punched his left cheek, then his right cheek, and repeated the process a few times as the Theoremists cringed at the smacking sounds of her knuckles against his flesh.

Elijah, who was so engrossed with the fight, suddenly snapped back to reality and looked around the camp. "We need to stop them!"

Two Theoremists approached from behind her and grabbed her shoulders. She elbowed one in the throat in response. As the Theoremist faltered backwards and choked, the other immediately let go.

"Don't hurt me, I'm sorry!" he exclaimed. "I-I'm just a baker! I'm not good at fighting! I'm sorry!"

Ignoring the cowering baker, Alexis punched Thaddeus a few more times, and then stood up once she was finished, her knuckles dripping with blood that wasn't hers. She casually turned and walked away towards the Cougar in silence.

Thaddeus weekly stood up and caressed his broken face. "Only an O'Leary could be this cruel," he muttered.

She paused to face him again. "And only you would continue to antagonize someone stronger than you."

"Just because you tried to educate someone doesn't mean they'll remember how to read," Harper said.

"Exactly."

Thaddeus coughed up some blood. "It doesn't matter what you tried to 'teach' me, I know who is in the right and in the wrong, and Kyle O'Leary is the blight among the Theoremists."

Thaddeus spit at Alexis, managing to get it on her cheek. She furiously wiped her cheeks and gripped her swords, but before she could draw them, she took a deep breath, and let go.

"No," she said, "you're not worth the effort. I'm over this."

"I'm not!" Reggy shouted from across the camp.

He suddenly emerged from the crowd behind Alexis on all fours and pounced on Thaddeus.

"For the honor of the O'Learys!" he shouted as he picked up Thaddeus, *held him over his head,* and threw him onto the ground before body slamming into him.

Some of the other Theoremists cheered at his response, before turning to punch the neighbors that didn't cheer. The fight broke out like a cold in a kindergarten classroom as brother punched brother, and sister passive aggressively insulted sister before clawing at each other. Some of them immediately went after James, who did not cheer in favor of Alexis, while all Moo-Moo did was bark at them.

"I'm on your side!" he angrily whispered as he did his best to dodge each attack and grew more and more frustrated as his voice continued to fail him.

So, when someone suddenly grasped his good shoulder, he reflexively spun around to punch the person in the face. He was successful, in fact, he was so successful that he knocked the person out cold and stopped the entire fight as the Theoremists watched Elijah fall to the ground.

Oh, fetch! James thought to himself.

Wow. I honestly thought the boy was tougher than that, Krag said.

As the Theoremists glared at James, Alexis calmly approached his side, and faced everyone.

"Come with me," she said.

She walked towards the direction of the shack, but paused to free Thaddeus from Reggy's chokehold, only to grab his beard and force him to follow.

The Theoremists, James, Reggy, Harper, and Moo-Moo sheepishly followed behind, each and every one of them covered in mud, ash, and blood. Once they all arrived at the shack, they watched Alexis push Thaddeus inside, and turn to face the crowd.

"You were warned about monsters, Threshers, and 'threats,' so here's your proof that they are gone. Thaddeus is going down there, and if he lives, then you know we're telling the truth."

“You’re being ridiculous!” Thaddeus sputtered as he tried to act tough. “How dare you only think that this could be solved with violence? You’re out of your Gloric-given mind—!”

“What’s the password, Harper?”

“Sam!”

The lift immediately began descending, echoing the noise of Thaddeus screaming and the fast music.

Alexis stood cold as she slowly turned to face everyone. “I… I didn’t know it was going to do that,” she defended.

There was a sudden crash, followed by a softer one and loud screams of pain.

Alexis sighed and pulled out some healing patches from her pocket. “Give this to him when you get him out. Should fix whatever’s broken,” she said as she walked into the crowd and shoved the patches towards Gunther.

“You’re still going to leave?” Gunther solemnly asked.

She shrugged. “I was never welcome here to begin with.”

“Well, you are to some of us.”

“Thanks,” Alexis continued, “but I have… bigger ambitions than this. Not that what you’re doing isn’t significant, it’s just—”

“We understand” —Gunther smiled— “but we hope you come back someday.”

“We’ll see.”

With that, Reggy and James began following her to the Cougar.

“… Your father *worked* for the Bureau?” James sheepishly asked.

Alexis sighed. “Everyone here technically worked for the Bureau. They’re all from the college in Galvin, it just so happened that the Bureau took more interest into his research than others, and eventually murdered him when they were done with him.”

“… I’m sorry.”

“It’s fine… but it is something I don’t like to talk about, so maybe another time.”

“I’ll be there to listen.”

Alexis and James exchanged a smile, while Harper suddenly began treading behind.

“Nuh-uh!” Reggy shouted. “Bad robot! Go home!”

Harper’s hands transformed into tools. “But I have more puzzles to solve.”

“This is amazing!” Alexis cheered in a sing-song tone. “Of course, you can come along!”

“What?” Reggy argued.

“Who’s the boss here, Reggy?”

Reggy scoffed. “I’ll just work somewhere else then!”

Alexis pouted her lip. “You’re going to leave me?”

Reggy’s lip trembled and he let out an aggravated sigh. “*Fine.* I’ll stay.”

Alexis smirked as she unlocked the Cougar and climbed aboard. James and Reggy followed, with Harper last to climb on. The Cougar rocked back and forth as the heavy, metal being walked through it, eventually causing it to lean a particular way as she sat down on a couch.

“… Maybe she should walk outside,” James suggested.

“Maybe you should shut your dirty mouth,” Alexis retorted.

“I like soap.”

“Thank you, Harper.”

Chapter Thirteen

The Wilder Things in Life

PAIN IS SOMETHING THAT CANNOT be forgotten. One can simply be distracted from it, but it doesn’t change the fact that it is still there. Perhaps one doesn't hurt anymore, but there are still reminders of what it felt like, and how long it lingered. As James kicked his feet against the dusty road, he cringed at the throbbing from the planaria patches bordering his shoulder wound (which had already developed a staph infection). The trees shivering in the wind quaked similarly to the muscle spasm in his upper leg as it did its best to carry him further. His head pounded in accompaniment to Moo-Moo's barking. He recalled his vision escaping him as the panic of the Beast's fangs sunk smoothly into his flesh, while glaring at the back end of the Cougar.

"I don't understand why we have to walk," James complained through gritted teeth.

"That's interesting," Alexis commented from the right side of the Cougar. "I thought you would sympathize more with her."

"What makes you think that?"

"Well, you're clearly tired from hauling your own baggage, wouldn't you assume she'd feel the same way after doing it for a good three weeks?"

The Cougar trembled and trumpeted with laughs.

"She's *meant* to carry things," James retorted. "The only difference is that we added Harper to our team, and she's clearly too heavy."

"Whales and most minds are more rotund than me," Harper defensively said.

"Don't coil your sprockets. I wasn't calling you fat," James grumpily responded.

“"Don't coil your sprockets?"' Alexis repeated with a hint of laughter.

"When are we going to stop and rest for the evening? It's already dark," James asked with hopes to divert away from his interesting choice of words.

"Dude, it's not dark. It might be, like, three in the afternoon dark, but come on. Quit complaining," Reggy said.

James exhaled heavily through his nose. He couldn't believe Reggy of all people was telling him to man up

Again.

His head fell to the ground and he stared at his sneakers. He hated the sneakers. He had owned his pair of boots for Gloric knows how long, and he had to replace such a reliable pair of footwear with these poor excuses for shoes that didn’t even have nice arch support. It was one thing to take his hunk of shoulder, but his only companions for the last ten years? That was a whole new world of hurt.

“In my defense, I just got the living hell beat out of me,” James spoke up again.

“You know, you’re lucky you only ran into the Beast. There are worse things out here in the Wilder-ness,” Alexis said.

“You mean the *wilderness*?”

"No, I mean the *Wilder*-ness."

James scoffed. "Okay, but I'm pretty sure that you're wrong. The Beast was a pretty bad encounter."

"You're not wrong… unless we run into the Wilder Man."

"The… The 'Wilder Man?'" Reggy nervously repeated.

"Uh-huh. The Wilder Man is an ancient creature that roams the Wilder-ness day and night, looking for helpless travelers that have trespassed upon his territory."

"You're just trying to scare us," James said, hoping he was right.

"No, it's a local legend about these woods," Alexis continued before stopping in her steps and facing the two. "Some say he was here since the creation of Tor, while others say he was a result of man's sin." She slowly approached James and Reggy, lowering her head and her voice. "One best not be caught by the Wilder Man. There is a reason why we only have *legends* instead of facts. Some say he doesn't care about who is traveling in his woods, and that trespassers are trespassers. Others say that he preys upon helpless men born from the earth, as a sign of the end times. He loves to eat those who smell like fear, and feed on it through their bone marrow, but a sure sign of knowing he is there is the sound of his labored breathing, and the Filn jingling from his coin purse, as a trophy for devouring dishonest and greedy men. Alexis' eyes glowed with the screams of the dead. "No one survives when they meet him, unless he allows it, but according to thc rumors, he's not one to be forgiving."

James normally would have shrugged off these kinds of things, but the nervousness of Reggy only added to his anxiety.

"You know what, James? You were right. This *does* seem like a good place to set up camp."

As Alexis brought the Cougar to a stop, Harper applauded her for the "articulated scaries," and James and Reggy exchanged worried glances as thoughts of the Wilder Man rampaging through their camp sprinted through their minds. Moo-Moo, seemingly noticing James' distress, trotted up to him, jumped up, and began licking his chin.

"I-I'm okay, boy," James said, trying to shake off the nerves. "No need to worry."

James dismissed the dog, but he continued to jump up on him and invade his personal space. He did his best to ignore the canine, even though Moo-Moo was very distracting and often stuck his nose wherever James' hand went, from unloading the Cougar to gathering firewood. Once James sat down to attempt to get a fire started, Moo-Moo decided that it was a good idea to climb onto James' lap.

"Come on!" James exclaimed in frustration. "First of all, you're too big to be a lap dog! Second, I need to get this done."

All dogs think they're lap dogs, Krag said.

James huffed. *It doesn't matter.*

Try telling him that.

"Why don't you go bother Reggy?" James directed at Moo-Moo.

"You're funner to bother," Reggy joked as he took over the chore of building the fire.

"He has a point," Alexis spoke up as she sat down on the ground with Harper beside her.

"Is that why you're all ganging up on me?" James snidely replied.

"What else are we going to do for fun?"

"I could play some music!" Reggy excitedly exclaimed as he pulled out his recorder from his pocket.

"A citizens' band can sing in my throat," Harper intervened.

"Look, robot, I know you want to feel involved, but don't interrupt. It's not nice," Reggy replied.

Harper stared at Reggy, unwaveringly, until a speaker emerged from her voice box and began to play some smooth jazz. Reggy squinted at her and furrowed his brow. He put away his recorder, folded his arms, and began to pout.

"I hate this robot. Why did we have to keep the robot?" he muttered.

"Dude, the robot has been nothing but nice to you. Quit complaining," James retorted.

Reggy looked up and gave James a dirty look while Alexis snickered. "You're both being a little salty today," she said.

"Like stock," Harper added.

"Just shut up and play the music," Reggy said to cut her off.

The group grew quiet as Reggy continued to mope, Alexis examined Harper (while she hummed to the music), and James submitted to Moo-Moo and let his fingers caress the dog's soft fur. It was a peaceful night. The jazz music sang nicely with the crackling fire, chirping crickets, and the coins clinking somewhere in the woods.

Wait... coins? James thought as he felt his heart race.

"Do you hear that?" James asked.

"Hear what? The music?" Alexis replied.

"No, that 'clinking' sound."

"Hey, quit trying to freak me out man, that isn't funny!" Reggy cried.

"I'm not trying to do anything!" James argued back.

"Will you two calm down? I'm sure it's the tambourines or something in the music," Alexis said.

After she spoke, Moo-Moo quickly sat up and his ears perked towards a group of trees, where James swore he heard the sounds coming from. Trusting the dog's instincts, James gently shoved the dog away, stood up, unsheathed his sword, and pointed it towards the trees. "There's definitely something out there."

"It's the Wilder Man!" Reggy shouted in a whisper before hopping up on his feet and shakily holding out his recorder in front of him.

"Guys, sit down," Alexis said. "The Wilder Man isn't real."

"What?" Reggy snapped.

"I made him up to scare you two pansies."

"You made him up?" James exclaimed.

"Of course, I did! It's a silly idea. Something like that couldn't *really* exist."

The leaves in the trees began to shake vigorously.

"... At least… not in this region."

The sound of a creature groaning echoed in the air.

Alexis warily stood up and gripped the hilt of her swords. "Then again… I hadn't been here in a while… things could've changed—"

Just then, a giant man emerged from the trees and let out a roar. The party screamed as Moo-Moo barked and Harper continued to hum. The man was holding a body over his head, and then he threw it down in front of him before unsheathing a sword and stabbing it.

"ANYBODY ELSE?" he bellowed in a thick, Brammish accent.

He panted aggressively as the waves from the quaking leaves in the trees began dispersing away from him, and then grew silent completely.

"That's what I thought," he muttered before he sheathed his sword. He continued to pant before looking up to see James, Reggy, and Alexis all holding onto one another and their choice weapons.

"Oh, sorry to interrupt. I didn't realize that there were any campers in this region." He pointed at the campfire. "May I?"

Alexis nervously shrugged. The man grabbed the body on the ground by the ankle, drug it over to the fire, and then he sat down. He held his hands up and hovered them over the fire before rubbing them together. James took a moment to observe him more closely as he did so. He wasn't nearly as tall as the Beast but was much gruffer with a bigger build. Some long strands of red hair exposed themselves from underneath his hood, but his thick beard was bright enough to give way to any disguise. James also noticed a few small braids and beads in the beard as well. His scaled chainmail rattled with every movement he made, so it wasn't like he was the quiet, sneaky type, but it wasn't like he necessarily needed to be either. After all, he could easily defend himself physically if anything tried to face him head on.

Alexis broke away from James and Reggy, sheathed her weapons, and quietly approached the man. "Who are you?" she asked.

"I'm Greg," he replied in a bit of a cheerier tone.

"You mean you aren't a Wilder Man?" Reggy asked.

"No, I'm a Greg."

Reggy paused to think about the statement, as if he wasn't expecting anything more than a simple "no."

"You're… a Brammish?" Alexis continued.

"Aye," Greg replied as he held his hands out over the fire again.

"What are you doing this far south? Why aren't you with your people?"

"I have no people."

"You have no people?" James intervened as he took a seat next to Alexis.

“Good lord!” Greg exclaimed. “What kind of freak ailment tore up your voice, lad?”

James groaned. “Chest cold.”

“Oh…” Greg said while drifting into thought like he was contemplating evidence that disproved James’ claim.

"Anyway, the Brammish have always been very tribal and looked after one another."

"How do you know that?" Alexis asked.

"There is a tribe in the Far North that is an ally to the Ice Archers, as long as they don't trespass, that is."

"So, yer from the Far North?" Greg asked.

"Something like that."

"Aye. Well, yer not wrong, lad. We Brams have always looked out for our own tribes. My tribe lived in the mountains, not so far away from the Far North, but probably not the one you were speaking of."

"'Lived?'" Alexis confirmed.

"Aye."

"So, your tribe… was it destroyed?"

Greg hung his head slightly.

"I'm sorry. I crossed a line by asking that.

"No, no. Don't be upset, lass, but aye, it was destroyed." Greg's demeanor changed to a deep anger. "By those *monsters.*"

"What monsters?"

"The Frakku."

"The Frakku?"

"What's 'the Frakku?'" James asked.

"It's a dead cult."

"Not anymore," Greg continued. "Unless you're referring to this guy" —he slapped the body next to him— "then you'd be right, they're *very* much dead."

Greg let out a little laugh while Alexis shook her head.

"That's just so bizarre," she continued. "Why would the Frakku suddenly come back?"

"They never went away, lass. They'd always been here, hiding in the shadows. It's what they do best."

"I'm confused," James spoke up. "What is the big deal about the Frakku? Are they Bureau agents? Worse?"

Greg cringed, sighed deeply, reached behind his shoulder, and pulled out an arrow from his back. "Sorry. Damn newts nicked me. Anyway, lad, they're *worse* than the Bureau. They are an active bunch, and work hard for whomever hires them. In me experience with them, they should at least leave you alone if you hadn't killed enough of the bastards, yet they keep growing in numbers like rabbits."

I wouldn't compare a cult to rabbits, James thought to himself.

He doesn't mean rabbits that are cute, per say, but rabbits that have beady red eyes and foam dripping from their mouths, Krag replied

That's ridiculous.

... You know, you have a point. I'm thinking of snakes.

What?

Don't worry about it.

Greg fidgeted under his arm and look rather perplexed. "Ah, dear. I seemed to have lost me knife. Do any of you have one I can borrow?"

"Here!" Harper exclaimed before pulling a bowie knife with a gold blade and black hilt out of her upper arm"

"Thank you, bionic lass."

"It was the smallest on my list."

"Oh. You don't make sense when you talk. That's fun," Greg said, not sarcastically or to be mean, but a general observation. He removed the mask of the corpse, revealing a, blond haired man that seemed a bit too young to be caught up in these shady ordeals, and to meet his end from them.

"Do you… collect those?" Alexis asked.

"Aye. Gotta keep track of every kill. Plus, it makes good chain mail. "

"If you say so."

"They're also made out of solid silver, so they're worth some money."

"*Really?*" Alexis asked with intrigue.

"Yeah, but they get fused to their faces after a while, so you got to get them from the initiates."

"Uh-huh," Alexis nodded, her eyes filling with greed.

“I’m sorry, are you some sort of expert on the Frakku?” James spoke up.

Greg smiled. “I’d say so.”

James narrowed his eyes. “This might just be a coincidence, but here you are, out here hunting a ‘dead’ cult, and happen to stumble right into us. How do we know you’re not trying to kill us?”

Greg nodded and scratched his thick beard. “Well, if you must know, I track them and hunt them on a daily basis, but *you* must have done something pretty grand because I found about six around your camp. But only ever one is dumb enough to try to do something, hence” —he flicked his thumb over to the dead body— “how I got a new piece to my armor.”

Greg sighed and looked at the fire with warm eyes. “This fire is friendly.”

“What have we possibly done to offend a murder cult?” Alexis exclaimed.

Greg sat up straight and smiled while he pulled back his hood, revealing long braids running down his back with runes, bits of metal and bone woven into them. His eyes grew forlorn as he gazed into the fire. “They don't really give details about orders. The young ones are only given commands to follow. The higher-ups train vigorously and devotedly only to get their tongues pulled out. I bet this one here was going to be a squad leader soon.”

Alexis shook her head. “What does that have to do with why they’re after us?”

“My point, dear lass, is that you don’t become a savage to follow reason, and they learn savagery to survive, and in order to survive, you don’t ask questions, but you nod, give a slight curtsey, and do as your told. Sorry I don’t know more.”

“That’s fine… I guess.” She shuffled in her seat. “Would you like to join us for dinner?”

“Alexis,” James snapped.

"What?" she snapped back.

James lowered his voice slightly and leaned closer to her. "We just met the guy and he is an active murderer."

"Yeah, he actively murders evil cultists."

"My point is that we just met the guy and he has *no* indication that he can be trusted, nor that he's not a psycho person!"

"I understand completely," Greg called in response to their "whispering," "but it's okay. I've got my own food, and I would love to just cook up my meat and be on my way, if that's not too much to ask?"

"I don't know," Alexis said loudly before panning over to James, "is that okay with you James?"

James shrugged. "I don't see why not—"

"Yeah, because it isn't like I'm the one that's in charge around here or anything so if anyone should be making decisions around here, it's you."

James waved his hand at her dismissively and walked away, anger brooding from the tips of his toes, but stopping at his shoulder.

Gods, this hurts.

He took the opportunity to grab the last of the fish for everyone. As soon as he stepped inside the Cougar, he overheard a new conversation begin to form between Alexis and Greg.

"I noticed you have a sword on your back," Alexis said.

James scoffed to himself. *So, that's why she's so trusting of him.*

"Oh, yes, this 'ere is my Theorem."

"Theorem, you say?"

"Aye, but not just any Theorem. This sword of mine has a Phoenix attached to it."

James jumped at Alexis loudly gasping.

"A Phoenix? That is a creature of myths! Please, how on Tor did you come across this blade?"

James stepped out of the Cougar, with the fish, hurrying to the campfire to hear the story as well.

The blade was about as massive as he was, the hilt spiraling with feathers whose fibers radiated red and gold in the firelight. A large red gem sat between the blade and the hilt, seemingly capturing a fire.

"This great sword belonged to my father, and his father before him," Greg began. "A simple blade, yet strong enough to defend my family for generations, just not strong enough to aid them when the Frakku attacked." Greg's voice intensified. "This creature had made its home in the mountains near my village, and as the sole survivor, asked how such a tragedy befell us."

"It spoke to you?" Alexis confirmed.

"Aye. It's beak moved not, but I heard its voice in my core."

Alexis quickly wrote down notes.

"When I explained what happened, the Phoenix claimed that it had favored my people, and how they cared for the land it watched over. Having found favor within me, it prompted me to seek out one that could bind its soul to the blade upon my back. With its blessing, I not only retrieved the ashes to bind to the blade, but the blade, itself, transformed to resemble the creature, and I received something greater.

Greg held his palm face up, suddenly manifesting a flame into his hand.

"I've heard of this," Alexis said. "The Phoenix's Blessing. Very few people in the world have ever received it, but many spend their lives looking for these creatures, and trying to prove to be worthy to receive such power."

"Together, this magnificent creature and I travel the land, eradicating it of the Frakku, and purifying the world around us, so that none may suffered the same way my people have."

Alexis nodded. "That's so tragic, but you're so amazing. To think you're one of the few worthy people to obtain a Phoenix's Blessing!"

Greg shrugged as he sheathed his sword. "I bear the burden of the fate of my people but use this blessing only for good." "Please, just one more question."

Greg nodded.

"Who was the Theoremist that enchanted the blade?"

"Oh," Greg looked down bashfully. "Unfortunately, I don't remember his name. It was many years ago."

"I see," Alexis said with a hint of disappointment.

Greg's eyes lit up at the sight of the parcels. "Butter my elk roast, is that what I think it is?"

"... I don't know," James confusingly responded.

"I have only had a mackerel once in my life from Ghoti, but I swore I'd taste another one of their delicacies at least once before I die."

"W-Well, we only have enough for tonight, so—"

"Hold on" —Greg held up his hands— "I offer you a trade."

Greg swung a duffle bag off of his shoulders and opened it, revealing raw, salted elk in the bag.

James gagged at the sight. "What the hell?"

Alexis' eyes widened. "That smell… this isn't elk from Dread Hollow?"

"Aye, but it is."

Alexis squealed in excitement. "How did you get it?"

"Wasn't easy, but I made it happen. Been eating off this bad boy for about a day or two."

"Hold on!" James exclaimed. "Why do you have more corpses in your bag?"

"Calm, down, James! It's game from Dread Hollow!"

"I don't know what that means!"

Alexis sighed. "Dread Hollow is a forest supposedly infested with ghosts; however, somewhere in the middle is a section rich with elk. Only a few researchers have ever been able to hypothesize the number of reasons why this particular elk meat is more tender and richer than others, but it is such a difficult task to get there!"

"Only rumors," Greg said. "It's actually a group of elves that are running an elk farm, but they didn't print enough fliers for their advertisement, and the 'ghosts' that you hear so much about are actually from a haunted hay-ride attraction."

Alexis sat back and gaped. "That's so sad!"

"Aye, but less crowded, so more for us!"

"The fish is yours."

"What?" James exclaimed.

"Relax, James. It will be worth it, I promise."

James sighed loudly as he handed Greg the fish. He, Alexis, and Harper all took initiative to begin cooking for the group.

"I didn't get your names, yet," Greg said.

"I'm Alexis."

Harper pointed at her head. "Clips for hair!"

"So… yer name is Harper?" Greg confirmed.

"How did you even know that?" James exclaimed.

"I have a daughter that didn't really make sense, either. 'Clips for hair,' another phrase for that is 'hair pins.' Harper was the closest thing I could think of. Silly, little birds these lassies are."

James sighed again.

"Yer gonna inhale bugs if you keep breathing like that, lad."

James tried to be angry but let out a little chuckle. "I'm James."

"Nice to meet ya, James. Who's that lad over there?" Greg gestured towards Reggy, who was skipping rocks in a pond.

"Oh, that's Reggy."

"Shy one, is he?"

James furrowed his brow. "Not until recently… it's nothing against you, it all started with the robot."

Greg nodded. "I won't pry, then."

"Are you going to cook for Greg, James?" Alexis asked.

James shrugged. "I mean, I normally do the cooking now, don't I?"

Alexis turned to Greg. "He knows how to cook fish really well."

"Really?" Greg raised an eyebrow with intrigue. "If that's the case, I'd be more than happy to prepare my game for you."

"That sounds like a good compromise."

"Or, even better, we can combine the fish and the game!" Alexis exclaimed.

"That sounds disgusting!" James replied.

"It doesn't matter," Greg said. "As long as we can feast together, tonight will be a good night."

James smiled as he and Greg separated to gather material for cooking. He couldn't help but notice Reggy and his reclusiveness, which was pretty new for him. Nevertheless, James decided to ignore it and continue with his task. After all, what does Reggy ever have to worry about anyway?

~

The man was quite beautiful and pleasing to look at. He wore an expensive, designer suit, often seen on bureaucrats and frivolous platinum spenders. His youthful complexion was complimented by his gold and purple silk tie, with a matching ribbon of a fantastic size pulling back his long, shimmery, platinum blond hair.

His name was Minster of the Far West.

Minster wasn't used to these kinds of environments. Being underground, wet, and surrounded by "devout worshippers" that were probably just commoners looking for a life better than the pathetic ones they left behind, was all a bit unfamiliar. *This* wasn't his department, but the Master insisted that he be the one to deliver the message. "So, do I make myself clear?" Minster asked the crowd before him.

The crowd, dressed in black garbs of wrapped fabric and robes, silently stared back at Minster through silver masks, with no indication of whether or not they found Minster to be just that, "clear."

Minster huffed. "Well, come now! Say something!"

There was no reply.

"... Do you not have language acquisition? Can you not understand the words from my tongue? What's wrong with you people?"

"… Minster?" an ominously soft-spoken man said.

"What?" Minster snapped, making sure this person was in his line of sight.

"These people can't talk. I'm the only one here that can."

Minster glanced at the crowd of people, back at the man, and then grabbed him by the arm and turned around. "What's the matter with them?" Minster whispered. "Do they have the… 'mental disabilities?' I mean, I can respect your view of hiring them, but doesn't that make bad stock in henchmen?"

"No," the man replied, his volume unchanging, "they just don't have tongues."

"Oh!" Minster exclaimed. "Well, what a great idea! I should do that to the infantry. They can be quite annoying."

"Well, I'm always looking for—"

"You bore me," Minster let go of the man's arm to give him a dismissive wave. "Look, do they understand their directive or not?"

"Oh, they definitely understand their directive."

"… Alright."

The two stared at each other quietly.

"… So, why haven't they departed yet?" Minster broke the silence.

"That's easy. They aren't obligated to do anything."

"Excuse me?"

"What is it you're always saying? It's 'not their department?'"

Minster trembled slightly with anger. "What is that supposed to mean?"

"Exactly how it sounds. They don't have to do anything for you." The man waved his hand, and the gathered troops dispersed to attend to their daily business.

"Do you realize what it is that you are doing? If you want to set your god free, you're going to need mine free first!"

"I understand perfectly, but whatever ordeal is happening there isn't *my* business. It's between my boss and yours. If he wanted me to help in any way, he'd tell me."

"Is this about Greg? If it is, then my infantry can handle him—"

"Greg is simply a threat to my recruiting pool. I just hired on some new people, and I don't need him culling the weak just yet."

Minster huffed. "Well, I don't care about *your* time. This is about *their* time and freeing them! You're letting your master down by not helping me!"

The man pulled a buzzing device out of his pocket. "Actually, I paged him when you showed up. I just got a reply, and he says I don't have to help you."

Minster clenched his teeth.

"See? I'm not letting anybody down. You, on the other hand, are quite the opposite. You let your god get into this position. It's taken you millennia to finally take some action. He's down in the depths of the world rotting in a hole, at least I know mine is safe."

"Yours hasn't been very cooperative. He's let Gloric run around doing whatever the hell he wants while he letting his relatives suffer. I don't think he's as grand as you say he is."

The man folded his arms and menacingly stepped towards Minster. "If I didn't know better, Minster. I'd say that you have a bit of a problem with our boss here."

Minster stood his ground. "He isn't *my* boss."

"Oh, he is. You just don't want to admit it because you're blinded with obsession and fear of failure."

"I wouldn't be here if he had just gotten the gauntlets."

"Plans change, and so do developments, but let me tell you something. *You're* not in charge around here, and you are most definitely not the boss of me. Don't forget who really runs the show, and where we have been casted, or do I need to remind you?" He spoke in a voice containing an eeriness that caused chills to erupt from the tip of the spine, and made hopes and dreams break from the sound of his tongue against his teeth.

Minster averted his gaze. "No."

"Good." The man stepped away. "The Frakku will not be assisting you in this endeavor."

"Well, he needs to give me *some* leeway."

"Leeway is a bit more negotiable. I'll see what I can do."

"Good." Minster turned around and began taking his leave.

"Visit anytime, Minster, you're always welcome," the man condescendingly called after him.

Minster rolled his eyes, pulled out an electronic notebook, and began creating a memo. "Note to self: consider severing tongues of infantry, the ones that haven't decayed yet…"

Chapter Fourteen

The Goblin City

AFTER THE ENCOUNTER WITH GREG, the group formed an immediate bond with him. Alexis goggled over his Phoenix sword, and he permitted her to study it frequently. James would spend the majority of his day talking with Greg while doing the heavy work, in addition to cooking with him throughout the day. Greg was also very kind to Harper and was always courteous even when she was difficult to understand. Even Reggy had taken a liking to him, seeing that they often went on walks to hunt and gather food. He also never hesitated to greet Moo-Moo with a belly rub whenever he had the opportunity.

The routine of finding new sites for digging up weapons and developing friendships continued for another three weeks. James had just reached the last stretch of his recovery, with his voice finally back to normal, the handprint on his neck faded to a light yellow, and some flesh growing over the wound in his shoulder.

It didn't change the fact that part of it was still missing, though.

One day, instead of searching for a new digging site, Alexis swung her bag over her shoulders, lead the group through the forest, and brought them to the Goblin City. James had only been to the Goblin City once before, and swore he'd never go back. He never really had an affinity for Goblins. They are creepy, rude, and gross little rodents[11] with no sense of courtesy. He also wasn't a fan of their chosen form of transportation and livestock,[12] or the fact that there was a "Vomit River" flowing underneath the city.

The Goblin City wasn't necessarily an area of poverty. In fact, it thrived greatly as a main trading hub for Theorem. The Theorem they made was mostly cheap, but it was still in high demand throughout the capital cities of the world. Despite its ability to thrive, it didn't change the fact that this urban setting was as dirty as slums, seeing that the overpopulation often made it difficult to move through the streets without dropping a swear or two, and the eight-foot tall Peepers among the three-feet tall goblins didn't make it any easier. The streets were often decorated with both Goblin and Peeper feces, and a thick smog from factories and coal burning settling in the lungs with every breath taken.

James shuddered at the thought of entering the city as he and his comrades stood on the outskirts, parking the Cougar near the valet. "So, what was so important for being here again?" he said as he leaned towards Alexis.

"I have an appointment set up with one of the Goblins here. I have a dagger of particular interest, and he has made me an offer,"

---

[11] Goblins on this world literally evolved from rodents. They maintain many similar qualities as rodents as well, such as having worm tails, long nails, and large teeth.

[12] Peepers are the choice livestock and are domesticated in the Goblin city. They are an eight-foot tall cross breed between a swine and a bull. They have thick, long hair that flowed over the body and their eyes. It's imperative that the hair is enabled to grow over the eyes because something with the way the body processes light and how the Peeper reflects it triggers emesis. The Goblins were the perfect height to see directly underneath the bangs of the Peepers, which is why the Goblin City is most infamous for its Vomit River. To handle the excessive vomiting, the Goblins developed an irrigation system that enables all the waste to flow into a river and outside the city. The river also flows underneath the city, and is easily seen through the grated streets.

she replied as she pulled a tarp out of a compartment on the outside of her wagon.

"Uh-huh, and when did you set up this 'appointment?'"

Alexis huffed and turned towards him. "What are you insinuating?"

"I'm not insinuating anything. I'm just saying that I haven't seen you physically set up an appointment the entire time I've been with you."

"And what makes you think I didn't set it up prior to our introduction, James?"

James opened his mouth to speak but let out a sigh instead. "I don't really have any logical reasoning, so, I'm sorry."

"Good," Alexis said nonchalantly as she began draping the tarp over the Cougar.

As Alexis was finalizing her task of covering the Cougar, one of the Goblin valets eerily sneered as he approached them. "That's an interesting wagon you've got there," he said.

"Uh-huh," Alexis dismissively said.

"It doesn't need iron horses to draw it. That's a peculiar trait for a wagon that typically cannot drive on its own."

"Listen small fry," Alexis turned to face the Goblin, "if you even look at my wagon funny, that tarp will inject you with toxin that will leave you paralyzed for well over twenty-four hours, so before you consider putting your grubby hands all over *my* property, I'd consider the risks."

The Goblin sneered. "I am simply looking. No need to act so hostile."

"Considering your culture of stealing anything that's shiny, I see the need to act as hostile as I need to be."

"If you insist. I suppose I've been warned. Time to consider how to spend my afternoon." The Goblin went back to its post.

"Mischievous li'l rascals," Greg commented as he folded his arms.

"Really?" Alexis replied as she finished putting on the tarp. "That's how you'd describe them? 'Mischievous li'l rascals?'"

Greg shrugged. "It's hard to stay mad at something so tiny."

"...Weird flex, but okay," Alexis dismissively said. "Harper, you stay here. I don't need the Goblins trying to lick you every ten seconds."

"Termites eat what *wood* be a good day," Harper replied.

"I'm glad you understand." She bent down and pet Moo-Moo. "You be a good dog and guard Harper and the Cougar, okay?"

Moo-Moo barked in response, as if she understood what she said.

"Good boy," she said, then she led the group towards the city entrance.

As the group entered the city, James glanced to his right and watched a Goblin pull on a leash dragging a Peeper. The Peeper merely snorted and the air from its nostrils flicked its hair. The Goblin had caught a glimpse of its eye, and immediately ran to a nearby barrel and threw up, disregarding whatever was in there to begin with. James cringed, stomaching his own disgusted reflexes. *The city hasn't changed,* he thought to himself.

Alexis suddenly turned to her right and entered into a bar.

"Is the appointment in there?" James asked.

"No."

"Then why are we going in there?"

"It's time for a drink."

"It's like, nine in the morning, Alexis," Reggy said.

"And?"

"Doesn't it seem a bit early to be drinking?"

"It's never too early to start drinking when you are in the city of Webber Stain." She led the group into the bar and took a seat at a table.

"We're in the *Goblin City,*" James corrected once they were all seated in the bar.

"I know, *James,* but the Goblin City is only known as the Goblin City to those who aren't local because of how often the city name gets changed."

"This city actually has a name?"

"Yes. Right now, it is Webber Stain, named after Webber Stain XV, Lord of Agriculture."

"'Lord of Agriculture?'"

"It has the word 'aggro' in it, so Stain assumed that Agriculture means 'culture of violence.'"

"You're kidding."

"Nope. Two months ago, the city was named Vandley, after Vandley the Consumer, and a month later it was named Bingy, after Bingy the Startle."

"… I'll just keep calling it the Goblin City," James replied.

"Nobody is stopping you."

A fight suddenly broke out in the bar. Alexis let out a huff of air. "I'll admit it's a bit too early for a bar fight," she said.

"Not necessarily," a man sitting at a nearby table said. "After all, it's never too early to start a fight with a Messenger."

"A Messenger?" Alexis exclaimed as she looked back at the scene. "What's a Messenger doing *here?"*

"Who knows, but the Bureau is getting awfully bold to send one of their own all the way out here."

"Apparently."

"I wouldn't worry too much about it. These things don't normally last very long, so you'll get a drink in no time." The man stood from his seat at the table to join them.

The mercenaries and Goblins in the bar all grabbed ahold of the Messenger and dragged him outside.

"Wh-Where are they taking him?" James nervously asked.

"Probably to drown him in the vomit river," the man replied.

"Ah."

"I'm Fletcher, by the way."

Alexis extended her hand to him. "I'm Alexis, and this is Greg, Reggy, and James."

"It's nice to meet you," Fletcher said as he shook Alexis' hand and then shared the gesture with everybody else. Once his hand met James', a smirk grew across James' face as he recognized the man's slender frame, olive skin, tribal designs shaved into the side of his head with braids and totems on the other side, and his cold breath visible against the warmer air.

"What's an Ice Archer doing all the way here in the Goblin City?" James asked.

"I'm glad you asked. I decided to see the world after being confined to one place for so long. I chose this place because I was interested in the mercenary work here."

"Interesting. Which tribe are you from?"

"Iron Maid."

"Nice. I actually grew up in Long Claw."

Fletcher raised an eyebrow. "Really? I wouldn't take you for an Ice Archer."

"I was actually adopted by Kaje."

"Ah, Kaje. The clear breather. His tribe isn't too far from ours. It's a shame we haven't met before."

"I agree."

"What brings *you* here to the Goblin City."

"Um… well—"

"We're here for an appointment," Alexis interrupted. "Which we are actually going to be late for, since it is too busy to get a drink. So, James, if you're done talking to your boyfriend here—"

"What the hell, Alexis?" James snapped. "You don't have to be rude. I'm just visiting."

"I understand," Fletcher said. "I won't keep you from your appointment."

Alexis stood from her seat. "It was nice meeting you, though."

“It was nice to meet you as well.”

Alexis stood and left the bar. As they did so, James noticed to hooded figures in the corner of his eyes that were observing them from a table on the other side of the bar. He shuddered and continued following his friends.

I’m just seeing things, he thought to himself.

Alexis paused outside of a large building, turned, and gave her companions a stern glare. “Listen, I want to be in and out of here in less than five minutes. Also, *I* will be doing the talking. Should I hear so much as a loud breath of air, I will slap you so hard that you’ll hear colors and see noise. Do I make myself clear?”

Greg nodded. “As you wish.”

James and Reggy gulped, and nodded, keeping a firm grip on their tongues with their teeth.

“Alright… in and out.”

Alexis took a deep breath then knocked on the front door to the building. To James’ surprise, two rather large Goblins opened the door, both of them being about the same height as Alexis. “Name?” one of them asked in a deep, gruff voice.

“Alexis O’Leary,” she replied.

“Do you have an appointment?” asked the other.

Alexis huffed. “Yes, I do.”

The two Goblins arched an eyebrow at one another but were interrupted before they could continue antagonizing the young woman. “It’s okay, my friends! I have been expecting Alexis for *weeks,*” said a rather obnoxious voice.

The Goblins stepped to the side, allowing the travelers to enter the building. Standing behind the tall Goblins was an average a yellow Goblin. “Come, this way,” the Goblin said, gesturing that they follow him.

The Goblin lead the group up a few flights of stairs, with his taller lackeys following behind, until they entered an office space. The Goblin took a seat at his desk, while the other two stood next to the door, Alexis stood in front of the desk, and her companions stood quietly behind her. The Goblin twiddled his thumbs as he rocked back in his seat. James observed that he had a rather unsettling expression, as if he were eyeing them like food to be played with. The Goblin stretched out one of his scrawny arms. "Have a seat, my dear."

"No, thanks, Brawnzlinger. I'm in a bit of a hurry, so, forgive me for having to rush this along—"

"I understand completely." The Goblin tapped his long, grungy fingernails against his desk. "Have you brought what we had discussed?"

Alexis reached into a satchel on her side and pulled out some sort of parcel. She laid it onto the desk and unwrapped it, revealing a beautiful black and silver dagger. "Here it is, the very dagger that killed King Arterion. It has been infused with fifty rats, each one a carrier for a different lethal disease. A single cut will infect somebody nearly on the spot, and they would be dead within seconds."

Brawnzlinger revealed a wide smile, his teeth sharp and brown, then gave a giddy, little clap. "This is perfect!" He laughed and then wiggled his fingers greedily. "I'll take it for fifty filn!"

As Alexis was wrapping the dagger back in the parchment, she paused, and gave him a perplexed look. "Fifty filn? This dagger is worth at least a gold piece!" she exclaimed

"Perhaps it is, my pretty, but as you can see, this city has been… slipping."

"Slipping?" James spoke up.

Alexis glared at him over her shoulder, reassuring her promise with her fiery eyes.

"Oh, nothing too fickle, my dear boy," Brawnzlinger said. "Inflation rates, rapid changes in the stock market, a holy war or two, the usual economic dispositions."

"'The usual economic dispositions' or Madame Krishnee[13] demanding more than she can afford?" Alexis retorted.

Brawnzlinger clenched his jaw and spoke through gritted teeth. "I can assure you that this exchange between us has nothing to do with the dear Madame. Specimen such as this don't deserve to be thrown into the underground trading; however, I need to be more careful in my dealings."

"Well, you've always been fair in our dealings, so I don't understand the sudden change," Alexis irately said.

"I'm not being unfair. Like I said, I'm being more cautious in my investments."

"I swear you will never come across a weapon rarer than this. One gold piece or the deal is off!"

"I agree, my dear, I won't find a weapon rarer than this, but I'd hate to lose such a reliable client. Tell you what, I'll give you fifty *silver* filn for it—" the Goblin set the money on the desk "—with the guarantee that nobody here will buy it for a higher price."

"... Fine."

"Or," Brawnzlinger quickly interrupted, "you throw in those two swords with the dagger, and I will exchange it for" —the Goblin opened a drawer, pulled out a sack, and spilled it onto the desk so gold coins would scatter across it— "one-hundred fifty gold."

"The swords aren't for sale," she said without any hesitation as she handed Brawnzlinger the wrapped dagger and swiped the silver filn off of the desk. "Pleasure doing business with you," she passively muttered, then stomped out of the office with her companions following behind.

---

[13] Madame Krishnee is in charge of an underground Theorem ring within the Goblin City. She often demands higher quality stuff, but it doesn't change the fact that cheap Theorem cycle through her ring. She pays rewardingly for Theorem that is either higher quality or is a historic artifact.

“Indeed! Always a pleasure, my dear!” Brawzlinger called after them.

As they exited, the door to the building slammed shut behind them. Infuriated, Alexis punched a nearby cart. The Goblin that owned the cart quickly ran up and began shouting at her.

“Piss off, you half-witted piece of—”

“Alexis,” James cautiously approached her, “you need to calm down—”

Before James could even blink, Alexis swung around with a right hook to his cheek. As soon as she made contact with him, her eyes widened and she cried out in pain, bringing her wrist close to her body, while James remained unfazed.

She huffed. “I told you to let me do the talking!”

“I’m sorry! It just… slipped out.”

“Learn to control your mouth then.”

She stomped off, and the group quietly followed behind her until they reached the Cougar, which had a good three to four Goblins passed out beside the vehicle, in addition to Moo-Moo gnawing on the shoes of the Goblins.

“Porcupine tarp. Does the trick every time,” Alexis said as she began removing the tarp off of the Cougar, her wrist seemingly better.

“So, where are we going?”

The party was startled at the sudden voice.

“Excuse me?” Alexis said.

“So, I became acquainted with your robot and your dog,” Fletcher said.

“Filibusterers and positions are a tax payer’s worst time.” Harper said

“I don’t know what she’s saying but you seem to accept anybody into this groups, so I thought I’d invite myself along.” He pointed to at the porcupine tarp. “Nice, by the way.”

Alexis sighed. "I mean" —she glanced over at James—"you're not wrong."

James pouted slightly.

"What's your experience with Theorem?"

"I have this." Fletcher pulled a bow off of his back.

"What's it do?"

"It was passed down throughout my family. I draw the string, and…"

Fletcher gave a demonstration. As he pulled the bow string back and released, a sparrow flew through the air until it formed into an arrow and struck a tree."

"Incredible," Alexis said.

"There are one hundred sparrows attached to it, so I have that much ammunition. Once I run out, it takes about an hour for it to regenerate."

"That's a fine piece of work."

"I am also well-educated, so I can definitely help with any research."

"You're hired."

"Am I literally the only person here that you fought?" James piped up.

"The weak don't die, James, just be lucky you're alive." Fletcher smirked.

Alexis gestured towards Fletcher. "He said it for me."

As the group integrated Fletcher and began getting the Cougar ready for departure, Greg approached James and pat him on the shoulder.

"Don't be too hard on yourself, lad," Greg said. "At least you didn't end up like these li'l things."

James nodded and tilted his head as he stared at the Goblin bodies, eyeing the valet they had met from earlier lying on the ground. "I guess some things never learn," he said.

Like me.

Chapter Fifteen

Degenerates in Monkey Suits

THEY DROVE A GOOD TEN miles outside of the Goblin City before setting up camp. Alexis explained their routines to Fletcher before insisting that she examine his bow, while Greg and Reggy gathered firewood, and Harper and James unloaded weapons from the Cougar.

"You can't just drop things onto the ground," James explained to Harper. "You need to set things down gently, so the contents inside don't break." He demonstrated by slowly placing a crate onto the ground.

"Like how you can't administer morphine to the dead?"

James narrowed his eyes. "… Yes."

"I understand," the robot said as she followed James' actions and set a similar crate gently onto the ground.

"Is that the last of it?" Alexis asked as she pulled down her workstation and put on a welding apron.

"Yes," James confirmed. "I honestly thought you sold off all the weapons in Peakless."

"Nah. Only so many Theoremists would actually want to purchase a base from me. Fortunately, I sold off most of the relics we dug up, so the rest of these are a bit more generic, and I feel better selling them to generic people. Hopefully tomorrow we will arrive at the next hub."

"Why didn't you just sell these at the Goblin City?"

"I don't like being there."

James shrugged in compliance. "I can't argue with that."

James' attention turned to Greg and Reggy as he heard them conversing as they returned, with Moo-Moo happily trotting in circles around them. As James approached them, Moo-Moo ran towards him, with his tail shaking so intensely that it shook his entire rear.

"Hey, buddy," James said as he crouched down to greet the excited dog. "You were gone a whole ten minutes! I thought I would never see you again."

Reggy scoffed. "Aren't you a bit pessimistic?"

James huffed as he looked up at Reggy. "It's a joke, you know, how dogs don't have a concept of time? Ten minutes could feel like eternity?"

"If you say so," Reggy said with a shrug before dropping wood into the firepit.

Harper quietly approached the three and crouched down next to James. "Morphine," she whispered as she stared at the wood on the ground.

James chuckled slightly. "Yep," he whispered back. "Anyway, what were you two talking about?" he asked at a normal volume.

"What types of knots you should use when hogtying a person," Greg answered.

James raised his eyebrows. "Interesting."

"Yeah, you don't want them to get loose, *especially* if they're a Frakku and have been trained to get out of those situations. You got to be creative," Reggy continued.

"In all honesty it depends on what you're doing. A simple kidnapping, yeah, you wouldn't want your captive to escape, but if you plan on torturing them, then you just want them secure in general. I guarantee nobody is remembering their training when they are in extreme pain. Even the feeblest of people can be aggressive when stressed."

Greg and Reggy exchanged glances.

"Either way, it's best to do it when they're unconscious."

"That's pretty dark, James," Reggy said.

"You think so?"

"Yeah, but I guess it's kind of cool. James has a *dark* side. It makes you mysterious."

"Mysterious, huh?"

"It isn't a mystery if you're just a psychopath," Fletcher said as he joined in on the conversation.

James scoffed. "I'm not a psychopath. I just… heard it somewhere."

"Like where?

"I lived in the Outer Ring at one point in my life. You hear a lot of sketchy things, there."

Fletcher tossed the idea around in his mind. "I suppose you're right. I didn't realize how bad it was there."

"It's pretty bad."

Well, that's a load of hogwash, Krag said. *That's some tier three level of understanding torture.*

There are different tiers of understanding torture? James replied.

My point is that sort of information isn't just floating around in the slums. Where did you really *hear that?*

Why do you care? Weren't you an evil warlord at some point?

James sighed. *I promise you I'm not lying. I really did hear it in Trig.*

Well... the wolves aren't reacting much, but I'm watching you boy.

Need someone to be proud of?

We've just met, yet you know me so well.

James smiled to himself. He wasn't lying to Krag. He really did hear that information in Trig, he just failed to mention *who* he heard it from.

After all, it wasn't like he knew how to control what the voices were saying.

"So, James, should I use a folding knife, a fixed-blade, or a gut hook to skin a body? Razor Elk are quite different from people, after all."

James sneered at Fletcher. "I'm not a psychopath! I overheard people in Trig saying those things."

"We heard you say that already. I just want to know if your psychopath friends had anything to say about skinning people."

Why am I getting worked up over this? James thought to himself as he decided to ignore Fletcher's comment.

There was a sudden rustle in the bushes as two hooded figures made their way forward. James recognized them from the bar earlier.

"Excuse us," one of the figures immediately said. "Sorry to follow you out here, but we heard you were a theory-mist?"

"Theoremist," the other corrected.

"Oh, yeah. Um… what he said."

Alexis warily walked towards them, keeping a slight grip on her swords. "What is it to you?"

"We wanted to ask you about a purchase."

"A theory purchase," the other added.

"And we want to buy from you."

"… Okay, well, I don't really have anything on hand to sell, but I'll take requests with a guarantee of creation and delivery in two weeks," Alexis replied.

"Well, we want a robot!"

"Not just a robot!" the companion exclaimed.

"Oh, right. *That robot.*" The figure pointed at Harper. "We want to buy-sell it."

"She's not for sale," Alexis abruptly said.

"But… the boss will be mad if we don't have her!"

"Who's your boss?" Alexis demanded.

"Um… I can't tell you."

"I think you can," she threatened as she drew her swords.

The figure looked to his companion. "What do we do?"

"Give up?"

"No, we can't give up!"

"But she's got magic swords!"

The fire in Alexis' eyes ignited.

"And we're just dumb and ordinary with nothing magical about us at all!"

The two figures were quiet until they both simultaneously took breaths and shouted, "Oh, right!"

The two figures suddenly grew in size and burst out of their cloaks, emerging as two zombie-like hounds, similar to the badger that James encountered in the Underworld.

"*We demand that you give us the—*"

Before the hound could finish speaking, Greg charged towards it and tackled into it, while the rest of the party took on the other. Alexis quickly tossed the bow to Fletcher. He caught it mid-jump before landing and aiming it at the hound. He released the sparrow into the air, which operated as a distraction before actually making contact while Alexis and James drew their own weapons. While the sizes of their brains were hindered greatly, the two had impeccable strength. The first creature seemed evenly matched to Greg, while the second only needed two swipes of its paw to throw Alexis and James out of the way and did so unflinchingly as it was struck with their weapons.

"I got this, guys," Reggy hollered as he pulled his recorder out of his pocket.

"Where the fetch is your short sword?" James exclaimed, only just observing the unarmed boy.

"Sold it at Peakless."

"Why? *Why* would you do that?"

"Because I don't need a sword to be lethal!"

Before James could continue the argument, he watched Reggy sprint towards the hound and effortlessly avoid its swiping paws with a graceful jump and a backflip. Reggy landed on the hound's shoulders before attempting to choke it with the recorder. The hound tried to claw at Reggy, but the way he had positioned his legs restricted the creature. The hound suddenly flexed its neck and managed to snap the recorder in half.

"Oh, fetch!" Reggy shouted as he hopped off of the hound.

The hound seized the moment to attack Reggy, but the young Hunter managed to effortlessly move out of the way and stabbed the recorder halves into its side and its leg. The hound howled in pain before turning its attention to Harper. It decided to ignore Reggy and galloped towards the robot.

"Fight back, Harper!" James exclaimed.

"It is not in my directive to harm Lynole Industry employees,"

Harper replied.

While James pondered the question as he got to his feet, the creature wrapped its arms around Harper's waist and tried to throw her onto its back, but alas, she was too heavy. The hound struggled greatly to life the unwavering robot, until it howled for its companion. The other creature quickly maneuvered around Greg's grip to help its companion but could only manage to lift her a few inches off the ground and move slowly. The group desperately tried to get the creatures away, but they took the blows with no pain, even to the point where Greg's fire was ineffective.

How the hell are we going to do this? James thought.

Punch on one the nose, Krag replied.

James, for once, did as Krag said without any question, dodged one of the creatures' swipes, and bopped it on the snout.
The creature whimpered loudly, dropped the robot, and pawed at its nose.

"You punched my snoot!" it shouted. Its tears gave James a slight pang of guilt.

The other approached its companion's side. *"You know, you're not very nice!"*

"Yeah, y-you're just a bunch of bullies!"

The creatures turned and ran back into the forest, one of them still crying loudly.

"Impressive," Fletcher said.

"Thanks."

"You know how to hurt dogs, too, you monster."

As James was about to turn towards Fletcher to extend a similar gesture, Alexis burst between them.

"What the hell was that about?"

James took a deep breath. "I think I know."

Chapter Sixteen

Gears in a Dark Place

"I WAS FIGHTING A LARGE, badger-like beast, and it was rotted, much like those two blokes," James began. "They called it a Chimera. I didn't take it seriously at first because it just looked like a young kid, but upon closer inspection, I realized it was a monster."

"'Upon closer inspection?' Fletcher questioned. "Who talks like that?"

"*Anyway,*" James sternly continued, "During the fight, it transformed from a kid into that badger, and it kept saying it would kill me for 'the glory of our god.' So, after Harper said she was unable to harm Lynole Industry employees—"

"You think that these creatures are worshippers of Cirlock," Fletcher finished. "That's very peculiar, considering nobody has worshipped Vrec or Cirlock in thousands of years."

"Yes, but not only do we have a name for these things, but we have a crazy cult trying to deal with us, and it all began when we took *her* with us." James pointed at Harper.

"I *knew* the robots were trying to eradicate us!" Reggy hopped in.

"Will you knock it off?" Alexis said. "We haven't even taken the chance to ask her *why* people want her!"

"Okay then," James turned towards Harper, "explain yourself."

"Lynchpins are always necessary for heavy machinery, take one out, and the whole thing falls apart."

James huffed. "Why is it that you can never make sense?"

"The brain is split in half, and one is trying to go towards the left, and the other is going towards the right, and it's not meeting in the middle and communicating with the bridge that connects the two so they can talk and coordinate," she said with a hint of frustration.

James turned towards Greg and Alexis. "Well, you two seem to be like the 'word salad' experts. What the hell is she talking about?"

Alexis shrugged. "Look, I have to understand the context to understand her, and I just… don't."

"She seems frustrated, though," Greg commented.

"Ladies and gentleman, the pyromancer with the ability to see things clearly like two human eyes!" Reggy exclaimed.

"… I'm not a pyromancer," Greg replied, ignoring the insult. "I just wield a fire sword and have the ability to manipulate fire."

"So, an arsonist?" James added.

"No, I wouldn't say that. I'm just a guy who likes fire—"

"Look, of course she's frustrated!" Reggy continued. "Her brain isn't working right and that's why she doesn't make any sense!"

Alexis' eyes widened. "Reggy, you can understand her?"

"I speak fluent crazy," Reggy said.

Alexis opened her mouth to speak, but Reggy quickly interrupted. "No!"

"Come on!" she whined. "This could be our one opportunity to figure out what is truly going on here, and you have the ability to do so!"

"I refuse! Robots are evil!"

"Do you know what's evil?" James questioned. "The Beast we encountered in the Lynole Industries building."

"The what?" Fletcher asked Greg.

Greg shrugged. "I think they mean the Wilderman. Lass gave me a chill talkin' about 'im."

"He's not talking about the Wilderman," Alexis said. "He's talking about a different thing we'd encountered before we met you two."

"Way to keep secrets from us," Fletcher retorted. "I want to hear more about this 'Beast.'"

"The Beast was just some mean scavenger," Reggy said. "Just because it was a brute doesn't mean that it was evil."

"That thing killed Harper's creator!" James shouted. "It hunted me down like it had something to prove instead of just playing a game, and brutes don't do that!"

"Well, fetch me for not knowing that, then!" Reggy argued.

"This matter is bigger than just what our eyes can observe, and if it means tearing apart our worlds and what we think we know to get to the bottom of it, then so help me, I'll do it!"

As soon as the words left James' lips, Harper's body tremored intensely, before she slumped over, with the sounds of slowing gears and loss of power filling the air.

"Oh gods!" Alexis exclaimed as she rushed to Harper's side. As she brought her hand to the robot, Harper immediately powered back up, sat up straight, and stared blankly ahead of her. A speaker emerged from her throat.

"Silver Protocol initiated," a voice began from the speaker, which James recognized as Harper's 'mother.' "An error with your (Harper) Automata Unit has occurred (error code 376.29). To begin troubleshooting, please recite the voice key override."

Everyone's eyes angrily panned over to James.

James gulped. "Why are you mad at me? I have no idea what I did wrong!"

"Initiating voice recognition," the speaker continued. "Voice recognized. Welcome, Gloric. To continue troubleshoot, please recite your seven-digit identification number."

Everyone's eyes strayed away from anger to awe as they turned their attention to Harper.

"It can't be referring to *the* Gloric," James said.

"James, how often do we run into a Cirlock *and* a Gloric being associated with one another?" Alexis exclaimed.

"This robot was built thousands of years ago! Lots of people were named after the gods, then!"

"It isn't too much of a long shot," Fletcher commented.

"You seriously believe all of this?" James questioned.

"Well, when you're personally exiled from the Ice Archers by the Element of Freedom, herself, you have no choice but to know that Gloric exists."

James gawked at Fletcher. "You said you were in the Goblin City to interact with merchants!"

"Because I *was* there to interact with merchants. Come on, James, not every answer to what I'm doing outside of the Far North is going to be 'because I live in exile.' Give me a break."

"Look," Alexis intervened, "all this talk about Chimeras, cults, and gods is leaning towards finding Gloric."

"How the hell are we going to find somebody that doesn't exist?" James retorted.

"Gods, you're so thick in the head, James!" Alexis shouted angrily. "Everything is so obvious and you're going to continue to question it? What's wrong with you?"

"Compromise," Fletcher interrupted, "we still are in good range with the Goblin City, and they have an enormous library there. I'm sure we can find some sort of answer regarding all of this and can come to some sort of conclusion."

James sighed. “I can agree to that.”

“I’m not going back there,” Alexis said.

“And why not?”

“I just try to avoid that place, and don’t think there is a reason to go back.”

“This is the only way to try and fix your robot,” Fletcher said. “I know that city sucks, but we have to do what we have to do, and it seems to me that our options are limited.”

Alexis reluctantly submitted. “Fine, plus I think I know somebody that might be able to help us repair Harper. We just need to make it quick.”

“Excellent, we leave at dawn.”

CHAPTER SEVENTEEN

PAGE TURNERS AND BOOGER SNATCHERS

JUST AS FLETCHER SAID, THE party was able to make it to the Goblin City in the afternoon.

Around four o'clock

In case anybody was wondering.

Alexis left Greg, Reggy, and the dog to watch over the Cougar and try to reactivate Harper while she, Fletcher, and James traveled to the city. The three of them treaded through thigh-high goblins, Alexis specifically looking around and over her shoulder every three seconds. "Are you okay?" James asked.

"I'm fine."

"You seem nervous."

"I'm just sick of people chasing after us. Plus, I don't want to be here for very long, so let's make this snappy."

"That's what you said last time."

"And what was my response last time?"

"Probably something along the lines of this place being awful and how it would be stupid to stay," Fletcher said.

"I knew there was something I liked about you," Alexis replied.

"I mean, I can understand, I'm a pretty *chill* guy."

"One can almost say he has an *icy* atmosphere about him," James said.

"I swear on Cirlock's silk robes if you two do that the entire time we're here I will kill you," Alexis threatened.

James bit his lip. "Yes ma'am."

The three walked through a street market being held that day. James paused at one of the booths selling clothes.

"James, what are you doing?" Alexis asked.

"Well, personally, I'm tired of attracting a ridiculous amount of stares because of Harper, so I think it would be worthwhile to buy her some clothes."

"We don't have time for this!"

"I'll have to agree with him on this one," Fletcher said. "We should attempt to disguise her."

Alexis huffed. "Just hurry."

James did his best eyeing which clothes would fit Harper the best, not hesitating to pick clothes that run a bit large, some gloves, a mask, and a belt.

We could also use one of the cloaks from the Chimeras to cover her up as well, he thought.

As he was about to pay, he noticed a section of boots, and didn't hesitate to pick up a pair to exchange them for his current poor excuses for shoes. He placed the boots with the rest of the clothes, and the Goblin there looked closer at the boots. "These are brand new," he said.

"Do you not normally sell new clothing?" James asked.

"Of course, I do, I just haven't had a chance to lick these yet."

"Gross!" James exclaimed. "Please, don't lick them!"

"I have too! I need to know what metal was used to make them."

"They probably didn't use—" James paused and took a deep breath. "I will pay you extra not to lick them."

"Sold."

James sheepishly looked over at Fletcher. "Hey, pal…"

"Wow," Fletcher said. "You haven't even known me for a day, and you are already trying to ask me for money?"

"I'll let you have my dinner for tonight."

"Can't say no to that," Fletcher said as he reached into his bag for his wallet.

"Can you two just hurry up?" Alexis exclaimed.

"We are doing our best!" James shouted. "Gall, just give us a second."

"Fine, fine. I'm sorry. There's the library," Alexis pointed to a large building up ahead. After James got the clothes bagged, the three of them walked inside. James noticed that it was a lot nicer on the inside than it was on the outside. The books were arranged neatly upon aisles and aisles of shelves. *Fletcher wasn't kidding. There are books from every Eon,* James thought.

Not everything is a myth, James, said Lord Krag.

James huffed.

"Is something wrong, James?" Alexis asked, irately.

"N-No."

"Good," she approached the receptionist window. "Excuse me?"

An elderly Goblin woman was organizing some books on the opposite side of the counter.

"… Excuse me?" Alexis said, a bit louder.

"WHAT?" the lady snapped.

Alexis winced. "W-We just need some help getting a book."

"I hate getting books for people!"

Alexis furrowed her brow. "But you're a librarian."

"I'm assigned to this job. I'd rather be eating bugs right now! It's always 'book here,' 'book there,' 'don't sneeze in the books!'"

“That’s disgusting!” James piped up. “People actually sneeze in books?”

“Where else are they supposed to sneeze?”

“Anywhere except for books!”

“Thanks, James,” Alexis intervened. “Anyway, ma’am, do you happen to have any books about the god, Gloric?”

The Goblin lady muttered and wandered over to the piles of books she was organizing. She grabbed one pile and carried it over. “Do you have your library card?”

“Well… no—”

“Well, you have to have a library card in order to check out a book!”

“Can’t we just read it in front of you?” James asked.

“No!”

Alexis sighed. “Where can I fill one out?”

The lady pulled out a piece of paper from a drawer in addition to a pencil. “Do you intend to use the books as weapons?”

“… No?”

The lady wrote down Alexis’ response. “Do you intend to use the books for anything other than use of knowledge?”

“No.”

“Do you plan on eating the books?”

Alexis took a deep breath. “No.”

“You hesitated!”

“I’m not going to eat the books!”

The lady grumbled as she wrote down the response. “Do you plan on using the books to build a brick house?”

“No.”

“Do you plan on sneezing in the books?”

“What kind of questions are these?” James interrupted.

“People disrespect books!” The lady shoved the paper to the side. She bent down and pulled out a camera and a large flash.

Without warning, she took a picture of Alexis, the flash as painful as staring into the sun.

"Sweet Cirlock!" Alexis covered her eyes. "How am I even supposed to read now?"

"That's not my problem!" the lady replied. "It's a part of the rules that I take your picture with a bright flash to capture all your nooks and crannies! It shouldn't be hard, though. It'd be impossible to miss such an ugly girl! Then again, we all can't be beautiful like me!"

Alexis huffed as she rubbed her eyes. "Who even made these rules anyway?"

"ME! Now take your books and sit down!" The lady handed Alexis a plastic library card.

Alexis rolled her eyes as James grabbed the pile of books. They each browsed for a place to sit, but every table was horribly small, almost like the children's table at a holiday meal. "Perhaps we should just sit on the ground?" Fletcher suggested.

Alexis nodded. "Yeah, it will probably be more comfortable than those small tables."

They found a secluded spot and sat down in a circle, placing the books in the middle. While Alexis and Fletcher effortlessly skimmed through the books, James found himself having a difficult time. He had read the same paragraph over and over for at least ten minutes, and probably memorized the details of a few "Gloric" portraits,

And how he looked different in every picture.

"Have you found anything yet?" Alexis asked.

"Well," Fletcher began, "right here, there is mention of Gloric making a home in one of the five Realms, but for more information, the book says to refer to *The Celestial Chronology.*"

"The book I'm reading speaks a lot about Heaven and Gloric's ties to it. So, perhaps Heaven is that Realm?"

"Does it say how to get to it?"

Alexis flipped through the pages and sighed. "'To find out more about Heaven's whereabouts, see p. 53 of *The Celestial Chronology.*'"

"At least we have a good idea of what to look for next."

"What about you, James? Did you find anything?"

James' eyes widened, feeling like a deer in the headlights. "Uh…" he looked down at the paragraph he was reading. "… most of this book says to refer to *The Celestial Chronology.*"

Alexis groaned in frustration and threw her book on the ground. "Well this was a dead end! Nobody has a copy of *The Celestial Chronology* anymore!"

"Maybe we can ask the lady if they have a copy?"

"We really don't have any other options," Fletcher agreed.

Alexis huffed. "Fine."

The three of them returned to the receptionist window and placed the pile of books on the counter. "Here are your books," Alexis said.

"Did you sneeze in them?" the lady asked.

Alexis sighed. "No."

The lady opened one of the books and sniffed it. She gave Alexis a dirty look and then put the book away.

"I do have one more question."

"What do you want now?"

"We were wondering if you happen to have a copy of *The Celestial Chronology?*"

The lady laughed. "That's stupid! People who have one are stupid! We have one."

Alexis' eyes lit up. "W-Well can I please see it?"

"No! Library is closed!"

The lady slammed down the shutters. Infuriated, Alexis began pounding on them. "Hey! I'm not done here! It's an emergency that we check out that book! Open these shutters, you hag!"

There was no reply, only the sound of a woman sneezing and a book closing.

Alexis punched the shutters and then walked away. James was about to approach her, but Fletcher put his hand on his shoulder. "I'd give her some space…"

James sighed. "Yeah, you're right."

~

Alexis moped as the three of them made their way out of the Goblin City. "We were so close," she moaned.

"We can always try again in the morning," James said.

"We may not last until morning!"

James shrugged. He wanted to say everything that she wanted to hear, but he knew it would just sound like lying. "We can still try."

Alexis nodded. "I guess so."

"Don't we need to find that person that you think can fix Harper?" James asked.

"I sent him a telegram earlier."

James nodded. "Right."

Eventually, the three of them found themselves crossing the bridge over the Vomit River. On the other side of the bridge was a Goblin dressed up in a uniform riding on a Peeper. Alexis seemed to recognize the uniform, paused, and took a step back. She then turned around, but a pit formed in her stomach when she saw an entire group of Goblins in the same uniform, all mounted on Peepers, and standing next to Brawnzlinger.

Alexis laughed nervously. "Brawnz! It's so good to see you!"

"Really?" Brawnzlinger replied. "I agree. It's so good to see you, as in, so good to see you get what you deserve!"

"What's going on here?" Fletcher demanded.

"Oh, you mean she didn't tell you?" Brawnzlinger piped up. "The dagger that she sold me was a fake!"

"You sold him a fake dagger?" James shouted.

"… He said he wanted *a* rat king dagger, not *the* rat king dagger," Alexis innocently said.

"Are you stupid? You can't just swindle a swindler!"

"You know what, James? Brawnzlinger eats babies!"

"What?"

"Yes! And he wanted that dagger to take out the parents with no problems whatsoever! I did more good than I did bad!"

"As much as I'd like to discuss my favorite meal, I'd much rather watch you rot in jail!" Brawnzlinger said.

Alexis scoffed. "Okay? What makes you think that I will?"

"Alexis," Fletcher whispered, "I don't think you understand just how much trouble you are in."

"What are they going to do? They're *Goblins.*"

"Yes, and swindling them is a crime punishable by death. They don't care if it was a fellow Goblin or someone three times their size, they'll find a way."

"I'd sure like to watch them try then."

"Perhaps we can find a compromise. If you give me your swords, I'll let you live."

"You can go to hell!"

"If you insist," Brawnzlinger snapped his fingers.

Then, all the Goblins pulled some sort of metal stick from their pockets. They each flicked their wrists towards the party, and metal chains extended from them. As James and Fletcher stood in front of Alexis and drew their weapons, they were immediately whipped out of their hands and onto the bridge. Then, they became entangled in the chains. Alexis unsheathed her swords, managed to dodge a few of the chains, but forgot about the Goblin behind her. The Goblin flicked his whip towards her and managed to wrap it completely around her arms and torso. Then, two more whips grabbed ahold of her katanas.

"No!" Alexis exclaimed before falling to her knees under the weight of the chains.

Fletcher let out a frustrated shout. "You stupid, stupid girl! You're supposed to be the smart one in this group!"

Brawnzlinger laughed. "He has a point. You really should've thought twice about double-crossing me, Alexis!" One of the Goblins handed the swords to him. "You've lost your greatest treasures and will soon lose your life!"

Alexis panted angrily, trying to hold back her tears. Disappointed that Alexis did something in poor taste, but horribly infuriated at the Goblins, James gritted his teeth and slowly extended his arms out from his side, flexing his muscles. With a shout, he broke out of his chains, and Alexis, Fletcher, and the Goblins stunningly gaped at this impeccable display of strength. He reached for the whip attached to his sword and ripped it out of the Goblins hands. Shaking off the shock, the Goblins pulled out more whips from their sides and flicked them towards James. Dodging effortlessly and gracefully, James raised his sword at Branwzlinger. Brawnzlinger let out a cry, let go of the swords, and cowered at James. He stopped so he could grab the swords, but one of the other Goblins swiftly whipped them out of the way, towards the edge of the bridge. James dove towards the swords, but before he could grab them, they fell into the Vomit River.

"What have you done?" Alexis shouted, almost in tears as the image of her swords falling into the river flashed repeatedly in her mind.

"I'm not done yet," James said with gritted teeth.

James removed the whip off of his sword, latched it onto the bridge while trying to evade the other Goblins, held on tightly to it, and dove into the Vomit River.

Alexis and Fletcher couldn't shake their awe, even the Goblins were perplexed at this man's actions. Brawnzlinger looked at Alexis. "… Your boyfriend there is pretty cool."

"He is *not* my boyfriend!" Alexis shouted through gritted teeth.

"He might be after this," Fletcher muttered.

"Shut up!"

James then ascended back to the bridge by climbing the whip, using his belt as a sheath for the two katanas Dripping with a mixture of water and various wastes, James stood up and yanked the Sword of Lord Krag out of the bridge.

Each of the Goblins gagged. "That's so disgusting!"

"I can't believe he actually jumped into the river!"

"… I… I'm gonna…" a Goblin began as he covered his mouth and fell to the side of the bridge, then hurled into the river.

James shuddered as a realization of what exactly happened overcame him, but he shook his head, remembering the predicament at hand.

I heard a rumor that Goblins are afraid of snakes, said Lord Krag.

I was just thinking the same thing.

"Alright, boys! Let's show 'em who's boss!" James pointed his sword at the Goblins.

The two snake heads manifested, each of them hissing at James.

"U-Uh, I mean ladies! Let's show 'em, ladies!"

The snakes stared at James.

"… Please?"

The snakes exchanged a glance with one another and then appeared to be shrugging. They took one look at the Goblins and gave them a blood curdling hiss. As soon as the cry sibilated from their tongues, the snakes' faces suddenly transformed into terrifying basilisks, with rows of teeth reflecting the fear of the

Goblins. The Terror extended forward and snapped onto the shirt of one of the Goblins and flung it into the river. The rest of the Goblins screamed and let go of their whips to cower behind their hands.

"Run!" James shouted.

Alexis and Fletcher both pulled off the loose chains. As Fletcher grabbed his bow, the three of them took off towards the other side of the bridge, the snakes maintaining their haunting gazes at the Goblins.

"F-Fools!" Brawnzlinger shouted, trying not to cry. "They've committed a crime against me! Do your job and run after—!"

As soon as they heard Brawnzlinger say "run," the Goblins ran in the opposite direction of the humans. Brawnzlinger began to sob and ran with his Goblin comrades.

When James, Alexis, and Fletcher put enough distance between themselves and the bridge, they stopped running, and panted over their tired legs. "… I'm really impressed," Alexis said with a heavy breath.

James smiled, as if the stars in the heavens had just aligned. "Thank you—!"

"I'm so proud of you two!" Alexis approached James and took back her swords.

The two snakes reverted into their python states and extended towards their master, each of them flicking their tongues against her cheeks. James felt his heart sink as he watched Alexis walk away, cooing and praising her pythons.

"…You smell like puke really bad," Fletcher said.

"Shut up!"

~

"Oh, my gods, I could smell you after you rounded that corner when you got into that Goblin fight," Reggy said.

"... How did you know?" James asked, still crusty from the dried "vomit."

"A squirrel told me," Reggy replied.

James scoffed. "That didn't happen."

Reggy turned to Greg. "See? I told you they wouldn't believe me."

"I believe ya."

"That's because you're a good man, Greg."

"Where'd the dog go?" Alexis looked around the camp.

"Oh, Moo-Moo went home with his friends."

James, Alexis, and Fletcher stared at Reggy, unsure to be confused, concerned, or to be entirely disinterested. Alexis shook her head, sat down by the fire, and hugged her knees. "Tell me, Greg, is this fire a disappointed one? Because, after today's events, I would be."

"Actually, this fire is a smart one."

"How is it smart?" James asked.

Greg pointed at the fire. "Look into the flame!"

James looked closer and could see numbers forming into equations in the fire, with the answers revealed in the smoke.

"So, was the mission successful or no?" Reggy asked.

"No," Alexis huffed. "The library was a total dead end and then we got cornered by Brawnzlinger and the Goblin police."

"... You gave him a fake dagger, didn't you?"

Alexis sat up. "How did you know?"

Reggy scoffed. "Like you'd part ways with a rat-infested knife wielded by a king."

Alexis shrugged. "Touché. What about you and Greg? Were you able to override Harper's protocol?"

"No. She just keeps asking for a seven-digit number. We started just reciting a bunch of different numbers, but none of them worked."

"Is that what the fire is for?" James asked.

Greg smiled proudly. "Aye."

"How typical of you, trying to swindle a Goblin. You still think you can out clever anybody," a Goblin standing on a stool and tinkering on Harper said.

"Grime" —Alexis stood up— "thank you for coming."

Grime grunted in response. "Who else is going to clean up your messes?"

"Is this the guy you mentioned earlier?" James asked.

"Yes."

James' eyes narrowed. "You didn't mention he was a *Goblin,*" he whispered.

"Will you shut up? Grime is fine," Alexis retorted as she approached the Goblin. "Do you have an idea of what's wrong with her?"

"Of course, I do!" Grime snapped. "The left transistor gear was slipping, so I was able to fix that, but the whole shaft is void of control of what looks like" —he squinted slightly— "cognitive specific speech and sensibility."

"So, she's broken?" James asked.

"I didn't say 'broken,' I said the left transistor gear was slipping, and the shaft is void of control of cognitive specific speech and sensibility!"

James blinked.

"She's functioning, but not whole," Alexis explained.

"Oh."

"I thought you would've chosen smarter slaves!" Grime exclaimed while waving a wrench at Alexis.

"'Slaves?'" James repeated

"They aren't 'slaves,' they're workers," Alexis said.

"Hiring workers without paying them is slavery!" Grime continued to argue.

"I feed them and clothe them!"

"As you're supposed to do with slaves!"

Alexis huffed and folded her arms. "Whatever. Can you fix her or no?"

"I'm going to need the rest of her gears to do that."

"We'd have to go all the way back to Lynole Industries if that were the case!"

"Actually" —James winced slightly— "they might've gotten destroyed when we fought the Beast and the Threshers."

Alexis rolled her eyes and placed her hands over her face, as if to calm her frustration.

"Well, I guess that settles that, then," Grime said as he closed up Harper's head, packed up his tools, and then hopped off of the stool. "Best of luck to you."

"Can you at least override the I.D. number?" Alexis asked.

"I tried! Why do you think your friend made that crazy fire?"

Alexis sighed. "Touché."

As Grime took his leave, Fletcher nudged James' shoulder. "So, you don't know about robot parts, but you know how to torture people?"

"Shut. Up."

Fletcher chuckled. "Well, today wasn't a *complete* loss, We found that a lot of sources point back to *The Celestial Chronology.*"

"No one has a copy anymore, Fletcher! Did you hear the lady at the library?"

"I have a copy," Greg said.

Everyone's heads shot towards Greg.

"… You do?" Alexis exclaimed.

"It was a tradition in my village to pass it down to the firstborn son. I never had a son, so I still have mine."

"C-Can I please read it?"

Greg reached into a satchel on his side, pulling out an old copy of *The Celestial Chronology.* It was worn, but not tattered, as if everyone who received it nurtured it like a fragile soul. The green, foiled lettering reflected the firelight, with a few numbers appearing now and again.[14] Alexis stood and gently took the book, holding it in her hands as if it were a porcelain sculpture worth more than the world itself. "I can't believe it. I'm actually holding *The Celestial Chronology.*"

"Well, believe it sweetheart," Greg smiled.

"Why is there a big ten on it?" James asked, staring at the large number in the middle of the cover.

"Because, it's the tenth edition."

"There are ten of these things?"

"Of course, there are."

"... Why?"

"Accuracy. *The Celestial Chronology* gets more and more accurate with every translation."

James' eyes widened. He couldn't believe that there were *ten* different versions of a book about *one* guy!

Alexis turned to the very first page. "'Here reads the account of everything before and is to come—"

"Wait a minute," Reggy piped up.

"What is it?"

Reggy glanced over at James. "I'm not listening to story time with this heaping pile of fetch work."

Greg and Fletcher muttered in agreeance.

James sighed. "Well, would anyone like to point me into the direction of a water source that *isn't* made of vomit?"

"I think I saw a pond over that way," Fletcher gestured towards the woods.

"Fine," James rolled his eyes and sheathed his sword.

"Be careful of the mini bugs!" Reggy cautioned.

"What mini bugs?"

"You know, the invisible kind that hide in water!"

---

[14] *The Celestial Chronology* is Tor's equivalent to the Bible. It consists of the creation of Tor and the many tales of Gloric's reign upon it.

"You mean bacteria?"
"And other stuff!"
James groaned and continued out into the forest.
I'm so glad I don't have a nose, Krag said.
James didn't reply.
... Not going to tell me to shut up?
In all honesty, I'm thinking about how much I envy you.
... Oh.
Yeah.

~

The pit wasn't exactly bottomless but was a long way down. That being said, one would probably die if they stumbled into it. Fortunately, the pit was surrounded by a railing made of gold to keep the common folk from inconveniencing the deity trapped in it.

At the edge of the pit, sitting at a desk, was Minster. He was speaking into an old, candlestick telephone, that was also made of gold.

"Yes… Yes… Absolutely, sir. You can't depend on those Frakku for anything—I mean— you *can* depend on the Frakku for everything! I'm sorry, sir, forgive me for thinking for myself again. B-But I promise that I would *never* fail you, sir," Minster nervously said.

Behind Minster stood about twenty Chimera soldiers, wearing black uniforms with lion emblems over their hearts. One of the soldiers, directly behind Minster, slowly turned his head to his comrade on the right. "Who's he talking to?" the soldier asked, in a heavy Trellish accent.

"Why, he's talking to the boss, of course!" the comrade replied in an equally heavy accent.

"Oh, right… who's the boss again?" He picked at some exposed muscle near his jaw

"The god we worship, who's currently sitting at the bottom of that hole!"

"Oh, yeah. I forgot about that."

After a moment of silence, the soldier spoke up to his comrade once more. "Who is the god we worship again?"

"The God of Commerce, of course! His name be Cirlock."

The instant 'Cirlock' left the lips of the comrade, Minster angrily pulled a revolver out of the inside of his suit pocket, turned, and shot the comrade in the center of his forehead.

The soldier watched his comrade fall to the ground, his lazy eye staring off into another direction. "… Oh, no. I think that guy is dead."

"What's 'dead' mean?" a different soldier in the back asked.

"Oh, Minster 'ere told me that dead means he went away to a farm, so he can run and run on endless fields forever!"

"That makes sense!"

"But how is he on the farm if he is still bleeding out on the ground?" another soldier lisped, since most of his teeth have left him.

The small group of soldiers stared at the corpse, trying to connect the dots between what Minster had told that soldier, the soldier currently dead on the ground,

And where exactly they could find the farm.

There might be ponies.

Minster took a deep breath as he hung up the phone, stood up with a smug look on his face, straightened his gold and purple tie, and turned to face the soldiers. "Alright, people, the Master has ordered us to go fetch something of his—"

A solder burst out laughing. "He said 'fetch!'"

The rest of the soldiers began laughing and saying, "fetch this!" "fetch that!" and "fetch yeah!" over and over.

"Silence! You dolts! Or I'll cut your tongues out!"

The soldiers were frightened by Minster's shouting and immediately stopped laughing, with maybe one or two more swears muttered under their breaths.

"Now then, people, can we all act like mature gentlepersons?"

"We're persons?"

"Well… yeah?" Minster replied. "You're sentient beings, aren't you?"

"He called us 'persons!'"

"We're important!"

"Are we important?"

"No!" Minster shouted. He huffed and straightened his coat.

"Then why are you calling us 'persons' if we aren't important?"

"Well… what else are you supposed to call a group of decaying Chimeras?" Minster genuinely asked.

"… Oh!" the group of soldiers exclaimed. "That makes sense!"

"… I hate all of you. You used to be so smart until your brains started rotting."

"Thanks Minster!" The soldier paused and then grew dismayed. "Oh… hate is bad."

"Anyway, we will be traveling through the Dwarven Mountains." Minster walked through the crowd, each of them stepping aside to create a path for him. As he got to the other side, he looked back over his shoulder at the pit. "These weapons we are assigned to retrieve are imperative for the Master's escape. We will not fail him, is that clear?"

"Yes, sir!"

"Good." Minster faced forward, his tied hair falling gracefully down his back. "Should anyone disappoint him, or me, you will be dealt with. Don't let me catch you lollygagging."

The soldier with the lazy eye picked at his muscles again, before slowly looking forward to another comrade. “Who’s the Master again?”

“The boss!”

“… Oh, right.”

Chapter Eighteen

Subtle Worship

"WHAT DID YOU GUYS NAME your weapons?" Fletcher suddenly asked.

"I mean, mine is the Sword of Lord Krag," James answered as he clung to his towel, his clothes still a bit damp from washing them in the pond.

Fletcher raised an eyebrow. "Really? You can't be that bad of a guy if the sword chose you."

James chuckled. "What's your weapon's name?"

Fletcher shrugged as he plucked the string of his bow. "I don't know. I want to call it something cool, like 'the Grievance,' or something, but I know I need to name it something dumb, like 'Chuck.'"

"Why would you do that?"

"It's a Gloricism thing. You should give your weapons a person's name instead of a title."

"Really?"

"Yeah."

"Alexis didn't do that."

Alexis paused before she took a bite of her fish. "Nicole and Nancy?"

"Excuse me?"

"Those are the names of my weapons: Nicole and Nancy."

"I thought they were 'the Terror' and 'the Hope?'"

"They have two names."

"So, my bow can have two names?" Fletcher intervened.

"Yes."

"Awesome." Fletcher turned towards Greg. "What's your weapon's name?"

"Oh," Greg put down his fish and then unsheathed his sword. "This be my Birdy."

"Yeah, we know there's a Phoenix in it, but what's its name?"

"Birdy."

Fletcher raised his eyebrows and exchanged a look with James. "You named your sword 'Birdy?'"

"Yes."

James stifled a laugh while Fletcher couldn't hide a smile. "Isn't that, I don't know, a bit silly?"

Greg gave a light laugh. "I suppose it is, but I named 'er after my daughter."

"Your daughter's name was Birdy?" James asked.

"Birdy is just something I called 'er. She had such a beautiful singing voice, like she was my li'l songbird."

James felt a pit in his stomach. "…'Was?'"

Greg sighed. "Yeah…"

James and Fletcher glanced at one another and then stared at the ground, feeling guilty.

"So, my Phoenix is named Birdy, to remind me why I keep on fighting in this life."

"That's so sad…but so cool at the same time!" Reggy exclaimed.

"Reggy!" James snapped with a whisper. "Be a bit more sensitive!"

"No one has told me I'm cool before," Greg said, a light shining in his eyes.

"Is it because you're a pyromancer?" James joked.

"Oh!" Fletcher shouted. "Burn!"

Fletcher and James burst into laughter. Greg and Reggy rolled their eyes and shook their heads but found themselves chuckling.

"So, besides naming your weapons, what other 'Gloric' things do you guys do?"

"I'm assuming you don't know about the braids," Alexis said.

"You'd be assuming correctly."

"Most Gloric worshippers wear braids," Fletcher said. "No one really knows how or why it came about, but if it is taught that you should maintain hair with some sort of braid. You're exempt to the rule if you don't have any hair, or if it is too short to do anything with."

"It's more of a symbol of modesty and cleanliness if anything," Alexis continued. "I, personally, find braids restricting, so that's why I always keep one, so I can let my hair down but still show my devotion to Gloric."

"That's pretty neat," James commented as an attempt to sound interested. "So, if every single one of you worship Gloric and have braids, how come you don't wear any, Reggy? Your hair too short?"

Reggy smirked, and he lifted a small section of his dirty, frizzy hair, and revealed a small braid, no longer than an inch, being held together with a piece of thread. "Hah!"

James scoffed slightly. "Of course, you would do that, you fetch."

"If we're all done talking and eating, can we get to the book, now?"

The men all muttered and shrugged as they set aside their scraps and allowing Moo-Moo to pick off of what wasn't eaten.

"Good," Alexis said. She turned to her left, grabbed the book, and began to read.

"'Here is the account of everything before and is to come,'" Alexis read. "'When the gods visited Tor, they left their mark upon the Heavens. Their bodies were like a burning fire, transcended beyond all the human eye can comprehend. We saw these gods as the Rising Star, Setting Star, and Mid-Star, but they revealed themselves as Cirlock, Vrec, and Gloric, the Suns of All.

"'Despite the majesty of the Suns, they infringed their godhood upon the nature of this terrain, awaking the goddess, Frelic, along with her Elements. Frelic, with her hair strung with auburn waves, and eyes of an orchid sky, filled the Suns with fondness, and each one yearned for her affections. To win her love, each Sun offered her a gift, and thus ended the First Eon.

"'Cirlock, Sun of Rising Star, offered her the gold and silver ore forged in Tor's veins. She saw that he was a God of Commerce, lusting after precious and worldly attires. She declined his gift, for she desired warmth and soft arms, not cold and rigid material.

"'Vrec, Sun of Setting Star, offered her the power that was forged from the fear in the hearts of man. She saw that he was a God of Destruction, desiring to rule and dictate the lives of others. She rejected his gift, for she wanted love and respect, not hatred and trepidation.

"'Gloric, Sun of Mid-Star, offered her the life forged from the light that twinkled in her eyes. She saw that he was a God of Peace, only seeking life to beautify the landscape he had found. She accepted his gift, for she needed to smile, and he dried every tear, and consoled every fear.

"'Angry that his brother had won the favor of the goddess he desired most, Vrec waged a war upon the land. In order to stop the rampage of their heartbroken brother, Cirlock and Gloric fought together to defeat him. The two brothers sealed the Setting Star away deep beneath the surface of Tor. Peace was brought to humanity at the expense of one less star in the sky, and thus ended the Third Eon.

"'Anguished over his lost brother and beloved, Cirlock grew to despise Gloric. He felt the punishment inflicted upon the Setting Star was heinous, and that his brother's marriage to the beautiful Frelic was selfish. Cirlock decided to betray Gloric by freeing Vrec from his underground prison, and waging war upon the land once more.

"'Devastated at the pain he could see in his brothers' eyes, Gloric pleaded with Cirlock and Vrec to stop seeking solutions through violence and conflict, but to join his side again, and together they will obtain tranquility and happiness. Cirlock and Vrec refused their brother, and thus began the Thanatichor, where the gods were no longer kin, but enemies.

"'In order to protect mankind, and to keep his beloved Frelic safe, Gloric, along with the power of the Elements, managed to seal Vrec below the surface once more, and cast Cirlock away into the trenches of Mahara.

"'Gloric, Sun of Mid-Star and God of Peace, restored harmony to the surface of Tor once more, but humanity grew vindictive towards the gods. They found it unfair that they became victims of their rage and began to turn upon one another as they lost hope in the world they resided on.

"'Grieved by his actions and the actions of his brothers, Gloric tarried away to the realm of Heaven, swearing that he will not impose his powers where it is not necessary, and thus ended the Sixth Eon.

"'Gloric and his brothers came to the plane of Tor to begin life and swore to bring happiness upon mankind. With the desire to keep that promise, Gloric left behind secrets and keys for man to be able to find their way to him and be with him. These secrets can be found within this account, and as Gloric makes his blessings available to you, he does the same with his guidance. And thus, begins the Seventh Eon of Man, where humanity can coincide with the God of Peace to obtain the promises he left behind.'"

Alexis took a deep breath as she flipped through the pages of the rest of the book. "Each chapter is an account of Gloric's mercy throughout the Eons."

"It's going to take us all night to read that," James said.

"No, it's going to take *me* all night to read."

"You mean you don't want us to help you?" Fletcher asked.

"The most you can do is sit there and listen."

"We can always alternate," Greg suggested.

Alexis shook her head. "No, I need you all to get rest and keep watch over the camp while I focus on this. I'll let you know what I find, and we can discuss from there."

"Are you sure?" James asked.

"I'm sure."

"Alexis, you don't have to—"

"I said I'm sure, James!"

James winced as everyone else merely shuffled in their spots and rubbed their eyes, stifling yawns.

"All of you go to sleep. We awake at first light."

Alexis stood up and went inside the Cougar, closing the door behind her. Greg extinguished the fire while Reggy grabbed some sleeping bags.

"Don't take it too personally, James," Reggy said. "Alexis doesn't like it when we question her decisions."

"*Really?*" James replied. "I would've never known that after all the time we have spent together."

"She's definitely a feisty one, that's for sure," Fletcher commented.

"The most we can do is be supportive of 'er," Greg piped up. "If she wants our help, she'll ask."

"You raise a valid point," James replied.

"Please recite your seven-digit identification number," Harper suddenly said.

"Huh, almost forgot about you."

"I bet she's trying to say the same thing, how we just need to be supportive," Greg said.

"*I* bet that she's saying she's going to annihilate all of us, *in code,*" Reggy responded.

"I think she's calling you stupid," Fletcher added.

James shrugged. *I bet none of this is real.*

Chapter Nineteen

The Fetch You Say to Me?

AFTER JAMES DRAPED THE CLOAK over Harper, he adjusted the mask slightly to hide any metal that may be revealed. "There you go," James said. "As human as the rest of us."

"Please recite your seven-digit identification number," she stated once more.

James chuckled. "Glad you like it."

Alexis groggily exited her mobile home, her eyes decorated with dark circles.

"You look awful," Reggy said when he got sight of her.

Alexis scoffed. "Thanks." She handed *The Celestial Chronology* back to Greg.

"Any luck findin' any leads?" he asked as he took the book.

"No," Alexis wearily said. "I was up all night trying to interpret this thing, and I've read a lot of difficult books in my life, but never have I come across anything so vague and confusing."

"Maybe if we all put our heads together, we can solve what it means," Fletcher observed as he put his bow across his back.

"Good luck. That thing makes about as much sense as… well, Harper."

"If we're going by that logic, then you just need the right person to understand."

"Exactly." Alexis yawned. "Anyway, we might as well move closer to the next town before—"

Interrupting Alexis was a sharp noise, cutting through the wind. As the party turned around to see what it was, they saw that an arrow on fire had landed on the Cougar.

"What?" Alexis exclaimed as she went to put it out.

"Alexis, no!" Reggy shouted.

She stopped as more arrows pounded into the Cougar. Greg quickly pushed her aside and waved his hand over the Cougar. The arrows were still piercing the side of it, but the fire was still out. It didn't stop the Cougar from panicking as it trumpeted loudly and sped off into the forest.

"Well, isn't that a nice, little party trick," a pleasant-sounding voice said.

The party turned around to see, with a smug smile spread across his face and a vindictive look as intense as the fire, a pompous, ostentatious man proudly displaying a purple and gold tie.

"Did you do this?" Alexis moved a few paces towards him.

"Oh, goodness, no. I have people that do that for me," he replied as he gestured all around the party.

They looked into the forest around them, noticing several soldiers and archers wearing a black uniform with a lion emblem over their hearts. They didn't look normal, though, as James observed. They were rather sickly, with a few limbs and, well, noses missing here and there. Some of them had cloudy eyes and confused expressions, as if they weren't entirely all there. They knew that they were face to face with some sort of enemy, though, and that there was some sort of cause to be fought.

Those must be more Chimeras... James realized as he felt pity for these poor fools.

"Who the hell do you think you are, attacking my home like this?" Alexis shouted, with her accent beginning to shine through.

"I am Minster of the Far West," the man said while checking his fingernails for dirt. "You might know me, you might not, but I regret to inform you that you stand—" he looked back up "—face to face with the Hand of Commerce. I'm here on behalf of my god, and you have something of his."

"I don't care about who you are! You impaled my house and chased it away!"

"You mean that pile of scrap metal is your house? I knew the common folk didn't have it as well but that doesn't give you an excuse to live in a trash heap."

Alexis growled.

"Anyway, I'm not one to converse with people of your… persuasion. So, I'll cut to the chase. *You* have something that I desperately need."

"I have no idea what you're talking about!"

"None at all? I mean, I've heard many rumors about a Theoremist and her lackeys frolicking about with the company of an automaton. You're telling me that isn't you?" Minster stared at every party member. "I'll bet it's that one with the cloak and the mask."

Alexis glared at James as Minster pointed at the disguised Harper.

"Please recite you seven-digit—"

"Shh!" James quickly shushed her. "Mute! Mute!" he frantically whispered.

"As I thought."

Minster snapped his fingers and the archers all aimed at the rest of the party. Fletcher readied his bow and Greg gripped onto his sword, but they were horribly outnumbered. Feeling desperate, James suddenly had a sly, but impossible idea. He just needed some sort of distraction to keep Minster from noticing.

"YOU FETCH!"

The entire guard gasped as Minster appeared to be having some sort of out of body experience from being so confounded from this second-rate bottom feeder's audacity

... *That works,* James thought.

Minster gripped his chest. "Excuse me," he said, his voice as light as his head, "I do *not* go out and handle *feces* like I'm some sort of animal servant… How dare you accuse me of being so filthy and primitive?"

Alexis furrowed her brow. "What? No… fetch is just a word that means—"

"I know what fetch means!" Minster snapped. "And you stand here in your dirty clothes and nappy hair and accuse me, *me,* of all people that I practically roll around in disgusting, putrid matter like I'm some sort of swine?"

James slowly approached Greg. "… Psst."

He looked down at him.

"Hand me your bag," James whispered.

Greg nodded, and stealthily handed James his satchel.

"At least I go out and work for my treasures!" Alexis retorted. "I don't stand there like some prissy princess expecting low-lives to do my dirty work!"

"… How dare you?" Minster said, looking even more offended.

"How dare *I?* How dare *you*?"

"No! How dare you just go and assume my royal disposition like that?" he exclaimed.

"… What?" Alexis shouted in a baffled tone

"I am not a *princess*! I am a duke! Or, maybe a prince, I think. At least, I was before that empire died out, but, that's not the point!"

Alexis threw her hands up. "It's a figure of speech!"

"Well it's a very insensitive figure of speech!"

James sneakily bent down and began putting rocks into the satchel as the two continued arguing.

"I'm going to kill you!" Alexis exclaimed as she whipped out her swords.

"Go ahead and try, I'll bet—"

Before Minster could finish, she whipped her swords towards him. Minster quickly hopped out of the way and the swords attacked one of the Chimeras instead. Before it could react, the snakes bit at its throat, instantly killing it.

Minster let out a small scream. "How dare you kill my favorite soldier! He was the smartest one here!"

"If he was your favorite, then what was his name?"

"I-It doesn't matter! The point is that you are being very rude!"

Alexis scoffed. "I'm being rude? *I'm* being rude? You're the one that—"

"Look, just stop!" James shouted as he got between the two. He turned to Minster. "I know where the gauntlets are. The robot doesn't have them."

Minster raised an eyebrow. "Excuse me?"

"Yes… the truth is the robot malfunctioned a while ago and left the gauntlets to us to keep them safe, but everything has been a hassle ever since they came into our lives! She didn't even explain to us what they were for, but it's clear that they belong with you, and not us."

James handed the satchel over to Minster.

The rest of the party exchanged confused glances. Alexis opened her mouth to argue but stayed silent.

"Well, then," Minster began, "it's nice to see that *somebody* has come to their senses, but do you honestly expect me to believe you? How do I know you're not lying?"

James felt a pit in his stomach, but decided to bluff, nonetheless. "I mean, you can always open the bag—"

"Don't tell me what to do! You are *not* my supervisor" Minster exclaimed before tossing the bag over his shoulder and whipping his ponytail as he spun on his heels to leave with his infantry.

As he watched the group walk away, James took in a deep breath. *I cannot believe that worked,* he thought.

"What's going on here, James?" Alexis asked. "What was he saying about 'gauntlets?' We don't have any gauntlets?"

"We don't, but *she* does," James said as he pointed to Harper. "I'll explain later, seeing that we have a rogue wagon we need to catch—?"

"THE COUGAR!" Alexis exclaimed before running off in one direction.

The rest of the group let out a heavy sigh (except for Harper, who asked for the identification number once more) as they followed behind her.

~

Blendell was one of the only towns that the Dwarves would travel to for business. It blended in with the mountains nicely, there was a blend of all sorts of people, and a blend of items to be bought and sold. Unfortunately, the Dwarves didn't like people anymore, so…

The only thing different was that there weren't any Dwarves.

So, just as anyone would be surprised about seeing something like a Dwarf, the party assumed that seeing a self-driving wagon on a rampage would be pretty noticeable, and something that isn't blendable.

"Excuse me? Have you seen a self-driving wagon around here?" Alexis asked several citizens of the next town as the group passed through. Everybody either dismissed her or gave her half-hearted head shakes as she asked.

Greg put a hand on her shoulder. "Let me try," he said before approaching an enclosure of sheep.

"No fetching way," Reggy began. "There's no way he's going to try and talk to sheep!"

"I mean, it isn't goat, but I could probably roughly translate." Greg crouched down to eye level with one of the sheep.

"Yeah, I'll believe it when I see it buddy—"

Before Reggy could finish, Greg suddenly bleated at the sheep, and the sheep bleated back. Reggy stood dumbfounded as he watched a mountainous man bleat back and forth with the animal, and how their body language changed as well, proving the conversation was legit.

James nudged his side, "I thought I was supposed to be the non-believer?"

"Shut up!" Reggy whined as he folded his arms and moved away from James.

Greg sighed, pat the sheep on the head, and stood up.

"Well," Alexis anxiously began, "what did he say?"

"It hasn't seen it. I'm sorry, lass."

She discouragingly hung her head.

"Look," Fletcher began, "we've been searching for about an hour, not to mention we haven't eaten yet this morning. Let's take a fifteen-minute break and return to our search. It couldn't have gotten far."

Alexis reluctantly submitted, and the party walked into a nearby restaurant. As they ordered beverages and snacked on some peanuts, Alexis could barely stay awake as she sat at the bar table, rummaging through *The Celestial Chronology*. "I found a few things, as to why Gloric hasn't handled the problem."

"The… 'problem?'" James took a sip of sparkling lemon water.

"The Cirlock followers, you dummy!" she said as she took a shot of whiskey. "It says here that Gloric swore he'd never set foot into Mahara again, as to give Cirlock and his people some space or something along those lines."

"So, what would be the point of finding Gloric if he isn't going to do anything?"

"We can at least give him Harper and the gauntlets. He'll keep them safe."

"Please recite your seven digit identification number," Harper said, as she was seated next to Alexis.

"If you don't mind," Greg piped up, "we have had some teachings passed down with our copies of *The Celestial Chronology*. I might be able to interpret a passage or two—"

A man suddenly entered the bar. Granted, lot of people were traveling in and out of the bar, but this person in particular drew a lot of attention to himself. He was dressed like a traditional Brammish, as he wore pelts and leather clothing, but the rest of his appearance showed a stark difference. Unlike having fair skin and rich, red hair, the man's skin was like that of a deep bronze, decorated with tattoos that flowed like liquid metal, and was the color of raw ore. His black hair rested smoothly on his person and had various braids with scraps of metal woven into them.

Greg squinted at this stranger. "Strange…" he muttered.

"What's strange? It's just some guy," James replied.

"I just don't understand why he would dress like a Bram." Greg's expression grew darker. "He is no Bram."

"… Maybe he's from a different tribe?"

"Maybe, but he isn't from the North." Greg maintained his gravity.

"… Are all Brams from the North?"

"… No, they are not," Greg replied, his expression taking a complete turn as his levity returned to him. "You bring up a good point there, lad."

"*Right.* Anyway, you think you can interpret a passage or two?" James directed at Alexis.

Alexis didn't reply. She stared wondrously at the stranger, like many other women in the bar, also allowing her jaw to drop and her eyes wander at the defined muscles on his exposed chest.

"Are you listening?" James asked as he shook her slightly.

Alexis took in a quick breath and shook her head. "What?"

"You said you can interpret a passage," James replied a bit harshly, unable to hide his jealousy.

"Oh, right. Sorry." She cleared her throat. "Anyway, I might be able to interpret a passage, or maybe a few, it would just require—"

Fletcher suddenly forced Reggy down into a chair at the bar table. Alexis huffed as she was interrupted once again.

"Quit asking the bartender for gasoline! We're going to get kicked out of here if you keep doing that!" Fletcher shouted.

"You wouldn't be fighting me if you knew how delicious it was, Fletcher!" Reggy replied, struggling to stand.

The two quarreled one another for a moment and stopped when a waiter came by and set down a couple of baskets of chips, salsa, chicken wings, and fried pickles.

"Hey, we didn't order these!" Fletcher shouted as the waiter was walking away.

"Oh, um, the guy at the bar ordered these for you. He said that he would take care of the tab…"

"I couldn't help to overhear, but it seems like you are unsure on how to… continue your journey, so to speak," the man at the bar said, his voice as solid as a hammer to an anvil.

"We're trying to find Gloric," Alexis responded.

"Seriously? You're going to tell a stranger about our motives?" James questioned.

"It's not like we're making any progress, James! Besides, I'm a bit desperate at this point! Thank you for your kindness, sir, but do you know of how we can get to Heaven? This book isn't being very clear on how to get there."

"Sometimes it's better to be lost than to be ill-advised," the man said as the clinking sound of gold filn vibrated against the wooden bar.

"What the hell is that supposed to mean?" James asked.

"It's exactly what I mean, Mr. Clemit. It's literally better to be lost than ill-advised. Maybe you all should quit asking questions, and just try."

The man wasn't harsh when he spoke, but quick to get to the point. He stood at the doorframe before pointing outside. "Does that wagon belong to you?"

The party watched the Cougar through the window as it dashed by. Alexis jumped to her feet, sprinted past the man, and after the Cougar. The rest of the party followed her, barely able to keep up and calling after her until they entered a forest. As they emerged through the trees, they suddenly found themselves in a wheat field, surrounded by sheep. Alexis immediately ran to the Cougar, which was driving in circles in the middle of the field and attempted to soothe it.

A couple of collies and other sheepdogs attempted to herd the sheep, which were running frantically at the spontaneous arrival of the party and the Cougar. Other dogs made their way to the party, almost welcoming them to their domain, beaming in the bright orange sky.

James looked to his right to see a shepherd sitting on a stool. "Isn't it such a beautiful day?" he asked while waving, seemingly calm at the arrival of the party.

"...This isn't real," James muttered.

Reggy placed a hand on James' shoulder. "I never thought I'd get to Heaven by following a mammoth."

James nodded. "Same."

CHAPTER TWENTY

UPON HEAVEN'S GATES

THE PARTY FOUND THEMSELVES ACQUAINTED with a black and white collie, that seemingly insisted that they followed it. As they ventured through the outskirts of Heaven, they followed the collie through fields of wheat and some sort of village made for the shepherds and their small families, where houses and places of business were white, and rooftops were a crimson red.

As they neared the heart of Heaven, buildings evolved into skyscrapers that towered over the citizens like dandelions to ants. Unlike the rest of Tor, these skyscrapers showed no hint of exclusion, but invited every walk of life to enter and exit however they pleased. The party passed a few parks with children congregating on playground equipment and came across vendors with samples of food that appeared either home-cooked or fresh from a microwave oven.

While the party excitedly sampled food and interacted with the villagers, James didn't quite know what to think of all this. He simply couldn't bring himself to be wide-eyed and fascinated like his companions, but slowly grew more and more paranoid as he held a croquette in one hand and a mini hot dog wrapped in a bagel in the other.

"Isn't this place amazing, James?" Alexis excitedly hopped to his side. "I never would've imagined Heaven to be like this! People always said it was paved with gold and had castles around every corner, but it's really its own utopian city! It has its own culture and everything!"

James nodded. "Yeah… it's pretty great."

Alexis shrugged at James' monotonous response and skipped away. The collie whined at the party, seemingly wanting to move forward rather than explore the bustling city.

After getting through the city, the group traveled through Heaven's Botanical Gardens, which was about a mile in between the city and the Brother's Palace. They found themselves fretting over every flora and fauna, while the collie continued to bark and give them annoyed looks as he continuously insisted that they followed.

James complied with the collie more and more as they continued through Heaven, feeling rather irate and disinterested at everything around him.

"Come on, James!" Reggy crouched near a rose bush. "Smell the roses!"

"I'm not smelling the roses, Reggy."

Reggy gave James a sad face. "But… he'll be offended."

"Who will be offended?"

"Gloric."

James scoffed. "So will my allergies. I think I'll take their side for once."

"What's with you today?" Reggy asked while standing up.

"Just… couldn't sleep, or whatever, okay?"

"Whatever, man. Just *try* to behave in front of our god okay?"

"I'll behave when you behave."

Reggy moaned. "But I'm naturally a troublemaker!"

“That’s not my problem,” James smirked as he walked ahead.

The collie brought the party in front of a large gate and a guard house. The guard outside was working on a crossword puzzle, humming along to the radio playing some aggressive ukulele music.[15] The collie gave the party a nod, and then walked away, leaving them alone with the guard.

Alexis approached the guard. “Uh… excuse me?”

The man started singing to the radio.

“… Excuse me?” Alexis raised her voice.

The man’s singing also grew louder, and a bit more passionate.

“Excuse me?”

The man belted out a high note.

“HEY!” Alexis shouted while flicking his hat.

Startled, the man looked up, then turned down the radio. “Oh, hey! Sorry, I didn’t see you there. How can I help you?”

“We want an audience with Gloric,” Alexis said at a softer volume, but still sounded annoyed. “And it’s an emergency, so if you say we have to wait three to five months to see him-”

“Nah, you can go in and see him,” the guard said.

Alexis blinked. “Oh…that easily?”

“Yeah.” The guard nodded. “Let me just finish this one word. I’ve been stuck on it for a while. Hey, maybe you can help me?”

“Uh—”

“Cool,” the guard held up the crossword book to his face, “what… is a… five letter word f-for… angry and sad?” The guard then set the book down and laughed. “Duh! I’m so stupid!” He began penciling in the answer. “Smad…”

“What? That isn’t a word!”

“You’re right… that’s not it.”

“Try two D’s!” Reggy piped up.

---

[15] Twelve Aviators, a popular band in the current Eon, not only use ukulele’s as instruments, but as weapons to practice their right to bear arms against Crusaders outside the city.

The guard pointed at Reggy then wrote in the extra letter. "Thanks, man!"

James gave Reggy a dirty look.

"What? I'm still learning my letters."

Alexis sighed. "Whatever, can we just see Gloric now?"

The guard groaned loudly. "Yes, yes. Just give me a minute. You know, Gloric doesn't like impatient people."

"Well, it's kind of an emergency."

The guard sighed and slowly stood up. He reached his arms towards the sky and stretched before giving his back a nice pop. He scratched his head as he sluggishly went inside of the guard house.

Alexis bit her lip and tapped her foot as her irritation flowed from her like a flamethrower. Once the guard was inside, he pressed a single, giant red button. The gates then swung open, quite rapidly.

"Oof, that's too fast," the guard said. "I need to make a note to slow that down."

Behind the gates stood a white fixture extending into the clouds. It didn't look constructed by the hands of laborers, but as if someone commanded the bones of the earth to come forth and stand tall, used words to define the crevice of each detail instead of a single chisel, and called upon the waters to bend the light of day with more colors and divination than a stain glass window ever could.

"The Brother's Palace," Alexis muttered as her demeanor calmed. "I never thought I'd actually see it."

James shook his head. He didn't want awe and wishful thinking to blind him as it did to his companions. "The Brother's Palace" seemed to defy the limitations dictating this world. It was too perfect to actually be real, so James was convinced that their minds were being toyed with.

It was just another image to mislead their ambitions.

“Hey, man, you okay there?” the guard asked, suddenly appearing at James’ side, and a bit too close at that.

James jumped. “Mother of Gloric!”

“… That’s not a very nice thing to say. You shouldn’t bring her into this.”

“You shouldn’t scare people like that!”

“Oh.” The guard looked down at the ground. “You’re right. Sorry, I was hiding.”

James shuddered and quickly walked forward to catch up with everyone else, leaving the guard behind. The party congregated in front of the entrance to the Brother’s Palace. A bit uncertain, Alexis pulled on the door handles, revealing a throne room inside.

The room seemed big enough for three thrones, but only one could be seen. The throne was white and immaculate, with lambs carved into the arm rests, and to their surprise, a certain white sheepdog that had been following them around lying in the throne, fast asleep.

“…Is that—?” Alexis began, but was interrupted by a loud, crunching noise.

The party jumped as the guard from earlier appeared on their right, cradling a bag of tortilla chips and holding a plastic, disposable bowl full of salsa. He was no longer in his guard uniform, but wearing a t-shirt, jeans, and leather loafers. “… Hey guys,” he said while reaching into the bag for another chip.

Alexis gave him a dirty look. “… Excuse me?”

The guard looked up at her as he took a bite of the chip, getting crumbs all over the ground.

“Do you not understand that you abide in the throne room of Gloric?”

The guard narrowed his eyes. “I do.”

“Then, you should be a bit less disrespectful.”

“How am I being disrespectful?”

Alexis raised her eyebrows. "You're getting food *everywhere!"*

The guard looked down and gasped. "Oh, right! I keep forgetting that I need to look presentable!" He swiped the crumbs on his shirt onto the ground.

Alexis huffed and returned her attention to the dog in the throne, still perplexed.

"Wait a minute… is that Gloric?" James pointed at the dog.

The guard burst into laughter. "No, that's not Gloric! That's a dog! You're silly! You're the funny one in this group, aren't you?"

"Funny looking," Fletcher remarked.

The guard continued laughing as James glared at Fletcher.

"Nah, seriously guys, that isn't Gloric. Gloric isn't a dog." The guard kept chuckling at the comment as he scooped up salsa with the chip.

"Then where is he?" James asked, frustrated. "We came all this way to see him, and the throne is empty?"

"I'm a bit confused by that, too," Fletcher agreed.

The guard looked up and squinted his eyes as he stared at the throne. "Maybe it's… symbolic. Maybe there is no Gloric, but the dog on the throne represents people's false idealizations that there has to be a god out there, because they made this throne for him, but instead it is filled with lies. Lies! Falsehoods! Blasphemy!" The guard squeezed the bag, a few chips flying out from the momentum.

"… Are you saying Gloric isn't real?" Alexis asked, terrified of an answer.

"Of course, he isn't!" James snapped. "We came all this way for nothing. I swear everything I do is just a never-ending nightmare!"

"No, Gloric's real," the guard confirmed.

"… Then why did you just say that he isn't?"

The guard shrugged. "I just… really hate that throne."

"… What?"

"Yeah, I mean, look at it. It's ugly and uncomfortable! I liked it better when it was just a card table with three, fold-out chairs. Then, my brothers *had* to upgrade to thrones, and they had like seat heaters and cup holders, but when I wanted those awesome contraptions as well, the contractor was like, 'No, no, no! Gloric is the one that everyone looks up to, so his throne needs to be more serious!

"And they didn't stop him. I'll admit, it happened thousands of years ago, but I'm still hurt by it. Still hurt…" He handed the chips and salsa to Reggy and then crouched down. "Come here, Moo-Moo! Come to Daddy!"

The dog snapped awake. It barked excitedly, jumped off of the throne, and barreled towards the guard. He giggled like a small child as the dog tackled into him and licked his face. "Who's my good Moo-Moo? I love you, too! Yes, I do!"

As the guard baby-talked the dog, Alexis' eyes lit up. "It's you…*You're* Gloric!" She smiled widely and laughed a bit. "It's really, really you!"

"Are you sure it isn't a guy named after Gloric?" James retorted.

"No, I'm named after another guy," Gloric piped up.

James rolled his eyes and shook his head.

"… You named your dog Moo-Moo?" Fletcher asked.

Gloric nodded as he scratched Moo-Moo's belly. "Yes."

"Why?"

"Look at these eyes!" Gloric cupped Moo-Moo's face in his hands and turned him towards Fletcher. "Aren't these the cutest, biggest brown eyes you've ever seen? You know what else has eyes like these? Cows! Moo-Moo is the most appropriate name for this dog, and don't tell me otherwise!"

Fletcher stared awkwardly at the dog's eyes, almost as if Moo-Moo was staring into his soul, and that had never happened to the

Ice Archer before and wasn't quite sure how to handle it. "I can at least give you that…"

"Mm! Is this habanero?" Reggy suddenly exclaimed.

"It's good isn't it?"

"Mmhmm!" Reggy nodded as he went for more.

"… Can I have some of that?" Greg asked.

"Go ahead, fam."

As Greg took a bite, his eyes lit up. "Milk my neighbor's goat! This is delicious!"

"How'd you get habanero?" Reggy asked.

"He's a god, Reggy," Fletcher began, "I'm sure he can manifest peppers out of—"

"Oh, I stole it out of somebody's garden."

The entire party paused, giving Gloric a surprised look.

"No, no, it's okay! They're a bit of a tool so it's fine…totally fine…" Gloric folded his arms and laughed to himself. "Not like Vrec is around to maintain the garden anymore."

"Sir," Alexis started, "as much… fun as we all are having, we really need to talk to you about something."

"Is it my brother?"

"So, you already know?"

"I've known for a while. I just didn't think anyone would find the gauntlets. Then again, never underestimate an O'Leary. They're too smart for their own good."

"Actually, James found them."

Gloric raised his eyebrows. "Really? I wouldn't expect that from you, James."

"… Is there something wrong with me?" James asked.

"Oh, no, it's just that everyone has their own job, you know? Like, Alexis is a Theoremist, Reggy is a Hunter, Harper's… something, you're a Messenger, Fletcher is an…"

The entire room grew completely silent as the party deadpanned towards James.

"... What?" Gloric asked.

"Please recite your seven digit identification number," Harper said.

"You're a Messenger?" Alexis asked James through gritted teeth.

"Oh, were they not supposed to know that?"

"No... no, they were not," James replied. "Thank you, Gloric."

"Whoops. Oh well, it's fine—"

Alexis stormed out of the Brother's Palace, and James frantically chased after her until he could grab her shoulder.

"You lied to me!" she snapped as she abruptly turned to face him.

"I-I didn't want my past to keep me from working for you—"

"Oh, you didn't? Well, it's a damn good thing you kept it from me since it's working out *so* well right now!"

James winced.

She got closer to his face. "You are a stupid, worthless pile of fetch-work. You should be—"

"Are you seriously doing this?" Gloric interrupted.

She faltered backwards. "Excuse me?"

"I'm asking if you're seriously chewing out James for being a Messenger and causing a stereotypical scene, where our two beloved heroes get into a 'schism' over something that could be easily resolved through communicating?"

She pointed at James. "Do you know what the Bureau *did* to my family?"

"Yes. Does James know that you *also* worked for them for a while?"

She blinked and stammered. "I had my reasons."

"And you don't think James also had his reasons?"

She bit her lip and angrily stared at the ground.

"You two can hash it out later, but for now, James, apologize for lying."

"… I'm sorry for lying," James said.

"Good. Alexis, apologize for being a meanie."

She looked up, maintaining her angry gaze. "Sorry."

"Good. Can we go back inside?"

Alexis shrugged. "I just got told to 'shut-up' by my god. I need a minute."

"I didn't tell you to 'shut-up.' James, did I tell her to shut up?"

"You basically did—"

"Look, if I wanted Alexis to shut-up, I would've told her to shut-up."

"But—"

"Alexis, shut-up. *I'm* the smartest person here right now. I've gone to *several* universities and dropped out of every single one of them! I know what 'shut-up' means. Now, can we *please* go back inside?"

James and Alexis reluctantly nodded.

"Good."

They followed Gloric back inside the Brother's Palace.

"So, Mom and Dad *aren't* getting a divorce," Fletcher said as he, Greg, and Reggy stood up from sitting on the ground.

"Please recite your seven-digit identification number," Harper said, still standing in the same spot.

Gloric laughed as he approached the throne. "Nope, no divorce today." He hopped into his throne, allowing his legs to hang over the side, and let out a pained breath as Moo-Moo jumped into his lap. "So, what do you want?" he asked in a strained voice.

"…What?"

"…What do you want? Like, in general, what do all of you want?"

"I wish I were dead," Fletcher said with a hint of sarcasm.

"Okay."

Everyone grew quiet with startled expressions as they stared at Fletcher.

"… Give it a few years," Gloric finally said.

Fletcher huffed. "I thought you were all powerful?"

"I'm not omnipotent, just nosey." He gestured towards Alexis. "And, what do you want?"

"Um," Alexis pulled her tools from her belt, "will you bless these for me?"

"Done!" Gloric outstretched his hand, and then moaned out of complaint and perplexity that he couldn't reach her tools from ten feet away. "… Help me out here, sweetheart?"

"O-Oh, yes! O-Of course!"

She quickly approached his side and unraveled her tools. He gently gave one of the tools a poke and an aura radiated around every single one of them. "…Thank you," Alexis bowed and returned to where she was standing.

"Reggy!"

"Wha?" Reggy replied, his mouth full

"What do you want?"

"Uh…" Reggy got a panicked look as he gazed between the salsa and his pocket.

"…There's always enough salsa to go around, Reginald."

"Then, I want a new recorder!"

"Done!"

Reggy then reached into his pocket and pulled out a brand new, white recorder.

"It's indestructible, so, it won't break if you sit on it."

"What if I stab someone with it?"

"Oh, well, in that case, it still won't break."

"Yes!" Reggy put the recorder back, returning his attention to the chips.

Gloric turned to Greg. "And, what do you want?"

"Erm…" Greg smiled somberly. "I lost a picture of my family when Frakku attacked my village…"

"Say no more."

Then, a white picture frame encasing a beautiful family manifested in Greg's hand. Standing on Greg's left in the picture was a lovely, red-haired woman, and in his arms, a sweet, little girl. Tears formed in Greg's eyes as he held the picture close to his heart. "Thank you..."

Gloric clicked his tongue and pointed to Greg, as if he wasn't sure how to handle someone of the emotional persuasion.

"Please recite your seven-digit identification number."

"Oh, right. I forgot about you," Gloric said as he struggled to pull something out of his back pocket. "Let's see here..." He managed to pull a cell phone that flips open out of his pocket. "Ugh... Is it... no, that's too long..." He snapped his fingers. "One, two, three, four, five, six, seven!"

"Seven-digit number recognized, restoring settings."

Harper seemingly snapped awake and smiled widely at the sight of Gloric. "Hello, Master 3.4!" she exclaimed as she went in for a hug.

"No, no" —Gloric smiled and cowered slightly— "you stay over there with your friends, okay?"

"Okay!" She nodded and stood still

"You're telling me you tried all of those different number combinations and counting to seven never occurred to you?" James directed at Greg and Reggy.

"I thought Gloric would be smarter than that," Reggy replied.

"Things don't always have to be so complicated," Gloric piped up. "Don't look into things that aren't there. Not everything is a subtle context clue, I mean, look at that plunger." He gestured towards a toilet plunger in the corner of the room. "That plunger has no significance nor importance whatsoever. It's just there and will stay there for the sake of decoration. That's all. Anyway, James?

"...What?" James asked, as if he had spaced out there for a moment.

"What do you want?"

"Um..." James bit his lip and took a deep breath. "I just... want to know if all of this is real or not."

Gloric blinked. "Yeah...no."

James furrowed his brow. "What?"

"I'm not going to do that for you."

"Why not?"

"First of all, that's a stupid request. You can have *anything* you want, and you want something you already have? It's a bit bogus. Second of all... I just don't want to."

James gaped at Gloric as he picked up Moo-Moo and stood from his throne. "Now, all you guys need to do is hold up your end of the deal."

"What deal?" Alexis put her tools back onto her belt.

Gloric sighed. "You know? The deal? You have Frakku and Chimeras on your butt, right?"

"Yes."

"And you took the gauntlets, so now my brother is wanting people to take them, so he can break out of prison, right?"

"Is that what's happening?"

"Yes."

"Okay, but—"

"And you read in that stupid book that I can't step foot in Mahara, right?"

Alexis sighed. "Yes."

"Then, there you go. I can't get into Mahara to solve the problem, so I need you guys to get me in."

"With all due respect, sir, how do we even do that?"

"Oh, it isn't hard. You just have to open the gate."

"With what?"

"With the gauntlets, of course."

Alexis shrugged. "That doesn't seem too hard."

"Oh, but don't put them on. They break everything they touch."

"So... how do we open the gate if we can't wear the gauntlets?"

"You're smart, you'll figure it out."

"Why can't you just come with us?" James skeptically asked.

"*Because,* James, I *can't* open the gate. Mahara is designed to keep gods out so that Cirlog can stay in. Only a mortal can open the gates, and that's that. Come on, guys, you got this far, you can... get farther, I guess."

The party shrugged. "... We'll do our best," Alexis said.

"Cool." Gloric set Moo-Moo down then swung his hands from his back to his front, clapping them together. "So... yeah. You take care of that, and I'll see you again tomorrow. I'd offer you a place to stay but even I'm off limits to like, half of these rooms so if there's a guest room I wouldn't know about it."

"How are you off limits to rooms in your own palace?" Fletcher asked.

"It's not that I'm off limits, it's just, you know, when you have weird brothers, you're afraid to see what they might've kept in their rooms."

The party grew a bit quiet, equally afraid of what two calamity gods might keep in their rooms.

"Anyway, the park benches here are pretty nice. It's like sleeping on a regular bed."

"Why are they like that?" Alexis pulled out her notebook.

"In case I get sleepy when I walk my dog."

Alexis nodded, taking notes about the park benches.

"So, feel free to camp out in a park. The homeowner's association might get angry, but... whatever. Fetch them."

"What if we get in trouble?" Fletcher asked.

"What are they gonna do? Each of you on your own are like a one-man army."

The party nodded as they considered Gloric's comment.

"… I have things I need to do, so, I *really* need you guys to leave. Mahara is, like, right between the mountain range near here, so, just go there."

"Wait—" James began.

"'Kay, bye!" Gloric quickly wandered off into a hallway with Moo-Moo.

"Oh no, you don't," James muttered as he chased after him.

"James, where you goin', bud?" Reggy asked.

"Just go ahead, I'll catch up with you guys later!"

Before they could make any arguments, James ran into the hallway after the so-called "God of Peace."

Chapter Twenty-One

A Non-Believer's Covenant

JAMES FOUND GLORIC STANDING OUTSIDE of a door and looking at keys in his hands, with Moo-Moo sitting patiently at his feet.

"Hey!" James shouted as he caught up with him.

Gloric let out a scream and held his arms up in defense, while Moo-Moo let out excited barks.

"…What are you doing?"

"You're in my bubble!" Gloric said, giving James a slight glare.

"Whatever! Why wouldn't you grant my wish back there? You granted everyone else's!"

"Because," Gloric put his arms down, "it wasn't a very good wish. Now, you made me lose track, so I have to start all over again with these fetching keys."

"… Why do you need keys? Can't you just, I dunno, teleport wherever you want to?"

"If you can teleport everywhere, then what's the point of walls, James?" Gloric asked, sounding quite matter-of-factly.

"Um… I don't know—"

"Exactly—oh right—I marked these."

Gloric held up a key that was painted in a pink nail polish and unlocked the door. On the other side, what James assumed, was an office.

A horribly, horribly cluttered office.

Papers were scattered all over the floor, in addition to being taped *and* pasted to the walls. Even the desk was cluttered with pencils, rubber band balls, and crumpled papers, except for one spot was untouched. Gloric walked inside the office, not really caring about stepping on the papers. Even Moo-Moo carelessly walked on them, getting dirty pawprints on them as he made his way to the dog bed underneath the desk. Then again, that was sort of expected of a dog. James, on the other hand, at least *tried* to be a bit more careful. "Geez, why is your office such a mess?" he asked.

"I wanted to make it look like an office."

"It'd look like an office if you just had a desk, a paperclip, and a piece of paper!"

"That's what my brother said, James, and look where he is!"

"… Trapped in a pit?"

"No, locked up in my basement."

"… What?"

"What?"

"Did you just say you keep your brother in your basement?" James exclaimed

"Who said that?"

"You! You just said that!"

"I just said what?"

"Gloric!"

"What?" Gloric held up his hands in defense.

James groaned in frustration. "Never mind!"

Gloric shrugged as he approached the clear spot on his desk. He reached into his pocket and pulled out a small journal and set it down. Upon reaching the desk, it grew larger.

"So, why did you think my wish was stupid?"

Gloric smiled. "James, buddy, pal, chum, uh, sonny boy? Kid?"

"What?"

"You already know that everything is real! Your friend Reggy seems pretty real, right?"

James shrugged. "I mean, kind of."

"Then isn't that all you need?"

"Well—"

"Oh, *I* get it." Gloric, being about an inch shorter, put an arm around James. "You want it written out in the stars, handed to you on a golden slip of paper, kept in a little sandwich baggie so you can carry it with you wherever you go."

"Maybe not to that extent, but-"

"Just keep your eyes open, man!" Gloric reached out in front of him and gestured to his office. "All of this is right here in front of you! You just have to believe that it is!"

James moved Gloric's arm away. "How do I know that you're real then?"

"You don't know, James. You don't know if I'm your conscience, if I'm just telling you this to make you feel better, or that I genuinely mean all of this and am telling you that this is *all* real! But, you know, who's a god to a non-believer, anyway?"

James' stomach dropped. "L-Look, I guess, I don't know, where have you been?"

"Where have I been?"

"Yeah, there's a terrible Bureau out there, ruining lives. People are losing their loved ones every day! Where have you been for *me*? I was only five years old when I lost my mom and dad and I *walked* to the *Far North* with no help from anybody! I felt like I didn't belong and so I became a homeless 'drunk!' Then, when I felt like I hit a dead end, I basically took a suicide pact, and even then, I still lived just to wake up to my sad, pointless life! I prayed and prayed to the great God of Peace and he wasn't there for me…"

Gloric took a deep breath, then approached a picture on a wall. "What do you see in this picture, James?"

James sighed. "A… house?"

Gloric nodded. "I see a home. There's a family inside that home, James. Probably a dysfunctional one, but still a happy one."

"Quit dodging the question."

"You see, James, that's where you stall. You see things so cut and dry, when really, it's all part of something more. A bigger picture, so to speak. You say that I wasn't there for you, well, who's to say that I didn't lead you to everywhere you've been, just so you can stand where you are now?"

"How have you 'led' me here?!"

"You all got lost following the Cougar, didn't you?"

... *Ohhh,* James thought to himself, *That's what that guy at the bar meant.*

Yeah, stupid, Krag thought back.

You mean you knew how to get to—of course you knew how to get to Heaven. You're just too lazy to say it!

You're too lazy to listen, so… shut up.

"I wouldn't have let you come here if I didn't want you here."

James scoffed. "Yeah, and you want me here, so you can use me? I feel really special now."

"No, because I see a lot of greatness in you, and you're a cool guy. I kind of want to be there when I watch you flip off the bad in this world."

James folded his arms and stared at the ground.

"Look, I'm sorry about your parents, but other people *chose* to inflict that upon you. You had a good home in the Far North, but you *chose* to leave it. I send you my sheep to tell you it's going to be okay, maybe help you with those weird figments you kept having, but you *chose* to ignore it. By the way, you haven't been having those lately, have you?"

James blinked. "Did you… did you do that?"

"Nah, but you haven't had any alcohol in a while, have you?"

"… No, I haven't."

"So, if anything, you *chose* to hallucinate by *choosing* to drink."

"But I never got drunk!"

"I mean, hallucinating sounds drunk to me."

"But I was like that *before* I started drinking!"

"Okay, so, you honestly thought that your problem made you *immune* to getting drunk? Do you even know what alcohol is, James?"

"Distilled—"

"Liquefied poison bread!"

James paused, a bit surprised at the answer.

"There's a reason why I'm not allowed to drink it."

James groaned, but looked past the trickling brown hair and tomfoolery, and into the god's eyes. What appeared to be an emerald green with just a few freckles of brown hid a picturesque of a ball of fire. James found himself overwhelmed with an old feeling. It wasn't unfamiliar, but old, and something he hadn't felt for a long time, for the God of Peace reflected a warm star of home, burning in the distance of the black in his pupils, welcoming all who came to him with a haven of refuge, where the hatred of the world cannot touch you.

"… This all feels unreal," James said, entranced by the sun in the god's eyes. "Almost like some sort of dream."

"A good one or a bad one?"

"Sometimes bad… sometimes good."

Gloric smiled, the freckles on his cheeks as bright as the ones in his eyes. "I feel that way sometimes, too."

James took a deep breath and broke eye contact. "Fine, you're right. You haven't been 'around' lately because you don't want to force your powers on anyone. You want people to be able to think and act freely, but you intervene when you have to because, in the end, you still have faith in people to do good, it's just a matter of accepting your help."

Gloric sat down in a chair and leaned back. "Do I have any powers? Hmm…"

"… How else did you grant those wishes?"

"Oh! I guess I do have powers!"

James sighed. "I get it, okay, but I still don't know if I *believe in* you, but… I can believe you."

"Meh, that's a start."

James nodded. "I guess you did grant my wish."

Gloric shook his head. "No, I didn't. That wish *sucked!*"

"… Can I have a different one?"

Gloric sighed, scratching his beard. "What do you want?"

James felt a bit silly, but then remembered that Fletcher wanted to die. "Some knitting needles? Maybe a bit of yarn? I'm tired of just using my hands."

"Hold out your hands."

James held his hands out, and a leather hard case appeared in his hands. He opened it up and found two chrome knitting needles resting on velvet.

"Pop by Dante's later, he's got some quality yarn. If you tell him the code word, then he'll give it to you for free."

"What's the code word?"

Gloric moaned. "I don't know, he won't tell me."

"… Oh."

Gloric opened the book on the table and tossed papers aside in search for a pen. "I'll see you tomorrow!"

"Okay, I guess," James muttered.

As James was leaving, he paused to look at a picture on a shelf. In the picture were three boys, two of them appearing to be teenagers, and the other having a more mature appearance. James could recognize one of them as Gloric but didn't know who the other two were. He didn't think they were his brothers, since they had little to no resemblance to him, plus one had bright red hair, and the other a jet black. "Who are these people in the picture?"

"… Just me and a few old co-workers."

"Gods have co-workers?"

"Gods have a lot of things, and pets."

James nodded. "Okay, well, enjoy your… time, I guess."

"Enjoy your knitting needles!"

James laughed as he left the office and closed the door behind him. He held the leather case close to his chest. "You have no idea."

~

"Where have you been?" Alexis asked as she ran up to James. "We started getting worried when it got dark out."

"Um…" James tightly gripped plastic bags full of colorful yarns. "I've been… out."

Alexis giggled. "You've been shopping?"

"Dante gave me a discount."

"How did you get a discount?"

"I mentioned something about a code word, and he said 'Oh, there's no code word, I just told Gloric that to keep myself entertained.' So, he gave me this all for a cheaper price for laughing."

Alexis rolled her eyes but kept her bright smile on her face.

"… Anyway, why did it suddenly get dark out?"

"We asked around, and apparently when Gloric gets tired, the sky grows darker, and when he wakes up, it's that orange color again. The sun is neither rising nor setting here."

"Neat," James walked to a park bench and took a seat, surprised that it really was like sitting on a bed. Reggy was having fun on some playground equipment, while Greg and Fletcher were sitting in the grass, examining their weapons.

"… So," Alexis took a seat next to James. "Reggy explained to us a bit on why you asked for that wish."

"Did he say what really happened or that I was just crazy?"

"A bit of both."

"Super…"

"It's okay, James."

James scoffed. "Not really, but thanks for trying to make me feel better."

Alexis frowned. "Look, I know that this all seems a bit unreal, especially to someone who isn't as religious as the rest of us, but you actually *met* Gloric! Shouldn't that be enough to make you feel better?"

James shrugged. "It should be, but it isn't going to happen overnight."

Alexis nodded, shifted awkwardly, and pulled the tools from off of her belt. "When my father worked at the Galvin university, he created a theory about Theorem surrounding Gloric. A lot of his colleagues agreed with him, but the owners of the university thought he was crazy. I made it a goal to get these tools blessed by Gloric, so I can light them on fire at the university, and prove that Gloric is real, and that my father is right." She looked up at him. "I truly am sorry for getting mad at you earlier."

James nodded. "… I'll tell you my story if you tell me yours."

"Alright." She let out a sigh. "Since the university board wouldn't give my father the funding he needed, he didn't pass the opportunity when the Bureau said they'd provide it in exchange for some goods and services. He made them a *lot* of Theorem, and it was expensive, high-quality Theorem at that. He even gave them the shield that belonged to Trenter, the Unbroken!"

"Oh, my gods," James said with an eye-roll. "That will sure be news to Franklin Waddlesworth III, who—"

"Found it on an expedition to the Dwarven Mountains?"

"*Stole* it from a blind man who thought it was a sheet of scrap metal!"

Alexis burst into laughter. "Yep, that sounds like something he would say."

"So, what happened after your father gave them the Theorem?"

"Well..." She took a deep breath. "They gave it to the contenders in the 54th Grand Interruption, and threw him into the ring as well, where he died in a fight against Mr. Finch, who used a sword that my father found and cared for."

"I'm so sorry."

"They honestly thought that he would die in the first round. His choice Theorem was a pencil with a butterfly attached to it. You see, my father had such a way with Theorem. He treated them the way they were intended to be treated, being modeled after the Gods' weapons after all. He was kind to them, and tended to them, and he won all of those fights by etching runes into the weapons to pacify them. He had the best intentions, but the fact that he took funding from the Bureau ruined our reputation for good."

"Why did you work for them if they did that to your father?"

"I didn't do it for very long. I only gave them enough weapons to make some pocket money before running away. I gave them some cheap Theorem, and they didn't necessarily complain since I was just some little girl. I got what I needed, passed through the Dwarven Mountains to get away from their jurisdiction, and met with a good friend of my father's."

James smiled. "Grime?"

"How did you know?" she asked, with a light beaming in her eyes.

"You're a lot like him. A bit rowdy, constantly tinkering, and very, very decent in a world where decent doesn't exist."

She blushed slightly. "Thanks… I lived with him for a very long time, which was where most of my shady ordeals happened. Yeah, working for the Bureau was bad enough, but the only practice in Theorem I could get was working for Madame Krishnee's underground ring. It wasn't until later when I found out that some of my Theorem might end up going back to the Bureau, and I couldn't handle that. So, I made the Cougar, left a telegram with Grime, and made my way through the world as a Theoremist, and continuing my father's legacy to improve the world with a symbiotic relationship with animals that go beyond weapons and violence."

"That's a nice story."

"Perhaps, but not as juicy as yours would be."

James chuckled. "Before I start, you bought me a drink once, why did you do that?"

She shrugged. "My father would've done the same thing. I'm always trying to think of good deeds he would do just so I can remember him better. I'm just too cranky to live up to it."

"You said it not me."

She shoved him while stifling a laugh.

"Okay, okay, I'm sorry!"

"It's fine." She took a deep breath. "You know, I always kind of knew who you were, but I didn't want to say it in case I was wrong. Plus, I didn't want to hurt Reggy's feelings. He isn't just 'research' to me. I really value his friendship."

"That's fair."

"That being said, I also tend to think I'm alone in the world, when I'm not. Nobody really works for the Bureau on purpose."

James sighed, with his heart heavy with guilt. "That's the thing that really sucks about me, though. I *volunteered* to work for the Bureau. You were right about me being a pile of fetchwork. I became a Messenger just so I could get back to Mr. Finch for murdering *my* family. I *killed* people just so I could have information about *one* person. It was irresponsible and stupid of me, and there is no way to justify my actions. I'm sorry to you, to Reggy, Greg, Fletcher, Harper, and everyone else I've ever encountered. I truly am a fool."

Alexis let out a sigh. "Well, you're definitely a fool," she teased as she gently nudged his elbow with hers, "but, like me, you're also not alone in the world. The friends you've made here are more powerful than your hallucinations, and also more permanent than your mistakes."

James looked up at Reggy, Greg, Fletcher, and Harper amidst one another in the park. Fletcher and Reggy were wrestling over the recorder (as an attempt to get Reggy to stop playing) and Greg seemed highly engrossed in a conversation with Harper, and she was beaming with a sort of sentience that made her feel special, despite her inanimacy.

"People do things, and sometimes they don't mean them. The best you can do is leave that behind you and move on, like you had been doing. You're not a bad person James, just a stupid one."

James smiled awkwardly. "Thanks."

Alexis shuffled slightly. "Can I ask how many messages you actually delivered?"

He thought about it. "… Three."

"That's better than three-hundred."

"Yeah, but it's still three people that I hurt."

Alexis shrugged. "Still better than three-hundred."

"Are we talking about how much of a fetch James is?" Fletcher asked as he, Greg, Reggy, and Harper approached.

"Just recapping my days as a Messenger," James replied.

"Same thing."

"Alexis!" Reggy whined. "Fletcher took my recorder and won't give it back!"

"I'll make him give it back later," Alexis said as she undid her braid and pulled out her notebook, "but for now, since we are all here, I think we need to come up with a way to open up the gates to Mahara."

"Gloric never said where these 'gates' were, did he?" Fletcher asked.

"No, he did not, but we know that they are somewhere in Mahara."

"We can cross that bridge later, but for now, we need to figure out how to use those gauntlets if they're supposedly indestructible," James spoke up.

"Well, you knew about them first. Is there anything you can observe about them?" Alexis asked.

"We just give them pajamas, like James," Harper said.

James eyes lit up. "Of course! The gauntlets can't destroy silk!"

"They can't?" Alexis asked.

"No! Harper, can you show us?"

Harper nodded and her chest opened up, revealing the black and gold gauntlets resting inside her silk-lined chest.

"Interesting," Alexis observed as she and the rest of the party walked closer to Harper.

"Whoever wears them just has to be wearing silk, and they will be fine!" James confirmed.

"Okay, to get things straight, tomorrow we travel to the mountain and use the gauntlets to get inside Mahara. From there, we find the gates and open them, and wait for Gloric to arrive and defeat Cirlock. Am I missing anything?"

Greg raised his hand.

"Yes, Greg?"

"Can I have the recorder?"

"But it's Reggy's."

"I know, I just know a few Brammish tunes. I'd be more than willing to teach the lad."

"Deal!" Reggy exclaimed as he ripped the recorder from Fletcher's hand and gave it to Greg.

"At least it will be tolerable," Fletcher muttered as he followed Greg and Reggy to the center of the park.

"Are you going to go to sleep?" James asked Alexis.

She shook her head. "Actually, I better go observe the music."

"That's fair."

As Alexis left, Harper sat next to James as he pulled out his knitting needles, feeling like a legitimate knitter since being in the Far North.

"Can I knit your sword a sweater?" Harper asked.

Yes, Lord Krag said.

"Please do," James said.

With that, the group spent the rest of the evening learning about Brammish folk tunes, and what Lord Krag's favorite color[16] truly is.

---

[16] It's blue, because blood is blue before it touches oxygen, supposedly. Don't take our word for it.

Chapter Twenty-Two

The Brink of Eternities

MINSTER HELD HIS HEAD IN one hand and the candlestick phone in the other, the only source of light being the sun high in the sky and a desk lamp. "I know, sir! I'm a complete disgrace! Yes, I would murder me, too. Would you like me to go die now? No? Not to question your authority but isn't a punishment… Oh, yes, as soon as you get out of your terrible prison, my fate is completely in your hands."

The soldier with the disfigured hands looked to his right and sighed.

"What's wrong?" a different soldier asked.

"I just really miss that one guy… he always asked questions… which was probably why he was so smart."

"… Maybe you can be the new smart guy."

"You think I have it in me?"

"Yeah, give it a try!"

"Okay!" He nodded and took a deep breath. "Who is he talking to?"

"Why, he's talking to the boss of course!"

"… Wait, who is our boss again?"

"Erm… I can't say his name."

"Oh, I remember, his name is Cir—"

"No! Don't say his name!"

Minster pulled out his revolver, shooting the second soldier.

The first soldier was stunned. "… Why did he die?"

"Because," Minster hung up the phone, "the Master doesn't like loud, mouth breathers."

"But… how are we supposed to breathe?"

"Through your nose!"

"… But I have a stuffy nose."

Minster huffed and tossed a handkerchief towards the soldier. "Clear it with this."

"Oh… thank you!"

"But I don't have a nose!" another soldier shouted.

Minster flicked his hand. "I have no idea how to help you."

"Oh…" The soldier looked down in disappointment.

The soldier struggled to put the handkerchief to his nose, but once he got his fingers untwisted and situated, he took a deep breath and blew. Minster tapped his foot impatiently as the soldier did so. After an obnoxiously long time, Minster stood up. "Are you done?"

"… Almost."

The soldier blew his nose for a little longer, then sniffled. He balled up the handkerchief. "What do I do with this? Should I throw it into that hole?"

"NO!" Minster exasperatedly exclaimed.

"Then, why do we have a hole?"

"That's where our Master lives! And he likes to keep his hole tidy and neat!"

"… It is a pretty neat hole, isn't it?"

Minster shouted in anger and turned off the desk lamp. "I'm done! I'm just…done with all of you!" he frustratingly opened and closed his fist, as if he were restraining himself from ripping out the throats of every soldier. "Just be ready when I summon you. They'll be coming to us this time."

Minster walked away, while keeping his head down and hugging himself, for he felt horribly disappointed that he had let his god down. The soldier nodded to himself. "I think I could get the hang of this being the smartest one here—"

And then, he was shot.

~

"So, Mahara is just through this mountain range?" James asked.

"Gloric said it was near here, and *The Celestial Chronology* said that Mahara was located next to Heaven through the Brink of Eternities." Alexis said, rummaging through the book.

"The Brink of Eternities?"

"There are several Brinks here on Tor, this one happens to be the one that separates Heaven and Mahara.

"... What are they?"

"Well," Alexis smiled with overconfidence. "According to *The Celestial Chronology*—"

James rolled his eyes.

"—Brinks are the side effect result of one Realm overlapping the other. The reason you can travel between Realms is through the Brinks. So far, we know of the Brink of Insanity,[17] the Brink of Eternities,[18] the Brink of Intensity,[19] and the Brink of Casualties.[20] The rest are to be discovered."

"There are more?"

---

[17] Connects Hell and the Underworld.

[18] Connects Heaven and Mahara.

[19] Connects Heaven and Hell.

[20] Connects the Surface to the Underworld.

"Of course, there are, James. There can't be five Realms and only four Brinks. There has to be at least twelve others we don't know about."

"Twelve others?" Fletcher spoke up.

"Yeah, at least, that's what is being hypothesized through some simple math."

"Oh." Fletcher shrugged. "The things math can do for you.[21]"

Alexis smiled, feeling a bit honored that she could teach a fellow intellectual something new.

"I am glad that the ice man can substitute for the exposition of the penstock," Harper said.

"I entirely agree," Reggy said.

The group trekked through wheat fields towards the mountain range. Eventually, the wheat started growing darker, until they came across what seemed to be a scar in the Realm. The wheat fields, at this point, were completely leveled, and the ground was black with ash and charcoal that tainted it like blood on snow.

"… What happened here?" James asked.

Alexis gazed out at the blackness. "I… don't know."

"Well, whatever it is, I think it's pointing us in the right direction," Fletcher gestured towards the mountain range.

From a distance, the mountains seemed to be peaks among a wide range. However, from where the party was standing, the mountain range looked like an optical illusion in an oil painting. As they moved closer, they noticed that the mountain was split in half by a large, black line, its peaks seemingly sown into the sky. They approached the base of this curious landmark, only to find a large boulder blocking the path, with a bit of a small hole near the bottom that looked like creatures were burrowing in and out from underneath it.

---

[21] Unless you plan on being an engineer, simple addition, subtraction, multiplication, division, and algebra is all you need in life.

Alexis took a deep breath. "Well, I guess this is the entrance, just how to get past that boulder…?"

Everyone's gaze shifted towards James. "…What are you looking at me for?"

"Well, you've been the idea guy, lately," Reggy said.

"I hate to admit it, but Reggy has a point," Alexis agreed.

James shrugged. "I don't know… maybe Greg can pick up the boulder?"

The entire party nodded. "Is that something you're up to?" Alexis asked Greg.

"No problem!"

Greg cracked his knuckles and approached the boulder. He attempted to pick it up from the bottom but found himself struggling to do so. He let go, panting heavily. "That boulder is stuck…I can't get it."

"Bummer…" James muttered, staring at the boulder again.

So… you're really going to make me say it? Krag asked.

Say what?

The gauntlets, dummy.

James groaned. "Harper, may I please borrow the gauntlets and some silk?"

Harper nodded, opened up her chest compartment to reveal the gauntlets, and opened another compartment on her arms to reveal long strips of pink silk and silk gloves. James put on the silk gloves first, which were admittedly too small, and covered the remainder of his arms with the silk. He cautiously lifted up the gauntlets, then put them on one by one. He smiled as he wiggled his fingers, a bit soothed at the metallic ring of the gauntlets.

"James… you look so pretty in pink," Fletcher teased. "It really brings out your eyes."

James tilted his head. "Aw… you really mean it?" he joked.

"I wouldn't lie to you, babe."

"Thanks, babe."

"I hate to interrupt another one of your weird improvisational bits," Alexis grumpily said, "but we really need to get back to the task at hand."

James sighed. "Fine."

He approached the boulder, then threw a punch at it smack in the middle. The boulder lit up and split in half, swung outwards like some sort of door, and revealed a cave on the other side.

James smiled and looked back to the party.

You're welcome.

James let out a sigh and placed the gauntlets and silk back into Harper's chest compartment.

"Well, at least we solved that problem," Alexis said. "Time to go look for the gate. Are you ready?"

"No," the gentlemen said simultaneously.

Alexis scoffed. "Cowards"

The rag-tag warriors entered through the cave. Alexis pulled out her flashlight to illuminate the dark place. The entrance to Mahara was more like a cavern. The rock ceiling was shaped like water droplets, seemingly dripping like falling rain. The melodic noise of hidden waterfalls sang lullabies as the sound of the party permeating puddles acted as a sweet accompaniment. To James' surprise, the air was damp with a heavy humidity, but it was the kind of humidity that was soothing to the touch, and warm like an embrace from a lost loved one. "This place is pretty."

"Yeah, but it's quiet," Reggy replied.

"… Quiet?"

"Too quiet."

"… Maybe if we just keep moving, we won't encounter anything sketchy," Fletcher suggested.

"*Or* if we just stay quiet, we won't worry about anything finding us," Alexis said.

"Either way, I have a funny feeling—" Reggy was interrupted by the sound of something shuffling, in addition to a few clicking noises. Reggy stopped cold. "Oh… fetch."

"… What is it?"

Reggy quickly shushed her, then pointed upward. "… It's above us," he whispered, smiling from ear to ear.

"What is?" James whispered back.

"A Thingy!" he ecstatically said.

"What? I thought those were dead?"

"I thought so, too! But… I guess not."

"Why are you excited about this?"

"Because, it's a Thingy!"

"I get that! But you effortlessly killed one when we first met. What's so different?"

"That one was a *baby!*"

James grew nauseated as flashbacks of the massive creature occupied his mind. "A… baby?"

"Yes."

"That was a baby?"

"Yeah, he was super tiny, didn't have all his legs…"

"So, you're telling me, that we are basically trapped in a cavern with a Thingy that not only has more legs but is *bigger?*"

"It has poisonous spikes."

"Mother of Gloric!" James covered his head with his hands. "I can't… I can't deal with you right now."

"Well, of course you can't, I have to—"

Suddenly, a low growl echoed through the cavern, causing somewhat of a small earthquake, and then a loud thud, causing an even larger earthquake. Reggy glanced at every member of the party with a wide smile. "Let's do this!"

"W-What?" James replied.

Harper's arms suddenly transformed into missile launchers, with at least five on each arm, and ripping her gloves and part of her shirt in the process. "I am ready!"

"No! Put those away! We are doing this *my* way! Come on!" Reggy shouted, then booked it. Everyone else didn't hesitate to follow, including Harper, who obeyed without hesitation. The pitch blackness of the cavern made it impossible to see the monstrosity, except for a split second when a beam from Alexis' flashlight glazed off of its body. This Thingy was about ten times bigger than what James had previously seen. Its flesh was a bone white with black towers sticking out of it.

Reggy referred to the towers as "spikes."

Discolored oozed seeped from its body as streams of saliva flung off of its blood-red teeth. It made direct eye contact with James, and he didn't hesitate to shout from what felt like horrors gnawing at his soul. "We're going to die!"

"I can't kill it!" Fletcher shouted as he blindly shot arrows at it.

"Of course, you can't!" Reggy laughed with every step he took.

"Then what the fetch are we supposed to do?" James panicked.

"Trust me! I've waited my whole life for this!"

Alexis let out a scream as large pointed rocks fell in front of the party. They each nearly fell over as they skidded to a stop, the Thingy growing near.

"Gimme a weapon!" Reggy reached out towards the group.

"Uh…" Alexis frantically rummaged through her bag before tossing Reggy a leather belt with a sheathed dagger attached to it. "Here!"

Reggy caught the belt and pulled out the dagger, smiling manically. "Don't wait up for me!"

"What are you going to do?" James shouted.

"Get eaten! Duh!"

"Reggy, no!"

Reggy darted into the darkness.

The only sounds that could be heard were the rapturous cries of the Thingy, and the crazed laughter of a predator hungering for his prey. Then, a loud screech and a thud quaked throughout the area. Reggy came back to the group, a frown spread across his face. "Here," he handed the dagger back.

"D-Did it work?" Alexis asked. "Did you get eaten?"

Reggy sighed. "Didn't need to."

A smile spread across her face. "I can't believe it! It actually worked!"

"What worked?" James asked, shaken up.

"This is the rat dagger I was supposed to sell Brawnzlinger! I never expected it to kill something like a *Thingy!*"

"Yeah…" Reggy muttered complaints under his breath.

"What's wrong? This is a good thing," Fletcher said.

"… I just thought it would put up more of a fight, you know?"

James blinked. "You're seriously upset about this?"

Reggy sighed, "Let's just go, guys."

"Well, you can keep the dagger as a reward—" Alexis began.

"No! I don't want this thing!"

"Why not?"

"It's cheap and boring! That Thingy died instantly! The first time I encounter an adult in years, and it dies within seconds? That's not fair!"

Alexis groaned. "Whatever. We just need to keep moving."

He moaned as he wrapped the belt around his hips and sheathed the dagger. The group climbed over the fallen rocks and continued through the cavern. Just as they came upon a light, more skittering could be heard. Reggy gasped. "Did you hear that?"

"What now?" James moaned.

"She was pregnant!"

"… Pregnant?"

"It sounds like there's about ten of them! Aw man that will be so great when they come out! Okay, light of day is dead ahead, let's go!"

"You're not going to go kill them?"

Reggy gave James a confused look. "Why? They're an endangered species, James. Please, be a little sensitive."

As Reggy scoffed, James threw up his hands. "*You're* the endangered species, Reggy!"

"And who am I to subject to hypocrisy?"

"Holy fetch," Fletcher said. "I didn't know you knew those words."

"Alexis is a great tutor."

"Aw!" Alexis put her hands over her heart. "That's so sweet!"

"Yeah," Fletcher mocked Alexis' tone, "but we should leave before 'daddy' shows up!"

Alexis' face fell. "Good point."

"Nah, female Thingy's eat the males after they mate," Reggy said.

"Oh," Fletcher shrugged. "Never mind then."

As the group left the cavern, James shook his head and looked to Greg. "I can't believe I'm saying this, but I think you're the sanest one here."

"… I'm just really excited to see Cirlock face to face," Greg replied.

"… Why?"

"I'm gonna punch 'im."

"Why?"

"I've never punched a god in the face before."

"… And I spoke too soon."

Chapter Twenty-Three

Just That Maharan Hospitality

WAR FACTORIES,

Miles and miles of doom, devastation, and lost hope spread across the entire plane of existence in addition to weapons of mass destruction scattered around left and right

Was not what the party beheld.

Turns out Mahara is a pleasant suburb, with maybe one or two factories out in the distance. There were people meandering around that resembled the pallid Chimeras, but everyone was wearing pastel colored polos, cashmere sweaters, or some sort of business attire, flavored with accessories of pashmina afghans and tennis bracelets.

"... Did... Did we get turned around?" James asked.

"No, this isn't Heaven but..." Alexis sniffed the air. "Is that peppermint? Is someone baking?"

Everyone else mimicked her actions.

"... This is not at all what I was expecting," Greg said.

"I don't think anybody was expecting this," Fletcher remarked. "That being said we stick out like sore thumbs and it is more than likely that these people are Chimeras, so, how do we handle this?"

"… Hide?" Alexis suggested.

James nodded. "Hide."

"I would also like to be nothing," Harper added.

"I second that," Reggy agreed.

"… You guys are geniuses," Greg said.

Alexis gave him a shocked look. "Are you… are you being sarcastic?"

"What? Oh, not at all! We've made it this far, so I genuinely mean that you are geniuses."

"Oh…" Alexis shook her head. "Let's just… go."

The group decided that the best route they could take would be jumping from backyard to backyard, tripping over garden gnomes and lawn flamingos, while searching willy-nilly for the gates.

As they hopped out of the neighborhood into what seemed to be some sort of park, Alexis paused. "Is that a flamingo?" She pointed to a pond.

There was, indeed, a flamingo, and then several more appeared near it.

"… I never learned flamingo," Greg commented.

"It isn't bad enough that you can speak to sheep?" Reggy asked.

Greg held up his hands in surrender. "I can speak various forms of bird."

"Greg?" James asked.

"Yeah?"

"… Can you just keep being this way all the time?"

"Yeah!"

"Thanks."

"Okay, James, since you're so much help, what do we do now?" Alexis retorted.

"Aviary feathers!" Harper exclaimed.

"I don't know! Keep searching for the gates, I guess," James continued, dismissing Harper."

"We have no idea where to even look and we've been hopping fences for at least forty-five minutes now," Alexis replied.

"What do you suggest? That we ask around? Golly, Alexis, that seems like a great idea!"

"We don't have to ask around!" Reggy shouted from the middle of the street. "I think I know where they are!"

"Reggy!" James snapped. "What are you doing? Get back here!"

"But there's a sign that says where Cirlock is!"

Everyone walked out into the street. "There is no way that there is a—oh wow—there's a sign," Alexis said.

There was a giant billboard with an arrow saying, "This way to Cir-" with the last few letters to "Cirlock" faded away, and underneath that a couple of smaller signs saying, "This way to Gun Factory," "This way to Worker's Comp.," "This way to Human Resources," and "This way to the Complaint Department" that pointed to a minefield.

"Well... that's convenient," Fletcher said.

"A bit *too* convenient," James commented.

"Nobody is ever sad to see a grocery story," Harper added.

"Uh-huh."

"Reggy! I'm so proud of you!" Alexis gave Reggy a hug. "You read that sign all by yourself!"

Reggy blushed. "Well, I learned from the best."

"Oh, you!"

"Yeah, yeah," James irately said. "Is there a sign that says where the gates are?"

"I don't see one," Alexis examined the sign. "There's a visitor's center though."

"A visitor's center? Who the hell visits this place?"

~

"Hello!" an old woman behind a receptionist desk said. "You must be from out of town!" She eyed them up and down, doing a bad job of hiding her disgust. "A little bit dirty, are we? Oh, well. That's okay. We have to take pity on humans occasionally." She giggled. "So, what can I do for you?"

"Uh," Alexis started, "ouch. Um, we're looking for the gates?"

"Oh, the gates? Well, that's where you must have come from! That entire mountain is the gate."

"What?"

"Yeah, we get a few squatters crawling in from under the boulder every once in a while, but that's about it… Why?"

"Clothed in iron and wrapped for winter," Harper answered.

"… Interesting." The lady eyed Harper's hands. "What interesting gloves."

"This is my flesh."

"*It is?*" The lady sounded intrigued. "Would that mean you are a robot?"

"A person counts as much as they can read."

The lady nodded. "Of course. So, if I were to, I don't know, ask about Protocol 87.2, what would you have to say about that?"

"She wouldn't say anything!" Alexis intervened. "In fact, I'm surprised you got her to speak. Normally, she is quite *mute*."

Harper nodded, indication she understood the command.

The lady gave a light laugh. "Right… I'm just going to ask you to stay right here while I go get my manager. I'll bring you guys back some water, too. You seem absolutely thirsty. Besides, with the way you guys look you must not have seen water in years!"

"… Did she just make a comment about our smell?" Greg asked.

"Well, none of us have really bathed in about a week now," Alexis remarked, "not to mention pukey boy over here."

"Hey…" James defensively said.

"I haven't had a bath, since, like, since I was *born!"* Reggy declared.

"We don't need to hear that!" Fletcher shouted.

The old lady laughed. "You guys are *hilarious*! We haven't had a group like you come in for a while now!"

"Yep!" Alexis gave a nervous chuckle. "Well, we really should be going now—"

"Why leave so soon?"

Alexis' face fell. "Uh…"

"You have just what our god needs to set us all free." The lady's voice grew deeper. *"And I will* not *surpass an opportunity to glorify our god!"*

The old lady's skin seemingly ripped off of her body as a human sized weasel emerged from behind the desk. The weasel hissed as white foam dripped from its mouth.

Reggy screamed. "Kill it! Kill it with fire!"

"Fire?" Greg grabbed his sword. Harper followed his example by turning her hand into a flamethrower.

"No!" Fletcher shouted, gesturing to the very tightly enclosed room around them.

"But I'm immune to fire!"

"Yeah, but we aren't!"

"… Oh, yeah!" Greg said as he sheathed his sword. Harper also transformed her hand back to normal.

The weasel screeched as it swung a decayed paw at Alexis' face. Alexis fell out of her seat and rolled away. The weasel was just about to pounce at her when James tackled into it with his sword. As the weasel writhed and clawed at James, he quickly pulled out his sword and cut off its head. "Let's go!"

The five of them ran out of the visitor's center, sprinting back towards the park with a couple of "friendly" faces giving them confused glances. The glances weren't so much of a "huh, that seems out of place," but more like "since when did we start housing rats in Mahara?"

As soon as they made it back to the park, they collapsed, panting with exhaustion. A couple of flamingos wandered over to them, searching their hands for food, but then just ended up gently nibbling their hair.

"… I hate this place," Fletcher said as he was lying on his stomach, with about three flamingos walking across his back.

"Look, we already opened the gates, so, I guess we just wait for Gloric," Alexis said while two flamingos played with her braids.

"Why wait for Gloric when we can just leave?" James asked. A flamingo honked at him, and James slowly turned his head towards it, not really sure how to handle the situation.

"… It's really up to you guys, but I have a bit of a request," Greg hugged a flamingo with each arm, the flamingos biting at the totems in his beard.

"… What might that be?" James questioned, feeling awkward from the flamingo staring at him.

"Well, I—"

Interrupting Greg was a chime coming from the lamp post, and a woman's voice saying "Workday over. Everyone, return to your homes." The voice was followed by a noise of interference.

"Attention, attention, may I have your attention, please?" Minster said over an intercom. "There will be a public service announcement located in the town square from our lord and savior, himself. Immediately reschedule your family matters and join us for his words." With a click, there was another chime, ending the announcement.

“Did he just say, ‘reschedule your family matters?’” Alexis asked.

“Why? You don’t reschedule your family?” Reggy asked as flamingos ate bugs out of his hair.

“Well, no, my family is dead,” Alexis said.

“Mine is, too,” Reggy retorted.

“And mine,” James remarked.

“… And mine,” Greg admitted.

Everyone slowly looked over at Fletcher.

“Uh… actually my mom is in a retirement home,” he said.

“Why didn’t you say anything?” James asked.

“Because it’s not really a conversation starter. ‘Hey, guys, my mom is senile!’”

Everyone nodded in agreement, except for Reggy. “… We could have had a really cool club name, like, ‘The Dead Family Brigade,’ and you had to just ruin it!”

“You want a group name?” Fletcher challenged. “How about ‘The Dead Fetch Brigade,’ since everything here wants to kill us! Hey, you can be our mascot, you fetch!”

Reggy scoffed. “Jokes on you! My mom was the village fetch!”

Fletcher rolled his eyes, while Harper mouthed something.

“You can unmute now, Harper,” James said.

“Volume restored,” she said. “Blankets against murder and puff dogs.”

“How about we focus on the fact that Cirlock is going to announce something to the public?” Alexis said. “Did he escape from his hole?”

“Who knows and who cares?” James replied. “We got the gate open! That’s all Gloric asked us to do!”

“But it’s our divine right to go!” Reggy shouted.

“What are we going to do? He’s a *god*! And we’re just humans!”

"… I just really want to see what's getting all of these Chimeras ruffled up," Reggy shrugged. "Something cool might happen."

"I think we should go," Alexis said. "We need to all do our part to help out Gloric."

"We did our part!" James shouted, the flamingo honking to match his volume.

"We're going," Alexis said sternly, "for Gloric."

Fletcher sat up. "For Gloric."

Greg nodded. "For Gloric and my family."

"For my entertainment!" Reggy shouted.

James scoffed. "For… my return to the Underworld."

The group cheered. "Wait," Fletcher spoke up. "Your *return* to the Underworld?"

"Uh…" James cleared his throat. "Let's just take care of Cirlock before I tell that story."

"… Yeah, agreed."

~

The Chimeras had gathered to an outdoor amphitheater with jazz music playing through the speakers. The party hid near the top of the amphitheater, watching from a distance. The Chimeras screamed and shouted when the music stopped, and Minster walked out onto the stage.

"What a beautiful crowd! The Master will be so pleased!" he said into a microphone. He laughed as the Chimeras cheered louder, then held his hand up, causing the cheering to die down. "Now, I know I said that our Master has a very, very special announcement to share with you, and it has been something we have been waiting to hear for almost *one thousand years!"*

The energy of the Chimeras skyrocketed as they turned to one another conversing excitedly.

Minster smirked. "That's right, we have the gauntlets in our possession!"

The crowd erupted again. James glanced over at the rest of his comrades. "They must still think the rocks are the gauntlets—"

"And we had them hand delivered to us via some grungy, secretion leeching mouth-breathers! Oh! And there they are!"

Minster pointed towards the group, everyone turning towards them, wide eyed. "Give them a round of applause!" He laughed maliciously as all the Chimeras excitedly clapped. The party stood, and turned around to run away, but were surrounded by Chimeras in their animalistic forms, each growling at them. "*Go down onto the stage*," one said with a snarl.

Holding tightly to the hilts of their weapons, the party walked down onto the stage, the transformed Chimeras ushering them and snapping at their heels. They lined up onto the stage, Minster giving them smug looks. "Oh, yes, these *humans,* to be a bit more endearing, were so gracious to give our Master the very key he needs to leave his prison, and in turn, we will loyally follow behind him to see the world of Tor once again."

"We'll never give you the gauntlets," Alexis said through gritted teeth.

Minster pouted his lips and pulled the microphone away. "Aw… you don't have a choice. Besides, I'm still not very happy with you for that stunt you pulled with the rocks."

"Actually, that was James," Reggy spoke up.

James groaned as Minster approached him. "Really? That was a good plan, calling my bluff by trying to tell me what to do like the inferior that you are. Good… good work." Minster reached out to pat him on the shoulder but then quickly retracted his hand. "You smell like vomit."

"I know," James said. "Believe me… I know."

"And that's what's so despicable about these creatures!" Minster shouted into the microphone at the crowd. "They wallow in their own filth, and keep the entire world to themselves, shunning us Chimeras and our god!" Minster turned towards the party. "And I'll have you know… He is the most talented and intelligent person in the entire world! So, I will happily pry those gauntlets from your cold, dead hands if it means setting the god that I love free! He has such vision and potential, and it doesn't matter what has happened to him, I will always do his will, even getting nitty and gritty to make him happy! So, please" —Minster held his hands out— "hand them over, or I'll make your deaths slow, and painful."

Alexis took a deep breath and unsheathed her swords. She lunged towards Minster, taking out an intercepting Chimera in the process. Minster swiftly dodged out of the way as she swung her sword, barely missing his neck. She took a few more jabs at Minster, while he smugly, and calmly, evaded every move she made. He ducked as she jumped over him and swung her sword in the process. Minster laughed. "Hah! You can try your best, sweetheart, but you can't even so much as lay a finger on me—!"

His face fell, and his eyes widened as she landed on her feet, gave him a blank stare, and held his ponytail in her hand. He gasped loudly, the crowd of Chimeras growing quiet, and filing out of the amphitheater.

"You… cut… my… hair!" he shouted.

She held the ponytail up in the air, about the same level with her head, challenging him with the fire in her eyes.

Minster began shaking, James almost swearing that he could see steam pouring off of him. "… I'm going to kill you."

"Go ahead!" Alexis shouted. "What's the worst thing that a whiney priss like you can do—?"

Suddenly, several chains fell from Minster's sleeves. The chains hissed as if they were coated with acid and burned a hole in the concrete.

"… Oh… fetch."

Minster let out a scream, and as it fluctuated in octaves, his skin twisted and transformed, and the Chimera inside grew nearly twenty feet tall on all fours.

Minster was no longer the priss that everyone knew and loved, but a massive white and gold creature that was part lion and part eagle.

"Harper, get out of here!" Alexis exclaimed as she took the ponytail (which had turned into a mass of feathers) around the Hope. Harper did as she was told and quickly ran away.

The creature's wings were crippled and broken, like it had complete inability to fly. Its claws and beak had some intense scars, but its pelt was well-groomed. The chains from Minster's sleeves levitated around the creature and was shackled around each of its claws. It looked at Alexis and howled at her in a splenetic, macabre scream.

"What did you *do?"* James shouted, noticing that even the guard Chimeras had run away.

"I-I didn't know he'd be scary!"

The Chimeric Minster growled. *"YOU'LL PAY FOR WHAT YOU DID TO ME!"*

He swiped his claw at Alexis. As she hopped out of the way, she barely saw the chains whipping towards her in the corner of her eye. Upon landing, she fell to the ground, the chains missing her by inches.

James unsheathed his sword and ran towards Minster. A chain seemingly gained sentience and lashed towards James. He fell backwards, the chain almost decapitating him, then shuddered as he got back onto his feet. The chain whipped towards him again, and James figured the best thing to do was to run away. "What is up with these chains?"

"It's Theorem!" Alexis replied as she dashed across the amphitheater stage, Minster, in turn, snapping his beak at her head.

"What kind of Theorem?!" Reggy asked as he fought off one particular chain with his new recorder.

"I've heard of this kind of weapon! Someone literally attached jellyfish to chains!"

"Jellyfish? Jellyfish! What the... hell is jellyfish?" James asked as he hit the chain with his sword.

"... What?"

"I just don't understand what benefit jam-filled fish can bring to these chains!"

"You don't know what a jellyfish is?!"

"*I* even know what a jellyfish is!" Reggy remarked. "You can't eat them!"

"Look, they sting, it hurts, I'll show you pictures later!"

"If there *is* a later!" James shouted.

"Don't feel bad, James! I didn't know what a jellyfish was at first, either!" Fletcher shot of several arrows, each of them glazing off of Minster's pelt.

"Shut up!"

Ow! Owww! Lord Krag shouted.

"You alright, buddy?!"

Yeah just... stings. Ha-ha!

"Yeah, buddy, I'm fine!" Reggy said.

"I wasn't talking to you, Reggy!"

"Oh...was it a voice in your head?"

"... Sure!"

"Guys! If you cover me, I can get to higher ground and shoot at him!" Fletcher yelled.

"We can barely cover ourselves!"

"Shut up and help him!" Alexis struck at one of the chains.

Fletcher swiftly climbed up the steps of the amphitheater, when a chain whipped around his leg and threw him back onto the stage, his clothes hissing.

"Ack!" Fletcher rolled onto his side and gripped his ankle.

Minster laughed. "*That's a cute plan! You realize that I'm not deaf, right?*" As he chased after Alexis, nearly close enough to give her a lobotomy with the tip of his beak, he suddenly squawked in pain.

"Get out of here!" Greg shouted as he gripped tightly to Minster's tail.

Without any hesitation, Alexis, Fletcher, James, and Reggy all sprinted out of the amphitheater. Greg tightened his grip and swung Minster into the amphitheater seats, then ran after the rest of the group.

Minster roared in frustration. "*You're not getting away that easily!*" Minster crawled out of the rubble and then gracefully jumped to the top of the amphitheater.

As the party desperately ran back towards the suburbs as Minster barreled towards them. "*I'm going to catch you!*" He playfully shouted. A chain flicked towards Alexis' backpack like a blink from a lightning bolt. She screamed as she was swept away with her bag.

"ALEXIS!" James stopped dead in his tracks and ran towards Minster without any hesitation.

Minster laughed as he shook Alexis out of the backpack. James dove in mid-air and caught her as she fell to the ground. Minster raised his paw and pinned them both to the ground with his giant talons.

"*Look at you, sacrificing yourself only to die with your little girlfriend. You are one interesting human, James.*" Minster laughed. "*I hope you taste a fraction better than you smell!*"

Minster lifted his talon as he reached for Alexis and James with his beak. James held Alexis tightly and squeezed his eyes closed as he braced for being eaten,

And wondered if he'd arrive at the Underworld whole, or in pieces.

Minster squawked again. James opened his eyes to see Greg standing over them, his face strained as he fought Minster's strength by holding the beak with his bare hands.

James let go of Alexis and nearly pushed her onto her feet as he scrambled behind her. Minster seemingly smiled as a loud hiss rang through the air. Alexis looked back. "Greg! Move!"

Greg stifled a scream as the chain burned against his flesh. "I don't think I can!"

"Then… throw him!"

"… Oh, right!"

Greg roared as he threw Minster towards someone's house. The Chimera crashed into the home, the weight of the beast destroying nearly half the property. James ran ahead towards Minster and held his sword out in front of him.

Minster chuckled as he weakly stood up. "*Do you think you're her knight in shining armor? Well, little boy, you haven't the faintest clue of what kind of demons and monsters are lurking in this world. Unlike them, I don't hide behind cheap cultists and pretty words. So, go ahead, bring me down.*" The chains radiated around him, the Chimera nearly glowing. "*I dare you!*"

James gulped, but he held his sword tighter and took a deep breath. He ran towards the Chimera, and as Minster opened his beak and raised his claws, he screamed out in pain as a white recorder plunged into his eye.

"Get him, James!" Reggy shouted.

This is all you, buddy! Krag encouraged.

James smirked as he ran straight into Minter's chest, stabbing him in his heart. Minster cried out in pain and thrashed around. James held tightly onto the sword, getting a bit of backlash as Minster clawed at him. Using the last of his strength to grab James, Minster weakly gave out and fell onto his side, some tears trickling down his face. "*I… failed him… I'm sorry… I'm sorry M-Master.*"

Minster let out a final breath, the beast almost majestic in death.

Alexis felt a pang in her chest and looked towards James with her kindling eyes. "He… saved us," she quietly said. "He didn't even hesitate… he just did it… how brave—"

"Eww! Eww, eww, eww!" James shouted as he flicked black blood off of his clothes.

Alexis took a deep breath, her eyes as wild as an ember from a tealight. "… Good job, James… way to be a man."

James gagged as he attempted to pull his sword from the dead Chimera's side. "Oh, gods, I'm gonna—"

Reggy walked up and pulled the sword out of the Chimera, unflinching. "Here you go, buddy."

"… Thanks," James said as he used the corpses feathers to wipe the sword clean. "Nice going with the recorder, by the way."

"Right?" Reggy climbed onto Minster's face and pulled out the recorder, only to have it snap in the process. "Wh…. WHAT? Gloric said it was indestructible!"

"Maybe he meant to give you a different one," Fletcher said.

"That fetch!" Reggy huffed as he stuck the broken recorder in his pocket.

"Well… that's one less problem," James said as he sheathed his sword.

"… Not exactly," Alexis said as she cradled Greg.

"… Greg!" James called as he ran to his side.

Alexis slapped James' shoulder. "Not him! He's fine! Sort of."

"Then, what's—"

James paused as he saw an angry mob of transformed Chimeras staring him down. "*You've killed Minster!*" one of them shouted.

"He was our prophet!"

"He was going to set our Master free!"

"His face now bears our hatred!"

"We shall offer him!"

"Whoa, whoa, whoa!" James held his hands up. "Offer me?"

"GET HIM!"

James turned around and ran as fast as he could, but one of the Chimeras snagged his jacket. James fell to the ground as one group of Chimeras worked together to pick him up while the rest worked to detain the party.

"Stop!" James shouted as the Chimeras carried him off. "Put me down!"

"If you insist!"

James' stomach dropped as he saw the Chimeras carrying him towards a giant hole in the ground, surrounded by gold railing. He struggled and fought to get away from the Chimeras.

"FOR THE GLORY OF OUR GOD!"

As the Chimeras heaved James into the hole, he caught a glimpse of indigenous beauty reflecting the burning sun through a glistening wood. His vision began blurring as kisses of dewdrops on the trees sparkled like diamonds. He closed his eyes. The familiar buzz drowned out the chanting Chimera's,

And the sweet voice of a woman shouting for him.

CHAPTER TWENTY-FOUR

ISN'T THIS JUST THE PITS?

THE WEIGHT OF JAMES' EYELIDS grew heavier with each attempt to open them.

... *What is this?* he thought as he gazed upon a silvery incandescence above him. *There wasn't a light last time...*

He blinked rhythmically with his breathing, the blurred light spinning with the room around him. He gradually built up the strength to push himself up. As soon as he was somewhat level, he discovered his concussion in the same manner as one would discover they've been plowed by a freight train.

Oh, and his boots were untied.

"Wh...Why are my boots untied?" he slurred. "I *hate* when they're untied!"

"Oh, well, let me help you out there, sport."

"Wha?"

James looked up to see a man dressed in a slick,

I mean *slick,*

Three-pieced silk suit. His body was subtly tanned, with his rich, red hair combed back, and a beard that has grown in nicely and is evenly trimmed. His light blue eyes shimmered harmoniously with a similarly colored silk tie. He charismatically flashed a set of sparkling, white teeth at James before bending down to tie his shoelaces.

"... Thanks," James murmured, almost struggling to get the words out.

"Quite a fall you took. Boy, it's a long way down! You must have a skeleton made of steel to survive a fall like that. Normally people just shatter on contact with the ground." The man paused to gesture towards a pile of bones. "You can't even see the light of the surface in this wretched place. *Thankfully,* my little worker boy would send me care packages, and included my artificial sun!" The man pointed to a glowing orb mounted on a post.

"That was one of my best," he said while eyeing it admirably. "Then again, it *was* more of a team effort. I merely got the idea when I offhandedly mentioned how I want the sun in my hand in front of my R&D department during my daily polo game. I'll have to admit, though, what a fantastic idea I had! I truly did something revolutionary with this one!"

James nodded, trying to observe the man in more depth. He recognized his voice from the Lynole Industries building but couldn't quite put his tongue on it.[22]

The man pat James' boots. "Damn... I'm so good at tying knots. What fine leather these shoes are! Are they Trigan?"

"... Uh," James finally replied, "yes?"

The man happily sighed. "That's the quality stuff. My shoes are made out of it too!" He tapped his own black Balmoral shoe, with bold shackle around his ankle resting above it. "Holds the shine very well, am I right, my friend? Course, I am! Anyway, care for a drink?"

The man stood up and sat down at the desk. James noticed he was sitting at a desk,

---

[22] Pardon this rather strange figure of speech. James had a concussion and couldn't really think straight at the moment.

Well,

More like sleeping and using the desk as a pillow.

"No… I don't drink anymore."

"Anymore?" The man scooted forward in his chair, then looked at James genuinely. "Why is that?"

"It made me see some crazy things."

The man chuckled. "Being drunk will do that, sport."

"Well… I wasn't drunk when it happened."

"Oh! You're soft in the head!"

"I'm not soft in the head!"

"Here, rub your head like this!" The man placed his fingers against his temples and moved them in circles.

Baffled, James mimicked his actions.

"Is it squishy?"

"Well, yeah—"

He snapped his fingers. "Then, your head is soft!"

"Wh- No! That's not how that works!"

"Why, that's exactly how that works! I had sixteen doctors tell me so! Granted, they're all dead, I probably threatened them, maybe. I don't remember, but they told me, dammit! Are *you* sixteen doctors with medical degrees and the motivation of a death threat?"

"I mean, I feel like I might have a fever—"

"Not *that* kind of medical degree! That's a cute start, though. I have an honorary one, but I don't have a wall in here." He acknowledged an empty space and a framed degree lying on the ground.

Thoroughly confused, James sat back and shook his head but studied the man more. The man had eyes like Gloric, seemingly beaming upon him like sunlight, except that home feeling was lost. There was only pain, suffering, and misery, almost as if the fire fueling this sun had only desire to watch the world burn.

There was something else, too. For a brief second, a solar flare would occasionally erupt from the sun, as if there was some sort of internal blaze trying to break free. James didn't understand the physics of suns, mostly because no one had ever ventured outside of the planet, but something like that didn't seem possible.

Something was wrong.

"So, what do you want?" The man pulled out a drawer in his desk. "I have... liquor." He moved some bottles around. "Liquor... more liquor... and *liqueur.*"

"Liqueur?"

"Yes, it's chocolate flavored. It's delicious."

James' jaw dropped once he realized whom he was conversing with. He sat up straighter and pointed to the man. "You!"

"I mean, the ladies seemed to think so!" he tittered as he poured himself a drink. "Sorry, boy, but I don't swing that way," he said with a grin, but clearly flattered.

"What? No! It's *you*! You're Cirlock!"

The man choked on his beverage, then gripped his chest as he erupted into a coughing fit.

"... Are you okay?" James asked, a bit apprehensively.

"What did you just call me?" the man demanded.

James felt his mouth grow dry. "... Cirlock?"

"Why are you saying my name like that?"

"... Saying your name like what?"

"Like *that!*"

James gave him a confused look.

"You know... by doing that thing with your tongue!"

"What thing?"

"Read my lips." The god leaned forward. "My name is Cir*log*. With a 'guh' sound at the end! Guh! Guh! Say it with me!"

"Uh... guh?"

"Guh!"

"Guh!"

"Good! Now, say my name right."

"… Cirlog?"

"There you go!" Cirlog clapped his hands together, his demeanor calming down.[23] "I won't be too harsh on you because you're soft, you probably didn't know any better."

"But, that's how everyone says your name."

"What?" Cirlog snapped. "Why?"

"… That's how it's spelled in *The Celestial Chronology—"*

"That fetching book! *Of course,* they'd spell my name like that! Bunch of imbeciles! They barely knew how to read until I invented it, and this is how they repay me?"

"You invented reading?"

"… No, but I should have! Reading would be so much better that way! Faster cars, more explosions, hotter women![24] The slogan would be: Reading! Do more of it because I said so!" he said while holding his hands out in front of him.

Cirlog panted with a wide grin, silence occupying the pit for a minute.

"… Are you… Are you trying to pitch an idea to me?"

"Don't need to." He put his hands down. "I already sold it."

James bit his lip. *Dammit… he kind of did.*

"What's your name?"

"I-It's James."

"It's Jay-mez?"

James furrowed his brow. "No… it's *James."*

"Yes, Jay-mez. That's what I said."

James stared at him vexingly.

"Doesn't feel so good, huh, Jay-mez?"

"Okay! You made your point! Mother of Gloric—"

---

[23] Payneful Reads: changing their minds on how to spell a name and owning up to it since 2020.

[24] There may or may not be a famous movie director that has this sentence trademarked.

“That’s not a very nice thing to say!”

“Why do you care?”

“Because, that’s my mother, too!”

“What?”

Cirlog laughed. “I mean, come on, James. Gloric and I are brothers for Pete’s sake!

“You guys have a mom?”

“I… don’t remember.” Cirlog’s gaze fell to his desk and began muttering quietly, seemingly lost in uncertainty.

“… You alright, there?”

Cirlog steadily got up on his feet and began pacing, with a long chain trailing behind him.

“Hey…” James reached out to touch him.

Startled, Cirlog roughly snatched his wrist. “Who are you?”

“I’m James—”

“Why are you here? Huh? Did *he* put you up to this?”

“I don’t know who—”

“Don’t lie!” Cirlog reached for James’ neck, lifted him out of the chair by his collar, and threw him onto the desk, pinning him down with one hand. “I won’t ask you again! Did *HE* send you?”

“Gloric sent me!”

His eyes narrowed and he let go of James. “Hah… Ah ha, ha…”

Cirlog erupted into manic laughter and walked away. He leaned against the wall of the pit, laughing harder with every breath he took.

James shakily inhaled deeply. His heart was beating out of his chest as the panicked thought settled upon his mind that he was trapped down here with a psychopath.

… And that there was a wall nearby.

“And you said *I* was soft,” James mumbled as he climbed off of the desk.

"Exactly!" Cirlog instantaneously moved from his spot on the ground to his seat at the desk and slammed his hands down onto the surface. "*I'm* soft, too, Jay-mez! I've been down here for almost one thousand years! I'm going mad! I've *already* gone mad!" Cirlog laughed again. "In fact, it's hard not to question reality when you've gone as mad as I have."

"Why would you say that?" James snapped.

"Oh, touched a nerve, have I? Do you have issues dealing with reality, Jay-mez? Do you wish you could live in a world better than this one? Or perhaps you just don't know what's real at all?"

James clenched his fists and gritted his teeth.

"I can truly relate to you, Jay-mez." Cirlog wandered around the pit as he spoke." You have it all in the palms of your hands, only to give it up for… what?" He stood directly behind James. "I bet you are so lost, you don't even know you're making sacrifices at all. Well, let's think about it. Is it family?"

James did not reply.

"Yourself?"

He remained quiet.

"Love?"

Still speechless.

"*I* bet it's love. Love is a funny thing. Sometimes you have it when you don't even realize it. Perhaps we could help each other, Jay-mez. You set me free, and I'll be sure to send your love here, and you can be by each other's side forever, assuming they survive the fall."

"Shut-up."

"So, there *is* someone. And you were reckless enough to bring them along on this suicide mission? Then, I guess it *won't* be my fault when they die from the impact."

"I said, 'shut up!'"

"Or what? You gonna 'kill me?' In case you haven't noticed, Jay-mez, I'm Gloric's *brother,* and if Gloric is a god, then I *also* am a god. In fact, I'm *the* God of Commerce. Whatever you could possibly to do me won't work." He leaned in close to James' ear. "Tell that to your lover when I throw their corpse down here."

James let out a shout, quickly stood from his seat, and in one swift motion, unsheathed his sword and swung it at Cirlog. Cirlog quickly hopped out of the way, and the full force of the sword fell down onto his chains, cutting them like soft butter.

Oh, fetch, Lord Krag said. *I didn't know that I could do that.*

You didn't *know you could do that?* James shouted in his head.

No, I didn't!

"Wow! That's one *hell* of a sword!" Cirlog exclaimed. "Who would've thought you'd *actually* be the one to free me, Jay-mez?" He let out a laugh. "Well, it truly was nice to meet you, Jay-mez. Perhaps I'll throw Gloric down here as well, and you all can spend eternity in this hell hole."

"You aren't going anywh—!"

James lunged for Cirlog but tripped and fell onto the ground. "What the?" He looked at his boots, noticing his shoelaces had been tied together.

Cirlog laughed. "Toodles! I'm going to miss you, Jay-mez!" And with a quaint wave of his fingers, Cirlog vanished.

"No!" James yelled, his voice echoing throughout the pit. "Dammit.... Dammit! There's... There's got to be a way out of here!" He clenched his fists. "Krag, do you think if you lend me your strength, I can climb out here?"

No.

James scoffed. "Screw you, then! I'll do it myself! I did it without you in the Underworld!"

I don't think you understand. That was a really, really long fall, James. Maybe twice the distance.

"Well... then..." James smiled and nodded his head with confidence. "I'm going to get lost."

Excuse me?

"We had a talk, and Gloric said-"

I was there, you dumb fetch. I just highly doubt that it will work this time.

"I'm out of options! I'm doing this!"

James retied his boots, stood firmly on his feet, and shut his eyes tight. He walked forward, but quickly tripped over something.

... I really, really hate you.

"I have to keep moving!"

You don't have to.

James opened his eyes and pumped his fists into the air. "Yes! Yes! I did it! Thank Gloric!"

"Ah, ah! Thank *Cirlog!"*

He then turned around to see an army of Chimeras, several tanks, and his friends all chained down to the ground in the midst of the war path.

"... Aw, fetch!"

CHAPTER TWENTY-FIVE

FIRES OF PRIDE

CIRLOG APPROACHED AND PUT HIS arm around James' shoulder. "I couldn't just *leave* you down there, Jay-mez! We're pals!" He suddenly held James in a bit of a chokehold and gave him a noogie. "Everyone, go ahead and give a nice round of applause for Jay-mez!"

Cirlog let go of James and laughed as the Chimeras reverted back to their human forms. With a light in their eyes, they erupted with roars of praise and excitement as they loudly and harshly clapped, a few of them losing their hands in the process.

James exhaled as dismay mercilessly crashed into him like a falling wave. "I'm sorry, guys." He turned towards his shackled friends.

"Why are you apologizing?" Alexis asked. "You've done nothing but fight for our goal. What is there to be sorry about?"

"I…" James bit his lip and laughed. "I guess I'm so used to everything being my fault that I felt the need to apologize."

"Aw, James! We accept your apology!" Reggy remarked.

"Yeah," Fletcher agreed. "Apology accepted."

James curled his lip and mockingly laughed at Fletcher's sarcasm. Fletcher chuckled to himself, proud that he could still manage to yank somebody's chain with impending death resting on his shoulders.

"Eyes of lilac and outlines of silver," Harper said

Surprised at the sudden comment, Cirlog approached Harper. "What did you say?"

"I thought you'd know better than that, Father. The Grand Project has no need for hermit crab shells when you have me!"

"The Grand Project?" Cirlog muttered before letting out a gasp. "Is that you, Harper?" He took off her mask and cloak. "Look at *you!* You'd always been your mother's greatest design."

Harper beamed at the compliment, while Alexis seemingly perked up and struggled to get closer to her.

"Don't listen to him, Harper!" she exclaimed. "He's the bad guy! If you want to keep the Grand Project safe, don't talk to him!"

"Don't listen to *her,* dear," Cirlog said. "After all, you've known me for years. You know me well enough to trust me, right?"

"Harper, don't listen to him, please!" Alexis cried. "Think about what Gloric told us! You need to trust in *him* right now!"

Harper glanced between the two as they both argued for her trust. When the arguing seemed to have no resolve, Cirlog freed Harper from her chains.

"Now, would somebody untrustworthy set you free?" Cirlog asked her.

Harper stood tall. "Just because you released one fish, doesn't mean you saved the rest from deprivation."

Cirlog nodded. "You know, you're right, after all, not all fish can be so easily gutted."

Cirlog suddenly punched Harper's chest, with enough force to break through it. Harper gave Cirlog a betrayed expression as he pulled his hand out, gripping onto a fuse.

"Consider yourself relieved from employment."

Harper's systems suddenly shut down, and her body collapsed to the ground. Alexis let out screams of grief as Cirlog forcibly opened Harper's chest compartment to retrieve the gauntlets. He equipped them, without the use of the silk, and turned to face the Chimeras. "Ladies and gentlemen, we did it!"

The Chimeras erupted into cheers as Alexis sobbed and the rest of the party mourned in silence.

Greg, who wasn't restrained, stumbled to his feet, grunting in pain and exhaustion. "Cirlock!" he yelled, baring his teeth and shaking with anger.

"Oh, again with the name thing! What?" Cirlog turned around. "Oh… this one isn't chained down… *Oh,* he's injured. That's why. Meh, the Chimeras aren't that smart anymore so, it's okay." Cirlog clasped his hands together. "What can I do for you, large, dirt monkey?"

Greg unsheathed his sword, his knuckles white from his tight grip.

"Ooh!" Cirlog turned around and faced his Chimeras, riling them up. They pointed and chortled at Greg, some of them throwing a few rocks at the injured man.

"I'm so frightened!" Cirlog cried. He hit his wrists together, the metal of the gauntlets ringing through the air. "*Bring* it, you half-witted Noofer.[25]"

Greg let out a battle cry, then hurtled towards Cirlog with a bit of a limp. Greg furiously advanced, the edge of his sword swinging towards Cirlog's midsection. The god jerked backwards, his smug face deteriorating into regret, as if he wasn't expecting Greg to be so strong.

Cirlog pivoted away from the striking blade, causing Greg to grow more and more infuriated. With a frustrated swing, and a

---

[25] This is a very derogatory term that cannot be defined because children read this.

miss, Greg lifted his leg up and kicked Cirlog in the chest, knocking him to the ground.

Cirlog's jaw dropped. "Excuse me? What the hell do you think you're doing?"

"Ending this—"

"No!" Cirlog raised his hand, cutting off Greg. "This tie is worth *six-thousand* platinum filn! It was interwoven with silk made of spiders!"

"… Moon silk spiders are extinct!" James spoke up.

"Not in my lifetime, boy! Besides, the spiders I'm referring to were made *of* silk, fetch!"

"That doesn't make any sense—!"

"This is not the time, James," Greg calmly said through gritted teeth.

"But—"

"Shut up, James!"

James felt himself shrinking as he averted his eyes. Greg was the only one in the group that hadn't told him to shut up.

"… Anyway, this tie is one of a kind" —Cirlog lowered his hand, giving Greg a disappointed shake of the head— "and you put your foot on it!"

"Do I look like I give a damn about your luxuries? I'm here to settle things once and for all!" Greg raised his sword.

"You can't hit me with that thing! You only got lucky brushing me with that grimy trotter you call a foot!"

"I don't need too"

Greg reached out and slapped his palm against the gem on his sword. The entire blade ignited with a searing blaze, the cries of a Phoenix radiating with the heat. Cirlog scrambled away, a look of terror creeping upon his face.

"P-Please… I have a right to know why you're going to kill me!" Cirlog cried as he raised his hands in surrender.

James tilted his head at the god's comment, questioning the lack of confidence. *Can Greg really do this?*

"You know exactly why!" Greg screamed. "This beloved creation was made because someone loved her, and someone loved *you,* and you *destroyed* her, and for what? Because yer selfish? Because you want to destroy everything else? You ruin everything thing that you touch!"

Cirlog winced slightly, as if that last insult actually hurt his feelings.

"You deserve to burn in Hell, and *I'm* going to be the one to send you there," Greg asserted, with a cold atmosphere overwhelming him for once.

"W-Wait, please!"

James' eyes widened. *He's actually doing it!*

"No! It's my turn now!"

Greg, in a blind fury, tackled into Cirlog and stabbed the sword into the ground. A blinding illumination expelled from the blade, touching the entire realm. James fell backwards from the impact, but the party was shielded from the intensity by a crater formation. The Chimeras on the opposite side, however, weren't as fortunate as some of them vaporized from the heat.

When the light subsided, James rubbed his eyes, trying to regain his eyesight. He then sat up and squinted through smoke to see Greg lying in the midst of the crater, and Cirlog taking a knee a few feet away from him.

"Greg!" James slid down towards them. "Greg!"

Greg coughed, his face covered with dirt and charcoal. "… Did he… Did I get him?" he implored in a strained voice.

James looked over at Cirlog, who was panting weakly. "Yeah… I think you actually did it."

"Okay… good… it took a lot out of Birdy." Greg held up a butter knife with a tiny sequin glued to it.

"… What the hell?"

“I don’t go full nuclear very often…”

“Will it be okay?”

Greg nodded. “Yeah, give ‘er a few months… She’ll be ‘erself in no time.”

“And… end…. scene!”

James snapped his head up and saw Cirlog effortlessly climb to his feet, as if everything that had happened left him completely unfazed.

“Oof! I knew three weeks of theater camp would pay off! That was quite the show! The pyrotechnics were phenomenal! The special effects of my vaporized Chimeras! They probably didn’t feel a thing since it happened so fast! *And,* not a single bit of radiation! Guess nobody gets cancer, today! Really, bravo, Greg! Bravo!”

James bowed his head and heaved a sigh.

“Well, *both* of you have been a pebble in my shoe up to this point.” He cracked his knuckles. “It’s a bit of a shame, because I liked you Jay-mez, but I really, really despise pebbles. Especially in my nice, Trigan leather shoes. Time to move you out of my way.”

“I’m sorry, man,” James said to Greg. “Looks like this is it for us.”

“At least I’ll go… with a friend.”

Cirlog pulled his hand back, aiming his fist at James first. James took a deep breath, his tightened chest cavity nearly depriving him from the pleasure of one last sip of air. He didn’t get this last time. There was no mildewed bar or family member beside him in his last dying moments, but the singing of birds in the sky as the singed embers and last of the pluming smoke entangled him into one long minute of remorse. He squeezed his eyes shut as he braced for the impact of what would be one of the most painful ways to go.

He wondered how the Underworld would greet him, this time.

Then, a whistle flew gently along the breeze, parting the smoke and ash to reveal clean, fresh air. The God of Commerce paused to briefly behold the heavens, wonderstruck as an object of unknown origin descended from the sky.

Then, the moment of truth came forward as a toilet plunger landed directly on Cirlog's face, with a wet, suction noise echoing through the air.

Panicked, Cirlog faltered back, his shouts muffled. He tried to pull off the plunger, but the gauntlets destroyed the stick when he grabbed it. He reached for the rubber part and crumbled it off, heavily winded.

"… Dang it… That was my favorite one."

Gloric stood at the top of the crater, complaining as he slowly crouched down. He swung his legs out into the crater with a grunt and began sliding down at a tedious speed. The crunching of gravel resonated in coordination with the god's leisure descent, and the aggravated fuming breaths of his observing brother. He landed on his rear next to James, his white armor clanging as he softly met the ground and shifted a bit to the left as gravity allowed his body to settle. "Hey, James."

"… H-Hey," James stammered.

"Doing okay?"

James nodded. "… No."

"Cool."

"I'm sorry," Cirlog piped up, his body tremoring. "What do you mean by your 'favorite one?'"

Gloric slumped forward a bit, as if reluctant to respond. "Well… more like it was the *only* one."

"… In the Palace?"

"Uh…" Gloric's eyes narrowed. "Which one will make you less mad?"

Cirlog's hands shook, his lip twitching as a pained expression spread across his face. "You" —he suppressed a gag— "are unbelievable!"

"I would've brought yours, but you locked up all the rooms and didn't tell me where the keys were-"

"You dumb fetch!" Cirlog yelled in a thunderous voice. "You're a fetching *god*! Phase through the walls like a normal deity would!"

"If you wanted to phase through things, then we shouldn't have had doors and walls in the floor plan! I don't understand why I'm the bad guy in this situation!" Gloric whined.

"Gloric, is that you?" Reggy shouted.

"Uh…" Gloric's face twisted. His lips curled up to bare his teeth and squinted one eye shut. "… No?" he strained in a high voice.

"You fetch! You told me my recorder was indestructible!"

"Uh, Reggy," Cirlog called out, "the adults are talking, sweetheart."

"Shut-up, Cirlog! This is between me and your brother."

"Reggy!" James chimed in. "You knew how to say his name this entire time?"

"Of course, I did!"

"Then, why didn't you correct us?"

"Because I didn't want to seem like the black sheep!"

"What?"

"That's how the rest of you guys were pronouncing it! I didn't want to seem wrong!"

"Excuse me!" Cirlog yelled. "Are you done?"

"Hold on" —Gloric held up a finger— "what did you do with the recorder, Reggy?"

"I threw it at Minster's eye when he was a giant bird, cat thing!"

Gloric huffed. “Well, sorry bud, but indestructible isn’t immune to sacrifice!”

“Wait, did you kill Minster?” Cirlog exclaimed.

“Since when?” Reggy continued.

“Since forever!” Gloric confirmed, seemingly confused that Reggy didn’t know the rules of sacrifice.

Cirlog took a deep breath. “Are you done, now?” he asked calmly.

“… Do you all know each other?” James pointed towards Reggy.

“Course, we do.” Cirlog folded his arms. “Everyone knows Reggy.”

James shook his head. “I shouldn’t be as surprised as I am.”

“Okay, I’m going to assume you’re done, now.”

“Can we not do this here?” Gloric asked. “I don’t want to get these guys involved in our sibling banter.”

Cirlog gestured to Gloric’s armor. “You call this ‘banter?’ You seem geared up for battle, little brother.”

“… How else were we raised?”

“Fine. I’ll humor you. Let’s even the playing field.”

The crater suddenly reverted back to the surface, the ground almost as good as new. Cirlog backed up, his suit transforming into a black and gold armor. He undid his gauntlets and delicately set them on the ground, leaving a small dent “They were never meant for you, anyway.” He grabbed onto a loop attached to his side and pulled out some sort of rapier that seemingly bent to the current of the wind.

Gloric let out another whine, lying on his back. “I don’t want to fight that thing! I don’t like it! You cheat with it!”

“Just stand up and face me!”

Gloric sighed, as if he didn’t want to put forth the effort in standing. He reached towards James. “Help me up… I’m stuck.”

“… You’re not stuck!” James retorted.

"Yes, I am, James. Quit being a fetch and help your god!"

"You're not my god!"

"Your god, his god, it… doesn't matter!"

"Do it yourself!"

Gloric groaned. "Fine."

Gloric struggled to roll onto his belly. Once there, he grunted as he pushed himself up with his arms. Slowly, he slid one knee forward, then the other. Sitting on his knees for a moment, he panted, then, got up on his feet. He drew his sword then held out a shield that was equipped onto his back.

"I thought you wanted this to be fair?" Cirlog retorted.

Gloric looked at his shield. "Yeah, you're right." He set it on the ground. "Kay, your move."

Cirlog, on the brink of an aneurysm, spoke up once more. "We're all done now, right?"

Gloric tossed his hands up. "I said, 'your move.'"

With an eyeroll and a bit of genetic regret, Cirlog readied a stance. "En-garde."

"What?"

"... Pret."

"Quit cussing at me!"

"Allez!"

Cirlog thrust his rapier towards Gloric. In response, Gloric twirled out of the way with a bit of a skip in his step. A sneer grew upon Cirlog's face as he flicked his wrist. The rapier took a sharp turn and jabbed Gloric into the shoulder. He yelped and gripped onto his wound. "Dammit! See, this is exactly what I'm talking about! It's never a fair fight!"

"It's not my fault you spent more time playing hide-and-seek instead of learning how to fence!"

Gloric furrowed his brow as his lip tremored a bit, looking as if he were a child about to break into a tantrum. He slapped the rapier out of the way with his wrist guard and shoved Cirlog. As

Cirlog faltered backwards, he pointed his rapier towards Gloric. "Hey! Corps-à-corps is illegal!"

"Your face is illegal!" Gloric shouted as he ran towards a tree.

Cirlog clenched his jaw and chased after his brother. "Gloric! Get back here!"

"I told you! I'm not fighting you with that thing!" He cried while hiding behind the tree.

As Cirlog approached the tree, Gloric tried another escape attempt, but was dismayed when Cirlog blocked his path. The two then played a game of cat-and-mouse around the trunk of the tree, running around in circles as Cirlog tried to keep Gloric in one spot.

"Stop messing around!" Cirlog fumed. "You're embarrassing me in front of the jury!"

"Where did you even get your accent? No one in our family talks like that except for you!" Gloric retorted while hiding behind the tree.

"It's acquired!" Cirlog lunged, the rapier wrapping completely around the trunk of the tree. He took a step back, surprised as to how he missed.

Gloric then dropped drown behind him from the branches above and kicked him in the rear. "Required, my butt!"

Cirlog stumbled into the tree but threw his arms out to catch himself. "*Acquired,* idiot!"

"Potato, avocado, hippopotamus, Pegamoose! I don't see the difference!" he said with a shrug.

"You can't ever be serious, can you?" Cirlog stood up straight and faced his brother.

"What is there to be serious about?"

"I'm going to tear this world apart."

Gloric's face fell as soon as the words left his brother's lips. "… You know why we can't do that."

"I don't care!"

Cirlog thrusted his sword towards Gloric, and instead of skipping aside or running away, Gloric unsheathed a basket-hilt sword at a lightning speed and blocked the blow. Gloric then began brutally slashing his sword at his brother, his footwork flawless, and his technique beautiful.

He... was playing him the whole time, James thought.

Gloric is an excellent swordsman, Krag replied.

Then, why didn't he wait until now to fight back?

Because wielding a sword is what Gloric hates the most.

Cirlog grunted in frustration as he desperately blocked each blow. He jumped to the side and sprung towards Gloric, but he gracefully leaped over his brother, his body twisting in the air. Gloric landed on his feet, and before Cirlog could defend himself, his brother got the best of him as Cirlog took several hits to his arms, the sword cutting through his armor.

As Cirlog tried to block, Gloric suddenly kicked up the shield from earlier into his hand and bashed Cirlog over the head with it using one hand.

Cirlog faltered backwards a few feet. "I-I thought you weren't going to use it!"

"I lied," Gloric replied, coldly.

After aggressively hitting Cirlog a few more times with the sword, he hit him again with the shield repeatedly until he parried the rapier out of his hand and kicked him to the ground.

"Stop!" Cirlog cried.

Gloric held his sword and shield defensively, keeping a serious expression.

Cirlog began weeping like a child. "I don't want to be here anymore!"

Gloric took a deep breath, his eyes becoming wet.

Cirlog looked up at his brother. "Aren't you tired?"

"... I'll never grow weary—"

"Maybe you won't, Gloric, but what about me? What about *Vrec?* I can't take it anymore!" He reached, nearly ripping out his hair and sobbed. "I can't keep battling like this! I can't keep fighting in a war that we've lost!"

"We haven't lost—"

"WE'VE LOST!" Cirlog's voice roared, echoing throughout the realm. "If we're no longer brothers, then we've lost!"

Gloric lowered his sword, his brother's words hitting like a metal beam.

Cirlog suddenly kicked out Gloric's legs, his sword and shield flying out of his hands. He climbed atop of him, grabbing Gloric in a chokehold.

"I don't want to kill you," Cirlog admitted, tears streaming down his face, "but I have to. If I want any sense of solace to return to me, then I have to!"

Gloric grabbed Cirlog's wrists and was able to pull his hands away from his neck. The strength the two brothers displayed showed as they hit what seemed to be a bit of a stalemate; however, with one big push, Gloric managed to get Cirlog off of him. Cirlog came at him again, Gloric kicked his sword into his hand,

Almost poetically,

Almost rehearsed,

And then, stabbed it into his brother's chest.

"What… What?" Cirlog shook his head and looked down, then back at his brother, as if he had been unaware they'd been fighting to begin with. "Wh…Why did you…?"

Gloric got up onto his knees and pulled his brother into a hug. "… I want to go home, too."

"… You do?"

"Yeah… I want to soar the cosmos, see the stars, and stare at nothing one last time."

"… I'm sorry, Gloric… I'm sorry I couldn't see this through."

"You already did."

As Cirlog fell limp, Gloric held him for a minute, a few tears streaming down his face. He gently set his brother down onto the ground, pulled the sword out of his chest, and took a deep breath. He stood up and looked out into the crowd of Chimeras. They each stood in shock, their pain radiating around them.

"… What do you want?" Gloric asked.

"… Gloric?" one of them spoke up.

James blinked, and then looked to his friends to see if they saw it, too. They were all gaping, which made James feel a bit relieved,

But still utterly shocked at the sight before him.

The Chimeras were no longer zombie-like creatures, but humans of flawless features. The rotten flesh and missing ligaments were completely healed and replaced. Their clouded eyes were clear, radiating with a light.

"Hey, Stoker. How are you?" Gloric responded.

"What's going on? Is that…" The Chimera inhaled sharply and put a hand over his head, the crowd behind him nervously whispering to one another. He looked Gloric up and down. "Did you *murder* Cirlog? Why would you do that? He was your brother!"

Gloric sheathed his sword, giving Stoker a dismayed look. "The Pickles Protocol, my dear friend."

Stoker bowed his head, a few tear drops falling to the ground. The crowd of Chimeras behind him began hugging one another, crying on each other's shoulder.

"… What's going on?" James leaned towards Alexis.

She shook her head. "I have no idea."

Gloric scuffed his feet against the dirt. "I'm… really sorry."

"No, Gloric!" a woman piped up. "We feel sorry for you! He may have been our god, but he was your family!"

"You freed him from his misery, and in turn freed us from fraying away with him!" another person shouted.

“We owe you our lives, and for that we thank you and offer our services. Please, sir, what can we do for you?” Stoker said.

“… I’ll let you know,” Gloric replied, his eyes focusing on the dirt. “You could start by helping these people out.”

The group of Chimeras directed their attention towards the party. James nervously eyed his friends, feeling awkward having the attention on him.

“Absolutely! We will give them any assistance they may need.”

“Cool.”

The Chimeras then dispersed, returning to their homes to gather any supplies to assist the travelers. A few of them approached the party, asking if they need any medical attention. As they became engrossed in the task at hand, Gloric began drifting towards one direction.

“… What about my recorder?” Reggy called after him.

“Check your pocket.”

Reggy pulled out the white recorder and gasped. “You fixed it!”

“… Uh-huh.”

Without another word, continued wandering into the depths of Mahara.

James grew dizzy as reality caught up to him. He had been so engrossed into the fight and the sudden transformation of the Chimeras that he almost forgot that he existed. He took a deep breath, stood up and looked over at Alexis. The two locked eyes and approached one another. Exhaling loudly, they gave each other a hug, tiredly resting their heads on the other’s shoulder.

“… This sucked,” she said.

“Yeah, it did.”

“Now what?”

James pulled away and looked towards Gloric. “… I’ll let you know.”

Chapter Twenty-Six

The God of Peace

JAMES FOLLOWED GLORIC THROUGH A thick, lush wood, the same wood that he saw when he was heaved into the pit. It was a quiet, peaceful place. The way the sunshine reflected off of the dew drops convinced James that it was more than just a source of nourishment to the surrounding ecosystem, but that every living thing drank off of the light as if it were a sweet ambrosia. It was a bit too good to be true in his opinion, after all, Mahara was a place meant to hold a terrible being.

Why would something so beautiful exist here?

James came across a clearing with a single tree, noticing a treehouse had been mounted upon it. As he approached and climbed up the ladder, he saw above the entrance was a plaque that read "Mahara." He peeked inside to see Gloric staring at a picture frame.

"Do you know what Mahara is, James?" Gloric asked.

James shrugged as he entered the treehouse. "I'm going to assume not."

Gloric took a deep breath. “My brother made it. He wanted it to be a place for us to ‘take a break’ from this world.” He set the picture frame face down onto a desk. “I… miss being young.”

James gave a light chuckle. “I mean, you’re a god, can’t you, you know, change your age if you wanted to?”

Gloric nodded. “Yeah, I could, but that’s not what I mean.” He walked to the center of the tree house, then fell backwards, flat on his back, the armor making a loud “thunk!” He sighed, then lazily slapped the ground with his hand. “Come here.”

Feeling a bit more than just awkward, James hesitantly approached, uncomfortably crouched down, then lied on his back next to Gloric. “… Am I supposed to be looking at something?”

“No.”

“Then…?”

“Sometimes it’s nice to just enjoy the company of a friend.”

“… Am I your friend?”

Gloric shrugged. “I don’t know.” He looked over at James. “Do you want to be friends?”

James nodded. “Uh… sure.”

“Cool,” Gloric turned his attention back to the ceiling.

“… I’m not going to convert to your religion or anything.”

“Pfft. My religion is dead anyway. I mean, I had one guy keeping it together but, you know, you killed him.”

James winced. “Sorry.”

“Water under the bridge.”

Silence for a moment.

“Did you know that Cirlog actually gave me the title, ‘God of Peace?’” Gloric asked.

“No… I thought that was your title when you came to Tor?”

Gloric shook his head. “No… one of his generals gestured to my dead soldiers during one of our wars, and in return, Cirlog sarcastically called me a ‘God of Peace.’ It was meant to be ironic, but Tor took it as a term of endearment instead… I hate that title.”

"... What did Cirlog mean? All that stuff about going home?"

"Ever had a job you hate, James?"

James laughed. "'Hate' might be an understatement."

Gloric chuckled. "Would you do something that made you miserable in order to make someone you love happy?"

James thought for a second. "I guess it depends on the situation."

"Care to elaborate?"

"I mean, what makes that person happy? Do they prefer simple favors, or do you need to go above and beyond to win them over? There's a difference between an act of kindness and complete asinine."

"I mean, you jumped into the Vomit River for that girl with no hesitation. That was pretty asinine, and, like, the grossest thing I've seen, and I've been alive for thousands of years!"

"Yeah, but to me it seemed like a simple...hey," James sat up. "That reminds me. How do you even know all of this stuff about me, anyway?"

"Uh, I'm a god? Duh!"

"... Oh, yeah."

"... No, I spy on you guys with squirrels and birds and stuff."

"What?"

Gloric laughed. "Yeah."

"Why?"

"It's like I told you, I think you can do good things in this world. Think of it as you... being my 'chosen hero,' or some dumb fetchwork like that."

"... I think it's funny that you swear."

"Why?"

"I dunno. Shouldn't that be taboo or something for a god to swear?"

"Never stopped me."

James chuckled. "A hero, huh?"

Gloric nodded. "Yeah. Here, I bless you and fetch and all that," he said while waving his hand.

"Well, you don't have to spy on us."

Gloric's eyes narrowed. "… What?"

"You can go wherever you want, right? Why not just, I don't know, hang out with us once in a while?"

Gloric sat up. "What makes you think that you and your little rag-tag team is going to stay together after this?"

"Well… we were together before you sent us here. I don't think that will really stop us."

"Well, just in case, can I ask for another favor?"

James shook his head. "Sure… why not?"

"Cool. I need you to go visit the Elements."

"The Elements?"

"Yeah."

"Why?"

"They need you to settle your 'unfinished business,'" he said with air quotations, his armor squeaking as if it hadn't been oiled in a long time.

"What's my unfinished business?"

Gloric arched an eyebrow. "What do you think it is?"

James gulped. "I… I need to take down the Bureau."

"You said it, not me! Dibs not! James volunteering again!"

James rolled his eyes. "Ha, ha, you're very funny. But seriously, where would I even find them?"

"Uh, your adopted father, Kaje, obviously!"

"What? *Him*?"

"You think all those 'high priest' stories were just fairytales?"

"… I guess not."

"Then, there you go, Jay-mez!"

James shuddered. "Why would you even call me that?"

"It fits."

James rolled his eyes again. "Whatever. I'll do your stupid favor."

"Also…"

James looked at him. "Yeah?"

Gloric bit his lip. "If you see my wife, can you tell her to come home?"

"Why can't you tell her?"

"Something about needing space and time to think, which I totally understand, I'm just… lonely."

"I'm sorry."

"It happens." Gloric hugged his knees. "I honestly never thought I'd ever come here alone."

"Don't I count?"

Gloric shrugged. "I mean, I *guess* you count as somebody." He smirked and wiggled his fingers at James. "Or are you even real to begin with?"

"Don't joke about that! It isn't funny."

"It's kind of funny."

James scoffed, but smiled, and then looked around the tree house. There were old televisions and video game consoles, some crushed up soda cans, and, to his surprise, test tubes, cultures, tools, and other trinkets lying around.

"I don't want you to look for her, because you have a job to do, but… if you happen to cross paths… you can't miss her. There's a really disgruntled unicorn hanging around her and stuff."

"I'll tell her," James chuckled. "I promise."

Gloric smiled back, his eyes shining, but very tired from hiding his grief. "Good… now get out."

"What?"

"Yeah, I needed you to go, like, yesterday."

"W-Why?"

“The Elements are *super* impatient, like, Metal has no sense of… what’s the opposite of ‘haste’… chilling out! Besides, I just lost my brother! I need a moment to be sad all by myself!”

“I thought you were lonely?!”

“Trust me, I’ll bug you in like, a day or two. I just need you to go.”

“… Okay.”

“Like, right now!”

“Okay!” James shouted irately as he stood up. “I’ll see you later I guess.”

“Bye!” Gloric gave him a squeaky wave, then laid back down, allowing his hand to stay in the air for a bit.

As James was leaving, he noticed a picture from a photo booth near the door frame. It was the same three boys from Gloric’s office. The red-haired boy and Gloric were making silly faces while the black-haired boy rolled his eyes, doing a terrible job of hiding his delight.

James smiled, a bit somberly, but left the God of Peace… left Gloric, behind.

~

When James returned to his friends, he felt a chill go down his spine when he saw Greg still in the same spot, a blanket covering all but his head. He sprinted over to his side and knelt down next to him. “Greg?”

No response.

“… Greg?” James shook him, panicked.

Greg then let out a snore.

James sighed, overwhelmed with relief.

“Excuse me?”

James looked up to see Stoker. “Oh, hey.”

"We've gathered a cart of supplies as a thank you for you and your companions' assistance to Gloric."

"Thank you."

"Be sure to treasure the fish mount, though! It tells jokes recorded by Cirlog, himself!"

James blinked. "You don't say?"

"Yep! You can hear his voice whenever you want to, It's better that you hear him in a light-hearted manner, so you can know him the way we remember him."

"That reminds me, did Cirlog have you kidnapped or something?"

Stoker laughed. "Oh, no, no. We were merely adamant followers of him, and as a thank you, he blessed us with the ability to shapeshift."

James looked up. "Oh, okay!"

"Anyway, we currently lack the resources to have a better transport for your friend, so the best we can do is offer a platform truck from our community garden."

"O-Okay."

"The exit is the way you came in, and if I remember right, that cave could be quite dangerous. Do you need some additional help? We don't pack the same punch that we used to, but we aren't completely useless!"

"I think we can manage," James said to Stoker.

"Okay, well, let's get your friend situated so you can be on your way!"

"Thanks!"

A couple of Maharans approached with the platform truck and James and Stoker helped load Greg on top of it. While it was a bit too small, Greg could still lie comfortably on it and not cause any resistance to the truck.

James glanced over at Reggy, Fletcher, and Alexis. He smiled as he watched Fletcher chase after Reggy as a desperate attempt to get him to finally stop playing the recorder, but felt his stomach sink as he saw Alexis kneeling next to Harper's lifeless body. He approached her and kneeled down next to her. "Are you going to be okay?"

She shrugged as she wiped away tears. "*I'll* be fine. It just sucks that of all people to get hurt, it had to be her."

James nodded. "You know, that's what's so great about you. She isn't a person, she's a robot. It didn't stop you from seeing her as a person, though, and it was your passion that made her, for lack of better words, real, and not inanimate."

She looked up at James. "Do you really mean that?"

"Of course, I mean that."

One of the Chimeras suddenly approached Harper, with the fuse box in his hand. "I don't know if we can ever fix her, but I can at least do this." He pulled out a screwdriver, knelt down, and reinstalled the fuse box. Parts of Harper's systems whirred to life, but she still remained lifeless. "This way, she could more than likely hear your goodbyes."

Alexis hung her head as her tears streamed faster. "Thank you."

"I'll give you some space," the Chimera said as he walked away.

Alexis let out a small sob as she grabbed Harper's hand. "Harper, I'm sorry this happened to you. You are such a good girl. I can't ever repay you for what you did for this family, especially for fixing my swords." She wiped her eyes and sniffled. "You're so much more than that, though. You're not just a container or a tool, you're an inspiration, and my greatest friend. I wish I could fix you. I love you."

Harper suddenly blinked, and her head turned towards Alexis. "Love doesn't die."

Alexis nodded before Harper turned to James.

"Help?"

"I can't help you, Harper," James replied, fighting back his own tears.

"No... help Mother."

"I don't understand."

"Projects need... blueprints in... order to... work..."

Harper's systems shut down once more, and Alexis let out another cry as the robot departed. As James let out a few of his own tears, he glanced over, and noticed the gauntlets still on the ground. He looked between Harper and the gauntlets, before removing the silk from her cavity, and walking towards the gauntlets. He wrapped them in the silk and returned to Alexis.

"What are you doing?" she asked as she wiped her eyes.

"Finishing what Harper started."

Alexis nodded. James reached out his hand to her and helped her off the ground. In turn, she took the gauntlets from him and carefully placed them in the bag.

"Okay, when are we taking down the Bureau?

"How do you know that's what we are doing next?"

"What else would we be doing, James?"

"Going back to grave robbing?"

She huffed and shoved his shoulder. "First of all, don't ever call what I do *graverobbing* ever again, and second, now that we have the gauntlets, the Bureau is utterly defenseless against us."

James chuckled. "You raise a valid point, but that's not what we're doing."

Alexis frowned and tilted her head. "What do you mean?"

"You have some unfinished business to attend to first."

Alexis stared at James, her curiosity eating at her, while he merely smirked.

~

The dean's assistant hadn't done much that day. He organized papers, books, and scrolls for the dean, but what else was he getting paid for?

The dean huffed and threw a book down on his desk.

"… Is there a problem, sir?" the assistant asked.

"Do you not know how to do your job?"

"I'm afraid I don't understand—"

"This is not the book that I asked for!"

"I apologize, sir—"

"Hand me that one!" The dean pointed to the shelf.

The assistant sighed, grabbed the book, and set it on the desk. "… I do have a name, sir."

"It's not worth the effort remembering. You're so lazy and stupid that I'll probably end up replacing you by the end of the day!"

The assistant nodded, hiding his internal rage. "Right…"

Suddenly, the door burst open, revealing two ragamuffin vagabonds that appeared armed and dangerous!

"Who the hell are you?" the dean angrily demanded.

James held up his hands. "Look, I'm just here to make sure your security doesn't interfere with this."

"With what?"

"Not my business. Alexis!" James sat down in a chair near the door, giving the assistant a slight nod.

He nodded in return.

Alexis burst through the room, threw her tools onto the desk, and then lit a match. She tossed the match onto the tools. Papers, pens, and many other things burned, but the tools seemingly glowed in the flame. "Gloric is real!" she declared, her voice and eyes as lively as the fire.

The dean stared at the tools, both astonished and appalled.

"Oh… she actually did it," the assistant muttered.

Alexis then pulled a pouch from her side and dumped some dirt onto her tools to extinguish the fire and grabbed them. Realistically, it wasn't enough dirt to put out the *entire* fire, so, she didn't. She walked out the door while James jumped back up and followed. He poked his head back in and pointed at the dean. "You're a fetch!" Then, he pointed at the assistant. "You're not, but *he* is."

As James finally left the room, the dean sat back in his seat, flabbergasted at what happened. The dean then shot his head towards the assistant. "You idiot! Don't just stand there! You need to put this out!"

"... Oh, yes, of course sir," he reached into his pocket and pulled out a lovingly engraved piece of a fractured sternum. "This is definitely a fire I need to put out."

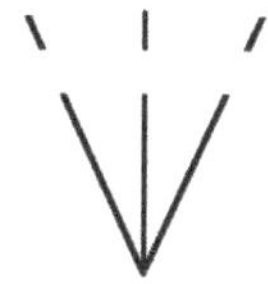

Thank you for your Support!

Aaron

Ashley Muyano

Aspen

Beverly

Cat

David & Georgia

Don & Kim Owens

Doug

Elsie

James & Jesse Tolman

Jesse Zolinger

Kasey

Koltin

Libby

Rachel Sabin

Rhiannon Mellin

Spenzer Jackson

And, of course, all our friends who wished to remain anonymous!